Nora Roberts publishe... ...udonym **J.D. Robb** in 1995, introducing readers to the tough as nails but emotionally damaged homicide cop **Eve Dallas** and billionaire Irish rogue, **Roarke**.

With the **In Death** series, Robb has become one of the biggest thriller writers on earth, with each new novel reaching number one on bestseller charts the world over.

For more information, visit **www.jd-robb.co.uk**

Become a fan on Facebook at **Nora Roberts and J.D. Robb**

The world can't get enough of J.D. Robb

'Definitely **ticks all the boxes** from beginning to end'
Bradford Telegraph & Argus

'Another **absolutely belting page turner** . . . you won't
be able to put it down'
Yorkshire Post

'This is **sheer entertainment**, a souped-up version of
Agatha Christie for the new millennium'
Guardian

'J.D. Robb's novels are **can't miss pleasures**'
Harlan Coben

'I can't wait to get out and **buy another**'
Coventry Telegraph

'Another **great read**, another bestseller'
Huddersfield Daily Examiner

'**Compelling** characters with a **dramatic** sci-fi twist'
Cambridgeshire Journal

'A **fast-paced, superbly crafted story** that is an amazing
– and possibly unique – combination of top-notch
suspense, detection, and intensely romantic sensuality'
Library Journal

'Robb serves . . . **classic whodunit** and noir'
Publishers Weekly

'**Great fun**'
Cosmopolitan

'A **consistently entertaining** writer'
USA Today

'Whether she writes as J.D. Robb or under her
own name, I love Nora Roberts. She is a woman
who **just doesn't know how to tell a bad story** . . .
an authentic page turner, with Eve Dallas – tough as
nails and still sexy as hell . . . If you haven't read
Robb, **this is a great place to start**'
Stephen King

Have you read them all?

Go back to the beginning with the first three In Death novels

For a full list of J.D. Robb titles, turn to the back of this book

Book One
NAKED IN DEATH

Introducing Lieutenant Eve Dallas and billionaire Roarke. When a senator's granddaughter is found shot to death in her own bed, all the evidence points to Roarke – but Eve senses a set-up.

Book Two
GLORY IN DEATH

High-profile women are being murdered by a knife-wielding attacker. Roarke has a connection to all the victims, but Eve needs his help if she's going to track down the real killer.

Book Three
IMMORTAL IN DEATH

With a new 'immortality' drug about to hit the market, Eve and Roarke must track down a vicious and evil drug dealer and killer – before it's too late.

Head to the end of the book for an exclusive extract from the **NEW J.D. Robb** thriller,

DELUSION IN DEATH

J.D. ROBB

SURVIVOR IN DEATH

piatkus

PIATKUS

First published in the United States in 2005 by G.P Putnam's Sons,
a member of Penguin Group (USA) Inc.
First published in Great Britain in 2005 by Piatkus Books Ltd
Paperback published in 2008 by Piatkus Books
Reprinted 2005, 2006 (twice), 2007, 2008, 2009, 2010, 2011
This reissue published by Piatkus in 2012

3 5 7 9 10 8 6 4

A CIP catalogue record for this book
is available from the British Library.

ISBN 978-0-7499-5742-1

Typeset in Bembo by Palimpsest Book Production Ltd,
Falkirk, Stirlingshire

Printed and bound by Clays Ltd, Elcograf S.p.A.

Papers used by Piatkus are from well-managed forests
and other responsible sources.

MIX
Paper from
responsible sources
FSC® C104740

Piatkus
An imprint of
Little, Brown Book Group
Carmelite House
50 Victoria Embankment
London EC4Y 0DZ

An Hachette UK Company
www.hachette.co.uk

www.littlebrown.co.uk

Eve Dallas – Personnel File

Name: Eve Dallas

Nationality: American

Rank: Homicide Lieutenant, New York Police and Security Department

Born: 2028

Height: 5 foot 9 inches

Weight: 120 lbs

Eyes: Golden brown

Hair: Light brown

ID number: 5347BQ

Service:
Began police officer training at the Academy in 2046, aged 18.

Family:
Between the ages of eight and ten, Eve lived in a communal home while her parents were searched for. Eve was found with no ID, no memory, and was traumatised having been a victim of sexual assault.

Why Eve is a cop:
'It's what I am. It's not just that someone has to look, even though that's just the way it is. It's that I have to look.'

So shalt thou feed on Death, that feeds on men,
And Death once dead, there's no dying then

WILLIAM SHAKESPEARE

Happy families are all alike; every unhappy Family is
unhappy in its own way

LEO NIKOLAEVICH TOLSTOI

Prologue

A late-night urge for an Orange Fizzy saved Nixie's life. When she woke, she could see by the luminous dial of the jelly-roll wrist unit she was never without that it was after two in the morning.

She wasn't allowed to snack between meals, except for items on her mother's approved list. And two in the morning was way between.

But she was *dying* for an Orange Fizzy.

She rolled over and whispered to her best friend in the entire galaxy, Linnie Dyson. They were having a school-night sleepover because Linnie's mom and dad were celebrating their anniversary in some fancy hotel.

So they could have sex. Mom and Mrs Dyson said it was so they could have a fancy dinner and go dancing and crap-o, but it was for sex. *Jee-zus,* she and Linnie were nine, not two. They knew what was what-o.

Besides, like they gave a woo. The whole deal meant Mom – the Rule Monster – bent the rules about school nights. Even if they'd had to turn the lights out at nine-thirty – were they *two?* – she and Linnie had the most magolicious time.

And school was still hours away, and she was thirsty. So she poked Linnie and whispered again. 'Wake up!'

'Nuh. Not morning. Still dark.'

'It is morning. It's *two* in the morning.' That's why it was so frosty. 'I want an Orange Fizzy. Let's go down and get one. We can split it.' Linnie only made grunting, mumbling noises, rolled away, and tugged the covers nearly over her head.

'Well, *I'm* going,' Nixie said in the same hissy whisper.

It wasn't as much fun on her own, but she'd never get back to sleep now, thinking of the Fizzy. She had to go all the way down to the kitchen because her mother wouldn't allow her to have an AutoChef in her room. Might as well be in prison, Nixie thought, as she scooted out of bed. Might as well be in prison in 1950 or something instead of her own house in 2059.

Mom had even put child codes on all the household AutoChefs so the only thing Nixie or her brother, Coyle, could program was health sludge.

Might as well eat mud.

Her father said, 'Rules is rules.' He liked to say that a lot. But sometimes he'd wink at her or Coyle when their mother was out and order up some ice cream or potato crispies.

Nixie sort of thought her mom knew and pretended she didn't.

She tiptoed out of her room, a pretty little girl, just going gangly, with a wavy mass of platinum blonde hair. Her eyes, a pale, pale blue, were already adjusted to the dark.

2

Still, her parents always kept a low light on in the bathroom at the end of the hall, in case anybody had to get up and pee or whatever.

She held her breath as she walked by her brother's room. If he woke, he might tell. He could be a complete buttpain. Then again, sometimes he could be pretty chilly. For a moment, she hesitated, considered sneaking in, waking him, and talking him into keeping her company for the adventure.

Nah. It was sort of juicy to be creeping around the house by herself. She held her breath again as she eased by her parents' room, hoping she could stay – for once – under her mother's radar.

Nothing and no one stirred as she crept down the stairs.

But even when she got downstairs, she was mouse quiet. She still had to get by Inga, their housekeeper, who had rooms right off the kitchen. Right off the target. Inga was mostly okay, but she'd never let her get away with an Orange Fizzy in the middle of the night.

Rules is rules.

So she didn't turn on any lights, and snuck through the rooms, into the big kitchen like a thief. It only added to the thrill. No Orange Fizzy would ever taste as frigid as this one, she thought.

She eased open the refrigerator. It occurred to her, suddenly, that maybe her mother counted stuff like this. Maybe she kept a kind of tally of soft drinks and snack food.

But she was past the point of no return. If she had to pay a price for the prize, she'd worry about paying it later.

With the goal in hand, she shuffled to the far end of the kitchen where she could keep an eye on the door to Inga's rooms and duck behind the island counter if she had to.

In the shadows, she broke the seal on the tube, took the first forbidden sip.

It pleased her so much, she slipped onto the bench in what her mother called the breakfast area, and prepared to enjoy every drop.

She was just settling in when she heard a noise and dived down to lie on the bench. From beneath it, she saw a movement and thought: *Busted!*

But the shadow slipped along the far counter, to the door of Inga's room, and inside.

A man. Nixie had to slap a hand on her mouth to stifle a giggle. Inga had a boogie buddy! And she was so old – had to be at least forty. It looked like Mr and Mrs Dyson weren't the only ones having sex tonight.

Unable to resist, she left the Orange Fizzy on the bench and slid out. She just had to look, just had to see. So she crept over to the open door, eased inside Inga's little parlor, and toward the open bedroom door. She squatted down on all fours, poked her head in the opening.

Wait until she told Linnie! Linnie would be so jealous.

With her hand over her mouth again, her eyes bright with laughter, Nixie scooted, angled her head.

4

And saw the man slit Inga's throat.

She saw the blood, a wild gush of it. Heard a horrible, gurgling grunt. Eyes glazed now, she reared back, her breath hissing and hitching into her palm. Unable to move, she sat, her back pressed to the wall and her heart booming inside her chest.

He came out, walked right by her, and out the open door.

Tears spilled out of her eyes, down her spread fingers. Every part of her shook as she crawled over, using a chair as a shield, and reached up to the table for Inga's pocket 'link.

She hissed for emergency.

'He's killed her, he's killed her. You have to come.' She whispered the words, ignoring the questions the voice recited. 'Right now. Come right now.' And gave the address.

She left the 'link on the floor, continued to crawl until she'd reached the narrow steps that led from Inga's parlor to the second level.

She wanted her mommy.

She didn't run, didn't dare. She didn't stand. Her legs felt funny, empty, like the bones in them had melted. She started to belly crawl across the hall, sobs stuck in her throat. And to her horror, she saw the shadow – two shadows now. One went into her room, the other into Coyle's.

She was whimpering when she dragged her body through her parents' bedroom doorway. She heard a sound, a kind of thump, and pressed her face into the carpet while her stomach heaved.

5

She saw the shadows pass the doorway, saw them. Heard them. Though they moved as if that's what they were. Only shadows.

Shuddering, she continued to crawl, past her mother's bedroom chair, past the little table with its colorful lamp. And her hand slid through something warm, something wet.

Pulling herself up, she stared at the bed. At her mother, at her father. At the blood that coated them.

1

Murder was always an insult, and had been since the first human hand had smashed a stone into the first human skull. But the murder, bloody and brutal, of an entire family in their own home, in their own beds, was a different form of evil.

Eve Dallas, NYPSD Homicide, pondered it as she stood studying Inga Snood, forty-two-year-old female. Domestic, divorced. Dead.

Blood spatter and the scene itself told her how it must have been. Snood's killer had walked in the door, crossed to the bed, yanked Snood's head up – probably by the mid-length blonde hair, raked the edge of the blade neatly – left to right – across her throat, severing the jugular.

Relatively tidy, certainly quick. Probably quiet. It was unlikely the victim had the time to comprehend what was happening. No defensive wounds, no other trauma, no signs of struggle. Just blood and the dead.

Eve had beaten both her partner and Crime Scene to the house. The nine-one-one had gone to Emergency, relayed to a black-and-white on neighborhood patrol. The uniforms had called in the homicides, and she'd gotten the tag just before three in the morning.

7

She still had the rest of the dead, the rest of the scenes, to study. She stepped back out, glanced at the uniform on post in the kitchen.

'Keep this scene secure.'

'Yes, sir, Lieutenant.'

She moved through the kitchen out into a bisected space – living on one side, dining on the other. Upper-middle income, single-family residence. Nice, Upper West Side neighborhood. Decent security, which hadn't done the Swishers or their domestic a damn bit of good.

Good furniture – tasteful, she supposed. Everything neat and clean and in what appeared to be its place. No burglary, not with plenty of easily transported electronics.

She went upstairs, came to the parents' room first. Keelie and Grant Swisher, ages thirty-eight and forty, respectively. As with their housekeeper, there was no sign of struggle. Just two people who'd been asleep in their own bed and were now dead.

She gave the room a quick glance, saw a pricey man's wrist unit on a dresser, a pair of woman's gold earrings on another.

No, not burglary.

She stepped back out just as her partner, Detective Delia Peabody, came up the steps. Limping – just a little.

Had she put Peabody back on active too soon? Eve wondered. Her partner had taken a serious beating only three weeks before after being ambushed steps outside her own apartment building. And Eve still had the image of the stalwart Peabody bruised, broken, unconscious in a hospital bed.

Best to put the image, and the guilt, aside. Best to remember how she herself hated being on medical, and that work was sometimes better than forced rest.

'Five dead? Home invasion?' Huffing a bit, Peabody gestured down the steps. 'The uniform on the door gave me a quick run.'

'It looks like, but we don't call it yet. Domestic's downstairs, rooms off the kitchen. Got it in bed, throat slit. Owners in there. Same pattern. Two kids, girl and boy, in the other rooms on this level.'

'Kids? Jesus.'

'First on scene indicated this was the boy.' Eve moved to the next door, called for the lights.

'Records ID twelve-year-old Coyle Swisher.' There were framed sports posters on his walls. Baseball taking the lead. Some of his blood had spewed onto the torso of the Yankees current hot left fielder.

Though there was the debris of an adolescent on the floor, on the desk and dresser, she saw no sign Coyle had had any more warning than his parents.

Peabody pressed her lips together, cleared her throat. 'Quick, efficient,' she said in flat tones.

'No forced entry. No alarms tripped. Either the Swishers neglected to set them — and I wouldn't bet on that — or somebody had their codes or a good jammer. Girl should be down here.'

'Okay.' Peabody squared her shoulders. 'It's harder when it's kids.'

'It's supposed to be.' Eve stepped to the next room, called for lights, and studied the fluffy pink and white bed, the little girl with her blonde hair matted with blood. 'Nine-year-old Nixie Swisher, according to the records.'

'Practically a baby.'

'Yeah.' Eve scanned the room, and her head cocked. 'What do you see, Peabody?'

'Some poor kid who'll never get the chance to grow up.'

'Two pair of shoes over there.'

'Kids, especially upper income, swim in shoes.'

'Two of those backpack deals kids haul their stuff in. You seal up yet?'

'No, I was just—'

'I have.' Eve walked into the crime scene, reached down with a sealed hand, and picked up the shoes. 'Different sizes. Go get the first on scene.'

With the shoes still in her hand, Eve turned back to the bed, to the child, as Peabody hurried out. Then she set them aside, took an Identipad out of her field kit.

Yes, it was harder when it was a child. It was hard to take such a small hand in yours. Such a small, lifeless hand, to look down at the young who'd been robbed of so many years, and all the joys, all the pains that went in them.

She pressed the fingers to the pad, waited for the readout.

'Officer Grimes, Lieutenant,' Peabody said from the doorway. 'First on scene.'

'Who called this in, Grimes?' Eve asked without turning around. 'Sir, unidentified female.'

'And where is this unidentified female?'

'I . . . Lieutenant, I assumed it was one of the vics.'

She glanced back now, and Grimes saw the tall, lean woman in mannish trousers, a battered leather jacket. The cool brown eyes, flat cop's eyes, in a sharply featured face. Her hair was brown, like her eyes, short, choppy rather than sleek.

She had a rep, and when that icy gaze pinned him, he knew she'd earned it.

'So our nine-one-one calls in murder, then hops into bed so she can get her throat slashed?'

'Ah . . .' He was a beat cop, with two years under his belt. He wasn't ranking Homicide. 'The kid here might've called it, Lieutenant, then tried to hide in bed.'

'How long you had a badge, Grimes?'

'Two years – in January, Lieutenant.'

'I know civilians who've got a better sense of crime scene than you. Fifth victim, identified as Linnie Dyson, age nine, who is not a fucking resident of this fucking address. Who is not one Nixie Swisher. Peabody, start a search of the residence. We're looking for another nine-year-old girl, living or dead. Grimes, you idiot, call in an Amber Alert. She may have been the reason for this. Possible abduction. Move!'

Peabody snagged a can of Seal-It out of her own kit, hurriedly sprayed her shoes and hands.

'She could be hiding. If the kid called it in, Dallas, she

11

could be hiding. She could be afraid to come out, or she's in shock. She could be alive.'

'Start downstairs.' Eve dropped on her hands and knees to look under the bed. 'Find out what unit, what 'link placed the nine-one-one.'

'On that.'

Eve strode to the closet, searched through it, pushed into any area of the room where a child might hide. She started out, moving toward the boy's room, then checked herself.

You were a little girl, with what seemed to be a nice family. Where did you go when things got bad?

Somewhere, Eve thought, she herself never had to go. Because when things got bad for her, the family was the cause.

But she bypassed the other rooms and walked back into the master bedroom.

'Nixie,' she said quietly, as her eyes scanned. 'I'm Lieutenant Dallas, with the police. I'm here to help you. You call the police, Nixie?'

Abduction, she thought again. But why slaughter an entire household to snatch a little girl? Easier to boost her off the street somewhere, even to come in, tranq her, carry her out. More likely they'd found her trying to hide, and she'd be curled up somewhere, dead as the rest.

She called for lights, full, and saw the smears of blood on the carpet on the far side of the bed. A small, bloody hand-print, another, and a trail of red leading to the master bath.

Didn't have to be the kid's blood. More likely the parents.

More likely, but there was a hell of a lot of it. Crawled through the blood, Eve thought.

The tub was big and sexy, double sinks in a long peachy-colored counter, and a little closet-type deal for the toilet.

A smudged and bloody swath stained the pretty pastel floor tiles.

'Goddamn it,' Eve mumbled, and followed the trail toward the thick, green glass walls of a shower station.

She expected to find the bloodied body of a small dead girl. Instead she found the trembling form of a live one.

There was blood on her hands, on her nightshirt, on her face.

For a moment, one hideous moment, Eve stared at the child and saw herself. Blood on her hands, her shirt, her face, huddled in a freezing room. For that moment, she saw the knife, still dripping, in her hand, and the body — the man — she'd hacked to pieces lying on the floor.

'Jesus. Oh Jesus.' She took a stumbling step back, primed to run, to scream. And the child lifted her head, locked glassy eyes on hers, and whimpered.

She came back, hard, as if someone had slapped her. Not me, she told herself as she fought to get her breathing under control. Nothing like me.

Nixie Swisher. She has a name. Nixie Swisher.

'Nixie Swisher.' Eve said it out loud, and felt herself settle. The kid was alive, and there was a job to do.

One quick survey told Eve none of the blood was the child's.

Even with the punch of relief, the stiffening of spine, she wished for Peabody. Kids weren't her strong suit.

'Hey.' She crouched, carefully tapped the badge she'd hooked to her waistband with a finger that was nearly steady now. 'I'm Dallas. I'm a cop. You called us, Nixie.'

The child's eyes were wide and glazed. Her teeth chattered. 'I need you to come with me, so I can help you.' She reached out a hand, but the girl cringed back and made a sound like a trapped animal.

Know how you feel, kid. Just how.

'You don't have to be afraid. Nobody's going to hurt you.' Keeping one hand up, she reached in her pocket with the other for her communicator. 'Peabody, I've got her. Master bath. Get up here.'

Wracking her brain, Eve tried to think of the right approach. 'You called us, Nixie. That was smart, that was brave. I know you're scared, but we're going to take care of you.'

'They killed, they killed, they killed . . .'

'They?'

Her head shook, like an old woman with palsy. 'They killed, they killed my mom. I saw, I saw. They killed my mom, my dad. They killed—'

'I know. I'm sorry.'

'I crawled through the blood.' Eyes huge and glassy, she held out her smeared hands. 'Blood.'

'Are you hurt, Nixie? Did they see you? Did they hurt you?'

14

'They killed, they killed—' When Peabody turned into the room, Nixie screamed as if she'd been stabbed. And launched herself into Eve's arms.

Peabody stopped short, kept her voice very calm, very quiet. 'I'll call Child Protection. Is she injured?'

'Not that I can see. Shocky, though.'

It felt awkward holding a child, but Eve wrapped her arms around Nixie and got to her feet. 'She saw it. We've got not only a survivor, but an eye witness.'

'We've got a nine-year-old kid who saw—' Peabody spoke in undertones as Nixie wept on Eve's shoulder, and jerked her head toward the bedroom.

'I know. Here, take her and—' But when Eve tried to peel Nixie away, the child only wrapped herself tighter.

'I think you're going to have to.'

'Hell. Call CPS, get somebody over here. Start a record, room by room. I'll be back in a minute.'

She'd hoped to pass the kid to one of the uniforms, but Nixie seemed glued to her now. Resigned, and wary, she carted Nixie down to the first floor, looked for a neutral spot, and settled on what looked like a playroom.

'I want my mom. I want my mom.'

'Yeah, I got that. But here's the thing: you've got to let go. I'm not going to leave you, but you gotta loosen the grip.'

'Are they gone?' Nixie pushed her face into Eve's shoulder. 'Are the shadows gone?'

'Yes. You have to let go, sit down here. I have to do a couple of things. I need to talk to you.'

15

'What if they come back?'

'I won't let them. I know this is hard. The hardest.' At wit's end, she sat on the floor with Nixie still clinging to her. 'I need to do a job, that's how I can help. I need to . . .' Jesus. 'I need to get a sample from your hand, and then you can clean up. You'd feel better if you got cleaned up, right?'

'I got their blood . . .'

'I know. Here, this is my field kit. I'm just going to take a swab for evidence. And I need to take a recording. Then you can go to the washroom over there and clean up. Record on,' Eve said, quietly, then eased Nixie back. 'You're Nixie Swisher, right? You live here?'

'Yeah, I want—'

'And I'm Lieutenant Dallas. I'm going to swab your hand here, so you can clean up. It won't hurt.'

'They killed my mom and my dad.'

'I know. I'm sorry. Did you see who they were? How many there were?'

'I have their blood on me.'

Sealing the swab, Eve looked at the child. She remembered what it was to be a little girl, covered in blood not her own. 'How about you wash up?'

'I can't.'

'I'll help you. Maybe you want a drink or something. I can—' And when Nixie burst into tears, Eve's eyes began to ache.

'What? What?'

16

'Orange Fizzy.'

'Okay, I'll see if—'

'No, I went down to get one. I'm not supposed to, but I went down to get one, and Linnie didn't want to wake up and come. I went down to the kitchen, and I saw.'

With blood smeared on both of them now, Eve decided washing up would have to wait. 'What did you see, Nixie?'

'The shadow, the man, who went into Inga's room. I thought . . . I was going to watch, just for a minute, if they were going to do it, you know.'

'Do what?'

'Sex. I wasn't supposed to, but I did, and I saw!'

There were tears and snot as well as blood on the kid's face now. With nothing else handy, Eve pulled a wipe rag out of her field kit and passed it over.

'What did you see?'

'He had a big knife and he cut her, he cut her bad.' She closed her own hand over her throat. 'And there was blood.'

'Can you tell me what happened then?'

As the tears gushed, she rubbed the wipe and her hands over her cheeks, smearing them with blood. 'He left. He didn't see me, and he left and I got Inga's 'link and I called Emergency.'

'That's stand-up thinking, Nixie. That was really smart.'

'But I wanted Mom.' Her voice cracked with tears and mucus flowing. 'I wanted Dad, and I went up the back way, Inga's way, and I saw them. Two of them. They were going into my room, and Coyle's room, and I knew what they would do, but I wanted my mom, and I crawled in, and I got their blood on me, and I saw them. They were dead. They're all dead, aren't they? Everybody. I couldn't go look. I went to hide.'

'You did right. You did exactly right. Look at me. Nixie.' She waited until those drenched eyes met hers. 'You're alive, and you did everything right. Because you did, it's going to help me find the people who did this, and make them pay.'

'My mommy's dead.' Crawling into Eve's lap, she wept and wept and wept.

It was nearly five A.M. before Eve could get back to Peabody, and the work.

'How's the kid?'

'No better than you'd expect. Got the social worker and a doctor with her. Cleaning her up, doing a physical. I had to swear an oath I wouldn't leave the house before she'd unclamp herself.'

'You found her, came when she called for help kind of thing.'

'She made the nine-one-one on the housekeeper's pocket 'link, from down there.' She caught Peabody up with Nixie's timetable.

'From what she was able to tell me so far, it jibes with how it looks to me – efficient professional job. Come in. Bypass or jam alarms and security. One takes the house-keeper. That's the first hit. She's isolated, on another floor, and they need to deal with her first, insure she doesn't wake up, catch a whiff and tag the cops. Other guy's probably upstairs, ready to move if anybody up there wakes up. Then they do the parents together.'

'One for each,' Peabody agreed. 'No noise, no struggle. Deal with the adults first. Kids aren't a big worry.'

'One takes the boy, one takes the girl. They're expecting one boy, one girl. It was dark, so the fact they killed the wrong kid doesn't necessarily mean they didn't know the family personally. They were expecting to find one small blonde girl, and they did. Job's done, and they walk out.'

'No blood trail leading out of the house.'

'Seal up in protective gear, strip it off when you're done. No muss, no fuss. You get time of deaths?'

'Oh two-fifteen on the housekeeper. Maybe three minutes later on Dad, Mom right after. Another minute or so for each kid. Whole deal took five, six minutes. Cold and clean.'

'Not so clean. They left a witness. Kid's messed up now, but I think we'll get more out of her. She's got a brain, and she's got spine. Doesn't scream when she sees her housekeeper get her throat cut.'

She put herself into the child, imagined those few minutes when murder cut quietly through the house.

'Terrified, she's got to be terrified, but she doesn't go running away so she can get caught and hacked up. She stays quiet, and she calls nine-one-one. Gutsy.'

'What happens to her now?'

'Safe house, sealed record, uniform guards, a rep from

19

Child Protection.' The cold steps, the impersonal stages. The kid's life, as she knew it, had ended at approximately two-fifteen. 'We'll need to see if she's got other family, or if there's legal guardianship. Later today, we'll talk to her again, see what more we can squeeze out. I want this house sealed up like a biodome, and we'll start running the adult vics.'

'Dad was a lawyer – family law – Mom was a nutritionist. Private practice, run primarily out of an office space on the lower level. Those locks are still in place, and it doesn't appear anything's been disturbed in that area.'

'We look at their work, their clients, their personals. This kind of hit, it's pro, and it's thorough. Maybe one or both of them – or the housekeeper – had a sideline that linked up with organized crime. Nutritionist, could be a front for Illegals. Keep the client thin and happy the easy way.'

'There's an easy way? A way that includes unlimited portions of pizza and no hideous stomach crunches?'

'A little Funk, a little Go as part of your basic food groups.' Eve lifted a shoulder. 'Maybe she screwed with her supplier. Maybe one of them had an affair with a wrong number that ended bad. You're going to wipe out a whole family, you've got one hell of a motivation. We'll see if the sweepers turn up something on scene. Meanwhile, I want to go through each room again myself. I didn't get much of a . . .'

She broke off when she heard the steady clip of shoes, and turned to see the social worker, sleepy-eyed but neat as a church, walk into the room. Newman, Eve remembered.

CPS drone, and from the looks of her not too happy with the early call.

'Lieutenant, the doctor has found no physical injuries. It would be best if we transported the minor subject now.'

'Give me a few minutes to arrange security. My partner can go up, pack some things for her. I want to—'

She broke off again. This time it wasn't a steady clip of shoes, but running bare feet. Still wearing the bloodied nightshirt, Nixie ran in, and threw herself at Eve.

'You said you wouldn't leave.'

'Hey, standing right here.'

'Don't let them take me. They said they were going to take me away. Don't let them.'

'You can't stay here.' She pried Nixie's fingers from her legs, crouched until they were eye-to-eye. 'You know you can't.'

'Don't let them take me. I don't want to go with her. She's not the police.'

'I'm going to have police go with you, and stay with you.'

'You have to. You *have* to.'

'I can't. I have to work. I have to do what's right for your mom and dad, for your brother and your friend. For Inga.'

'I won't go with her. You can't make me go with her.'

'Nixie—'

'Hey.' Voice pleasant, a non-threatening smile on her face, Peabody stepped in. 'Nixie, I need to talk to the lieutenant for a minute — just over here. Nobody's going anywhere yet, okay. I just need to talk to her. Dallas?' Peabody walked to the far side of the room, where they were still in Nixie's line of sight.

Dallas joined her.

'What? Can I make a break for it?'

'You should take her.'

'Peabody, I need to do a more thorough on-scene.'

'I've done one, and you can come back and do your own.'

'So I ride with her to the safe house? Then she wigs on me when I have to leave her with uniforms. What's the point?'

'I don't mean take her to a safe house. Take her home. No place safer in the city — probably on the planet — than your place.'

Eve said nothing for ten full seconds. 'Are you out of your mind?'

'No, and just listen first. She trusts you. She knows you're in charge, and she trusts you to keep her safe. She's the eye witness, and she's a traumatized kid. We'll get more out of her, bound to, if she feels safe, if she's settled, at least as much as she can be. A few days, like a transition, before she ends up in the system. Put yourself in her shoes, Dallas. Would you feel better being with the icy, kick-ass cop, or the bored, overworked CPS drone?'

'I can't babysit a kid. I'm not equipped.'

'You're equipped to pull information out of a witness and this would give you full access. You wouldn't have to go through the annoyance of clearance from CPS every time you want to question her.'

Thoughtfully now, Eve glanced back at Nixie. 'Probably only be a day, two tops. Summerset knows about kids. Even if he is an asshole. How much more traumatized could she get looking at his ugly face, considering? Basically I'd be housing a witness. Big house.'

'That's the spirit.'

Eve frowned, studied Peabody's face. 'Pretty clever for somebody who's only been back on the job for a couple of days.'

'I may not be up for chasing down suspects on foot quite yet, but my mind? Sharp as ever.'

'Too bad. I was hoping concussion and coma might have honed that area, but you get what you get.'

'Mean.'

'I could be meaner, but it's five in the morning and I haven't had enough coffee. I gotta make a call.'

She stepped away, and saw Nixie tense out of the corner of her eye. Eve just shook her head, and pulled out her pocket 'link.

Five minutes later she was signalling the social worker.

'Absolutely out of the question,' the woman said. 'You're not qualified or approved to transport a child. I'm required to accompany—'

'What I'm doing is taking a witness into protective custody. She doesn't like you, and I need her settled in order to interview her more thoroughly.'

23

'The minor subject—'

'The kid had her family whacked in front of her eyes. She wants me. I say she gets what she wants – and as a ranking member of the New York City Police and Security Department, I'm seeing that she's taken to a safe place, and kept safe and secure until her safety is no longer an issue or other arrangements can be made. You can buck me on this, but why would you?'

'I'm obliged to consider what's in the best interests of—'

'The minor subject,' Eve concluded. 'Then you know that it's in her best interests to feel safe, to avoid more stressful situations. She's scared shitless. Why add?'

The woman looked back. 'My supervisor won't like it.'

'Your supervisor can deal with me. I'm taking the kid. Go file a report.'

'I need the location, the situation where—'

'I'll let you know. Peabody? Pack what you figure Nixie needs.' She walked back to Nixie. 'You know you can't stay here any more.'

'I don't want to go with her. I don't want—'

'And you've had it hit really hard tonight that you can't always have what you want. But for right now, you can come with me.'

'With you?'

While Newman stalked away, Eve drew Nixie across the room. 'That's right. I can't stay with you, because I've got to work. But there'll be people there who'll look out for you. People I trust, so you can trust them, too.'

'But you'll be there? You'll come back?'

'I live there.'

'Okay.' Nixie took Eve's hand. 'I'll go with you.'

2

All things being equal, Eve would rather have been transporting a three-hundred-pound psycho hopped on Zeus in the back of her police issue than a little girl. She knew how to handle a homicidal chemi-head.

But it was a short ride, and she'd be able to pass the kid off soon enough, and get back to work.

'After we notify . . .' Eve glanced in the rearview, and though Nixie's eyes were drooping, she left off *next of kin*. 'We'll set up in my home office. I'll swing back to the scene later. For now, we'll work with your record.'

'EDD's picking up all the home and personal 'links and comps, and they'll run a check on house security.' Peabody shifted so she could keep Nixie in the corner of her eye. 'Maybe they'll have something by the time we do a second pass through the scene.'

Had to get back in the field, Eve thought. Work to do. Interviews, reports, runs. She needed to get back to the scene. Her concentration had been fractured by finding the child. She needed to get back there, get the vibe.

Walked in the front door, she thought, going back in her head. Kid was in the kitchen, would've seen if someone

26

had come in the back. Through the front, through security like it wasn't there. One up, one down. Fast and efficient.

Housekeeper first. But she wasn't the target, she wasn't the goal. Otherwise, why go upstairs at all? The family was the target. Parents and kids. Don't even deviate for a second and scoop up an expensive wrist unit lying in plain sight.

Straight kill, she thought. Impersonal. No torture, no talk, no mutilation.

Just a job, so— 'You live here?'

Nixie's sleepy question broke Eve's rhythm as she drove through the gates toward home.

'Yeah.'

'In a castle?'

'It's not a castle.' Okay, maybe it looked like one, she admitted. The vastness of it, the stones gleaming in the early light, with all those juts and towers, all that space of green and the trees shimmering with the last sparks of fall.

But that was Roarke for you. He didn't do ordinary. 'It's just a really big house.'

'It's a mag house,' Peabody added, with a smile for Nixie. 'Lots of rooms, tons of wall screens and games, even a pool.'

'*In* the house?'

'Yeah. Can you swim?'

'Dad taught us. We get to go on vacation for a week after Christmas to this hotel in Miami. There's the ocean, and there's a pool, and we're going to . . .'

She trailed off, teared up, as she remembered there would

27

be no family vacation after Christmas. No family vacation ever again.

'Did it hurt, when they got dead?'

'No,' Peabody said, gently.

'Did it?' Unsatisfied, Nixie stared hard at the back of Eve's head. Eve parked in front of the house. 'No.'

'How do you know? You never died before. You never had somebody take a big knife and cut you open in your throat. How do you know—'

'Because it's my job.' Eve spoke briskly as Nixie's voice rose up the register toward hysterics. She shifted, looked back at the child. 'They never even woke up, and it was over in a second. It didn't hurt.'

'But they're still *dead*, aren't they? They're all still dead.'

'Yeah, they are, and that blows wide.' Typical, Eve thought, letting the fury roll off her. Anger usually held hands with grief. 'You can't bring them back. But I'm going to find out who did it, and put them away.'

'You could kill them.'

'That's not my job.'

Eve got out of the car, opened the back. 'Let's go.'

Even as she reached out a hand for Nixie's, Roarke opened the front door, stepped out. Nixie's fingers curled into hers like little wires.

'Is he the prince?' she whispered.

As the house looked like a castle, Eve supposed the man who'd built it looked like its prince. Tall and lean, dark and gorgeous. The flow of black hair around a face designed to

28

make a woman whimper with lust. Strong, sharp bones, full, firm mouth, and eyes of bold and brilliant blue.

'He's Roarke,' Eve answered. 'He's just a guy.'

A lie, of course. Roarke wasn't just anything. But he was hers. 'Lieutenant.' Ireland cruised out of his voice as he came down the steps and walked toward them. 'Detective.' He crouched. Eve noted that as he looked into Nixie's eyes he didn't smile.

He saw a pretty, pale little girl, with dried blood in her sunlight blonde hair, and bruises of fatigue and grief under eyes of quiet blue.

'You'd be Nixie. I'm Roarke. I'm sorry to meet you under such terrible circumstances.'

'They killed everybody.'

'Yes, I know. Lieutenant Dallas and Detective Peabody will find who did this horrible thing, and see that they're punished for it.'

'How do you know?'

'It's what they do, what they do better than anyone. Will you come inside now?'

Nixie tugged on Eve's hand, kept tugging until Eve rolled her eyes and bent down. 'What?'

'Why does he talk like that?'

'He's not from around here, originally.'

'I was born across the sea, in Ireland.' Now he did smile, just a little. 'I've never quite shaken the accent.'

Roarke gestured them inside the spacious foyer, where Summerset stood, with the fat cat sprawled at his feet. 'Nixie, this is Summerset,' Roarke said. 'He runs the house. He'll be looking after you, for the most part.'

'I don't know him.' And eyeing Summerset, Nixie cringed back against Eve.

'I do.' It was a big cup of bile to swallow, but Eve gulped it down. 'He's okay.'

'Welcome, Miss Nixie.' Like Roarke, his face was sober. Eve had to give them both credit for not plastering on those big, scary smiles adults often wore around vulnerable kids. 'Would you like me to show you where you'll sleep?'

'I don't know.'

He reached down, picked up the cat. 'Perhaps you'd like some refreshment first. Galahad would keep you company.'

'We had a cat. He was old and he died. We're going to get a kitten next . . .'

'Galahad would be pleased to have a new friend.' Summerset sat the cat down again, waiting while Nixie loosened her grip on Eve's hand and moved closer. When the cat bumped his head against her leg, a ghost of a smile trembled on her lips. She sat on the floor, buried her face in his fur.

'Appreciate this,' Eve said to Roarke under her breath. 'I know it's a major.'

'It's not.' There was blood on her as well. And the faint scent of death. 'We'll talk of it later.'

'I need to go. I'm sorry to dump this on you.'

'I'll be working here most of the morning. Summerset and I will deal well enough.'

'Full security.'

'Without question.'

'I'll get back as soon as I can, work out of here as much as possible. Right now, we need to go notify the parents of the minor female vic. Peabody, you have the Dysons' address?'

'They're not home.' Nixie spoke with her voice muffled against Galahad's fur.

'Nothing wrong with your hearing,' Eve commented, and walked across the foyer. 'Where are they?'

'They went to a big hotel, for their anniversary. That's why we could have a sleepover on a school night, me and Linnie. Now you have to tell them she's dead instead of me.'

'Not instead of. If you'd been in the room, you'd both be dead. Where does that get you?'

'Lieutenant.' The irritated shock in Summerset's voice had her doing no more than lifting a hand to jab a finger at him for silence.

'She's not dead because you're not. This is going to be hard on the Dysons, just like it is on you. But you know who's to blame for what happened.'

Nixie looked up now, and those quiet blue eyes hardened like glass. 'The men with the knives.'

'Yeah. Do you know what hotel?'

'The Palace, because it's the best. Mr Dyson said.'

'Okay.' It was the best, Eve thought, because it was one of Roarke's. She shot him a look, got a nod.

'I'll clear the way.'

'Thanks. I've got to go,' she said to Nixie. 'You're going to hang with Summerset.'

'The men with knives could come looking for me.'

'I don't think so, but if they do, they can't get in. There's a gate, and it's secure, and the house is secure. And Summerset? I know he looks like a bony, ugly old man, but he's tough, and you're safe with him. This is the deal if you're staying here,' she added as she rose. 'It's the best I've got.'

'You're coming back.'

'I live here, remember? Peabody, with me.'

'Her bag's right here.' Peabody gestured to the duffle she'd packed. 'Nixie, if I forgot anything you want, or you need something else, you can have Summerset contact me. We'll get it for you.'

Eve's last look was of the child sitting on the floor between the two men, and seeking comfort from the cat.

The minute she was outside, Eve rolled her shoulders, rolled the weight off. 'Jesus' was all she said.

'I can't imagine what's going on inside that kid.'

'I can. I'm alone, I'm scared and hurt, and nothing makes sense. And I'm surrounded by strangers.' It made her sick, just a little sick, but she pushed past it. 'Check in with EDD, see where they are.'

As she drove back toward the gate, Eve used the dash 'link to contact Dr. Charlotte Mira, at home.

'Sorry. I know it's early.'

'No, I was up.'

On screen Eve could see Mira dab a white towel at her soft sable hair. There was a dew – either sweat or water – on her face.

'Doing my morning yoga. What's the matter?'

'Multiple homicide – home invasion. An entire family, save the nine-year-old daughter. Sleepover friend murdered through mistaken ID. Kid's a witness. I've got her stashed at my place.'

'Yours?'

'Fill you in later, but that's how it stands. I'm heading over to notify next of kin on the daughter's friend.'

'God's pity.'

'I know you've probably got a full slate, but I'm going to need to interview this kid today. I'm going to need a shrink – sorry.'

'No problem.'

'I'm going to need a psychiatrist on hand, one who's got experience with children and police procedure.'

'What time do you want me?'

'Thanks.' And relief rolled in where the weight had rolled off. 'I'd prefer you, but if you're squeezed I'll take your best recommendation.'

'I'll make room.'

'Ah.' Eve checked her wrist unit, tried to gauge the timing. 'Can we make it noon? I've got a lot to push through before then.'

'Noon.' Mira began to make notes in a mini memo book. 'What's her condition?'

'She wasn't injured.'

'Emotional condition.'

'Ah, she's fair, I guess.'

'Is she able to communicate?'

'Yeah. I'm going to need an eval for Child Protection Services. I'm going to need a lot of things for the red tape brigade. I'm on borrowed time here since I went over the rep's head. Have to notify the supervisor there. Soon.'

'Then I'll let you get to it, and see you at noon.'

'EDD's on scene,' Peabody said when Eve ended transmission. 'Their team's going through security and checking 'links and data centers on site. They'll transport the units to Central.'

'Okay. Next of kin on the other vics?'

'Grant Swisher's parents divorced. Father's whereabouts currently unknown. Mother remarried – third time – and living on Vegas II. Works as a blackjack dealer. Keelie Swisher's parents are deceased – back when she was six. Foster care and state schools.'

And that, Eve knew, was just tons of fun. 'When we've talked to the Dysons, contact Grant Swisher's next of kin and inform. She may have legal guardianship of the kid, and we'll need to deal with that. You got an addy on Swisher's law firm?'

'Swisher and Rangle, on West Sixty-first.'

'Close to the hotel. We'll hit there after the Dysons. See how it goes and tap in another pass at the scene if it fits.'

     ★   ★   ★

This, as hard as it was, she knew how to do. Shattering the lives of those left behind was a job she did all too often. Roarke had, as promised, cleared the way. Since she was expected, she avoided the usual wrangle with the doorman, the time-consuming conversation with desk clerks and hotel security.

She almost missed it.

But she and Peabody were efficiently escorted to the elevators and given the Dysons' room number.

'Only child, right?'

'Yeah, just Linnie. He's a lawyer, too, corporate. She's a pediatrician. Reside about two blocks south of the Swishers. Daughters go to the same school, same class.'

'You've been busy,' Eve commented as they rode up to the fortysecond floor.

'You were wrapped up with the kid awhile. We detectives do what we can.'

Out of the corner of her eye, Eve saw Peabody shift her stance, wince just a bit. Ribs still bothering her, she thought. Should've taken a few more days medical. But she let it pass.

'Get any financials on the Swishers?'

'Not yet. We detectives are not miracle workers.'

'Slacker.' Eve stepped off, walked straight to 4215. She didn't allow herself to think, to feel. What good would it do?

She pressed the buzzer, held her badge up to the security peep. Waited. The man who answered was wrapped in a plush hotel robe. His thatch of dark brown hair stuck up in wild tufts and his square, attractive face held the sleepy, satisfied look of someone who'd just enjoyed some early morning nookie. 'Officer?'

'Lieutenant Dallas. Matthew Dyson?'

'Yeah. Sorry, we're not up yet.' He cupped his hand over a huge yawn. 'What time is it?'

'Just after seven. Mr Dyson—'

'Is there a problem in the hotel?'

'Can we come in, Mr Dyson, speak to you and your wife?'

'Jenny's still in bed.' The sleepy look was fading into mild irritation. 'What's the problem?'

'We'd like to come in, Mr Dyson.'

'All right, all right. Hell.' He stepped back, waved at them to shut the door.

They'd sprung for a suite – one of the dreamy, romantic ones with banks of real flowers, real candles, fireplace, deep sofas. There was a bottle of champagne upended in a silver bucket on the coffee table. Two flutes, and she noted, some lacy portion of female lingerie draped like a flag over the back of the sofa.

'Would you get your wife, Mr Dyson?'

His eyes were brown like his hair. And irritation flashed into them. 'Look, she's sleeping. It's our anniversary – or was yesterday – and we celebrated. My wife's a doctor, and she works long hours. She never gets to sleep in. So tell me what the hell you want.'

'I'm sorry, we need to speak with both of you.'

'If there's a problem with the hotel—'

'Matt?' A woman opened the bedroom door. She was sleep-tousled and robed, and smiling as she shoved a hand through her short, disordered blonde curls. 'Oh, I thought you must've ordered room service. I heard voices.'

'Mrs Dyson, I'm Lieutenant Dallas, NYPSD. This is my partner, Detective Peabody.'

'The police.' Her smile became uncertain as she walked to her husband, hooked an arm through his. 'We weren't that loud last night.'

'I'm sorry. There was an incident at the Swishers' early this morning.'

'Keelie and Grant?' Matt Dyson went stiff and straight. 'What kind of incident? Is everyone all right? Linnie. Did something happen to Linnie?'

Fast, Eve knew. Like a short-armed punch to the face. 'I'm sorry to tell you that your daughter was killed.'

While Jenny's eyes went blank and frozen, Matt's went hot with rage. 'That's ridiculous. What is this, some sort of sick joke? I want you out of here, I want you to get out.'

'Linnie? Linnie?' Jenny shook her head. 'This can't be true. This can't be right. Keelie and Grant are too careful. They love her like their own. They'd never let anything happen to her. I need to call Keelie.'

'Mrs Swisher is dead,' Eve said flatly. 'Persons unknown entered the residence last night. Mr and Mrs Swisher, their housekeeper, their son Coyle, your daughter were murdered. Their daughter Nixie was overlooked, and is now under protective custody.'

'This is a mistake.'

Jenny squeezed a hand on her husband's arm as he began to shake. 'But they have security. They have good security.'

'It was compromised. We're investigating. I'm sorry for your loss. I'm extremely sorry.'

'Not my baby.' It wasn't a cry so much as a wail as Matt Dyson crumbled, as he turned to his wife and collapsed against her. 'Not our baby.'

'She's just a little girl.' Jenny rocked, herself, her husband, as her shattered eyes clung to Eve's. 'Who would hurt an innocent little girl?'

'I intend to find out. Peabody.'

On cue, Peabody stepped forward. 'Why don't we sit down? Can I get you something. Water? Tea?'

'Nothing, nothing.' With her arm still wrapped around her husband, Jenny sank with him onto the couch. 'Are you sure it was my Linnie? Maybe—'

'She's been identified. There's no mistake. I'm sorry I have to intrude at this time, but I need to ask you a few questions. Did you know the Swishers well?'

'We . . . Oh God, dead?' The barrage of shock had turned skin to paste. 'All?'

'You were friends?'

'We were, God, like family. We . . . Keelie and I shared patients, and we . . . we all . . . the girls, the girls are like

38

sisters, and we – Matt.' She encirled him, rocked again. Said his name over and over.

'Can you think of anyone who wished them harm? Who wished anyone in the family harm?'

'No. No. No.'

'Did any of them mention being worried about anything? About being threatened or bothered by someone.'

'No. I can't think. No. Oh God, my baby.'

'Was either of them involved with someone, outside of the marriage?'

'I don't know what you . . . Oh.' She closed her eyes as her husband continued to weep on her shoulder. 'No. They had a good marriage. They loved each other, enjoyed each other. Their children. Coyle. Oh my God. Nixie.'

'She's all right. She's safe.'

'How? How did she get away?'

'She'd gone downstairs for a drink. She wasn't in bed at the time of the murders. I don't believe she was seen.'

'She wasn't in bed,' Jenny said softly. 'But my Linnie was. My baby was.' Tears flooded her cheeks. 'I don't understand. I can't understand. We need to . . . Where is Linnie?'

'She's with the Medical Examiner. I'll arrange for you to be taken to see her, when you're ready.'

'I need to know, but I can't.' She turned her head so her shoulder rested on her husband's as his did on hers. 'We need to be alone now.' Eve dug a card out of her pocket, laid it on the coffee table. 'Contact me when you're ready. I'll arrange the rest.'

She walked away from their grief, and she and Peabody rode down to the lobby in silence.

The law offices boasted a comfortable waiting area, divided by theme rather than walls into distinct parts. A child's corner, with a minicomp and a lot of bright toys, flowed into a section designed, Eve imagined, with the older child in mind. Mag vids, puzzles, trendy comp games. Across the room, adults could wait their turn in pastel chairs, and watch vids on parenting, sports, fashion, or gourmet cooking.

The receptionist was young, with a cheerful smile and a shrewd eye. She wore her streaked red and gold hair in what Eve assumed to be a stylish fringe of varying lengths.

'No appointment, but then cops don't usually need one.' She made them as cops before badges were shown, and angled her head. 'What's up?'

'We need to speak to Rangle,' Eve said and pulled out her badge for form.

'Dave's not in yet. He in trouble?'

'When do you expect him?'

'He'll swing in any minute. Early bird. We don't open for business until nine.' She made a point to gesture to the clock. 'Still nearly an hour shy.'

'That makes you an early bird, too.'

The woman smiled, toothily. 'I like coming in early, when it's quiet. I get a lot done.'

'What do you do here?'

40

'Me, personally? Manage the office, assist. I'm a paralegal. What's up with Dave?'

'We'll wait for him.'

'Suit yourself. He's got an appointment at . . .' She turned to a data unit, tapped the screen with short, square-shaped nails painted gold like the streaks in her hair. 'Nine-thirty. But he likes to get here, line up his ducks beforehand like me. Should be in soon.'

'Fine.' Because she wanted Peabody off her feet, Eve gestured her partner to the chairs, then leaned casually on the reception counter. 'And you'd be?'

'Sade Tully.'

'Got an eye for cops, Sade?'

'Mother's on the job.'

'That so? Where?'

'Trenton. She's a sergeant, city beat. My grandfather, too. And his daddy before him. Me, I broke tradition. Seriously, is Dave in trouble?'

'Not that I know of. Anybody else here, in the office?'

'Dave's assistant isn't due until ten. Health appointment. Receptionist generally clocks in about quarter to nine. Grant Swisher, Dave's partner, should be in pretty soon. Grant's between assistants, so I'm filling in that slot. We got a droid clerk, but I haven't activated it yet today. Law student comes in about noon – after class – today. Well, if you're going to hang, you want coffee?'

'I would. We would,' Eve corrected. 'Thanks.'

'No prob.' Sade popped up, walked two steps to an AutoChef. 'How you take it?'

'Black for me, sweet and light for my partner.' As she spoke, Eve wandered, gave herself the chance to study the setup. Friendlier than most law offices, she decided. Little touches of hominess in the toys, the cityscape wall art. 'How long's your mother been on the job?'

'Eighteen. She freaking loves it, except when she hates it.'

'Yeah, that's the way.'

Eve turned when the outer door opened.

The man who came in was black and trim, in a trendy suit of rusty brown with pencil thin lapels and a flashy striped tie. He carried a jumbo cup of takeout coffee in one hand, and was biting into a loaded bagel.

He made a *mmm* sound, nodded to Eve and Peabody, winked at Sade.

'Minute,' he managed with his mouth full, then swallowed. 'Morning.'

'Cops, Dave. Want to talk to you.'

'Sure. Okay. Wanna come back?'

'We would. Sade, would you join us?'

'Me?' The paralegal blinked, then something came into her eyes. A knowledge of trouble, bad trouble. She might have broken tradition, Eve thought, but she had cop in the blood. 'Something happened. Did something happen to Grant?'

No point in going back to an office, Eve decided. 'Peabody, on the door.'

'Yes, sir.'

'I'm sorry, Grant Swisher is dead. He, his wife, and his son were killed last night.'

Coffee streamed out of Dave's cup as it tipped in his hand and spilled a pool onto the company carpet. 'What? What?'

'An accident?' Sade demanded. 'Were they in an accident?'

'No. They were murdered, along with their housekeeper and a young girl named Linnie Dyson.'

'Linnie, oh God. Nixie.' Sade was around the counter and gripping Eve's arm in a flash. 'Where's Nixie?'

'Safe.'

'Mother of God.' Dave staggered to the sofa, slid onto it, crossed himself. 'Merciful Jesus. What happened?'

'We're investigating. How long have you worked with Swisher?'

'Um, God. Ah, five years. Two as a partner.'

'Let's get this out of the way. Can you give me your whereabouts between midnight and three A.M.?'

'Shit. Shit. Home. Well, I got home just after midnight.'

'Alone?'

'No. Overnight guest. I'll give you her name. We were up and . . . occupied until around two. She left about eight this morning.' His eyes were dark, and when they met Eve's again, they were shattered. 'He wasn't just my partner.'

Sade sat beside him, took his hand. 'It's just what she has to ask, Dave. You know. Nobody thinks you'd hurt Grant or his family. I was home. I've got a roommate,' she added,

43

'but she wasn't home last night. I was talking to a friend on the 'link until just after midnight. She's got man trouble. You can check my machine.'

'Appreciate it. I'm going to want the name of your overnight guest, Mr Rangle. It's routine. Ms. Tully, you said Mr Swisher was between assistants. What happened to his assistant?'

'She just had a baby last month. She took maternity, but was planning to come back, so we did the temp thing. But a few days ago, she opted for professional mother status. There wasn't any friction, if that's what you're after. God, I'll have to tell her.'

'I'll need her name, and the names of all the staff. Just routine,' Eve added. 'Now I want you to think, to tell me if you know of anyone who'd wish Mr Swisher or his family harm. Mr Rangle?'

'I don't have to think. I don't.'

'A client he'd pissed off?'

'Honest to God, I can't think of anybody who's ever walked in that door who would do something like this. His kid? Coyle? My God.' Tears swam into his eyes. 'I played softball with Coyle. The kid loved baseball. It was like his religion.'

'Swisher ever cheat on his wife?'

'Hey.' When Dave started to rise, Sade pressed a hand on his thigh.

'You can never say a hundred percent, you know that. But I'd give you a ninety-nine point nine percent no, and that goes for her, too. They were tight, they were happy.

44

They believed in family, since neither of them had much of one before they hooked up. And they worked to keep it together.'

Sade took a steadying breath. 'You work as close as we work in this firm, you know that kind of thing. You get the vibes. Grant loved his wife.'

'Okay. I want access to his office, his files, his client list, court transcripts, the works.'

'Don't make her get a warrant, Dave,' Sade said quietly. 'Grant wouldn't if it had been one of us. He'd cooperate. He'd help.'

He nodded. 'You said Nixie was safe. She wasn't hurt.'

'No. She wasn't injured, and she's in protective custody.'

'But Linnie . . .' He passed a hand over his face. 'Have you told the Dysons?'

'Yes. Do you know them?'

'Yeah, God, yeah. Parties at Grant's, weekends at this place they have in the Hamptons on time share. Grant and Matt and I golfed a couple times a month. Sade, can you make calls, close things down for the day?'

'Sure. Don't worry.'

'I'll show you Grant's office – sorry, I can't remember if I got your name.'

'Dallas, Lieutenant Dallas.'

'Um, they didn't have close family. Arrangements . . . Will we be able to make arrangements?'

'I'll see if I can clear that for you.'

★　　★　　★

When they got back in their vehicle, they had a box full of discs, several files of hard copies, Swisher's office calendar, address, and memo books.

Peabody strapped in. 'Picture's coming clear of a nice, happy family, nicely secured financially, good circle of friends, close relationships with associates, satisfying careers. Not the sort you expect to get murdered in their beds.'

'Plenty of layers to pick through. A lot of families might look happy on the surface, even to friends and coworkers. And they hate each other like poison in private.'

'Cheery thought.' Peabody pursed her lips. 'That makes you the cynical cop, and me the naive one.'

'That's about right.'

3

She felt squeezed for time, but going back to the scene, moving through it, *feeling* it was essential. A nice three-story single-family, she thought, bumped up against other nice two- or three-story single- or multiple-families in a tony Upper West Side neighborhood.

More solid than flashy.

Kids went to private schools, one live-in domestic. Two full-time careers, one outside the home, one based in it. Two front entrances, one rear.

Security, she noted, on all doors and windows, with the addition of decorative – but efficient – riot bars on the below street level where Keelie Swisher based her office.

'They didn't come in from below,' Eve noted as she scoped out the house from the sidewalk. 'Security was active on the office entrance, and on the rear.' She turned, scanned the street, the curbs. 'Parking's a bitch in neighborhoods like this. You need a permit, curb scanners verify. If you park at the curb without one, it's an automatic ticket. We'll check, but I can't see these guys making it that easy for us. Either they walked from another point, or had a permit. Or they live right around here.

47

'Walked, more likely walked. Block or two anyway,' she said as she crossed, opened the useless little iron gate and stepped up to the door. 'Walked to the front door. Jammed the security, the alarms, the cameras, the ID pads by remote before they moved into scanning distance. Had the codes, or knew how to bypass locks quickly.'

She used her police master to deactivate the seal, open the locks. 'Not a lot of people on the street around here that time of night, but some. You could have some. Walking a dog, taking a stroll, coming home from a night out. People watch people in this kind of area. Had to be slick, move fast, and casual.'

She stepped inside the narrow hall that separated living from dining areas. 'Whatcha got? A couple of bags, likely. Nothing big or bold. Soft black bags, probably, to carry the weapons, the jammers, protective gear. Couldn't gear up outside, too risky. Right here, I'd wager, right here just inside the door. Pull on the gear, split up. One upstairs, one straight back to the housekeeper. No talking, just business.'

'Hand signals maybe,' Peabody suggested. 'Night vision equipment.'

'Yeah. Tools in the pouch, but you know the route, the routine. You've done sims. Bet your ass you've done sims.' She walked back toward the kitchen, imagining the dark, the utter quiet. Straight back, she thought. Been here before or had a blueprint. She flicked a glance toward the table and benches where Nixie had been. 'Wouldn't see the kid, wouldn't be looking.'

She went into a crouch, and had to angle her body to see the police marker where Nixie's soda had been found. 'And even if you glanced around, you wouldn't see a little girl lying on the bench. Attention's this way, toward the housekeeper's rooms.'

Inga had been neat, as she'd expect of someone who made her living cleaning up other people's debris. She could see the order under the disorder caused by the sweepers. Catch the fresh scents, and the death scents, under the smear of chemicals.

And she imagined Nixie creeping in, the excitement of a child hoping to catch adults in a forbidden act.

In the bedroom, blood patterned the walls, the bedside table and lamp, pooled on the sheets, had dripped to the floor.

'She liked the right side of the bed, probably a side sleeper. See?' Eve moved into the murder zone, gestured to the spatter pattern.

'He walks up to this side, has to – or wants to – lift her head up. The spatter shows that her head was turned a little, so her body's on her left side, facing away from the bed – the way he left her after he cut her throat. Her blood's on him now, but he doesn't worry about that. Take care of that before he leaves. Walks right out again, walks right by the kid.'

Illustrating, Eve turns, heads out. 'Must've passed inches away from her. Smart kid, scared kid. She doesn't make a peep.'

Turning again, she studied the bedroom. 'Nothing out of place. He doesn't touch anything but her. Isn't interested in anything but her, and the rest of the mission.'

'Is that how you see it? A mission?'

'What else?' Eve shrugged. 'Leaves, work's done here. Why doesn't he take the back steps?'

'Ah . . .' Peabody frowned in concentration, looked at the layout. 'Positioning? Master bedroom's actually closer to the main stairs. That's probably where his partner was stationed. Does another sweep by going around that way.'

'Adults have to come first, have to be done at the same time.' Eve nodded as they made the trip around. 'He probably has a way to signal his partner that the first wave is complete and he's on his way.'

She glanced at the blood, the occasional drops of it staining floor or carpet, stair treads. 'He leaves a little trail, but no big. It's her blood, not his. This down here, on the right, will all be the housekeeper's. They removed the bloody gear, stuffed it in the bags before they came down again.'

'Cold,' Peabody commented. 'No hand slapping, no good job. Slice five people, strip off the gear, and move on.'

'Straight up, straight in while the kid pulls it together enough to get the pocket 'link and call nine-one-one. "Y" off in here, in the main bedroom, one to each side of the bed. Same pattern as the housekeeper. They've got a rhythm down. Terminate the targets, move out and on.'

'They slept back-to-back,' Peabody pointed out. 'The ass-to-ass snuggle. McNab and I do that, mostly.'

Eve was seeing them, husband and wife, mother and father, sleeping butt-to-butt on the big bed with its sea green sheets, its downy quilt. Sleeping in a tidy, relaxing room, with its windows facing the back patio. Him in black boxers, her in a white sleepshirt.

'Lift the head, expose the throat. Slice, drop, head out. No chatter. They're out and heading for the two other bedrooms as the kid's coming up the stairs. They've already designated who takes which room. Split off. One takes the boy – going in as Nixie crawls across the hall behind them.'

Eve walked out as she spoke, and into Coyle's room. 'Boy's a sprawler, flat on the back, covers kicked off. Don't have to touch this one to do the job. Take him out while he's flat.'

She saw it in her head, the cold horror of it as she walked across the hall to the other bedroom. 'Girl's room, girl in bed. Too sure of yourself to think twice. Too steeped in the routine to deviate. Just cross over. Why would you notice the shoes, the extra backpack? You're not looking at anything but the target. She's mostly buried under the covers – stomach sleeper. Yank her up, by the hair probably. A lot of blonde hair, as advertised. Slice her throat, dump her back, walk away.'

'Not as much spatter here,' Peabody commented. 'He probably took most of it on his person, and the rest went on the bed and covers.'

'Steps out into the hall, coordinating with his partner. See the blood in this spot. From their gear, dripping off

51

the gear as they strip it off. Shove it in the bags with the knives. Go downstairs and out, clean. Walk away. Mission accomplished.'

'Except it wasn't.'

Eve nodded. 'Except it wasn't. And if they'd taken a few more minutes, just a few, if they'd taken time to pick up a few goodies on the way out, or linger over the job, the black-and-white would have pulled up before they walked out. As it was, it was close. The kid acted fast, but they acted faster.'

'Why kill the kids?' Peabody asked. 'What threat were they?'

'For all we know at this point, one or both of the kids was the main target. Saw something, heard something, knew something – was into something. We can't assume the adults were the primary. The point is they all had to go, the entire household. That's where we start.'

She was late for Mira, but it couldn't be helped.

Eve found her sitting in the parlor, drinking tea and working on her PPC.

'Sorry. I got hung up.'

'It's all right.' Mira set the PPC aside. She wore a simply cut suit in a smokey color that wasn't quite blue, wasn't quite gray. Somehow her shoes managed to be the exact same in-between tone. There were twists of silver at her ears and a trio of hair-thin chains around her neck.

Eve wondered if she had to strategize to put herself together with such elegant perfection, or if it came naturally.

'She's sleeping. The child,' Mira said. 'Summerset has her on monitor.'

'Oh, good. Okay. Listen, I've got to get some real coffee or my brain's going to melt. You good?'

'Fine, thanks.'

Eve walked over to a wall panel and, opening it, revealed a mini AutoChef. 'You got the report.'

'Yes, it's what I was going over when you got here.'

'It's sketchy yet, but I haven't had time to fill in the fine points. Peabody's getting the clearance for the minor victims' data – heading to their schools, see what we can find there.'

'Do you expect to find anything there? Do you think the children were the targets?'

Eve lifted a shoulder, then closed her eyes and let the jolt of coffee do its work. 'The boy was old enough, certainly, to be involved in illegals, gangs, and all sorts of bad behavior. Can't discount that. Or the possibility he and/or his sister witnessed something or were told something that required their termination. Odds are higher it was one of the adults, but it's not a certainty, especially this early on.'

'There was no additional violence, no destruction of property.'

'None, and if anything was taken from the premises, we don't know about it yet. The timing was quick and slick. Teamwork, timetable. Damn good job.'

'From anyone else, I'd say that was a cold and heartless

remark.' Eve's eyes flattened. 'From their point of view, it was. Cold, heartless, and a damn good job. Except they missed. They'll know they missed soon, once the media gets going on this.'

'And they may try to finish the job,' Mira said with a nod. 'So you brought the child here.'

'One of the reasons. This place is a fucking fort. And if I keep CPS at a distance, I've got unlimited access to the eye witness. Plus, the kid freaked at the idea of going with the social worker. She's no good to me if she's hysterical.'

'Remember who you're talking to,' Mira said mildly. 'You would have managed full access even if she'd been placed under CPS and put in a safe house. Feeling for her doesn't make you less of a cop.'

Eve slid one hand into her pocket. 'She called nine-one-one. She crawled through her parents' blood. Yeah, I feel for her. I also know a kid who can do that can stand up to what comes next.'

She sat across from Mira. 'I don't want to push the wrong buttons on her. I could do that, and if I do, she's going to pull in, shut down. But I need details from her, information from her. Everything I can get. I need you to help me.'

'And I will.' She sipped her tea. 'My preliminary profile of your killers is that they were indeed a team. Have likely worked together before, and have certainly killed before. They would be mature, and likely have some training. Military or paramilitary, or organized crime. There was nothing personal in this act, but the murder of the children

– a family as a unit – is certainly personal. I'm sure it wasn't a thrill kill, nor was it sexual.'

'For profit?'

'Very possibly, or because they were given orders, or simply because it had to be done. The motive?' She sipped her tea thoughtfully. 'We'll need more on the victims to speculate on the why. But the who? They'll be experienced, and they'll trust each other. They're organized and confident.'

'It was an op. That's how it ran for me. An operation, planned and practiced.'

'You think they had access to the house before last night?' Mira asked.

'Maybe. In any case, they knew the layout, where everyone slept. If the housekeeper was primary, there was no reason to take the second floor and vice versa. So it was a clean sweep.'

Eve checked her wrist unit. 'How long do you figure she'll be out? The kid?'

'I couldn't say.'

'I don't want to hold you up.'

'And you're anxious to get to work yourself.'

'I haven't talked to the ME, or finished my report, harassed the lab, or yelled at the sweepers. People are going to think I'm on vacation.'

With a smile, Mira rose. 'Why don't you contact me when . . . Ah,' she added when Summerset stepped into the doorway. 'Lieutenant, your young charge is awake.'

'Oh. Right. Fine. You still got time to start this now?' she asked Mira.

'Yes. Where would you like to speak with her?'

'I figured my office.'

'Why don't you bring her down here? It's a nice, comfortable space, and might help put her at ease.'

'I'll bring her down.' Summerset faded out of the doorway, and left Eve frowning.

'Am I going to owe him for this?' she wondered. 'For, you know, riding herd or whatever you'd call it. Because I'd really hate that.'

'I think you're fortunate to have someone on premises who's willing and able to tend to a young, traumatized girl.'

'Yeah, shit.' Eve sighed. 'I was afraid of that.'

'It might help to remember the child's welfare and state of mind is priority.'

'Looking at him on a regular basis might send her back into shock.' But when Nixie came in, the cat on her heels, she had her hand firmly in Summerset's bony one, releasing it only when she saw Eve.

Nixie walked directly to her. 'Did you find them?'

'Working on it. This is Dr. Mira. She's going to help—'

'I already saw a doctor. I don't want to see a doctor.' Nixie's voice began to rise. 'I don't want—'

'Throttle back,' Eve ordered. 'Mira's a friend of mine, and she's not only a doctor, she works with the cops.'

Nixie slid her eyes toward Mira. 'She doesn't look like the police.'

'I work with the police,' Mira said in calm, quiet tones. 'I try to help them understand the people who commit crimes. I've known Lieutenant Dallas quite a while. I want to help her, and you, find the people who hurt your family.'

'They didn't hurt them, they killed them. They're all dead.'

'Yes, I know. It's horrible.' Mira's gaze and her tone stayed level. 'The worst thing that can happen.'

'I wish it didn't.'

'So do I. I think if we sit down and talk, we might be able to help.'

'They killed Linnie.' Nixie's bottom lip began to tremble. 'They thought she was me, and now she's dead. I wasn't supposed to go downstairs.'

'We all do things we're not really supposed to sometimes.'

'But Linnie didn't. I was bad, and she wasn't. And she's dead.'

'Not so very bad,' Mira said gently, and taking Nixie's hand led her to a chair. 'Why did you go downstairs?'

'I wanted an Orange Fizzy. I'm not supposed to have them without permission. I'm not supposed to snack at night. My mom—' she broke off, knuckled her eyes.

'Your mom would have said no, so yes, it was wrong of you to go behind her back. But she'd be very glad you weren't hurt, wouldn't she? She'd be happy that, this once, you broke the rules.'

'I guess.' Galahad leaped into her lap, and Nixie stroked his wide back. 'But Linnie—'

'It wasn't your fault. Nothing that happened was your fault. You didn't cause it, and you couldn't have stopped it.'

Nixie looked up. 'Maybe if I'd yelled really loud, I'd've woken everyone up. My dad could've fought the bad guys.'

'Did your father have a weapon?' Eve demanded before Mira could speak.

'No, but—'

'Two men with knives, and him unarmed. Maybe if you'd yelled he'd have woken up. And he'd still be dead. Only difference is they'd have known someone else was in the house, hunted you down, and killed you, too.'

Mira shot Eve a warning look and turned her attention back to Nixie. 'Lieutenant Dallas told me you were very brave and very strong. Because she's both of those things, I know she's telling the truth.'

'She found me. I was hiding.'

'It was good that you hid. It was good that she found you. I know what Lieutenant Dallas just said is hard for you to hear, but she's right. There was nothing more you could have done last night to help your family. But there are things you can do now.' Mira glanced at Eve, signalling her.

'Listen, Nixie,' Eve said, 'this is rough, but the more you can tell me, the more I know. This is my recorder.' She set it on the table, sat across from Mira and the child. 'I'm going to ask you some questions. Dallas, Lieutenant Eve, in interview with Swisher, Nixie, minor female, with Mira, Dr. Charlotte, in attendance. Okay, Nixie?'

58

'Okay.'

'Do you know about what time it was that you got out of bed?'

'It was more than two o'clock. Like ten after, about. I had my Jelly Roll on.'

'Wrist unit,' Mira translated.

'What did you do when you got up? Exactly.'

'I went downstairs – really quiet. I thought, for a minute, since Linnie didn't want to wake up, I'd get Coyle. But maybe he'd tell, and I liked being up by myself. I went to the kitchen and got an Orange Fizzy out of the friggie, even though I'm not supposed to. And I went to sit down and drink it in the breakfast area.'

'What happened then?'

'I saw the shadow come in, but it didn't see me. I got down on the bench. It went into Inga's room.'

'What did the shadow look like?'

'It looked like a man, I guess. It was dark.'

'Was he tall or short?'

'As tall as the lieutenant?' Mira prompted and gestured for Eve to stand up.

'Taller, probably. I don't know.'

'What was he wearing?'

'Dark stuff.'

'What about his hair?' Eve tugged her own. 'Short, long?'

On a short sigh, Nixie nuzzled the cat. 'It must've been short, 'cause I couldn't really see it. It was . . . it was . . . covered. Like.' She made a gesture, as if pulling something over her head. 'It covered him up. His whole face, and his eyes, they were all black and shiny.'

Protective gear, Eve surmised. Night goggles. 'Did you hear him say anything?'

'No. He killed her, with the knife. He killed her, and there was blood. And he didn't say anything.'

'Where were you?'

'On the floor, at the door. I wanted to look inside and see . . .'

'It was dark. How could you see?'

Her eyebrows came together a moment. 'From the window. The streetlight through the window. He had a light.'

'Like a flashlight?'

'No, a little dot, a little green light. It was blinking. On his hand. On his . . . here.' She closed her fingers around her wrist.

'Okay, what happened then?'

'I got against the wall. I think. I was so scared. He killed Inga, and he had a knife, and I was so scared.'

'You don't have to be scared now,' Mira said. 'You're safe now.'

'He didn't see me, like I wasn't there. Like hide-and-seek, but he didn't look for me. I got the 'link and I called. Dad says if you see somebody getting hurt, you call Emergency and the police will come and help. You gotta call, you gotta be a good neighbor. My dad—' She broke off, bowed her head as tears dripped.

'He would be very proud of you.' Mira reached for her own bag, took a tissue from it. 'Very proud that you did just what he taught you, even when you were scared.'

'I wanted to tell him, to tell him and Mom. I wanted Mom. But they were dead.'

'You saw the man again, and someone else,' Eve prompted, 'when you went upstairs. You went up the back way.'

'The man who killed Inga was going into Coyle's room.'

'How do you know? Nixie, how do you know it was the man from Inga's room who went into Coyle's?'

'Because . . .' She looked up again, blinking against the tears. 'The light. The green light. The other didn't have one.'

'Okay. What else was different?'

'The one who killed Inga was bigger.'

'Taller?'

'A little bit, but bigger.' She flexed her arms, indicating muscle. 'Did they talk to each other?'

'They didn't say anything. They didn't make any noise. I couldn't hear anything. I wanted Mom.'

Her eyes went dull again, and a tremor shook her voice. 'I knew what they were going to do and I wanted Mom and Dad, but . . . And there was blood, and it got on me. I hid in the bathroom, and I didn't come out. I heard people come in, but I didn't come out. You came.'

'Okay. Do you remember, before any of this happened, if your parents said anything about being concerned, about anybody who was mad at them, or if they'd seen somebody hanging around who shouldn't be?'

'Dad said Dave said he was going to beat him unconscious with his nine iron because he won the golf game.'

'Did they fight a lot, your dad and Dave?'

'Nuh-uh, not for real.' She knuckled her eyes. 'Just ripping.'

'Was there anybody he did fight with? Not just ripping?'

'No. I don't know.'

'Or your mom?' When Nixie shook her head, Eve eased into a dicey area. 'Did your mom and dad fight, with each other?'

'Sometimes, but not like bad. Gemmie's mom and dad used to yell at each other all the time, and Gemmie said they threw things. And they got divorced because her dad couldn't keep his pants zipped. That means he screwed around.'

'Got that. But your parents didn't fight like that.'

'They didn't, and they didn't screw around either. They danced on the beach.'

'Sorry?'

'In the summer, when we went to the beach and got the house. Sometimes they went out to walk at night, and I could see them from my window. They'd dance on the beach. They weren't going to get divorced.'

'It's good to have a memory like that,' Mira said. 'When you start to feel too sad, or scared, you can try to see them dancing on the beach. You did very well. I'd like to come back and talk to you again some time.'

'I guess it's okay. I don't know what I'm supposed to do now.'

'I think you should have some lunch. I have to go soon,

but Lieutenant Dallas will be here, working upstairs in her office. Do you know where the kitchen is?'

'No, the house is too big.'

'Tell me about it,' Eve muttered.

Mira rose, held out a hand. 'I'll take you back, and maybe you can help Summerset for a little while. I'll be back in a minute,' she said to Eve.

Alone, Eve paced to the windows, to the fireplace, back to the windows. She wanted to get to it, start the process. She needed to set up her board, do the runs, write her report and file it. Calls to make, people to see, she thought, jingling loose credits in her pocket.

Shit, how was she going to deal with this kid?

She wondered if the cops who'd had to interview her all those years ago had been equally unsure of their footing.

'She's coping very well.' Mira came back into the room. 'Better than most would. But you should expect mood swings, tears, anger, difficulty sleeping. She's going to require counseling.'

'Can you handle that?'

'For the moment, and we'll see how it goes. She may require a specialist, someone trained primarily in children. I'll look into it.'

'Thanks. I was thinking I should check the department, Youth Services, find a couple of officers who I can assign to her.'

'Take it slow. She's dealing with a lot of strangers at once.'

She touched Eve's arm, then picked up her bag. 'You'll handle it.'

Maybe, Eve thought when Mira left. Hopefully. But at the moment, she had plenty of doubts. She headed upstairs, detoured into Roarke's office.

He was at his desk, with three of his wall screens scrolling various data, and his desk unit humming. 'Pause operations,' he said, and smiled. 'Lieutenant, you look beat up.'

'Feel that way. Listen, I didn't have a chance to really run all this by you. I know I just more or less dumped some strange kid on you and blew.'

'Is she awake?'

'Yeah. She's with Summerset. I did a second interview with her, with Mira in attendance. She holds up pretty well. The kid, I mean.'

'I've had the news on. The names haven't been released yet.'

'I've got that blocked – for the moment. It's going to break soon.' Knowing his wife, he went to the AutoChef, programmed two coffees, black. 'Why don't you run it for me now?'

'Quick version, because I'm behind.'

She gave him the details, brief and stark.

'Poor child. No evidence, as yet, that anyone in the household was into something that could bring down this kind of payback?'

'Not yet. But it's early.'

'Professional, as I'm sure you've already concluded. Someone trained in wet work. The green light she saw was most likely the jammer – green for go – as the security had been bypassed.'

'Figured. On the surface, these people seem ordinary, ordinary family. Straight arrows. But we haven't done much scratching on that surface yet.'

'Sophisticated electronics, special forces–type invasion, quick, clean hits.' Sipping coffee, he ignored the beep of his laser fax. 'In and out . . . in, what, ten or fifteen minutes? It's not something for nothing. Home terrorism would have left a mark, and the targets would have been higher profile. On the surface,' he added.

'You still have some contacts in organized crime.' A smile ghosted around his mouth. 'Do I?'

'You know people who know people who know scum of the earth.' He tapped a fingertip on the dent in her chin. 'Is that any way to talk of my friends and business associates? Former.'

'Damn straight. You could make some inquiries.'

'I can, and I will. But I can tell you I never associated with child killers. Or anyone who would slaughter a family in their sleep.'

'Not saying. I mean that. But I need every angle on this. The little girl? The one he killed in place of the kid downstairs? She was wearing a little pink nightgown with – what do you call it – frills around the neck. I could see it was pink from the bottom. The rest was red, soaked through with blood. He'd slit her throat open like it was an apple.'

He set his coffee down, walked to her. He put his hands on her hips, laid his brow on her brow. 'Anything I can do, I will.'

'It makes you think. You and me, we had the worst most kids can get. Abuse, neglect, rape, beatings, hate. These kids, they had what it's supposed to be, in a perfect world: nice homes, parents who loved them, took care of them.'

'We survived,' he finished. 'They didn't. Except for the one downstairs.'

'One day, when she looks back on this, I want her to know the people who did this are in a cage. That's the best I can do. That's all I can do.'

She eased back. 'So, I'd better get to work.'

4

Her first step was contacting Feeney, captain of the Electronic Detectives Division. He popped on her 'link screen, wiry ginger hair threaded with silver, saggy face, rumpled shirt.

It was a relief to her that his wife's recent attempt to spruce him up with eye-popping suits had gone belly-up.

'I'm catching up,' she said briskly. 'You got word on the Swisher case, home invasion?'

'Two kids.' His face, comfortably morose, hardened. 'When I got wind, I went to the scene myself. I got a team working on the 'links and data centers. I'm doing the security personally.'

'I like getting the best. What can you tell me?'

'Good, solid home system. Top of the line. Took some know-how to bypass. Camera shows squat after one hundred fifty-eight hours. Remote jammer, with secondary jam as the system had an auto backup.'

He tugged on his earlobe as he read data from another screen. 'Visual security shuts down, backup pops within ten seconds, with alarms both in-house and at security center. Compromised the works.'

'They knew the system.'

67

'Oh yeah, they knew the system. Deactivated camera alarm, lock alarm, motion alarm. I'm going to pin it for you, but my prelim indicated entrance ten minutes after the camera blanked, four minutes after the secondary jam.'

'Ten minutes? That's a stretch of time. Might've held, insurance the system didn't make the signal, in-house, to the security company. Four after hitting the secondary. Is that as slick as I think it is?'

'Slick enough. They worked fast.'

'Did they know the code?'

'Can't tell you that yet.' He lifted a mug to his lips that had MINE printed on it in murderous red. 'Either knew it or had a first-class code breaker. Couple of kids not safe in their own bed, Dallas, it's a fucked-up world.'

'It's always been a fucked-up world. I'm going to need all the transmissions, in and out, personal and household. All security discs.'

'You'll have them. I'm putting weight on this one. Got grandchildren that age, for Chrissake. Whatever you need on this one, you got it.'

'Thanks.' Her eyes narrowed as he sipped again. 'That real coffee?' He blinked, eased the mug out of sight. 'Why?'

'Because I can see it on your face. I can see it in your eyes.'

'What if it is?'

'Where'd you get it?'

He shifted. Even with her screen view she could tell he squirmed. 'Maybe I swung by your office, to update you, and you weren't there. And maybe since you've got a damn unlimited supply of the stuff I got myself one lousy mug. Don't see why you have to be so stingy when you've—'

'You help yourself to anything else while you were there? Such as candy?'

'What candy? You got candy in there? What kind?'

'That's for me to know, and you to keep your hands off. I'll get back to you.'

Thinking of coffee and candy reminded her she'd missed breakfast and lunch. She ordered up data on Grant Swisher, then strode into her office kitchen to grab a nutribar and another hit of caffeine.

Settling, she ordered the data on wall screen, and scanned.

Swisher, Grant Edward, DOB March 2, 2019. Residence 310 West Eighty-first, New York City, September 22, 2051 to present. Married Getz, Keelie Rose, May 6, 2046. Two children of the marriage: Coyle Edward, DOB August 15, 2047, male. Nixie Fran, DOB February 21, 2050, female.

Three of those names would be listed as deceased by end of the day in Vital Records, she thought.

She read through the basic data, requested any and all criminal records, and got a pop for possession of Zoner when Grant Swisher had been nineteen. Medical was just as ordinary.

She dug into finances.

He did well. Family law paid enough to handle the mortgage on the house, a time share place in the Hamptons, private schools for both kids. With the wife's income factored in, you had a cozy buffer for a live-in domestic, family vacations, restaurants, and other recreational activities – including a hefty golf tab – and enough left over for a reasonable savings or emergency account.

Nothing over the top, she mused. Nothing, from the looks of it, under the table.

Keelie Swisher, two years younger than her husband, no criminal, standard medical, had a master's degree in Nutrition and Health. She'd put it to use, prior to children, with a position on staff at a high-end city spa. After the first kid, she'd done the professional mother gig for a year, then gone back to the same employment. Repeated the routine with kid number two, but instead of going back as an employee, she'd opened her own business.

Living Well, Eve mused. Didn't sound much like Nutrition, but it must have worked. She tracked the business, shaky first year, middling second. But by the third year, Keelie Swisher had developed a solid clientele, and was cruising.

She ran the boy. No criminal, no flag for sealed juvenile records. No flags on the medical to indicate violence or abuse – though there were some bumps, some breaks. Sports related, according to the medicals. And it fit.

He had his own bank account with his parents listed on it. She pursed her lips over the regular monthly deposits, but the amounts weren't enough to arrow toward illegals sales or criminal profits.

She found the same pattern, with smaller amounts, in Nixie's account.

She was pondering it when Peabody came in carrying a white bag, stained with grease and smelling like glory. 'Picked up a couple of gyros. Ate mine, so if you don't want yours, I'll be happy to take it off your hands.'

'I want it, and nobody should eat two gyros.'

'Hey, I lost five pounds when I was on medical. Okay, I put three back on, but that's still two by anybody's math.' She dropped the bag on Eve's desk. 'Where's Nixie?'

'Summerset.' Eve dumped the nutribar she'd yet to open in her desk drawer and pulled out the gyro. She took a huge bite and mumbled something that sounded like 'Slool ressa.'

'Got the school records on both.' Translating, Peabody pulled out two discs. 'Their school officials were pretty broken up when I notified. Nice schools. Coyle did well, no suspicious dips in grades or attendance. And Nixie? That kid's a blade. Aces all the way. Both scored high on IQ tests, but she's a level up from her brother, and makes the most of it. No disciplinary problems on either. A couple of warnings about talking in class or sneaking game vids, but no major. Coyle played softball and basketball. Nixie's into school plays, does the school media flash, school band – plays the piccolo.'

'What the hell is that?'

'It's a wind instrument. Kinda like a flute. These kids have a lot of extracurricular, good grades. Didn't have time to get in trouble, from my view.'

'They both have their own bank accounts, and make regular monthly deposits. Where do kids get up to a hundred bucks a month?'

Peabody turned to the wall screen, scanned the data. 'Allowance.'

'Allowance for what?'

She looked back, shook her head at Eve. 'Their parents probably gave them a weekly allowance, spending money, saving money, that sort of thing.'

Eve swallowed more gyro. 'They get paid for being a kid?'

'More or less.'

'Nice work if you can get it.'

'Household like that, the way this is shaping up, the kids probably had regular chores, even with a full-time domestic. Keeping their rooms clean, clearing the table, loading the recycler. Then you got your birthday or holiday money, your school report money. Being a Free-Ager, we did bartering more than pay, but it comes to the same.'

'So if everybody stayed a kid, nobody'd have to get a job. They could have seen something at school,' she continued before Peabody could comment. 'Heard something. Something off. We'll take a look at teachers and staff. We can run the adults' business associates and clients, fan out from there to friends, neighbors, social acquaintances. These people weren't picked out of a hat.'

'Doesn't feel like it, but can we discount straight urban terrorism?'

'It's too clean.' Roarke had it right on that one, she thought.

'You want to terrorize, you're messy. Kill the family, rape and torture first, wreck the house, slice up their little dog.'

'They didn't have a little dog, but I get you. And if it was terrorism, some whacked-out group would be taking credit by now. Did we get any reports in? EDD, sweepers, ME?'

'I talked to Feeney. He's on it. Fill you in on the way.'

'To?'

'Morgue, then Central.' She rose, stuffing the last of the gyro in her mouth.

'Want me to let Summerset know we're leaving?'

'Why? Oh. Hell. Yeah, do that.' She crossed to the door joining her office with Roarke's. 'Hey.'

He was rising from his desk, slipping on one of his dark suit jackets. 'I'm heading out,' she told him.

'So am I. I've rearranged a few things. Should be back no later than seven.'

'I don't know when.' She leaned against the jamb, frowning at him. 'I should put the kid in a safe house.'

'This house is safe, and she's fine with Summerset. A more detailed media bulletin's come through. It doesn't list the names, as yet, but reports on an Upper West Side family, including two children, killed early this morning, in their home. Lists you as primary. Details to follow.'

'I'll have to deal with that.'

'And so you will.' He came to her, cupped her face, kissed her. 'You'll do your job, and we'll figure out the rest. Take care of my cop.'

★ ★ ★

As she'd expected, the chief medical examiner had taken charge of the Swisher homicides. It wasn't the sort of detail Morris would pass to someone else, however qualified or skilled.

Eve found him, suited up, over the body of Linnie Dyson.

'I've taken them in order of death.' Behind his micro-goggles his dark eyes were cool and hard.

There was music playing. Morris rarely worked without it, but this was somber, funereal. One of those composers, she imagined, who'd worn white wigs.

'I've ordered tox screens on all victims. Cause of death is the same in all. There are no secondary wounds or injuries, though the minor male vic had several old bruises, two fresh, with minor lacerations – long bruising scrapes on his right hip and upper thigh. His right index finger had been broken, set, and healed at some point within the last two years. All injuries look consistent to me with a young boy who played sports.'

'Softball primarily. Fresh deal sounds like he got it sliding into base.'

'Yes, that fits.'

He looked down at the little girl, at the long slice in her throat. 'Both minor vics were healthy. All vics had a meal at approximately seven p.m., of white fish, brown rice, green beans, and mixed-grain bread. There was an apple dish with wheat and brown sugar topping for dessert. The adults had a glass of white wine, the children soy milk.'

'The mother, the second adult female, was a nutritionist.'

'Practiced what she preached. The boy had a cache some-where,' Morris added with a faint smile. 'He'd consumed two ounces of red licorice at about ten p.m.'

Somehow it cheered her to know it. At least the kid got a last taste of sweet. 'Murder weapons?'

'Identical. Most likely a ten-inch blade. See here.'

He gestured to the screen, magnified the wound on the child's throat. 'See the jags? There, on the edge of the diagonal. Swipe down, from his left to his right. Not a full smooth blade, or a full jagged. Three teeth serrating from the handle, the rest smooth-bladed.'

'Sounds like a combat knife.'

'That would be my take. It was employed by a right-handed individual.'

'There were two.'

'So I'm told. Eyeballing it, I'd have said the same hand delivered the killing blows, but as you can see.. .' He turned to another screen, called for pictures, split screen on Grant and Keelie Swisher. Magnified the wounds.

'There're slight deviations. Male vic's wound is deeper, more of a slicing motion, more jagged, while the female's is more of a draw across. When all five are put up . . .' He nodded as the screen shifted to show five throat wounds. 'You can see that the housekeeper, the father, and the boy have the same slicing wound, while the mother and the girl have the more horizontal drawing across. You'll want the lab to run some reconstructs, but it's going to be a ten-inch blade, twelve at the max, with those three teeth near the handle.'

'Military style,' she stated. 'Not that you have to be military to obtain one. But it's just one more piece of the operation. Military tactics, equipment, and weapons. None of the adults did military time, or appear to have any connection to the military. Can't link any of them, at this point, to paramilitary or game playing.'

Then again, she thought, sometimes a cozy family was the perfect cover for covert or dark deeds.

'I've cleared the Dysons.' Eve glanced back at Linnie. 'Have they seen her yet?'

'Yes. An hour ago. It was . . . hideous. Look at her,' he urged. 'So small. We get smaller, of course. Infants barely out of the womb. It's amazing what we enlightened adults can do to those who need us most.'

'You don't have any kids, right?' Eve asked.

'No, no chick nor child. There was a woman once, and we were together long enough to consider it. But that was . . . ago.'

She studied his face, slickly framed by black hair pulled cleanly back in one sleek tail that was bound in crisscrossing silver twine. Under the clear, protective suit, stained now with body fluids, his shirt was silver as well.

'I've got the kid, the one they didn't get. I don't know what to do with her.'

'Keep her alive. I would think that would be priority.'

'Got that part handled. I'll need those tox reports, and anything that pops, as soon as.'

'You'll have them. They wore wedding rings.'

76

'Sorry?'

'The parents. Not everyone does these days.' Morris nodded toward the scribed band Eve wore on the ring finger of her left hand. 'It's not very fashionable. Wearing them is a statement. I belong. They'd made love, about three hours prior to death. They used a spermicide rather than long-term or permanent birth control, which tells me they hadn't ruled out the possibility of more children in the future. That, and the rings, Dallas? I find that both comforts and angers me.'

'Anger's better. Keeps you sharper.'

When she walked toward Homicide in the massive beehive of Cop Central, she spotted Detective Baxter at a vending unit, getting what passed for coffee. She dug out credits, flipped them to him. 'Tube of Pepsi.'

'Still avoiding contact with vending machines?'

'It's working. They don't piss me off, I don't kick them into rubble.'

'Heard about your case,' he said as he plugged in her credits. 'And so did every reporter in the city. You got most of them hassling the media liaison and hammering for an interview with the primary.'

'Reporters aren't on my to-do list right at the moment.' She took the tube of Pepsi he offered, frowned. 'You said most. Why is Nadine Furst of Channel 75 even now sitting on her well-toned ass in my office?'

'How do you know? Not about the ass, anybody could see Furst's got an excellent ass.'

'You've got cookie crumbs on your shirt, you putz. You let her into my office.'

With some dignity, he brushed off his shirt. 'I'd like to see you turn down a bribe of Hunka-Chunka Chips. Every man has his weakness, Dallas.'

'Yeah, yeah. I'll kick your well-toned ass later.'

'Sweetheart, you noticed.'

'Bite me.' But she studied him as she broke the tube's seal. 'Listen, how's your caseload?'

'Well, as you're my lieutenant I should say I'm ridiculously overworked. I was just coming in from court when I was distracted by Furst's ass and cookies.'

Keying in his code, he ordered a tube of ginger ale from the machine. 'My boy's writing up the three's on one we caught last night. Double D that went nasty. Guy'd been out drinking and whoring, according to the spouse. They got into it when he crawled home, smacked each other around – as per usual according to the neighbors and previous reports. But this time she waited until he'd passed out, then cut off his dick with a pair of sheers.'

'Ow.'

'Fucking A,' Baxter agreed, and took a long gulp. 'Guy bled out before the MTs got there. Damn ugly mess, let me tell you. And the guy's dick? She'd stuffed it in the recycler, just to make sure it didn't get in any more trouble.'

'Pays to be thorough.'

'You women are cold and terrifying creatures. This one?

She's damn proud of it. Says she's going to be a hero to neofems throughout our fair land. Maybe so.'

'You got that closed. Anything else hot?'

'We don't have any more actives than we can handle right now.'

'Anything you don't feel comfortable passing on?'

'You want me to dump my caseloads on somebody else. I'm your boy.'

'I want you and Trueheart on witness duty. My residence.'

'When?'

'Now.'

'I'll get my boy. They did two kids?' His face sobered as they walked toward the bull pen. 'Did them while they slept?'

'It'd have been worse if they'd been awake. You and Trueheart are baby-sitting the eyewitness. Nine-year-old female. Keep it off the log for now. I still have to report to Whitney.'

She moved through the bull pen, then into the glorified closet that was her office.

As predicted, Nadine Furst, Channel 75's on-air ace, sat in Eve's ratty desk chair. She was perfectly groomed, her streaky blonde hair swept back from her foxy face. Her jacket and pants were the color of ripe pumpkin, with a stark white shirt beneath that somehow made the whole getup more female.

She stopped recording notes into her memo book when Eve walked in. 'Don't hurt me. I saved you a cookie.'

Saying nothing, Eve jerked a thumb, then took the chair Nadine vacated. When the silence went on, Nadine cocked her head. 'Don't I get a lecture? Aren't you going to yell at me? Don't you want your cookie?'

'I just came from the morgue. There's a little girl on a slab. Her throat's cut from here, to about here.' Eve tapped a finger on both sides of her own throat.

'I know.' Nadine sat in the single visitor's chair. 'Or I know some of it. A whole family, Dallas. However hard-shelled you and I might be, that gets through. And with a home invasion like this, the public needs some of the details, so they can protect themselves.'

Eve said nothing, just lifted her eyebrows.

'That's part of it,' Nadine insisted. 'I'm not saying ratings aren't involved, or I don't want my journalistic teeth in something this juicy. But the sanctity of the home should mean something. Keeping your kids safe matters.'

'See the media liaison.'

'The ML doesn't have squat.'

'Should tell you something, Nadine.' Eve lifted a hand before Nadine could sound off. 'What I've got at this point isn't going to help the public, and I'm not inclined to give you the inside edge. Unless . . .' Nadine settled back, crossed her exceptional legs. 'Name the terms.'

Eve stretched out, flipping the door shut, then turned around in her chair so that she and Nadine were face-to-face. 'You know how to slant reports, how to spin stories to influence the public who you love to claim has a right to know.'

'Excuse me, objective reporter.'

'Bullshit. The media's no more objective than the last ratings term. You want details, you want the inside track, one-on-ones, and your other items on your reporter's checklist? I'll feed you. And when this goes down and I get them – and I will get them – I want you to bloody them in the media. I want you to skew the stories so these fuckers are the monsters the villagers go after with axes and torches.'

'You want them tried in the press.'

'No.' It wasn't a smile that moved over Eve's face. Nothing that feral could be called a smile. 'I want them hanged by it. You're my secondary line, if the system gives them a loophole even an anorectic blood-worm has trouble wiggling through. Yes or no.'

'Yes. Was there sexual assault on any or all of the victims?'

'None.'

'Torture? Mutilation?'

'No. Straight kills. Clean.'

'Professional?'

'Possibly. Two killers.'

'Two?' The excitement of the hunt flushed onto Nadine's cheek. 'How do you know?'

'I get paid to know. Two,' Eve repeated. 'No vandalism, destruction of property, no burglary that can be determined at this time. And at this time, it is the opinion of the primary investigator that the family in question was target specific. I've got a report to write, and I have to speak to my commander. I'm cooking on three hours' sleep. Go away, Nadine.'

'Suspects, leads?'

'At this time we are pursuing any and all blah, blah, blah. You know the drill. Disappear now.'

Nadine rose. 'Watch my evening report. I'll start bloodying them now.'

'Good. And Nadine?' Eve said as Nadine opened the office door. 'Thanks for the cookie.'

She set up her office case board, wrote her report, read those submitted by EDD and Crime Scene. She drank more coffee, then closed her eyes and went through the scene, yet again, in her mind.

'Computer. Probability run, multiple homicides, case file H-226989-SD,' Eve ordered.

Acknowledged.

'Probability, given known data, that the killers were known by one or more of the victims.'

Working . . . Probability is 88.32 percent that one or more of the victims knew one or more of the killers.

'Probability that the killers were professional assassins.'

Working . . . Probability is 96.93 percent that the killers were professional and/or trained.

82

'Yeah, I'm with you there. Probability that killers were hired or assigned to assassinate victims by another source.'

```
Working . . . Wholly speculative inquiry with
insufficient data to project.
```

'Let's try this. Given current known data on all victims, what is the probability any or all would be marked for professional assassination?'

```
Working . . . 100 percent probability as
victims have been assassinated.
```

'Work with me here, you moron. Speculation. Victims have not yet been assassinated. Given current known data – deleting any data after midnight – what is the probability any or all members of the Swisher household would be marked for professional assassination?'

```
Working . . . Probability is less than five
percent, and therefore these subjects would
not be so marked.
```

'Yeah, my take, too. So what don't we know about this nice family?' She swiveled around to the board. 'Because you're dead, aren't you?' She shoved another disc in the data slot. 'Computer, do a sort and run on subsequent data pertaining to Swisher, Grant, client list. Follow with sort and run on Swisher, Keelie, client list. Highlight any and all subjects with criminal or psych evals, highlight all with military or paramilitary training. Copy results to my home unit when complete.'

Acknowledged. Working . . .

'Yeah, you keep doing that.' She rose, walked out.

'Peabody.' She gave a come-ahead that had Peabody pushing back from her desk in the bull pen.

'I've got a complaint. How come Baxter and most of the other guys always get the good bribes? How come being your partner means I get shafted on the goodies?'

'Price you pay. We're heading to Whitney. Do you have anything new I should know about before we report?'

'I talked with McNab. Purely professional,' Peabody added quickly. 'We hardly made any kissy noises. Feeney put him on the household 'links and d and c's, and Grant Swisher's units from his office. He's running all transmissions from the last thirty days. So far, nothing pops. Did you see the sweepers' report?'

'Yeah. Nothing. Not a skin cell, not a follicle.'

'I'm doing runs on the school staff,' Peabody continued as they squeezed onto an elevator. 'Pulling out anything winky.'

'Winky?'

'You know, not quite quite. Both schools are pretty tight. You gotta practically be pure enough for sainthood to work there, but a few little slips got in. Nothing major at this point.'

'Pull out military, paramilitary backgrounds. Even those – what are they? – combat camps. Those recreational places where you pay to run around playing war. Take a hard look at teachers in the e-departments.' Eve rubbed her temple as they stepped off the elevator. 'The housekeeper was divorced. Let's eyeball the ex. We'll get the names of the kids' pals. See if any of those family members should be checked out.'

'He's waiting for you.' Whitney's admin gestured even as Eve strode toward her desk. 'Detective Peabody, it's good to have you back. How are you feeling?'

'Good, thanks.'

But she drew in a deep breath before they entered Whitney's office. The commander still intimidated her.

He sat, a big man at a big desk, his face the color of cocoa, his short cropped black hair liberally dusted with gray. Peabody knew he'd done his time on the streets, nearly as much time as she'd been alive. And he rode his desk with the same fervor and skill.

'Lieutenant. Detective, it's good to see you back on the job.'

'Thank you, sir. It's good to be back.'

'I have your writtens. Lieutenant, you're walking a thin line taking a minor witness into your own custody.'

'Safest place I know, Commander. And the minor was emotionally distressed. More so at the prospect of going with CPS. As she's our only witness, I felt it best to keep her close, to have her monitored, and to attempt to keep her emotionally stable in order to gain more information from her. I've assigned Detective Baxter and Officer Trueheart to witness protection, off the log.'

'Baxter and Trueheart.'

'Baxter's experience, Trueheart's youth. Trueheart has a kind of Officer Friendly way about him, and Baxter won't miss the details.'

'Agreed. Why off the log?'

'At this time the media is unaware there was a survivor. It won't take much longer, but it gives us more of a window. Once they know, the killers know. These men are trained and skilled. It's highly possible this was an operation executed under orders.'

'Do you have evidence of that?'

'No, sir. None to the contrary either. There is, at this time, no clear motive.'

It was going to be the why, Eve thought, that led to the who. 'Nothing that pops in any of the victims' data or background,' she added. 'We're beginning further runs, and I will continue to interview the witness. Mira has agreed to supervise, and to counsel.'

'Nothing in your report indicates this as a spree killing or home terrorism.'

'No, sir. We're running like crimes through IRCCA, but haven't hit anything with these details.'

'I want your witness under supervision twenty-four/seven.'

'It's done, sir.'

'Mira's name will have considerable weight with CPS.

I'll add mine.' The chair creaked when he leaned back. 'What about legal guardians?'

'Sir?'

'The minor. Who are her legal guardians?'

'The Dysons, Commander,' Peabody said when Eve hesitated. 'The parents of the minor female who was killed.'

'Jesus. Well, they're unlikely to give us any trouble over the situation, but you'd do better to get their permission, officially. Doesn't the child have any family left?'

'Grandparent. One on the father's side who lives off planet. Maternal grandparents are dead. No siblings on either side.'

'Kid can't catch a break, can she?' Whitney muttered.

She caught one, Eve thought. She lived. 'Detective Peabody? You spoke with the grandmother.'

'Yes, Lieutenant. I notified next of kin. At that time, I was told the paternal grandmother was not legal guardian in case of parental death or disability. And, to be frank, while shocked and upset, she made no statement to indicate she intended to come here and attempt custody of the minor.'

'All right then. Dallas, speak with the Dysons at the first opportunity, and tidy this up. Keep me updated.'

'Yes, sir.'

When they were walking back toward the elevator, Peabody shook her head. 'I don't think now's the best time – for the Dysons. I'd let that slide another twenty-four anyway.'

The longer the better, Eve thought.

Security and streetlights were popping on by the time Eve headed back uptown from Central. Normally, the vicious traffic would have given her plenty of reason to snarl and bitch, but tonight she was grateful for the distraction, and the extra drive time.

It was gelling for her.

She could see the method, the type of killers. She could walk through the scene over and over in her mind and follow the steps. But she couldn't find motive.

She sat in stalled traffic behind a flatulent maxibus and circled around the case again. Violence without passion. Murder without rage.

Where was the kick? The profit? The reason?

Going with instinct, she called up Roarke's personal 'link on her dash unit.

'Lieutenant.'

'What's your status?' she asked him. 'Healthy, wealthy, and wise. What's yours?'

'Ha. Mean, crafty, and rude.'

His laugh filled her vehicle, and made her feel slightly less irritable. 'Just the way I like you best.'

'Location, Roarke?'

'Maneuvering through this sodding traffic toward hearth and home. I hope you're doing the same.'

'As it happens. How about a detour?'

'Will it involve food and sex?' His smile was slow, and just a little wicked. 'I'm really hoping for both.'

Odd, damn odd, she thought, that after nearly two years of him that smile could still give her heart a jolt. 'It might later, but first on our lineup is multiple murder.'

'Teach me to marry a cop.'

'What did I tell you? Hold on a minute.' She leaned out the window, shouted at the messenger who'd nearly side-swiped her vehicle with his jet-board. 'Police property, asshole. If I had time I'd hunt you down and use that board to beat your balls black.'

'Darling Eve, you know how that kind of talk thrills and excites me. How can I keep my mind off sex now?'

Eve pulled her head back in, eyed the screen. 'Think pure thoughts. I need to do another walk-through of the crime scene. I wouldn't mind having another pair of eyes.'

'A cop's work is never done, and neither is the man's who's lucky enough to call her his own. What's the address?'

She gave it to him. 'See you there. And if you beat me to the scene, for God's sake don't tamper with the seal. Just wait. Oh, shit, parking. You need a permit. I'll—'

'Please' was all he said, and signed off.

'Right,' she said to dead air. 'Forgot who I was talking to for a minute.'

She didn't know how Roarke dispensed with such pesky details as parking permits, and didn't really want to. He was just stepping onto the sidewalk when she arrived. She pulled up behind his vehicle, flipped on her on-duty light.

'Pretty street,' he said. 'Especially this time of year with the leaves scattered about.' He nodded toward the Swisher house. 'Prime property. If they had any equity in it, at least the child won't be penniless as well as orphaned.'

'They had a chunk, plus standard life policies, some savings, investments. She'll be okay. That's one of the deals, actually. She'll be set pretty well, coming into the bulk of it when she hits twenty-one. They both had wills. Trust-fund deal for the kids, supervised by legal guardians and a financial firm. It's not mega-dough, but people kill for subway credits.'

'Did they make contingencies for alternate beneficiaries should something happen to the children as well?'

'Yeah.' Her mind had gone there, too. Wipe out the family, rake in some easy money. 'Charities. Shelters, pediatric centers. Spread it out, too. Nobody gets an overly big slice of the pie. And no individual gets much above jack.'

'The law firm?'

'Rangle, the partner, gets the shot there. His alibi is solid. And if he has the connections, or the stomach, to order a hit like this, I'll toast my badge for breakfast. This family wasn't erased for money. Not that I can see.'

He stood on the sidewalk, studying the house as she did. The old tree in front, busily shedding its leaves onto the stamp-sized courtyard, the attractive urban lines, the sturdy pot filled with what he thought were geraniums beside the door.

It looked quiet, settled, and comfortable. Until you saw the small red eyes of the police seal, the harsh yellow strip of it marring the front doors.

'If it were money,' he added, 'one would think it would take a fat vat of it to push anyone to do what was done here. The erasing, as you put it, of an entire family.'

He walked with her to the main entrance. 'Put my ear to the ground, as requested. There's no buzz about a contract on these people.'

Eve shook her head. 'No. They weren't connected. But it's good to cross that off the list, at least the probability of it. They didn't have ties to any level of the underworld. Or government agencies. I played around with the idea that one of them had a double life going, thinking of what Reva dealt with a couple months ago.' Reva Ewing, one of Roarke's employees, had had the misfortune of being married to a double agent who'd framed her for a double murder. 'Just doesn't slide. No excessive travel; not much travel at all without the kids. Nothing that sends up a flag on their 'links or comps. These people lived on schedules. Work, home, family, friends. They didn't have time to mess around. Plus . . .'

She stopped, shook her head. 'No. I'll let you make your own impressions.'

'All right. By the way, I've arranged to have my ride picked up. That way I can have my lovely wife drive me home.'

'We're ten minutes from our own gate.'

'Every minute with you, Darling Eve, is a minute to treasure.'

She slid a glance toward him as she uncoded the seal. 'You really do want sex.'

'I'm still breathing, so that would be yes.'

He stepped inside with her, scanning when she called for lights. 'Homey,' he decided. 'Tastefully so. Thoughtfully. Nice colors, nice space. Urban family style.'

'They came in this door.'

He nodded. 'It's a damn good system. Took some skill to bypass without tripping the backups and auto alarms.'

'Is it one of yours?'

'It is, yes. How long did it take them to get in?'

'Minutes. Feeney figures about four.'

'They knew the system, possibly the codes, but certainly the system. And what they were about,' he added, studying the alarm panel. 'It's a tricky one, and would take good, cool hands, and just the right equipment. You see, the backups are designed to engage almost instantly if there's any sort of tampering. They had to know they were there, and deal with them simultaneously, even before they read or input the codes.'

'Pros then.'

'Well, it certainly wasn't their first day on the job. Likely they had an identical system to work with. That would take time, money, planning.' He stepped back from the panel, trying to ignore the outrage he felt that one of his designs had failed to serve. 'But you never supposed this was random.'

'No. What I put together from the scene and the witness report is that one went upstairs – or at least stayed back – while the other went through here.'

She led the way, moving directly to the kitchen. 'It was dark – some glow from security and streetlights through the windows – but they had night vision. Had to. Plus the witness described blank, shiny eyes.'

'Which could be a child's imagination. Monster eyes. But,' he said with another nod, 'more likely night vision. Where was she?'

'Over there, lying on the bench.' Eve gestured. 'If he'd looked, taken enough time to do a sweep through the kitchen, he'd have seen her. The way she tells it, he just walked straight to the domestic's door.'

'So he knew where he was going. Knew the layout, or had been here at some time.'

'Checking on household repairs, deliveries, but that doesn't feel like it. How do you get the layout of the whole house if you, what, install a new AutoChef or fix a toilet? How do you know the layout of the domestic's quarters?'

'Someone involved with the domestic?'

'She wasn't seeing anyone, hadn't been for several months. A few friends outside the family, but they pan out. So far.'

'You don't think she was the primary target.'

'Can't rule it out, but no. He moved straight in,' she

repeated, and did so. 'Sealed all the way. Had to be. Sweepers didn't find a fricking skin cell that wasn't accounted for. Witness said he didn't make any noise, so I'm thinking stealth shoes. Went directly to the bed, gave the head a quick yank up by the hair, sliced down, right-handed.'

Roarke watched her mime the moves, quick and sure, cop's eyes flat. 'Combat knife from Morris's report – lab should be able to reconstruct. Then he lets her drop, turns, walks out. Witness is there, just outside the doorway, down on the floor, back to the wall. If he looks, he sees. But he doesn't.'

'Confident or careless?' Roarke asked.

'I'd go with the first. Added to it, he's not looking because he doesn't expect to see anything.' She paused a moment. 'Why doesn't he expect to see anything?'

'Why would he?'

'People don't always stay tucked in through the night. They get up to whiz, or because they're worried about their work and can't sleep. Or because they want a damn Orange Fizzy. How come you're this thorough, this much a pro, but you don't sweep an area when you enter?'

Frowning, Roarke considered, studied the layout again. Yes, he thought as he pictured himself moving through the house in the dark. He would have. Yes, and he had on those occasions when he'd lifted locks and helped himself to what was behind them.

'Good question, now that you pose it. He – they – expect everything, everyone in their proper place because that's how it works in their world?'

'It's a theory. Goes out,' she continued, 'goes back to the main stairs and up. Why? Why, when there are back stairs right over there.'

She gestured to a door. 'That's how the witness got up to the second floor. Back stairs. Peabody's take was that the front steps were closer to the adults' room, and it's not implausible. But you know what, it's a waste of time, steps, and effort.'

'And they wasted nothing. They didn't know there was a second set of steps.'

'Yeah. But how did they miss that detail when they knew everything else?'

Roarke walked over to the door, ran a hand over the jamb, examined the steps. 'Well, they're not original.'

'How do you know?'

'The house is late nineteenth century, with considerable rehab work. But these are newer. This rail here, it's manmade material. Twenty-first-century material.' He crouched down. 'So are the treads. And the workmanship's a bit shoddy. I wouldn't be surprised if this was a home job – something they added themselves without all the permits and what have you. Without filing the work, so it wouldn't show on any record, any blueprint your killers might have studied.'

'How smart are you? You're right. They're not on the on-file blueprints. I checked. Still, that doesn't mean one or both of the killers wasn't in the house, wasn't even a friend or neighbor. This is the domestic's room, and her stairs.'

'That would, however, go further to eliminating the housekeeper as primary target. And it would be less likely the killers were close acquaintances of hers, or privy to her quarters.'

'She was excess. It was the family that mattered.'

'Not one of them,' he put in, 'but all.'

'If it wasn't all, why kill all?'

She took him back through, following the assumed path of the known killer. 'Blood trail from domestic's, through here, up the right side of the steps. More concentrated blood pattern here, see?'

'And none coming back down the stairs. Removing protective gear here, before going down.'

'Another point for the civilian.'

'I think you should have another term for me. Civilian's so ordinary, and just a bit snarky when you say it. Something like "nonpolice specialist on all things".'

'Yeah, sure, my personal NPS. Focus in, ace. They'd done the adults before the witness got up to this level. She saw them walking away from this room, then split off. One in each of the other bedrooms. Two more rooms up here – one a home office, the other a playroom deal.

Kids' bathroom, end of hall. But they went straight for the bedrooms. You couldn't be a hundred percent from a blueprint which room was which up here.'

'No.' To satisfy his curiosity, he walked over, glanced into one of the rooms. Home office – work station, mini-friggie, shelves holding equipment, dust catchers, family photos. A small daybed, all coated now with the sweepers' residue.

'This is certainly large enough to be used as a bedroom.'

She let him wander, watched him step to the doorway of the boy's room and saw his face harden. Blood spatter on sports posters, she thought, blood staining the mattress.

'How old was the boy?' he asked. 'Twelve.'

'Where were we at that age, Eve? Not in a nice room, surrounded by our little treasures, that's for bloody sure. But Christ Jesus, what does it take to walk into a room like this and end some sleeping boy?'

'I'm going to find out.'

'You will, yes. Well.' He stepped back. He'd seen blood before, had shed it. He'd stood and studied murder when it was chilled. But this, standing in this house where a family had lived their ordinary lives, seeing a young boy's room where such a tender life had been taken, left him sickened and shaken.

So he turned away from it. 'The office has as much space as this bedroom. The boy could easily have been across the hall.'

'So they had to surveil the house – or know it from the inside, enough to know who slept where. If they cased it from outside, they'd need to watch the patterns. Which lights went on, what time. Night vision and surveillance equipment, and they could see through the curtains easy enough.'

She moved to the master bedroom. 'Morris tells me the same hand that did the domestic did both males. The other took the females. So they had their individual targets worked out in advance. No conversations, no chatter, no excess movements. Thought about droids, assassin droids.'

'Very costly,' Roarke told her. 'And unreliable in a situation like this. And why have two – double the cost and detail of programming, when one could do it all? That's if you had the wherewithal and the skill to access an illegal droid, and program it to bypass security and terminate multiple subjects.'

'I don't think it was droids.' She walked out, into the little girl's bedroom. 'I think human hands did this. And no matter how it looks on the surface, no matter how cold and efficient, it was personal. It was fucking personal. You don't slice a child's throat without it being personal.'

'Very personal.' He put a hand on her back, rubbed it gently up and down. 'Sleeping children were no threat to them.' There were demons in this house now, he thought. Brutal ghosts of them with children's blood staining their hands. Lurking ones in him, and in her, that muttered, constantly muttered, of the horrors they'd survived.

'Maybe the kids were the targets. Or there's the possibility one or more of the household had some information that was a threat, so they all had to go in case that information had been shared.'

'No.'

'No.' She sighed, shook her head. 'If the killers were afraid of information or knowledge, they would need to ascertain, by intimidation, threat, or torture, that the information hadn't been passed outside of the household. They would need to check the data centers, the whole fricking house, to be certain such information wasn't logged somewhere. The tight timing – entrance, murders, exit, doesn't leave room for them to have searched for anything. It's made to look like business. But it's personal.'

'Not as smart as they think,' Roarke commented. 'Because?'

'Smarter to have taken the valuables, to have torn the house up a bit. The entire horror would point more to burglary. Or to have hacked away at the victims, to make it seem like a psychopath, or a burglary gone very wrong.'

She let out a half laugh. 'You know, you're right. You're damn right. And why didn't they? Pride. Pride in the work. That's good, that's good, because it's something, and I've got nothing. Fucking bupkus. I knew there was a reason I liked having you around.'

'Any little thing I can do.' He took her hand as they started downstairs. 'And it's not true you have nothing. You have your instincts, your skill, your determination. And a witness.'

'Yeah, yeah.' She didn't want to think about her witness quite yet. 'Why would you wipe out an entire family? Not *you* you, but hypothetically.'

'I appreciate the qualification. Because they'd messed with mine, had been or were a threat to what's mine.'

'Swisher was a lawyer. Family law.'

Roarke tilted his head as they went out the front door. 'That's interesting, isn't it?'

'And she was a nutritionist, did a lot of families, or had clients with families. So maybe Swisher lost a case – or won one – that pissed one of his clients or opposings off. Or she pushed the wrong buttons on somebody's fat kid, or had a client die. And the kids went to private schools. Maybe one of the kids screwed with somebody else's kid.'

'A lot of avenues.'

'Just have to find the right one.'

'One of the adults might have had an affair with someone else's spouse. It's been known to annoy.'

'Looking there.' She slid behind the wheel of her vehicle. 'But it's not solidifying. These two, they had what looks like a pretty solid marriage, and a lot of focus on family. Took trips together, went out together. Like a group. The picture I'm getting doesn't leave much time for extra-marital. And sex takes time.'

'Done well, certainly.'

'I haven't found anything in their data, their possessions, their schedules that points to an affair. Not yet, anyway. Neighborhood canvass didn't shake out anything,' she added as she pulled away from the curb. 'Nobody saw anything. I figure one of them lives in the area, or they had a bogus permit, or – Jesus – they took the goddamn subway, hailed a cab a couple of blocks away. I can't pin any of it down.'

'Eve, it's been less than twenty-four hours.'

She glanced in the rearview, thought of the quiet house on the quiet street. 'Feels longer.'

★　　★　　★

It was always weird, in Eve's opinion, to have Summerset materialize in the foyer like a recurring nightmare the minute she walked in the door, but it was weirder yet to see him there, with a small blonde girl at his side.

The kid's hair was shiny, wavy blonde, as if it had been freshly washed and brushed. Who did that? Eve wondered. Did the kid deal with her own hair, or had Summerset done it? And the thought of that gave her the heebies.

But the kid looked comfortable enough with him, even had her hand in his, and the cat at her feet.

'Isn't this a fine welcome?' Roarke shrugged out of his coat. 'How are you, Nixie?'

She looked at him – all blue eyes – and nearly smiled. 'Okay. We made apple pie.'

'Did you now?' Roarke bent to pick up the cat when Galahad slithered over to rub against his legs. 'That's a favorite of mine.'

'You can make a little one with the leftovers. That's what I did.' Then those eyes, big and blue, lasered into Eve's. 'Did you catch them yet?'

'No.' Eve tossed her jacket over the newel post, and for once Summerset didn't snark or sneer at the habit. 'Investigations like this take some time.'

'Why? Screen shows with cops don't take very long.'

'This isn't a vid.' She wanted to go upstairs, clear her mind for five minutes, then start back over the case, point by point. But those eyes stayed on her face, both accusing and pleading.

'I told you I'd get them, and I will.'

'When?'

She started to swear, might not have choked it back in time, but Roarke played a hand gently down her arm and spoke first. 'Do you know, Nixie, that Lieutenant Dallas is the best cop in the city?'

Something, maybe it was speculation, passed over Nixie's face. 'Why?'

'Because she won't stop. Because it matters so much to her that she takes care of people who've been hurt, she can't stop. If someone of mine had been hurt, I'd want her to be the one in charge.'

'Baxter says she's a major butt-kicker.'

'Well, then.' Now Roarke smiled fully. 'He'd be right.'

'Where are they?' Eve asked. 'Baxter and Trueheart?'

'In your office,' Summerset told her. 'Dinner will be served in fifteen minutes. Nixie, we need to set the table.'

'I'm just going to—'

This time Roarke took Eve's hand, squeezed. 'We'll be down.'

'I've got work,' Eve began as they went up the stairs. 'I don't have time to—'

'I think we need to make time. An hour won't hurt, Eve, and I'd say that child needs as much normalcy as we can manage. Dinner, at the table, is normal.'

'I don't see what's more normal about shoveling in food off a big flat surface than shoveling it in at your desk. It's multitasking. It's efficient.'

'She scares you.'

She stopped dead, and her eyes went to lethal slits. 'Just where the hell do you come off saying that?'

'Because she scares me, too.'

Temper flickered over her face for a moment, then everything relaxed. 'Really? *Really?* You're not just saying that?'

'Those big eyes, full of courage and terror and grief. What could be more frightening? There she stands, such a little thing, all that pretty hair, tidy jeans and jumper – sweater,' he corrected. 'And that need just radiating out of her. We're supposed to have the answers, and we don't.'

Eve let out a breath as she looked back toward the stairs. 'I haven't even figured out all the questions.'

'So we'll have dinner with her, and do what we can to show her that there's normalcy and decency left in the world.'

'Okay, okay, but I need to debrief my men.'

'I'll meet you downstairs. Fifteen minutes.'

She found normal in her office, where a couple of cops – who'd obviously raided her AutoChef – were chowing down while they studied murder. On her wall screens, each Swisher bedroom, each victim, was displayed while Baxter and Trueheart chomped on cow meat.

'Steak.' Baxter forked up another bite. 'Do you know the last time I had real cow? I'd kiss you, Dallas, but my mouth's full.'

'Summerset said it was okay.' Trueheart, young and fresh in his uniform, offered her a hopeful grin.

She merely shrugged, then turned so that she, too, had full view of the screens. 'What's your take?'

'Big red check to everything in your report.' Baxter continued to eat, but his expression was sober now. 'Slick job. And a mean one. Even without the eyewit, I'd have said two or more to pull it off, and even then it went down damn fast. The tox came in from the ME. No illegals, no drugs of any kind in any of them. No illegals on the premises. Even the pain remedies were herbal and holistic.'

'Fits with the adult female's career choice,' Eve murmured. 'No defensives, no struggle, no missing valuables.'

'No trace,' she added. 'Sweepers got zip. You dump your currents?'

'With pleasure.' Baxter stabbed his fork into another bite of steak. 'Carmichael now hates me like a case of genital warts. Made my day.'

'The two of you are relieved here. Report back at oh eight hundred. Double duty. You babysit, and start running the names I pulled out of the Swishers' client lists. Anybody with so much as a parking violation gets a deeper look. We look at them, their family, their friends and associates, their next-door neighbors, and their little pets. We look until we find.'

'The housekeeper?' Baxter asked.

'I'll do her tonight. We look at them all, kids included. School, activities, neighbors, where they shopped, where they ate, where they worked, where they played. Before we're done, we'll know these people better than they knew themselves.'

'A lot of names,' Baxter commented. 'It's only going to take one.'

Though she now had steak and murder on her mind, Eve ate roasted chicken and tried to keep her conversation away from the investigation. But what the hell were you supposed to talk to a kid about over dinner?

They didn't use the dining room often – well, she didn't, she admitted. So much easier to grab something upstairs. But she couldn't call it a hardship to sit at the big, gleaming table, with a fire simmering in the grate, the scent of food and candles in the air.

'How come you eat so fancy?' Nixie wanted to know.

'Don't ask me.' Eve jabbed a fork toward Roarke. 'It's his house.'

'Do I have to go to school tomorrow?'

Eve blinked twice, then realized the question was directed at her, and Roarke wasn't stepping in to field the ball.

'No.'

'When do I go back to school?'

Eve felt the back of her neck begin to ache. 'I don't know.'

'But if I don't do my work, I'll get behind. If you get behind, you can't be in the band or the plays.' Tears started to shimmer.

'Oh. Well.' Shit.

'We can arrange for you to do your school work here, for now.'

Roarke spoke matter-of-factly. As if, Eve thought, he'd been born answering thorny questions. 'You enjoy school?'

'Mostly. Who'll help me with my work? Dad always did.'

No, Eve thought. Absolutely not. She wasn't moving into that area if somebody planted a boomer under her ass.

'The lieutenant and I weren't the best of students. But Summerset could help you, for the time being.'

'I'll never get to go home again. Or see my mom and dad, or Coyle or Linnie. I don't want them to be dead.'

Okay, Eve decided. Maybe she was a kid, but she was still the eyewit. The case was back on the table along with the chicken.

Thank God.

'Tell me what everybody was doing. The whole day before it happened.' When Roarke started to object, Eve only shook her head. 'Everything you remember.'

'Dad had to yell at Coyle because he got up late. He's always getting up late, then everybody has to rush. Mom gets mad if you rush your breakfast because it's important you eat right.'

'What did you eat?'

'We had fruit and cereal in the kitchen.' Nixie cut a spear of asparagus neatly, and ate without complaint. 'Inga fixes it. And juice. Dad had coffee, 'cause he gets to have one cup. And Coyle wanted new airskids, and Mom said no, and he said that sucked, and she gave him the look because you're not supposed to say "suck," especially at the table. Then we got our things and went to school.'

'Did anyone use the 'link?'

'No.'

'Did anyone come to the door?'

She ate a bite of chicken in the same tidy way. Chewed and swallowed before she answered. 'No.'

'How did you get to school?'

'Dad walked us, because it wasn't too cold. If it's too cold, we can take a cab. Then he goes to work. Mom goes downstairs to work. And Inga was going shopping because Linnie was coming after school and Mom wanted more fresh fruit.'

'Did either your mother or father seem upset by anything?'

'Coyle said "suck" and didn't finish his juice, so Mom was down on him. Can I see them even though they're dead?' Her lips trembled. 'Can I?' It was a human need, Eve knew. Why should it be different for a child? 'I'll arrange it. It may take a little while. You do okay today with Baxter and Trueheart?'

'Baxter's funny, and Trueheart's nice. He knows how to play a lot of games. When you catch the bad guys, can I see them, too?'

'Yes.'

'Okay.' Nixie looked back down at her plate, nodded slowly. 'Okay.'

I feel like I've been in the Interview box, getting sweated by a pro. Eve rolled her shoulders when she walked into her office.

107

'You handled it, and very well. I thought you'd over-stepped when you asked her to go over the day before the murders, but you were right. She'll need to talk about this. All of this.'

'She'll think about it anyway. She talks, maybe she'll remember something.' She sat at her desk, brooded a minute. 'Now here's something I never thought would come out of my mouth – and if you ever repeat it, I'll twist your tongue into a square knot, but thank God Summerset's around.'

He grinned as he eased a hip onto the corner of her desk. 'Sorry, I don't think I quite heard that.'

Her look, her voice, went dark. 'I meant it about the square knot. I'm just saying the kid's easy with him, and he seems to know what to do with her.'

'Well, he raised one of his own, then took me on besides. He has a soft spot for troubled children.'

'He has no soft spots whatsoever, but he's good with the kid. So yay.' She dragged a hand through her hair. 'I'll be talking with the Dysons again tomorrow. Depending on how things go, we could be moving her into a safe house with them in a day or two. Tonight, I'm going to focus on the housekeeper, see where that takes me. Need to send a memo to Peabody,' she remembered. 'She's already hit the school, so she can swing by there in the morning, get the kid's work and whatever. Listen, let me ask you, why would you want, I mean, actually *want* to do the school thing if you had an escape hatch?'

'On that, I have absolutely no idea. Maybe it's like your work is to you, mine is to me. Somehow essential.'

'It's school. It's like prison.'

'So I always thought, too. Maybe we're wrong.' He leaned over, traced his finger down the dent in her chin. 'Want some help with this?'

'Don't you have work?'

'A bit of this, a bit of that, but nothing I can't do while assisting New York's best cop.'

'Yeah, that was a good one. You know the security at the scene. Maybe you could tag Feeney at home, exchange data. See if you can figure out what kind of equipment these bastards needed to bypass. And where they might've come by it.'

'All right.' This time he brushed her cheek. 'You've put in a long day already.'

'I've got another couple hours in me.'

'Save some for me,' he said, and walked into his own office.

Alone, she set up a second murder board, programmed a short pot of coffee, then ordered Inga's data on-screen.

She studied the ID photo. Attractive, but in a nonthreatening, homey sort of way. She wondered if Swisher had specified nonthreatening, nothing too young and pretty to tempt her husband.

Whatever the requirements, the match seemed to have worked. Inga had put plenty of years in with the Swishers. Enough, Eve noted, to see the kids grow up.

None of her own, Eve saw. One marriage, one divorce, full-time domestic since she was in her twenties. Though Eve couldn't understand why anyone would volunteer to clean up for someone else, she supposed it took all kinds.

Her financials were steady, reasonable considering her occupation, and her outlays within the normal range.

Normal, normal, normal, Eve thought. Well, Inga, let's go deeper. An hour later she was circling her board.

Nothing, she thought. If there were hidden pockets, they were expertly concealed. Inga's life had been so utterly normal it was bordering on boring. She worked, she shopped, she took two vacations a year – one with the family she worked for, and the other, at least for the last five years, with a couple of other women to the same relaxation spa in upstate New York.

She'd check with, and on, the other women, but nothing had popped out on them when she'd run their data.

The ex lived in Chicago, had remarried, and had one offspring, male. He was a drone for a restaurant supply company, and had made no on-record trips to New York in over seven years.

The idea that the housekeeper had heard or seen something dire while buying plums or cleaning supplies just seemed ludicrous.

But life was full of the ludicrous that ended in bloody murder.

She acknowledged Roarke when he came in. 'Nothing jingles my bell on this one.' She nodded toward the screen.

'Still a lot of legwork to do to cover the bases, but I think she's going down as innocent bystander.'

'Feeney and I are of the same opinion regarding the bypass equipment. It could have been homemade by someone expert in the field, with access to prime materials. If it was purchased, it had to come from military, police, or security sources. Or black market. It's not something you'd find in your local electronics store.'

'Doesn't narrow the field much, but it jibes.'

'Let's shut it down for the night.'

'Nothing much more I can do.' She ordered her machine to save, file, close. 'I'm going to start here tomorrow, then leave Baxter and Trueheart on wit duty.'

'I'll take it to some of my R&D people tomorrow, see if anybody in my brain trust comes up with something more specific on the security system.'

'None of the vics had any military or security training – or as far as I've found, any connections thereto.' She pushed it around in her head as they walked toward their bedroom. 'I can't find any link with organized crime, with paramilitary. As far as my data shows, they didn't gamble, fool around, were not overly political. The closest to an obsession I can get is the woman's devotion to nutrition.'

'Maybe something had come into their possession, even by accident, that had to be reclaimed.'

'Then if you're so damn good at B&E, you go in when the house is empty and you take it. You don't go in, kill everybody. The only thing taken from the house was lives.'

The Swishers are dead because someone wanted them dead.'

'Agreed. What do you say we have a glass of wine and relax for a bit?' She nearly refused. She could just think, let it all wind around in her head awhile. Pace and let it play until something jiggled loose, or she was too damn fried to do anything but pass out for a few hours.

Their lives would never be like the Swishers'. She didn't want them to be, didn't think she could handle trying to navigate something quite that straightforward. But they did have a life. And lives deserved attention.

'I'd say you've got a pretty good idea. I've got to let it simmer.' She tapped the back of her head. 'Since boiling it up front isn't doing the job.'

'How about this for a better idea?' He shifted so they faced each other and a dip of his head had his teeth closing lightly over her jaw. 'Getting me naked is your usual idea.'

'But with variation, and that's the key.'

It made her laugh. 'Sooner or later even you have to run out of variations.'

'Now there's a challenge. Why don't we take that wine down to the pool, have a little water sport?'

'I'd say your ideas get better and—' She broke off, and sprinted when she heard Nixie scream.

6

She didn't know which room, so could only race toward the sounds of a child screaming. At a turn in the corridor, Roarke passed her. She kicked in so together they shot through an open door.

The bedroom was washed by soft light. The bed was a four-poster with a mountain of pillows and a lacy white spread. Someone – Summerset, she imagined – had placed yellow flowers, cheerful and bright, on a table by the window. As she bolted in, Eve nearly tripped over the cat, who was either in retreat or on guard.

In the middle of the sumptuous bed, the little girl sat, her arms lifted and crossed over her face as she shrieked as if someone was whaling on her with a hammer.

Roarke reached Nixie first. Later Eve would think it was because he was used to dealing with a female in the grip of nightmares, while she was simply used to having them.

He plucked Nixie straight up and into his arms, holding her, stroking her, and saying her name even when she struggled and slapped at him.

Eve had yet to speak or decide what best to do, when

113

the elevator on the far wall whizzed open, and Summerset strode out.

'Natural,' he said. 'Expected.'

'Mommy.' Exhausted from the fight, Nixie let her head drop on Roarke's shoulder. 'I want my mommy.'

'I know, yes, I know. I'm sorry.'

Eve saw him turn his head to brush his lips over Nixie's hair. That, too, seemed natural. Expected.

'They're coming to get me. They're coming to kill me.'

'They're not. It was a dream.' Roarke sat, Nixie curled in his lap. 'A very bad dream. But you're safe here, as you can see. With me, and the lieutenant and Summerset.'

He patted the bed, and the cat gathered his porky self and leaped up nimbly. 'And here, here's Galahad as well.'

'I saw the blood. Is it on me?'

'No.'

'We'll get a soother in her.' Opening a wall panel, Summerset pressed buttons on a mini AutoChef. 'She'll be the better for it. Here now, Nixie, you'll drink this for me, won't you?'

She turned her face into Roarke's shoulder. 'I'm afraid in the dark.'

'It's not very dark, and we'll have more lights if you like.' Roarke ordered them up another ten percent. 'Is that better, then?'

'I think they're in the closet,' she whispered, and her fingers dug into his shirt. 'I think they're hiding in the closet.'

That, Eve thought, was something she could do. She

went directly to the closet, opened it, did a complete search while Nixie watched her. 'Nobody can get into this place,' she spoke flatly. 'Nobody can get past us. That's the way it is. It's my job to protect you. That's what I'll do.'

'What if they kill you?'

'A lot of people have tried. I don't let them.'

'Because you're a major butt-kicker.'

'You bet your ass. Drink the soother.'

She waited, watched, while Nixie drank, while Summerset took over. He sat on the bed, talking to the child in a quiet voice until her eyes began to droop.

And waiting, watching, Eve felt raw and scraped inside. She knew what it was to be chained in nightmares where something unspeakable came for you. The pain and the blood, the fear and the agony.

Even after it was over, the dregs of it stained the edges of your mind. Summerset rose, stepped away from the bed. 'That should help her. I have her room on monitor, should she wake again. For the moment, sleep is the best thing for her.'

'The best thing is me finding who did this,' Eve stated. 'Yeah, her parents will still be dead, but she'll know why, and she'll know the people who did it are in a cage. That happens, it'll be better than a soother.'

She walked out, straight to her own bedroom. Cursing, she sat on the arm of the sofa in the sitting area to drag off her boots. It relieved a little tension to heave them across the room.

Still, she was glaring at them when Roarke came in.

'Will she have them all of her life?' Eve pushed off the sofa. 'Will she relive that in her dreams all her life? Can you ever get rid of the images? Can you cut them out of your head like a fucking tumor?'

'I don't know.'

'I didn't want to touch her. What does that say about me? For Christ's sake, Roarke, a little kid, screaming, and I didn't want to touch her, so I hesitated. Just for a minute, but I hesitated, because I knew what was in her head, and knowing it, put him in mine.' She yanked off her weapon harness, tossed it aside. 'So I'm standing there, looking at her and seeing my father, and the blood. All over me.'

'I touched her, and you showed her there were no monsters in the closet. We each do what we do, Eve. Why ask yourself for more than you can do?'

'Goddamn it, Roarke.' She whirled around, spun by her own demons. 'I can stand over a body and not blink. I can grill witnesses, suspects, and not break stride. I can wade through blood to get where I need to go. But I couldn't cross the room to deal with that kid.' It sat in her belly like lead. 'Am I cold? God, am I that cold?'

'Cold? Sweet Jesus, Eve, you're nothing of the kind.' He went to her, laying his hands on her shoulders. Firming his grip when she started to shrug him away. 'You feel too much, so much I wonder how you stand it. And if you have to close off certain things at certain times, it's not coldness. It's not a flaw. It's survival.'

'Mira said . . . she said to me not long ago that once – before I met you – she'd figured I had maybe three years left before I burned out. Before I couldn't do the job any more.'

'Why?'

'Because the job was it. It . . .' She lifted her hands, dropped them. 'It was all I had at the center of it. I didn't – maybe couldn't – let anything else in. And maybe, no matter how much I felt, there was too much cold with it. If things had gone on that way – I think I'd have been more than cold . . . I'd've been brittle by now. I've got to do what I do, Roarke, or I couldn't survive. I've got to have you, or I wouldn't *want* to survive.'

'It's no different for me.' He pressed his lips to her brow. 'Winning was my god, before you. Winning, whatever it took. And no matter how much gain you stuff in your pocket, there are still empty spaces. You filled them for me. Two lost souls. Now we're found.'

'I don't want the wine.' Craving the connection, she locked her arms around him. 'Or the pool.' Crushed her mouth to his. 'Only you. Only you.'

'You have me.' He swept her up. 'Now and always.'

'Fast,' she said, already tugging at the buttons of his shirt as he carried her to bed. 'Fast and rough and real.'

He climbed the platform, and didn't lie her down so much as fell with her, pinning her arms as they hit the sea of bed. 'Take what I give you, then.'

His mouth covered her breast over her shirt, teeth nipping

so that the pricks of heat stabbed through her. Filled all the cold, dark corners.

She reared up, ground herself to him, let herself be overpowered.

For a moment, for a shuddering moment, that lusty desperation flooded her, washing away all the doubts, the fears, the smears of the day. Now just her body and his, hard and eager, strong and hot.

When he freed her hands to take more of her, she tangled her fingers in his hair, dragged his head up so that her mouth fixed urgently to his.

There was his taste, those firm, full lips, that quick and clever tongue. The scrape of his teeth, small, erotic bites that stopped just short of pain.

Feel me, taste me. I'm with you.

Her hands were more impatient now, greedier now, as they pulled at his shirt. As he pulled on hers.

Her skin was like a fever and her heart a thundering storm under his hands, his lips. The demons that haunted her, those monsters they both knew forever lurked in closets, were cast out by passion. For now, for as long as they had each other.

The violence of her need whipped at his own, burning like a sparking wire in the blood.

He dragged her up, fixing his teeth into her shoulder, ripping what was left of her shirt away. She wore his diamond, the sparkling teardrop on a chain around her throat. Even in the dark he could see its fire. Just as he could see the gleam of her eyes.

The thought passed through his mind that he would give anything he had – life and soul – to keep her looking at him with everything she was in those strong, brown eyes.

She pulled him back with her, so that they rolled now, a sweaty tangle over the midnight ocean of the bed.

She locked her legs around him, locked those eyes on his. 'Now,' she said. 'Now. Hard and fast and . . . Yes. Oh God.'

He drove into her, felt her clamp around him, a wet, velvet vice, as she came. Felt that long, lean body shudder and shudder as he plunged. Still her hips pistoned, taking him in deeper, driving him brutally on.

'Don't shut your eyes. Don't.' His voice was thick. 'Eve.'

She lifted her hands, and though they trembled, they framed his face. 'I see you. I see you. Roarke.'

And her eyes were open, on his, when they fell.

In the morning she was relieved it didn't appear on the 'normal' list to have breakfast with Nixie. It might've been small, even cowardly, but Eve didn't think she could face the questions, or those steady, seeking eyes, without a couple of quarts of coffee first.

She did what was normal for her instead and took a blistering shower, and a quick spin in the drying tube while Roarke did his usual scan of the stock reports on-screen in the bedroom.

With the first cup of coffee down, she opened her closet and pulled out a pair of pants.

'Have some eggs,' Roarke ordered.

'I'm going to go over some data in my office before the rest of the team get here.'

'Have some eggs first,' he repeated, and made her roll her eyes as she shrugged on a shirt.

She marched over, picked up his plate, and shoveled in two forkfuls of his omelette.

'I didn't mean mine.'

'Be more specific, then,' she said with her mouth full. 'Where's the cat?'

'With the girl, I'd wager. Galahad's shrewd enough to know she'll be more likely to share her breakfast with him than we are.' To prove it, Roarke took the plate back. 'Get your own eggs.'

'I don't want any more.' But she nipped a piece of his bacon from the plate. 'I expect to be in the field most of the day. I might need to relieve Baxter and Trueheart, pull in a couple of uniforms. That a problem for you?'

'Having a house full of cops? Why would that be a problem for me?'

The dry tone made her smile. 'I'm going to see the Dysons. Could be we'll move her by tonight, or tomorrow anyway.'

'The child is welcome as long as need be, so that goes for whoever you need to look out for her. I mean that.'

'I know. You're nicer than me.' She leaned down, kissed him. 'I mean that.'

She reached over for her weapon harness, strapped it on.

'With the Dysons as legal guardians, I can bypass Child Protection and get them moved into a safe house without any sort of data trail.'

'You're concerned whoever did this to her family will want to clean up the loose end.'

'It's a good bet. So her location will be need-to-know, with no paperwork.'

'You told her you'd arrange for her to see her family. Is that wise?' Eve picked up the boots she'd thrown in temper the night before. 'She'll need to. Survivors of violent crimes need to see the dead. She'll have to wait until it's safe, and until Mira clears it, then she'll have to deal. It's her reality now.'

'You're right, I know. She looked so small in that bed last night. It's the first I've dealt with this, specifically. A child who's lost so much. It wouldn't be the first for you.'

After dragging on the boots, she remained sitting on the arm of the sofa. 'Not many firsts left in my line. You've seen this at Dochas,' she said, thinking of the shelter Roarke had built. 'And worse than this. That's why you made the place.'

'Not quite so personally. Would you want Louise to help in this?'

Louise Dimatto, crusader and doctor, head of Dochas – she'd be a plus, Eve thought, but she shook her head. 'I don't want to pull anyone else in, not at this point anyway. Especially a civilian. I've got to get set up before the rest get here. If you get anything on the security system, let me know.'

'I will.'

She leaned down, brushed his lips with hers. 'See you, ace.'

She was revved to work, ready to do what she knew how to do. While Baxter and Trueheart plowed through some drone work, Feeney, his EDD team – along with their civilian expert – pushed on the security angle, she and Peabody would continue the interview process.

It was likely, she thought, that the killers had been hired, and were even now out of the city. Even off planet. But once she found the root, she'd work her way up the stem, then break off those branches.

And that root was buried somewhere in the lives of an ordinary family.

'Ordinary family,' she said when Peabody walked in. 'Mother, father, sister, brother. You know about that.'

'And good morning to you, too.' Peabody all but sang it. 'It's a lovely fall day. Just a bit brisk, with the trees in your beautiful, personal park just – what is it – burnished with that last stand of color. And you were saying?'

'Jesus, what happy bug jumped up your ass?'

'I started out my day with what you could call a bang.' She showed her teeth. 'If you know what I mean.'

'I really don't want to know. Really don't.' Eve pressed the heel of her hand against her left eye as it twitched. 'Why do you do that? Why do you insist on making me see you and McNab having sex?'

Peabody only flashed a wider grin. 'Gives my day an extra bounce. Anyway, I saw Nixie for a minute downstairs. How'd she do last night?'

'Had a nightmare, took a soother. Would you also like to discuss fashion, or any current events while we're chatting?'

'No happy bug up your ass,' Peabody grumbled. 'So,' she said when Eve merely studied her with steely eyes, 'you said something about families.'

'Oh, I see we're ready to work now.' Eve gestured to the board where, in addition to the on-scene pictures, she'd pinned photos of the family, alive and smiling for the camera. 'Routines, families have routines. I had Nixie take me through the morning before the murder, so I've got a sense of theirs: breakfast together, hassling the kids, father walks them to school on his way to work, and so on.'

'Okay.'

'So, somebody surveilling them would get a good sense of their routine, too. Easy enough to snatch and grab one of them, if one of them is the problem. A little persuasion and you know if you've got a problem. Tells me the whole family was the problem. That's one.'

She stepped back from the board. 'Two, they have contact with a number of people during the course of this routine: clients, coworkers, neighbors, merchants, friends, teachers. Where do one or more of them cross with someone who not only wants them dead, but has the means?'

'Okay, from what we know, no one in the family felt

threatened or worried. From that we can deduce, no dangerous type came up to one of them and said: "I'm going to kill you and your whole family for that." Or words to that effect. From the profile on this family, if they'd been scared, they'd have made a report. They were law abiders. Law abiders generally believe in the system, and that the system will find the way to protect you from harm.'

'Good. So while there may have been an argument or a disagreement, none of the adults in the household took it seriously enough to take those steps. Or it happened long enough ago they no longer felt threatened.'

'Oh. There might have been a previous threat, a previous report,' Peabody responded.

'Start looking.' She turned as Baxter and Trueheart came in.

Within the hour, she had her team on their respective assignments and was driving out of the gates. 'Dysons first,' she told Peabody. 'I want to handle that one, then we'll do formal interviews with the neighbors.'

'I'm not finding any official complaints filed by any of the Swishers or the domestic. Not in the last two years.'

'Keep going. Somebody who could do this would have a lot of patience.'

The Dysons had a two-level apartment in a security-conscious building on the Upper West Side. Even before Eve swung toward the curb, she spotted a pair of media vans.

'Goddamn leaks,' she muttered, and slammed out, leaving Peabody to flip the on-duty light.

The doorman had called out reserves – a smart move, Eve thought – and had two burly types helping him hold off the reporters.

She flashed her badge, saw the relief on the doorman's face. Not the usual reaction. 'Officer.'

The minute he said it, the hungry horde swung on her. Questions shot out like laser blasts and were ignored.

'A media conference will be scheduled later today, at Central. The liaison will give you the details on that. Meanwhile, you will remove yourselves from this entrance or I'll have the lot of you arrested for creating a public nuisance.'

'Is it true Linnie Dyson was killed by mistake?'

Eve reined in her temper. 'In my opinion, the murder of a nine-year-old child is always a mistake. My only statement at this time is that all resources of the NYPSD will be utilized to identify those responsible for the death of that child. This case is open and active and we are pursuing any and all possible leads. The next one who asks me a question,' she continued as they were hurled at her, 'will be banned from the official media conference. Moreover, you will be cited for obstruction of justice and tossed in the tank if you don't get the living hell out of my way so I can do my job.'

She strode forward; they scrambled back. As the doorman pulled open the door for her, he muttered, 'Nice work.'

He came in behind her, leaving the two wide-shoulders to deal with any loitering press.

'You'll want to see the Dysons,' he began. 'They've asked not to be disturbed.'

'I'm sorry. They'll have to be.'

'I understand. I'd appreciate it if you'd let me call up first, let them know you're down here. Give them a couple of minutes to . . . Mother of God.' His eyes filled with tears. 'That little girl. I saw her every day. She was a sweetheart. I can't believe . . . Sorry.'

Eve waited while he pulled out a cloth, mopped at his face. 'You knew her, and the Swisher girl. Nixie.'

'Nixie Pixie.' He balled the cloth in his hand. 'I'd call her that sometimes when she came over to visit. Those kids were like sisters. The reports this morning are saying she's okay. That Nixie, she's alive.'

She judged him to be six feet, and in fighting trim. 'What's your name?'

'Springer. Kirk Springer.'

'I can't give you any information right now, Springer. It's against procedure. You see a lot of people come in and out of here, a lot of people pass on the street. Have you noticed anybody hanging around, maybe a vehicle that was parked in the vicinity that wasn't familiar?'

'No.' He cleared his throat. 'Building's got security cameras on the entrance. I can get clearance, get you copies of the discs.'

'I'd appreciate it.'

'Anything I can do. That kid, she was a sweetheart. Excuse me, I'll call upstairs.' He paused. 'Officer?'

'Lieutenant.'

'Lieutenant. The Dysons, they're good people. Always got a word for you, you know? Don't forget you on your birthday or Christmas. So anything I can do.'

'Thank you, Springer.' When he walked away to make the call, Eve said, 'Run him.'

'Sir, you don't think—'

'No, but run him anyway. Get the names of the other doormen, and the security staff, the building manager, the maintenance staff. Run the works.'

'It's 6-B, Lieutenant.' Springer's eyes were still teary when he came back. 'To the left of the elevator. Mrs Dyson's waiting for you. Again, appreciate you dispersing the hounds out there. These people deserve their privacy.'

'No problem. Springer, you think of anything, give me a heads-up at Central.'

When they stepped into the elevator, Peabody read off from her pocket unit. 'He's married, two kids, Upper West Sider. No criminal. Employed here the last nine years.'

'Military or police training?'

'No. But he'd have to have security orientation – personal and building – to rate a gig on a building like this.'

With a nod, Eve stepped off, turned left. The door to 6-B opened before she rang the bell.

Jenny Dyson looked older than she had the day before. Older, pale, with that distant look Eve saw in accident victims struggling between shock and pain.

'Mrs Dyson, thank you for seeing us.'

'You found him. You found the man who killed my Linnie.'

'No, ma'am. Can we come inside?'

'I thought you'd come to tell us. I thought . . . Yes, come in.' She stepped back, glanced around her own living space as if she didn't quite recognize it. 'My husband, he's asleep. Sedated. He can't . . . They were so close, you see. Linnie, she's Daddy's girl.' She pressed a hand to her mouth, shook her head.

'Mrs Dyson, why don't we sit down?' Peabody took her by the arm, led her to a long sofa done in a striking, in-your-face red.

The room was bold, splashy colors, big shapes. A huge painting that looked to Eve to represent some sort of swollen sunset in shades of searing red and gold and vivid orange dominated the wall behind the sofa.

There was a wall screen and a mood screen, both turned off, tables in sheer and glossy white, and a tall triple window, with its red curtains tightly closed.

In the excited cheer of the room, Jenny Dyson seemed only more pale. More a faded outline of a woman than flesh and blood.

'I haven't taken anything. The doctor said I could, probably should, but I haven't.' Her fingers worked as she talked, linking together, pulling apart. 'If I did, I wouldn't feel, would I? What I need to feel. We went to see her.'

'Yes, I know.' Eve sat across from her, in a chair of lively purple. 'The doctor said she wouldn't have suffered.'

'No. I understand this is a very difficult time—'

'Do you have children?'

'No.'

'I don't think you can understand, I really don't.' There was a hint of anger in the tone – the how-dare-you-presume-to-understand. Then it fizzled into dull grief again. 'She came from me, from us. And she was so beautiful. Sweet and funny. Happy. We raised such a happy child. But we failed. I failed, you see. I didn't protect her. I didn't keep her safe. I'm her mother, and I didn't keep her safe.'

'Mrs Dyson.' Sensing a meltdown, Eve spoke sharply. Jenny's head snapped up. 'You're right, I can't understand, not really, what you feel, what you're going through, what you have to face. But I do know this. Are you listening?'

'Yes.'

'This isn't about what you did or didn't do to protect Linnie. This isn't your failure, not in any sense. This was beyond your control, beyond your husband's, beyond anyone's but the men who did this thing. They're responsible, and no one else. And this I do understand, the way you can't, at least not now. Linnie is ours now, too. We can't protect her now, but we will serve her. We will stand for her. You have to do the same.'

129

'What can I do?' Her fingers kept moving. Together, apart. Together, apart.

'You were friends with the Swishers.'

'Yes. Good friends. Yes.'

'Did either of them say anything to you about being worried, even uneasy, as regarded their safety.'

'No. Well, sometimes Keelie and I talked about what a madhouse the city can be. All the precautions you have to take to live here. But there was nothing specific.'

'What about their marriage?'

'I'm sorry?'

'You were friends. Would she have told you if she had a relationship outside of the marriage, of if she suspected her husband did?'

'They – they loved each other. Keelie would never.' Jenny touched a hand to her face – temple, cheek, jaw – as if assuring herself she was still there. 'No, Keelie wasn't interested in anyone else, and she trusted Grant. They were very steady, family-oriented people. Like us. We were friends because we had a lot in common.'

'They both had clients. Any trouble there?'

'There were irritations, of course. Some difficulties. Some people would come to Keelie looking for miracles, or instant gratification. Or they'd sign up with her when they'd have been better off just going to a body sculptor, because they weren't willing to alter their lifestyle. And Keelie's philosophy was about health and lifestyle. Grant handled a number of custody cases that weren't always pleasant.'

130

'Any threats?'

'No, nothing serious.' She stared beyond Eve to the red wall of curtains. 'A client demanding their money back from Keelie, or filing suit because they didn't get the results they wanted when they were stuffing their faces with soy chips. And Grant would get the sort of outrage or anger lawyers deal with because they're lawyers. But for the most part, their clients were satisfied. Both of them built a solid base because of referrals and word of mouth. People liked them.'

'Were they ever involved in anything or with anyone illegal? This isn't about protecting them,' Eve added.

'They believed in doing the right thing, in setting an example for their children. Grant used to joke about his wild college days, and how he'd once been arrested for possession of some Zoner. How it scared him enough to straighten him out.'

She curled her legs up in a way that told Eve the gesture was habitual, thoughtless. 'They didn't have a strong family base, either of them. It was important to them to make one, and to raise their own children on that base. The closest either of them would have come to doing something against the law was jaywalking or cheering too loudly at one of Coyle's games.'

'How did you arrange to have Linnie stay the night in their house?' Jenny shuddered once. She uncurled her legs, sat very straight with her busy fingers twisted tight in her lap. 'I . . . I asked Keelie if she'd be able to have Linnie over after school, keep her for the night. A school night. Normally,

131

she didn't allow sleepovers on school nights. But she was happy to do it, pleased that Matt and I were able to get the suite, have the anniversary celebration.'

'How long ago did you arrange it?'

'Oh, six, seven weeks. We're not spur-of-the-moment people. But we didn't tell the girls until the night before, in case something came up. They were so excited. Oh God.' She clutched her belly and began to rock. 'Linnie said, she said, it was like a present for her, too.'

'Nixie came here a lot, too.'

'Yes, yes.' She kept rocking. 'Play dates, study dates, sleepovers.'

'How would she get here?'

'How?' She blinked. 'One of them would bring her, or one of us would pick her up.'

'She and Linnie ever go out by themselves?'

'No.' Her eyes were wet now, and Jenny wiped at them in the same absent way she'd curled her legs up on the cushion. 'Linnie would complain sometimes because a lot of her schoolmates were allowed to go to the park by themselves, or to the vids or arcades. But Matt and I felt she was too young to be on her own.'

'The Swishers, with Nixie?'

'The same. We had a lot in common.'

'With Coyle?'

'He was older, and a boy. I know that's sexist, but it's the way it is. They kept a tight rein on him, but he could go out with his friends, on his own, as long as they knew where. And

132

he had to carry a pocket 'link so they could check on him.'

'Did he ever get in any trouble?'

'He was a good kid.' Her lips trembled. 'A very good kid. His biggest rebellion, that I know of, was sneaking junk food, and Keelie knew about it anyway. He was sports mad, and if he screwed up, they'd limit his activities. Coyle wouldn't risk not being able to play ball.'

When Eve sat back, Peabody touched Jenny on the arm. 'Is there someone we can call for you? Someone you want to be here with you?'

'My mother's coming. I told her not to, but then I called her back. My mother's coming.'

'Mrs Dyson, we're going to need to talk about arrangements for Nixie.'

'Nixie?'

'You and your husband are her legal guardians.'

'Yes.' She pushed a hand through her hair. 'We — they wanted to make sure Nixie and Coyle had . . . I can't, I can't think—' She shot off the sofa when her husband came down the curve of the stairs like a ghost.

His body swayed; his face was slack with drugs. He wore only a pair of white boxers. 'Jenny?'

'Yes, baby, right here.' She dashed toward the stairs to enfold him.

'I had a dream, a terrible dream. Linnie.'

'Shh. Shh.' She stroked his hair, his back, staring over his shoulder at Eve as he bowed his body to hers. 'I can't. I can't. Please, can't you go now? Can you go?'

7

Marriage, to Eve's mind, was a kind of obstacle course. You had to learn when to jump over, when to belly under, and when to stop your forward motion and change direction.

She had work, and at the moment would have preferred that forward motion. But figured when you dumped a strange kid on a spouse, you should at least give him a heads-up when it looked like the stay might be extended.

She took five minutes personal – as personal as she could manage on a pocket 'link while standing on the sidewalk.

She was surprised he answered himself, and guilty when she caught the flicker of annoyance in his eyes at the interruption.

'Sorry, I can get back to you later.'

'No, I'm between – but just. Is there a problem?'

'Maybe. I don't know. Just a gut thing, and I thought I should let you know the kid might be around a little longer than I expected.'

'I told you she's welcome as long as . . .' He glanced away from the screen, and she saw him raise a hand. 'Give me a minute here, Caro.'

'Look, this can wait.'

'Finish it out. Why do you think she won't be with the Dysons in the next day or so?'

'They're in bad shape, and my timing didn't help. Mostly, it's a gut feeling. I'm thinking about contacting the – what is she – the grandmother? – when I find a minute. And there's a stepsister, his side, somewhere. Just a backup. Maybe a temporary deal until the Dysons are . . . better equipped or whatever.'

'That's fine, but meanwhile she's all right where she is.' He frowned. 'You're thinking it might be considerable time before they're able to take her. Weeks?'

'Maybe. Family member should take the interim. I could bring CPS in, but I don't want to. Not if I can avoid it. Maybe I didn't read the Dysons right, but I figured you should know the kid might be around longer than we thought.'

'We'll deal with it.'

'Okay. Sorry to hold you up.'

'No problem. I'll see you at home.'

But when he clicked off, he continued to frown. He thought of the child in his home, and the dead ones. He had half a dozen people waiting for a meeting, and decided they could wait a few moments. What good was power if you didn't flex its muscles now and again?

He called up Eve's file on the Swishers from her home unit, and scanned the names of the family connections.

They started knocking on doors, working their way east then west from the Swisher home. A lot of doors remained unopened, people in the workforce. But those that did open shed no light.

Saw nothing. Terrible thing. Tragedy. Heard nothing. That poor family. Know nothing.

'What are you seeing, Peabody?'

'A lot of shock, dismay — the underlying relief it wasn't them. And a good dose of fear.'

'All that. And what are these people telling us about the victims?'

'Nice family, friendly. Well-behaved children.'

'Not our usual run, is it? It's like stepping into another dimension where people bake cookies and pass them out to strangers on the street.'

'I could use a cookie.'

Eve walked up to the next building, listed in her notes as a multi-family. 'Then there's the neighborhood. Families, double incomes primarily. People like that are going to be beddy-bye at two in the morning, weekday.'

She took another moment to look up and down the street. Even in the middle of the day, the traffic was pretty light. At two in the morning, she imagined the street was quiet as a grave.

'Maybe you catch a break and somebody's got insomnia and looks out the window at just the right time. Or decided to take a little stroll. But they're going to tell the cops, if they spotted anything. A family gets wiped out on your block, you're scared. You want to feel safe, you tell the cops if you saw anything off.'

She rang the bell. There was a scratching sound from the intercom as someone inside cleared their throat.

'Who are you?'

'NYPSD.' Eve held her badge to the security peep. 'Lieutenant Dallas and Detective Peabody.'

'How do I know that for sure?'

'Ma'am, you're looking at my badge.'

'I could have a badge, too, and I'm not the police.'

'Got me there. Can you see the badge number?'

'I'm not blind, am I?'

'As I'm standing out here, that's impossible to verify. But you can verify my ID if you contact Cop Central and give them my badge number.'

'Maybe you stole the badge from the real police. People get murdered in their own beds.'

'Yes, ma'am, that's why we're here. We'd like to speak with you about the Swishers.'

'How do I know you're not the ones who killed them?'

'Excuse me?'

Eve, her face a study in frustration, turned to look at the woman on the sidewalk. She was carrying a market sack and wearing a great deal of gold-streaked red hair, a green skin-suit, and a baggy jacket.

'You're trying to talk to Mrs Grentz?'

'Trying being the operative. Police.'

'Yeah, got that.' She bounced up the stairs. 'Hey, Mrs Grentz, it's Hildy. I got your bagels.'

'Why didn't you say so?'

There was a lot of clicking and snicking, then the door opened. Eve looked down, considerably. The woman was barely five feet, skinny as a stick, and old as time. On her head was perched an ill-fitting black wig only shades darker than her wrinkled skin.

'I brought the cops, too,' Hildy told her, cheerfully. 'Are you arrested?'

'No, they just want to talk. About what happened with the Swishers.'

'All right then.' She waved a hand like she was batting at flies and began to walk away.

'My landlady,' Hildy told them. 'I live below. She's okay, except for being – as my old man would say – crazy as a shithouse rat. You ought to go on in and sit down while she's in the mood. I'm going to stick her bagels away.'

'Thanks.'

The place was jammed with things. Pricey things, Eve noted as she made her way between tables, chairs, lamps, paintings that were tilted and stacked against the walls.

The air had that old-lady smell, what seemed to be a combination of powder, age, and flowers going to dust.

Mrs Grentz was now perched in a chair, her tiny feet on a tiny hassock and her arms crossed over her nonexistent breasts. 'Whole family, murdered in their sleep.'

'You knew the Swishers?'

'Of course I knew the Swishers. Lived here the past eighty-eight years, haven't I? Seen it all, heard it all.'

'What did you see?'

'World going to hell in a handbasket.' She dipped her chin, unfolded one of her bony arms to slap a gnarled hand on the arm of the chair. 'Sex and violence, sex and violence. Won't be any pillar of salt this time out. Whole place, and everything in it, is going to burn. Get what you ask for. Reap what you sow.'

'Okay. Can you tell me if you heard or saw anything unusual on the night the Swishers were killed?'

'Got my ears fixed, got my eyes tuned. I see and hear fine.' She leaned forward, the tuned-up eyes avid. 'I know who killed those people.'

'Who killed them?'

'The French.'

'How do you know that, Mrs Grentz?'

'Because they're *French*.' To emphasize her point, she slapped a hand on her leg. 'Got their der-re-airs kicked the last time they made trouble, didn't they? And believe me, they've been planning a payback ever since. If somebody's murdered in their own bed, it was the French who did it. You can take that to the bank.'

Eve wasn't sure the little sound Peabody made was a snicker or a sigh, but she ignored it. 'I appreciate the information,' Eve began, and started to rise.

'Did you hear someone speaking French on the night of the murders?'

At Peabody's question, Eve sent her a pitying look.

'You don't *hear* them, girl. Quiet as snakes, that's the French for you.'

139

'Thank you, Mrs Grentz, you've been very helpful.' Eve got to her feet.

'Can't trust people who eat snails.'

'No, ma'am. We'll let ourselves out.'

Hildy stood just outside the doorway, grinning. 'Buggy, but somehow fascinating, right? Mrs Grentz?' She lifted her voice, moved into the doorway. 'I'm going on down.'

'You get my bagels?'

'All put away. See you. Keep walking,' she instructed Eve, 'and don't look back. You never know what else is going to pop into her head.'

'You got a few minutes to talk with us, Hildy?'

'Sure.' Still carrying the market bag, Hildy led the way out, down the stairs, and around to her own entrance. 'She's actually my great-great-aunt – through marriage – but she likes to be called Mrs Grentz. The mister's been dead thirty years. Never made the acquaintance myself.' Though below street level, the apartment was bright and cheerful with a lot of unframed posters tacked to the walls and a rainbow scatter of rugs on the floor. 'I rent from her – well, her son pays the rent. I'm a kind of unofficial caretaker – her and the place. You saw upstairs? That's nothing. She's loaded. Wanna sit?'

'Thanks.'

'Seriously loaded, like millions, so I'm here to make sure the security's always on, and that she doesn't lie around helpless if she trips over some of that furniture and breaks her leg. She's got this alarm deal on.' Hildy pulled a small receiver out of her pocket. 'She falls, or if her vitals get wonky, this beeps. I do some of the marketing for her, listen to her crab sometimes. It's a pretty good deal for the digs. And she's okay, mostly, sort of funny.'

'How long have you had the place?'

'Six months, almost seven now. I'm a writer – well, working on that – so this is a good setup for me. You guys want something to drink or anything?'

'No, but thanks. You knew the Swishers?'

'Sort of, the way you do when you see the same people all the time. I knew the parents to nod to, like that. We weren't really on the same wave.'

'Meaning?'

'They were totally linear, you know. Put the *con* in conservative. Nice. Really nice. If they'd see me out, they'd always ask about Mrs Grentz, and if I was doing okay. Not everybody bothers with that. I knew the kids a little more.'

She held up a hand, shut her eyes a minute. 'I'm trying to put it in its place, to get to "they're where their destiny took them to," that place. But Jesus!' Her eyes opened again, swam a moment. 'They were just kids. And Coyle? I think he had a little crush on me. It was really sweet.'

'So you saw them around the neighborhood.'

'Sure. Coyle mostly. They didn't let the little girl run around as much. He'd volunteer to run to the market, or walk with me there. Or I'd see him out boarding with some friends, and wave, or go out to talk.'

'Did you ever see him with somebody you didn't recognize from around the neighborhood?'

141

'Not really. He was a good kid. Old-fashioned, at least from the way I was raised. Really polite, a little shy, at least with me. Way into sports.'

'How about the comings and goings? Writers notice things, don't they?'

'It's important to observe stuff, file it away. You never know.' Hildy twirled a hunk of her colorful hair around her finger. 'And I did think of something I didn't remember before, when the other cops came by to ask stuff. It's just – I couldn't keep anything in my head when I heard about it. You know?'

'Sure. What do you remember now?'

'I don't know if it's anything, but I started thinking about it this morning. That night . . .' She shifted, gave Eve a weak smile. 'Listen, if I tell you something I did that's not a hundred percent legal, am I going to get in trouble?'

'We're not here to hassle you, Hildy. We're here about five people who were murdered in their beds.'

'Okay.' She drew a long breath. 'Okay. Sometimes, if I'm up writing late, or if Mrs Grentz has been a particular pain – I mean, you got a load right? She's funny, but sometimes she wears.'

'All right.'

'Sometimes, I go up on the roof.' She pointed a finger at the ceiling. 'There's a nice little spot up there, and it's a place to hang out, look around, sit and think. Sometimes I go up there to, you know, smoke a little Zoner. I can't do that in here. If Mrs Grentz was to come down – and she does sometimes – and smell it – she's got a nose like a blood-hound – she'd wig. So if I'm in the mood for a toke, not like every night or anything . . .'

'We're not Illegals, and we're not concerned if you had a little recreational Zoner.'

'Right. So I was up there. It was late because the book had been chugging. I was just hanging up there, about ready to go down, because the long night plus the Zoner made me sleepy. I just sort of looked around, like you do, and I see these two guys. Nice builds – that's what I thought, you know. Prime meat. I didn't think anything much of it, even when the cops came by and I heard about the Swishers, but I was thinking back, and I remembered.'

'Did you see what they looked like?'

'Not so much. Except they were white guys, both of them. I could see their hands, and a little bit of their faces, and they were white. I didn't really see faces, couldn't from the angle up there. But I remembered how I thought, "Look at the beef," and how they walked, side-by-side, almost like they were marching. Not talking or anything, like you do if you're out walking with a pal late at night. Just one, two, three, four, all the way to the corner.'

'Which corner?'

'Um, west, toward Riverside.'

'What were they wearing?'

'Okay, I've thought about this, really hard. Black, top to toe, with – what do they call those wooly hats you pull down on your head?'

'Watch cap?'

'Yeah, yeah! Like that. And they each had a bag, long strap, cross-body. I like to watch people, especially if they don't know. And they really were built.'

'How old were they?'

'I don't know. Honest. I didn't see their faces. They had those caps pulled down, and hell, I was checking the bods. But the other thing I thought later? I never heard them. I mean, they didn't just not talk, I didn't hear their footsteps. If I hadn't gone over to the rail just as they were passing below, I'd never have known they were down there.'

'Let's go up to the roof, Hildy.' Eve got to her feet. 'Take us through it again.'

'It's a break,' Peabody said when they were out on the sidewalk again.

Eve was staring up at the roof. 'Not much of one, but a break.'

'It's details. And details count.' She walked back down to the Swisher house, looked up toward the roof where they'd recently stood with Hildy. 'Probably would have seen her, if they'd looked. Seen her standing up there, or the silhouette of her, when they got closer. But they were done, confident. Maybe scanned the street, yet careful to keep out of the brightest beams of the security lights. Walked – marched. No hurry, but disciplined – to the corner of Riverside. Had a ride somewhere, you bet they did. Legally parked, street or lot. Street's better, no paperwork of any kind if you snag a street spot, but you can't count on finding a space, so maybe a lot.'

'Stolen ride?' Peabody suggested.

'Be stupid. Stupid because it leaves a trail. You steal something, the owner gets pissy and reports it. Maybe take a vehicle out of long-term somewhere, put it back. But why? You've got all this equipment, expensive equipment. You've got money or backing. You've got a ride of your own. It won't be anything flashy.' She rocked back and forth on her heels. 'Nothing that catches the eye, and the driver obeys all traffic regs.' She walked west as she visualized it. 'Do the job, walk out, walk away. No hurry, no noise. Eyes tracking left and right – that's training. Don't think to look up, though, and that's sloppy. Just a little sloppy, or cocky. Or under it, they were revved from the kill. Pro or not, you've got to get a little revved. Walk straight down, no conversation. Go straight to the ride, no detours. Stow the bags for later cleaning or destruction. Back to HQ.'

'Headquarters?'

'Bet that's how they referred to it. Someplace to be debriefed, or to exchange their war stories, to practice, to clean up. And I'll bet you it's squared away.'

She had their scent. She knew it wasn't a logical term, but it was the *right* term. She had their scent, and she would track it until she had them.

She stood on the corner of Eighty-first and Riverside, looking north, and south, and further west. How far had they walked? she wondered. How many people had seen them walking away from that death house, fresh blood in their bags?

Just a couple of guys heading home after a quick night's work. 'Tag Baxter,' Eve ordered. 'I want some names.'

Her name was Meredith Newman, and she was overworked and underpaid. She'd be happy to tell you so, given the opportunity. Though she liked to think of herself as a contemporary martyr, long suffering and sweating blood for the cause.

Once, in her younger days, she'd visualized herself as a crusader, and had worked and studied with the fervor of the converted. But then a year on the job had become two, and two had become five, and the caseloads, the misery and uselessness of them, took their toll.

In her private fantasies, she'd meet a handsome, sexy man, *swimming* in money. She'd quit. Never have to drag herself through the endless paperwork, the disheartening home checks. Never have to see another battered woman or child.

But until that fine day, it was business as usual.

Now she was heading toward a routine home check, where she fully expected to find the two kids filthy, the mother stoned or on her way toward oblivion. She'd lost hope that it would ever be any different. She'd lost the will to care. The number of people who eventually turned themselves around and became decent, contributing members of society was about one in fifty, in her estimation.

And she always seemed to pull the other forty-nine.

Her feet hurt because she'd been stupid enough to buy a pair of new shoes, which she couldn't afford. Not on her salary. She was depressed because the man she'd been seeing on and off for five weeks had told her she depressed *him*, and had broken things off.

She was thirty-three years old, single, no boyfriend, a joke of a social life, and so sick and tired of her job she wanted to kill herself.

She walked with her head down, as was her habit, because she didn't want to see the dirt, the grime, the people.

She hated Alphabet City, hated the men who loitered in doorways and rubbed their crotches when she passed by. She hated the smell of garbage – urban perfume – and the *noise*. Engines, horns, voices, machinery all pulsing against her ear drums.

Her vacation wasn't scheduled for eight weeks, three days, twelve hours. She didn't know if she could make it. Hell, her next day off was three days away, and she didn't know if she could make that.

She wouldn't.

She didn't pay any attention to the squeal of brakes, just more of the cacophony of the city she'd come to loathe like a wasting disease.

The little shoulder bump was just another annoyance, just more of the innate rudeness that infected everyone who lived in this shit hole.

Then her head spun, and her vision went gray. She felt, as if in a dream, the sensation of being lifted off her feet and thrown. Even when she landed in the back of the van, with the tape slapped over her face and her eyes, it didn't seem real. Her body had barely registered the need to scream when the faint nudge of a pressure syringe had her going under.

By midafternoon, Eve and Peabody had spoken with three of Keelie Swisher's clients and two of her husband's. They were working geographically and took another of Keelie's next.

Jan Uger was a hefty woman who smoked three herbals during their twenty-minute interview. When she wasn't puffing, she was sucking on one of the brightly colored candy drops in a dish beside her chair.

Her hair was done up in a huge glossy ball, as if someone had slicked it up, around, then sprayed it with silicone. She had long jowls, a trio of chins, sallow skin. And a pisser of an attitude.

'A quack.' She puffed, jabbed with her smoking herbal. 'That's what she was. Said she couldn't help me if I didn't keep up the regimen. What am I, in Christing boot camp?'

'You were, at one time,' Eve prompted.

'Did three years, regular Army. Where I met my Stu. He put in fifteen, serving our country. I spent those years being a good Army wife and raising two kids. Was the kids put the weight on me,' she claimed and chose another candy. 'I tried diets, but I've got a condition.'

Which was, Eve decided, the inability to stop putting things in her mouth.

148

'Our insurance doesn't cover body sculpting.' She worked the candy around in her mouth, gave it a couple of good crunches. 'Cheapskates. Except on the provision you see a licensed nutritionist for six months, and they sign off for you. So, that's what I did, went to that quack, listened to her bullshit. And what happened?'

She sucked so hard on the candy in her fury, Eve wondered it didn't lodge in her throat and choke her to death.

'I'll tell you what happened. I gained *four* pounds in two months. Not that Stu minds. More to love, is what he says. But I did the drill, and would she sign off? No, she would not!'

'You had a problem with that.'

'Damn right. She said I didn't qualify. Who was she to say? What skin off her nose is it to sign the damn paper so my insurance will foot the bill? People like that make me sick.'

She lit another cigarette, scowled through smoke that smelled like burning mint.

'You argued with Mrs Swisher?'

'Told her just what I thought of her and her Christing *regimen,* and said I was going to sue. Would have, but her husband's a damn lawyer, so what's the point? Everybody knows they stick together like a pile of shit. Sorry they're dead, though,' she added as an afterthought.

'Your husband's retired military now, and employed with . . .' Eve pretended to check her notes.

'He's security at the Sky Mall. Hard to live on retirement, plus my Stu, he likes to get out and do a job. Better insurance there, too. He works there another eighteen months, and I can get the sculpting, on them.'

Keep eating, sister, and it's going to take more than sculpting. It's going to take an airjack to whittle you down. 'Meanwhile, you were both very dissatisfied with Mrs Swisher.'

'Of course we were. She took our hard-earned money and did nothing for it.'

'That's upsetting, and feeling unable to sue successfully, you must have wanted to be recompensed in some other way.'

'Told everybody I knew she was a Christing quack.' Her triple chins wagged with satisfaction. 'I got plenty of friends, and so does Stu.'

'If it'd been me, I'd have wanted something more personal, more tangible. Maybe you and your husband went to Mr or Mrs Swisher to complain, to demand your money back.'

'No point.'

'Was your husband home last night? Between one and three A.M.?'

'Where else would he be at one o'clock in the morning?' she asked hotly. 'What is this?'

'A homicide investigation. Your husband's military records indicate he was an MP.'

'Eight years. So what?'

'I wonder, when he complained to his buddies about Mrs Swisher's treatment of you, they must have gotten heated up – on your account.'

150

'You'd think, wouldn't you? You'd think. But people don't have much sympathy for a woman with my condition.'

'That's a shame. You don't have any friends, or relatives, who could front you the money for the body work?'

'Shit.' She blew out smoke, reached for another candy. 'Who are we going to know with that kind of money? I was an Army brat, and my father died serving his country when I was sixteen. Stu's family's mostly factory workers out in Ohio. You know what sculpting costs?' she demanded. Then she swept her gaze over Eve, curled her lip. 'How much did it cost you?'

Eve paused outside the building. 'Do you think I should've been insulted?' she wondered. 'The "how much did it cost you" crack?'

'She probably meant it as a kind of compliment. But still, I've got a great-aunt who's half French and I was sort of insulted with Mrs Grentz's French cracks.' She slid into the vehicle. 'This one gets checked off.'

'Yeah. No way she's smart enough, no way they have the resources. Husband's military record's clean, and even the MP stint wouldn't give him the kind of training we're after. And he's too old, too weighty himself according to his ID data.'

'Could just be pulling the strings, but—'

'Right. Hard to believe anyone married to her, living in a place full of smoke and candy, is disciplined and clever enough to outline an operation like this one.'

'Or working as a security drone at the mall, chasing off

kids, mostly. Bad-mouthing and complaining, that's what these people do.'

'And they don't kill off an entire family because they're pissed off at somebody. No,' Eve agreed. 'She was irritating, and he's likely the same, but they're not masterminds or cold-blooded kid killers.'

'You know what else? I don't think whoever did this, or is behind it, made any noise. I mean, none of this, I'll-sue-your-quack-ass business. I know we have to check those out, but that's not going to be the hit.'

Eve kept her attention on the road as she drove. 'Why?'

'Because he has to think ahead, right? Has to be controlled and organized. Whenever this happened – I mean whatever it was that made him target these people – he had to pull it out. Because he'd have been thinking payback. Someday, somehow. But you don't leave a trail.' Now Eve turned her head. 'My pride in you bubbles in my heart. Unless it's that soy dog you talked me into earlier.'

'Gosh, Dallas, a blush rises to my cheeks. Unless that, too, is the soy dog.' She thumped a fist on her chest, gave a small, somehow ladylike belch. 'Guess it was the dog.'

'Now that we've established that, let's have the next on the list.' Peabody called up the list, the next name, the location, and the directions from the dash menu. Then leaned forward, stroking the dash and crooning. 'Nice vehicle, pretty vehicle. Smart vehicle.' She slid her gaze toward Eve. 'And who got the nice, pretty, smart vehicle for us?'

'You've already milked that one, Peabody.'

'Yeah but – Aww, and see, look at its little 'link beeping.' Shaking her head, Eve answered the beep. 'Dallas.'

'A little tit for tat coming your way,' Nadine said, 'so don't forget it. Scanner picked up a snatch-and-grab report. Female on Avenue B, tossed in the back of a van quick as a wink.'

'Unless she's dead, she's not my table. Sorry.'

'Cold, cruel, true. Thing is, one of the witnesses recognized her, and actually bothered to say so to the uniforms responding. Said she was a social worker named Meredith Newman. I get wind of that and I think, hey, isn't that the name of—'

'The CPS drone on the Swisher case.'

'I'm heading down there, to do some interviews. Thought you'd want to know.'

'We're on our way. Don't talk to anybody on scene, Nadine. I need a shot first. You're going to give me tit,' she added when Nadine's mouth opened. 'Don't be stingy with it.'

She broke off, whipped around a corner, and headed south.

8

Eve spotted the Channel 75 van parked in a loading zone on Avenue B. She whipped by it, then double-parked beside the black-and-white already at the curb.

She spotted Nadine as well – it was hard not to when the perfectly streaked hair and the vivid royal blue of the reporter's on-air suit sprang out like an exotic bloom against the faded forest of dingy shirts and smudgy concrete.

She was cozied up with a trio of the daily doorway lurkers but peeled off toward Eve.

'I never said I wouldn't ask questions,' Nadine said immediately. 'But I've kept it off record. For now. Your uniform's inside with the woman who claims to have seen the grab and recognized the grabee. Hi, Peabody. How are you feeling?'

'Better and better, thanks.'

Eve sent a hard stare at the van. 'Keep the cameras off.'

'Public street,' Nadine began. 'Public—'

'Nadine, do you know why I often give you an inside track? Because it's not just the story with you. You actually give more than a passing thought to the people in the story.

And you wouldn't, not even for ratings, sacrifice those people to get your pretty face on air.'

Nadine blew out a long breath. 'Shit.'

'Keep the cameras off,' Eve repeated and strode toward the lingering lurkers. 'What did you see?' she began. 'What do you know?'

The skinniest of the lot, a mixed-race stick with a pitted complexion, grinned – illustrating that his dental care was slightly below the standard of his skin care – and rubbed his thumb and forefinger together.

'Detective Peabody.' Eve spoke in mild tones, her eyes cold as a shark's. 'In your professional opinion, did this individual, who has possibly witnessed a crime, just solicit a member of the NYPSD for a bribe in exchange for information regarding that crime?'

'That does appear to be the case, Lieutenant.'

'Me and my 'sociates need some jack. You give, you gets.'

'And, Detective, what would be my most usual response to such a solicitation?'

'Your response, Lieutenant, would be to haul said individual, and possibly his associates, into Central, possibly charged with obstruction of justice and impeding a police investigation. You would also determine if subject and/or his associates had sheets. If so, you would then spend considerable time ruining their day and potentially making their lives, for the short-term at least, a stinking hell.'

'That's exactly correct, Detective. Thank you. You catch any of that, asshole?'

He actually looked hurt. 'No jack?'

'That is also exactly correct. Now I'll repeat: What did you see, what do you know?'

'You gonna take me in I don't say?'

'Two correct answers in a row. Want to try for three?'

'Well, shit. I seen the big nose sluffling along, coming along looking like she smell something she don't like. Ain't worth two looks, but we just hanging, so I start to give her a blow. Then the van thing, it flies up. Fast! And the two dudes, they pop out the back. Got one on each sida her. Lifts her up, toss her in, slam, bam, gone. We and my 'sociates, we'da taken them on but they was rat fast, man. You gets?'

'Yeah, I get. What did they look like? The men who popped out the back?'

'Like ninjas, man.' He looked at each of his pals for nods of agreement. 'Like a coupla kick-face ninja dudes in black threads with the mask thing.'

'How about the van?'

'Black, too.'

'Make, model, plate?'

'Hell, what I know? I don't drive no van. Big and black, and moved slick as goose shit. Musta been a dude in the front, but I didn't see nothing. Wasn't lookin'. And the big nose? She don't even squeak. Got her grabbed and stashed so fast, she don't even squeak. We chill now?'

'Yeah, we're chill now. Name?'

'Man.' He shuffled his feet. 'Ramon. Ramon Pasquell. I

156

got legitimate parole, man. I be looking for a job now, but I'm standing here jawing you.'

'Right. Ramon, if you or your associates remember anything else, you can contact me at Central.' She handed him a card and a twenty.

'Hey!' No amount of joy lighting his face could make it any less ugly. 'You fridge for a big nose.'

'Sweet talker,' she said and walked into the building.

'You don't have a big nose,' Peabody pointed out. 'In fact, it could be called narrow and elegant.'

'Big nose – nosey – cops, CPS, probation officers, and so on. We're all big noses to mopes like Ramon.'

'Ah, I gets. Report has the witness on the third floor. Cable, Minnie.'

It only took one glance at the grimy, dented door of the single skinny elevator to have Eve taking the grimy stairs instead. She had a moment to wonder why the stench of urine and puke always seemed to permeate the walls in such places when a uniform stepped out of a door on the third floor.

She noted he made them as cops even before he eyed the badge she'd hooked in her belt. 'Lieutenant, you're quick. I just called for detectives.'

'Belay that, Officer. This incident may be related to one of our cases. She going to give me anything worthwhile?'

'Saw the whole thing. She's excitable, but she saw the grab, recognized the victim. Meredith Newman. Child Protection. I contacted CPS, and it checks. Newman was due here for a home check.'

'Okay. Rescind the request for a detective. I'll contact Central after I've talked to the wit. I'd like you to wait downstairs. I've got your unit boxed in anyway. I'll want your report when I'm done up here.'

'Yes, sir.'

As he went down, Eve glanced at Peabody, noted the beads of sweat on her partner's face. Should've risked the elevator, she thought. 'You holding, Peabody?'

'Yeah, I'm fine.' She dug out a tissue, wiped her face. 'Still get a little winded, but the exercise is good for me. I'm good.'

'You're otherwise, I want to know. Don't pussy around.' Eve stepped up to the door, knocked. She could already hear the shouts, the crying, the voices. A trio of voices, if she wasn't mistaken. And two of them kids.

It seemed to be her week for kids. 'Police, Ms. Cable.'

'I just talked to the police.' A woman, looking harassed – and who wouldn't with one kid on the hip and the other pulling at your leg? – opened the door. Her hair was a short, spiky blonde, her build going toward bottom heavy. And her eyes had the rabbit pink hue of a funky-junkie.

'Lieutenant Dallas, Detective Peabody. We'd like to come in.'

'I told the other guy the works. Jeez, Lo-Lo would ya stop for two seconds. Sorry, the kids're riled up.'

'This Lo-Lo?' Peabody smiled. 'Hi, Lo-Lo, why don't you come on over here with me.'

Kids responded to Peabody, Eve noted. And this one, a pint-size with hair as blonde and spiky as her mother's, peeled off her mother's leg, put her hand in Peabody's, and walked off babbling.

There wasn't far to go. The room was a little L, with a kitchen forming the jag. But there were a few toys scattered around, and the kid arrowed toward the pile to share them with her new pal.

'I saw from the window, there.' Minnie pointed, shifting the smaller child on her hip. This one had eyes as big and unblinking as an owl's, and a crop of smokey brown curls. 'I was watching for her, for Ms. Newman. She don't – didn't think I'd clean up, she didn't think I'd kick the funk. But I did. Been off it six months now.'

'Good.' And if she hadn't been on it too much longer than she'd been off, her eyes might one day lose the red rims and pinkish whites. 'They were going to take my kids. I had to clean up for my kids, so I did. Not their fault I got screwed up. I'm off the funk, and I go to meetings. I get spot checked, and I'm clean. I need Ms. Newman to say I can keep my temp professional mother status. I gotta have the money, gotta pay the rent and the food, and—'

'I'll contact CPS and tell them I was here, saw you were clean, and your children cared for. Your place is clean,' she added.

'I made sure. It gets messy, with the kids, but I don't let it get dirty. I get some more money together, I'm going to

159

move us to a better neighborhood. But this is the best I can do now. I don't want to screw up my kids.'

'I can see that. CPS will send another rep out. You won't lose your status due to these circumstances.'

'Okay.' She turned her face into the little one's neck. 'Sorry. I know I shouldn't be so into what's going on with me when that lady got herself grabbed like that. But I don't want to lose my kids.'

'Tell me what you saw.'

'I was standing there, at the window. I was nervous, because she didn't like me. That's not right,' she corrected. 'She didn't care. Didn't give a dried-up turd.' She winced, looked over at her older girl. 'I try not to use bad language in front of the kids, but I forget.'

'Don't worry about it.' Eve stepped to the window. There was a clear view of the street. She could see the black-and-white, and her own vehicle. And the shaking fists of drivers who were fighting the logjam the double-parking caused. 'Here?'

'Yeah. I'm standing there, with Bits on my hip, like now. I'm telling her and Lo-Lo they have to be good. My eyes.' She touched a finger just below her left. 'You've been on the funk, even when you're off awhile, they get worse when you're nervous or upset, or just tired. Guess I was all. I saw her coming, walking from that way.'

Stepping closer, Minnie pointed. 'Had her head down, so I didn't see her face at first. But I knew it was her. I was going to get back – so in case she looked up she wouldn't see me watching – but I saw the van. It just flew up, you know? Real fast. Squealing when it stopped. These two guys jumped out the back, and they were on her so fast. Pow! Grabbed her up, right off her feet. I saw her face then, just for a second. She hardly looked surprised, but it was—' She snapped a finger. 'Tossed her through the open doors, jumped in after her, and were gone.

'I called right away. It might've taken me just a minute, because I was so surprised. I mean it was so fast, then it was like it never happened. But it did. I called nine-one-one and I said what I saw. They won't think I had anything to do with it, will they? Because she was coming here, and I'm a junkie?'

'You don't sound like a junkie to me, Minnie.' A smile lit up in her red-rimmed eyes.

'Cute kids,' Peabody commented on the way down. 'Looks like that woman's pushing against the odds. Good chance she'll make it.'

Eve nodded. The junkies she knew – including vague memories of her own mother – cared more about the next fix than any child. Minnie had a shot.

She stepped back onto the street, signalled to Nadine. 'Do your interviews. But keep our names out. I don't want whoever did this to know we suspect a connection to the Swisher murders.'

'And you do.'

Eve started to say 'off-record,' but decided it would be an insult under the circumstances. 'No. I know there is. But we make that known, Newman is dead. Probably is anyway, but that would seal the deal. And it wouldn't hurt to pump up the human interest regarding Minnie Cable – recovering funk addict, working to stay clean and do right by her kids, so on. She stood up, called this in. But make it clear, Nadine, like crystal, that she was unable to give any description of the perpetrators.'

'Was she?'

'No. Couple of guys, dressed in black. Masked, moved fast. She couldn't make height, age, weight, race, nothing. Just make it clear on-air.'

'Got that. Hey!' She strode, high heels clipping, as Eve walked away. 'Is that all I get?'

'All there is, at this point. Nadine?' She paused long enough to glance around. 'Your heads-up is noted, and appreciated. Officer,' she continued, stepping up to the uniform. 'Give me your report.'

Eve sat in the double-wide cube at Child Protection and fought not to squirm. She hated places like this. An atavistic loathing with an unreasonable current of fear rushed through her. She knew it was unreasonable, knew its root was in a monster spinning horror tales to make her believe he was the lesser of evils.

Lies, of course, vicious lies to keep her in control.

How long did it take to shed the fear-skin of childhood? Did we ever?

The woman sitting at the workstation in the cube didn't

162

look like a monster. *They'll toss you in a pit, little girl. Black and deep and full of spiders.* She looked like someone's plump and comfortable grandma. At least the way Eve envisioned plump and comfortable grandmas. Her hair was in a neat circle around a round, rosy-cheeked face, and she wore a long, shapeless print dress. She smelled like berries. Raspberries, Eve thought.

But when you looked in her eyes, the cozy granny was nowhere to be seen. They were dark and shrewd, tired and concerned.

'She hasn't checked in, and doesn't answer her 'link.' Renny Townston, Newman's supervisor, frowned at Eve. 'All our reps – male and female – are issued panic alarms. They often visit rough neighborhoods, and rougher subjects. They're given standard defense training and are required to update that training, along with their other job qualifications, annually. Meredith knew how to take care of herself. She's no rookie. In fact . . .'

'In fact,' Eve prompted.

'She's on the edge of the board, in my opinion. A year, maybe two left in her for this job. She does the job, Lieutenant, but she's lost the heart. Most do after a few years. In six months, if it doesn't turn around, all she'll be doing is putting in time. The fact is . . .'

'The fact is?'

'She should never have allowed you to override her on the Swisher matter. Never have permitted you to take that child out of her care or supervision. She didn't even demand the location, and barely followed up on the matter the following morning.'

'I pushed pretty hard.'

'And she didn't stand up to it, to you. At the very least, she should have gone with you and the child, reported in. Instead, she went home, and didn't file the report until morning.'

Annoyance, then worry, pursed Townston's lips. 'Now, I'm afraid one of her clients grabbed her up. They blame us, you know, same as you cops get blamed, for their own screwups and failings.'

'How about her personal life?'

'I don't know much about it. She isn't a chat-in-the-breakroom sort. I know she was dating someone for a while recently, but that's over. She's a loner, which is part of the problem. Without a life outside, you don't make it to retirement age.'

Though she knew it was a time waster, it was a routine one, so Eve took the data on Newman's case files. She took the names, the addresses. And with Peabody, went next to Newman's apartment.

The living/kitchen area was larger than Minnie Cable's, but lacked the color and life of clutter. It was clean to the point of sterile with its blank, white walls, engaged privacy screens, its straight-lined sofa and single chair.

There was a data unit on a workstation in the bedroom – bed tidily made – and two boxes of discs, clearly labeled.

'Kinda sad, isn't it?' Peabody glanced around. 'Thinking about the different places we've been in today. Say, Mrs Grentz's insane treasure house, the wild space where Hildy lives below. Even Minnie Cable's pitiful little rooms. People lived there, you could see. Stuff happened there. This is like a vid set. Single professional female with no life.'

'Why didn't they take her here, Peabody? Why risk a street grab when they can slide into a secured family dwelling and kill five people in less time than it takes to get pizza delivered?'

'Um. They'd be in a hurry. They'd want to get her fast, see what she knows.'

'Part of it. Yeah, part of it. Maybe this place looks dead, feels dead, but she was smart enough, careful enough to rent in a building with good security. Still, no real problem for our boys. But they didn't wait until she got home, didn't take her here. They want her awhile. That's what I'd want. Want to make sure they get it all out of her, and that might take some time. Take privacy. And there's more.'

She turned a circle, thinking. 'Because they can. They know how to move fast, to do a job like this fast, so any potential witnesses see mostly a blur. Couple of guys in black, big black van. Pow, pow. Might not have figured that anybody'd do more than scratch and spit over it in that neighborhood, too. Nobody reports, it takes more time for anybody to realize Newman's among the missing. Longer yet to make any connection to the Swisher murders.'

Eve looked at the blank walls, the lonely, neatly made

bed. 'They've got her somewhere, right now. When they're done with her, she'll be as dead as this room.'

Eve pulled out her communicator. When Baxter came on, she snapped: 'Private communication. Get to a secure location or go to text only.'

'Just me and Trueheart here, Dallas. Kid's downstairs. We've got her on monitor.'

'The social worker on her case has been grabbed. Unsubs match description of our suspects. I don't want the wit out of your sight.'

'She isn't and won't be. Do you expect they'll come after her?'

'If they can find out where she is, they'll try. I want her inside, at all times. Stay on this until the next time you hear from me.'

She clicked off, called Roarke. 'They've got the social worker,' she said when he went to private. 'She doesn't know the location, and it's a big leap. But I've alerted Baxter.'

'Understood. I'll pass this on to Summerset,' he added in a tone that told her he was in a meeting. 'I can be there myself in thirty minutes.'

'I don't think they can move faster – and Newman just knew I took her, not that I took her home, but watch your back. They put the kid with me, they put you with me. Another grab isn't out of the question.'

'I'll offer you the same advice, and say that in both cases it's unnecessary.'

This time it was Roarke who ended transmission.

'Scoop up her discs, address books, memo books. Contact EDD for a pickup on her equipment. Let's do this by the book.'

'How long do you think she's got?'

Eve looked around the stark, soulless room. 'Not long enough.'

When Meredith surfaced, she thought there was an ice pick dead center of her forehead, radiating sharp shards of pain. The headache was so blinding, she assumed at first that was the reason she couldn't see.

Her stomach rolled a bit, as if she'd eaten something past its expiration date, but when she tried to press her hand to it, her arm wouldn't move.

From somewhere, far off, she heard voices. A watery echo of voices. Then she remembered. She'd been walking on Avenue B, on her way to a home check, and something . . . someone . . .

The fear came fast, spearing through the pain. When she tried to scream, the only sound she could make was a wild, whimpering moan.

She was in the dark, unable to move her arms, her legs, her head. Unable to see or speak, and when something brushed her cheek, her heart punched against her ribs like a fist.

'Subject's conscious. Meredith Newman, you are in a secured location. You will be asked questions. If you answer these questions, you will not be harmed. I'm going to

167

remove the tape from your mouth at this time. Once I do, tell me if you understand.'

Having the tape ripped off in the solid dark brought on a scream that was more from utter terror than pain. She was slapped, open-palm, on one cheek, followed by a quick answering backhand on the other.

'I said tell me if you understand.'

'No. I don't. I don't understand. What's the matter? Who are you? What—' She screamed again, her body straining against the restraints as pain exploded. Like a thousand hot needles jabbed into her bones.

'It will hurt every time you refuse to answer, any time you lie, any time you don't do as you're told.' The voice was quiet, flat. 'Do you understand?'

'Yes. Yes. Please, don't hurt me.'

'We'll have no reason to hurt you if you answer our questions. Are you afraid, Meredith?'

'Yes. Yes, I'm afraid.'

'Good. You've told the truth.'

She couldn't see, but she could hear. She heard little beeps and pings, his breathing – steady. No, someone else, too. She could hear, she thought, movement – but not where the breathing was. Two of them. *There'd been two of them.*

'What do you want? Please tell me what you want.'

There was another jolt, shocking, quicker, that left her gasping. She thought she smelled something burning, like raw meat. And thought, through the shocking pain, she heard a woman laugh.

'You don't ask questions.'

A second voice. A little deeper, a little harsher than the first. Not a woman. Must have imagined. What does it matter?

God, oh God, help me.

Her eyes wheeled, and she saw there was faint light, just a slit of light to her left. Not in the dark. Thank God, not in the dark. Her eyes were taped as her mouth had been.

They didn't want her to see them. Didn't want her to be able to identify them. Thank God, thank God. They weren't going to kill her.

But they would hurt her.

'I won't. I'll answer. I'll answer.'

'Where is Nixie Swisher?'

'Who?'

The pain struck like a fiery ax, slicing her up the center. Her screams burst into the air, and tears of shock spilled down her cheeks. Her bowels went to water.

'Please, please.'

'Please, please.' It was a woman's voice, a sneering mimic of her own. 'Jesus, she shit herself. Pussy.'

Meredith screamed again when the icy water struck her. She began to weep now, thick, wet sobs, as she realized she was naked, wet, soiled.

'Where is Nixie Swisher?'

'I don't know who that is.'

And sobbing, she braced for the agony that didn't come. Her breath came in pants now, her eyes tracking back and forth, from the dark, to the sliver of light, to the dark, to the light.

'Your name is Meredith Newman.'

'Yes. Yes. Yes.' Her skin was on fire, her bones were like ice. 'God. God.'

'Is Nixie Swisher one of your cases, as an employee of Child Protection Services?'

'I – I – I get so many. There are so many. I can't remember. Please don't hurt me, please, I can't remember.'

'Register blue,' one of them said from behind her. 'Overworked, Meredith?'

'Yes.'

'I understand that. The system sucks you up, sucks you dry. The wheel of it runs over and crushes what's left of you. Revolution comes because of all it crushes. You're tired of the wheel, aren't you?'

'Yes. Yes.'

'But it's not done with you yet. Tell me, Meredith, how many families have you destroyed?'

'I—' Tears spilled into her mouth. She swallowed the salt of them. 'I try to help.'

Impossible, unspeakable pain seared into her. Her screams were mindless pleas for mercy.

'You're a cog on that wheel. A cog on the wheel that crushes out the lifeblood. But now it's turning around to crush you, isn't it? Do you want to escape, Meredith?'

She tasted vomit on her tongue, in her throat. 'Yes. No more, please, no more.'

'Nixie Swisher. Let me refresh you. A girl, a young girl who wasn't in her bed as she was told to be. Disobedient child. Disobedient children should be punished. Isn't that right?'

She opened her mouth, unsure. 'Yes,' she said, praying it was the answer he wanted.

'Do you remember her now? Do you remember the little girl who wasn't in her bed? Grant and Keelie Swisher, deceased. Executed for heinous acts. Their throats were slit, Meredith. Do you remember now?' His voice had changed, just a little. There was a fervor that hadn't been there before. Part of her brain registered the fact while the rest gibbered in fear. 'Yes. Yes, I remember.'

'Where is she?'

'I don't know. I swear I don't know.'

'In the blue,' the other voice reported. 'Jolt.'

She screamed and screamed and screamed as the pain tore into her. 'You reported to the Swisher residence on the night they were executed.'

Her body continued to shudder. Spittle dribbled down her chin. 'Did you speak with Nixie Swisher?'

'Interview, exam. Exam, interview. Standard. No injuries, no molestation. Shocky.'

'What did she see?'

'I can't see.'

'What did Nixie Swisher see?'

'Men. Two men. Knives, throats. Blood. We'll hide now. Hide and be safe.'

171

'Losing her.'

'Stimulant.'

She wept again, wept because she was back, aware, awake, and the dregs of pain still lived in her. 'No more, please. No more.'

'There was a survivor of the Swisher execution. What did she tell you?'

'She said . . .' Meredith told them everything she knew.

'That's very good, Meredith. Very concise. Now where is Nixie Swisher?'

'They didn't tell me. The cop took her. Against procedure, but she had weight.'

'As her caseworker, you must be informed of her location. You must supervise her.'

'Over my head. Under the table. I don't know. Cop took her. Police protection.'

She lost track of the pain now, of the times it ripped through her like burning arrows. Lost track of the times they brought her back from the edge of oblivion, pounded her with questions.

'Very well, Meredith. I'll need the address of every safe house you know. Every hidey-hole the system digs.'

'I can't – I'll try,' she screamed against the next wave of agony. 'I'll try to remember.' She blurted out addresses between sobs and whimpers. 'I don't know all of them, I don't know all. Only what they tell me. I'm not in charge.'

'Just a cog in the wheel. Who took Nixie Swisher?'

'The cop. Homicide cop. Dallas. Lieutenant Dallas.'

'Yes, of course. Lieutenant Dallas. That's very good, Meredith.'

'I've told you everything. Everything I know. Are you going to let me go?'

'Yes, we are. Very soon.'

'Water, please. Could I have some water?'

'Did Lieutenant Dallas indicate where she could take Nixie Swisher?'

'No, no. I swear, I swear. Into her custody. Not regs, but she pushed it through. I wanted to get home. It was a bad place to be. I wanted to get out. Supposed to check into the safe house with the subject, but Dallas overrode me. I let her.'

'Have you been in contact with Lieutenant Dallas since that night?'

'No. The bosses took it over. They don't tell me. It's high-profile. It's sensitive. I'm just—'

'A cog on the wheel.'

'I don't know anything. Will you let me go now?'

'Yes. You can go now.'

The knife slashed so fast, so cleanly across her throat, she never felt it.

9

Eve walked into her own home as if she were walking into an op. 'No one comes in, no one goes out,' she snapped to Summerset, 'without my clearance. Savvy?'

'Certainly.'

'Where's the kid?'

'In the game room with Officer Trueheart.' Summerset hitched back the cuff of his black jacket to reveal a wrist unit. Not a time piece, Eve noted, but a monitor. On it, she saw Trueheart and Nixie battling it out on one of Roarke's classic pinball machines.

'I took the precaution of pinning a homer on her sweater,' he added. 'If she moves from one location to another, it signals.'

Despite herself, Eve was impressed. 'Sweet.'

'They will not lay a hand on that child.'

She looked at him. He'd lost a child, a daughter, not that much older, really, than this one. Whatever else she thought of him, she understood he would stand as Nixie's shield.

'No, they won't. Roarke?'

'He's here. In his private office.'

'Right.' The office where he kept his unregistered – and therefore illegal – equipment. However much she trusted

Peabody, there were lines. 'Head up, will you,' she said to Peabody. 'Give Baxter the current. I'm going to update Roarke, then we'll conference. My office.'

As her partner started up the steps, Eve moved out of the foyer and to the elevator. There she paused. 'I need them alive,' she said to Summerset. 'Best-case scenario.'

'One of them alive would do.'

She turned back. 'She will be protected. Extreme measures, including termination, will be employed if necessary. But consider this before you get your juices up. Two men grabbed Meredith Newman off the street — and one to drive, so that makes three. There may be more. I don't get one healthy, that I can sweat, she may never be safe. The more of them I get healthy, the better chance I have to get them all. To get the why. Without the why, she may never be safe. And she'll never know. You don't know the why, you don't always heal.'

Though his face remained unreadable, Summerset nodded. 'You're quite right, Lieutenant.'

She stepped into the elevator, ordered Roarke's private office.

He knew when she came through the gates, and that she'd come up before much longer. So he closed the file, went back to evaluating his security.

He didn't think it was appropriate right at the moment to tell her one of the tasks he'd chosen for the unregisters was in-depth — and technically illegal — background checks on all of Nixie's family connections.

175

The grandmother was out. She'd had a few misdemeaner illegals charges, any number of cohabs, and had a part-time licensed companion standing.

Perhaps the moral judgment was ironic as he was currently an official guardian for the child and had done worse. Considerably worse.

But he was making it nonetheless. He wouldn't see a child turned over to a woman of that sort. She deserved better.

He'd found Grant Swisher's biological father. It had taken a bit of time, but the moral judgment there had come swiftly.

The man was rarely employed, had done a short stint for petty theft, and another for jacking vehicles.

The step-sister looked more promising. She was married, a corporate lawyer out of Philadelphia. Childless. No criminal on record, and financially solvent. She'd been married, to another lawyer, for seven years.

The child could have a home with her, temporarily, even permanently should it become necessary. A good home, he thought, with someone who'd known her parents, who felt some connection.

He sat back, tipped back in the chair. It was none of his business. Not a bit of it.

The hell it wasn't. He was responsible for that child now, whether he'd chosen to be or not. Whether he wanted to be or not.

He had stood outside her bedroom, had seen what had nearly been done to her.

He had stood outside her brother's room, had seen what

had been done. A young boy's blood drying to rust on the sheets, the walls.

Why was it that seeing it made him see his own? He didn't think of those days, or so rarely it didn't count. He wasn't − wouldn't be − haunted by nightmares as Eve was. He was done with those days, and what had been.

But he thought of them now, had thought of them too many times since he'd been inside the Swisher home.

He remembered seeing his own blood. Coming to, barely. Obscene pain swimming through him as he stared at his own blood on the filthy ground of the alley after his father had beaten him half to death.

More than half, come to that.

Had he meant to kill him? Why hadn't he ever wondered that before? He'd killed before.

Roarke looked at the photo of his mother, of himself as a baby. Such a young, pretty face she'd had, he thought. Even bruised by the bastard's fists, she'd had a pretty face.

Until Patrick Roarke had smashed it, until he'd murdered her with his own hands and tossed her in the river like sewage. And now her son couldn't remember her. He'd never remember her voice, or her scent. And there was nothing to be done about it.

She'd wanted him, this pretty girl with the bruised face. She'd died because she'd wanted to give her son family.

Those few years later, had Patrick Roarke, God rot him, meant to leave his own son for dead, or had he simply used his fists and feet as usual?

A lesson for you, boy-o. Life's full of hard lessons.

Roarke dragged his hands through his hair, pressed them to his temples. Christ, he could hear the cocksucker's voice, and that would never do. He wanted a drink, and nearly rose to pour himself a whiskey, just to take off the edge.

But that was a weakness — drinking because you wanted to blunt the edge. Hadn't he proved every day, every bloody day of the life he'd been given that he wouldn't be weak?

He hadn't died in that alley, as poor young Coyle had died in his bed. He'd lived, because Summerset had found him, had cared enough to take a broken boy in — a nasty little son of a bitch, as well.

He'd taken him in, and tended him. And given him a home.

In a human world, even one of murder and blood, didn't an innocent girl like Nixie Swisher deserve that much? Deserve more than he'd been given?

He'd help her get it, for her sake — and for his own. Before his father's voice got too loud in his head.

He didn't get the whiskey. Instead he pushed aside the memories, the questions, and as much of the sickness of heart as he could manage, and waited for his wife to step into the room.

The room was full of light, the wide windows uncovered. She knew no surveillance device could penetrate the privacy screens on them. Unless he'd built them himself, she thought. Then he'd have built better screens.

At the wide black U of the control console, he sat, jacket

discarded, sleeves rolled up, the silk of his hair tied back with a cord.

Work mode.

The console always looked a bit futuristic to her, just as the man who piloted it could remind her of a pirate at the helm of a spaceship.

Lights flashed on that glossy black like jewels as he worked the controls, manually, and by voice.

On the wall screens were different areas of his domain, and the various computer responses gave brisk reports.

'Lieutenant.'

'I'm sorry about this. I'm sorry about what I may be bringing here.' He stopped what he was doing. 'Pause operations. You're upset,' he said, as coolly as he'd spoken to the equipment. 'So I'll forgive that insulting remark.'

'Roarke—'

'Eve.' He rose, crossed the wide black floor toward her. 'Are we a unit, you and I?'

'Doesn't seem to be any way around it.'

'Or through it.' He took her hands and the contact steadied him. 'Or under it, over it. Don't apologize to me for doing what you felt was right for that child.'

'I could've taken her to a safe house. I second-guessed myself on that half a dozen times today. If I had, Newman would know some of the locations. If they get them out of her . . . hell, not if, when. There are cops scrambling right now to move people out of what should be secure locations. Just in case.'

Something flickered in his eyes. 'A minute.' He moved back, fast, to the console, switched on a 'link. 'Dochas,' he snapped into it. 'Code Red, immediate and until further notice.'

'Oh Christ.'

'It's handled,' he said, turning from the 'link. 'I have built-in procedures for just this sort of thing. It's unlikely they'll believe you would take her there – with so many others. Less likely yet they can find it. But it's handled. Just as this is.'

He stepped back to her, nodded toward the screens. 'I have every inch of the wall and gate secured.'

'A teenager once got over using a homemade jammer.'

The fact that he looked momentarily perturbed by the memory lightened her load. 'Jamie is no ordinary teenager. Nor was he able to get through the secondaries. And I've upgraded since then. Believe me, Eve, they won't get in.'

'I do believe you.' Still she paced to the window, to look out, to see the walls for herself. 'Newman doesn't know I brought the kid here. Went over her on it, and didn't tell her, mostly because she irritated me. Just a little slap. My balls are bigger than your balls kind of thing. Petty.'

'Being petty – and I do love that about you – has added another layer of protection over Nixie.'

'Dumb luck. But why argue with dumb luck? I've had her supervisor picked up, taken into protective. Had all the paperwork buried.' She huffed out a breath. 'I've got Mira locked down, too, just in case her involvement leaks. She's not happy with me.'

'Her safety's more important than her happiness.'

'Put surveillance on Peabody's place. She's mine, so they may go for her.'

'She and McNab can stay here.'

'One big, happy family. No. We deviate from routine too much, they'll know we're waiting for them to make a move.'

'Eve. You and I both know they're unlikely to move on this house tonight, even if they believe the child is here. They're careful, they're organized. They're controlled. They would have to obtain or simulate my system. Believe me when I say that alone would take them weeks. Then they'd have to find the chinks — of which there are none — they'd have to practice. If you haven't run a probability on that, as I have, I'd be very surprised.'

'A little over twelve percent.' She turned to him, framed now by the wide, wide glass. 'But we don't take chances.'

'And the probability they'll try for you?' He lifted his eyebrows when she said nothing, when he saw the faint irritation on her face. 'Ninety-six.'

'You're right behind me, pal, at ninety-one.'

'Bloody annoying to have you slip by me by five percent. You were working up to asking me — and I use that verb tongue in cheek — to lock myself down in here. Are we going to argue about that so that I have to throw that five percent probability in your face?'

Thoughtfully, she rocked back and forth on her heels. 'I had a pretty good argument worked out.'

'Why don't you save it for another time?'

'I can do that.'

The in-house 'link signalled. 'This is Roarke,' he said from where he stood, his attention still on Eve.

'As per her instructions, I'm informing the lieutenant that Captain Feeney and Detective McNab are requesting entrance at the gate.'

'You verify ID visually and by voice print?' she asked Summerset. 'Of course.'

'They're cleared to come through. I want to go talk to my team,' she said to Roarke. 'Okay if that includes you?'

'I wouldn't have it any other way. Give me a couple of minutes to finish in here. I'll be along.'

She walked to the elevator, stood looking at the door when it opened at her command. 'Roarke? The thing is about probabilities, they don't always factor in every element. They can't fully and successfully analyze every human emotion. The computer doesn't factor in that if someone got to you, it would take me down. If they used you, bargained your life, there isn't much I wouldn't do to get you back. So you factor that in, and I figure you've cut ahead of me on the probability scale.'

She entered the elevator quickly, closed the door before he could respond.

Eve let them settle in first, go through the chatter, the greed for food. She even ignored the cooing flirtation between her partner and EDD ace Ian McNab, the recent cohabs.

The fact was, Peabody's color had been off since they'd hauled up the steps to interview Minnie. The cooing, however unseemly, had her pinked up again.

And while they settled, Eve organized the conference in her head. 'Okay, boys and girls.' She remained standing. She handled such meetings better on her feet. 'If everyone's had their afternoon snack, maybe we can get started.'

'Uptown grub.' McNab scooped up the last of leftover apple pie. His skinny frame was festooned – Eve figured that was the word for it – in a neon orange skin-tank with sizzling blue pants that had some sort of silver clamps running up the outside of each leg. The over-shirt was a headache of dots, outdone only by the glowing checks covering his airboots.

His shining blond hair was pulled back from his thin, pretty face. The better to show off the trio of orange and blue coils adorning each ear.

'I'm glad you approve, Detective. Now maybe you can give your report. Unless, of course, you'd like seconds.'

Sarcasm, even delivered in mild tones, could hit like a hammer. He swallowed the last of the pie quickly. 'No, sir. Our team has reviewed and completed search-and-scans on all 'links, all d and c's owned or used by any and all of the vics, and the survivor. We found no transmissions on the 'links other than ordinary communications from and to the Swishers and their domestic. While there were numerous transmissions over the last thirty days, they check. Friends, clients, each other, personal and business transmissions. A list of all, with transcription, is now on disc for your file.'

'Thirty days?'

'The Swishers cleared their 'links every thirty. That's common. We're digging in, and will retrieve the deleted transmissions prior to the thirty. As to the data centers, the files are pretty much what you'd expect.'

'What would I expect, Detective?'

He was warming up, she could see, losing the stiffness her reprimand had caused. He slouched more comfortably in his chair and began to gesture as he spoke. 'You know, Dallas, games, to-do lists, meal planning, appointments, birthday reminders. Family stuff, school stuff, upcoming vacation data. Got case files from each of the adult's business units, comments, reports, financials. Nothing pops out. If they had trouble, or suspected they might have trouble, they didn't make a record of it. They didn't discuss it with anyone via 'link.'

He glanced toward the murder board, the death photos, and his eyes – a misty green – hardened. 'I've been spending a lot of time with that family the last few days. My opinion – from their electronic records and transmissions – they didn't have a clue.'

She nodded, shifted to Feeney. Beside the fashionable McNab, he looked blessedly dull. 'Security.'

'Bypassed and shut down. Remote and at site. Diagnostic scan couldn't locate the source, but when we took the system apart we found microscopic particles – fiber-optic

184

traces. They hooked in – portable code-breaker, most likely. Had to be prime equipment to read the code, to get through the failsafes without tripping any alarm. Equipment and operator had to be prime to do it in the time frame we're working with. We're looking for at least one suspect who has a superior knowledge of and skill with electronics, and the equipment to match.'

Since Feeney looked to him for confirmation, Roarke nodded. 'Their equipment would have had to have been small, possibly palm-sized. From your description, Lieutenant, of the men seen walking away from the location of the murders.'

'They each had a bag, but no,' she confirmed, 'nothing large.'

'Your ordinary, even better-than-average, B and E man isn't likely to have access to a palm-sized breaker in the range capable of reading that system, certainly not at that speed. As the system showed no signs of tampering, the men you're looking for probably didn't have the burglary skills to go manual.'

'Meaning they had to rely on equipment, not . . .' She lifted her hands, wiggled her fingers. And made him smile.

'Exactly. The equipment would also have to be tailored specifically for that system. The time frame means it was tailored prior to their arrival.'

'Confirming they knew the system, knew what they'd find, and had studied it either by duplicating or purchasing the same system, or spending time on site.'

'The only way they could have studied it on site thoroughly enough to have pulled this off means they had considerable time – hours – both inside the house and outside, with no one questioning them.'

Eve pursed her lips at Roarke. 'Hours?'

'It's a solid system, Dallas,' Feeney commented. 'They didn't get through by eyeballing it.'

'Then it's unlikely they ran sims with the Swisher's actual system. Peabody, you've done a search of purchases of that security system?'

'Yes, sir, and it's a whale of a list. I've started on it, dividing it into city, out of city, out of state, out of country, and off planet. I've then eliminated purchases made before the Swishers obtained their system. I've started runs on purchases in city, and have eliminated approximately another six percent.'

'By what process?'

'Well, by separating out single female purchasers and married with family, then checking those to determine if they had any maintenance and repair on the system since the purchase date. Profile indicates the killers are not family men, and the probability run gave me in the nineties that this process was the most efficient. At this time.'

'Have you run those systems purchased that were not installed by the company?'

Peabody opened her mouth, then closed it long enough to clear her throat. 'No, sir. I'll do so.'

'Split the list between all members of this team. Probability

186

or not, do not – at this time – eliminate families or single females. Maybe one of them has a girlfriend, or a female accomplice. Maybe he's a licensed installer. Maybe he's just the handy neighbor who says, "Hey, I'll take care of that for you and save you some dough." These are home security systems, but there's no law saying a business couldn't purchase one. Let's get on this.'

She leaned back against her desk, remembered the coffee she'd poured before she'd begun. She picked it up, drank it lukewarm. 'Baxter. Client lists.'

'Both the Swishers had a good thing going. Successful in their professions. Family law firm was busy, and Swisher had a good win rate. His caseload weighs heavy on protection of children's rights, custody suits, divorce, while his partner takes more of the straight abuse, palimony, cohab dissolutions, and competency stuff. But they both have a mix, and both have a good percentage of pro bono work.'

He cocked his ankle onto his knee, brushed the line of the pants of his well-cut suit smooth. 'She was no slouch either. Lots of referrals. Liked to do families or couples, but didn't turn away the individual. She would also work on a sliding scale, ratio of fee to income. Not just fatties,' he added. 'Dug into various eating disorders, health conditions. Consulted with her client's health care provider, and made house calls.'

'House calls?'

'She'd visit the client's home and workplace. Do a study on their lifestyle, recommend changes, not just in eating habits, but in exercise, entertainment, stress levels, the works. That kind of treatment didn't come cheap, but like I said, she had a lot of referrals. Satisfied customers. You got your dissatisfied, too, both sides.'

'Do a cross-check. See how many times their clients crossed. Do another, see which cases Swisher's firm worked on where Meredith Newman was listed as CPS rep. It could be interesting data. Trueheart.'

'Sir.' Long and lanky, and almost tenderly young in his uniform, he came to attention.

'You've been spending time with the witness.'

'She's a nice kid, Lieutenant.'

'Any further data from her?'

'Sir, she doesn't talk much about it. She's broken down a couple of times. Not hysterical, just sits down and cries. I'm trying to keep her busy. She seems comfortable with me, and with Summerset, though she asks about you.'

'Asks what?'

'When you're coming back, what you're doing. When you're going to take her to see her parents and her brother. If you've caught the bad guys yet. I don't know much about, well, I guess you'd say child psychology, but I'd say she's holding on to herself until you do. Catch them. To date, she hasn't said anything that would add to her previous statements.'

'All right. Moving on to Meredith Newman. CPS reps in cases like this are kept confidential. However, it's not that complicated to access the data. Anyone with serious interest

188

and reasonable hacking capabilities could slither into the CPS files like a snake through grass. Feeney, I'll want your department to check the d and c's for any evidence of hacking. Maybe we'll get a bounce. The subject was abducted off the sidewalk on Avenue B, daylight grab, with witnesses. The speed and success of the grab indicates the suspects have some experience in daylight abductions. It also indicates there were three. It's unlikely these two would trust their vehicle to auto under the circumstances. We must assume Newman's connection to Nixie Swisher was the motive for the grab. We must assume that the perpetrators had experience in making grabs of this nature, in electronics and security, in stealth assassinations.'

'Military or para,' Feeney said. 'Espionage or special forces. Average citizens, they're not.'

'If they were military, it's likely we'll find they washed out – or were promoted to fucking general because of their particular skills. One way or the other, these men have been in the field, and they've gotten wet. They're not rusty, either, so they've kept in the game.'

'Paramilitary seems more probable,' Roarke commented. 'There's testing in standard military that would question the personality type or predilection of killing for personal gain or satisfaction – particularly children.'

'Mercenaries kill for personal gain, and are often attached to military ops.'

'True enough.' But he shook his head at Eve. 'That's most usually monetary. Where is the monetary gain here?'

'We might not have found it yet, but let's say I agree. And I agree that it takes a certain kind of personality to slit a child's throat while she sleeps. That's terrorist tactics, and fringe at that. I think that's where this arrow's going to point.'

'More cross-checking then,' Baxter put in. 'Known terrorists or members of fringe organizations.'

'Look for teams. Two or more who are known to work together, or known to have trained together. Then we need to put one of them, at least, in New York during the last few years.'

'Could be hirelings,' Baxter pointed out. 'Brought into New York to do the job.'

'Low odds. Hirelings would've been smoke an hour after the Swisher hit. But they're still in New York, still here to grab up Newman. One or both of them targeted the Swishers, and for a reason. This means, at some point, one or more of them crossed paths with one or more of the Swishers. Security and wet work, and they're in shape. No desk jockeys or data crunchers. These are field operatives. Males, between thirty and sixty to start. White or light-skinned males. Either they or their organization has deep pockets. Look for the money.'

She rubbed the back of her neck, finished off the cold coffee. 'They've got a place, in or near the city. Headquarters. They'd need something local, and they'd need something private. The only logical motive for grabbing Newman would be for information on Nixie Swisher. They'd need somewhere they could take her, work it out of her.'

'We'll be cross-checking until the blood runs out of our ears. Not complaining, Lieutenant,' McNab said quickly. 'You can't look at that board and complain. Just feels like the time's dripping away.'

'Then you'd better get busy.' She checked her wrist unit. 'Baxter, you're all right where we set you up?'

'It's prime.'

'Trueheart, maybe you could spell Summerset with the witness for fifteen. Mira's due here shortly, then she'll take her. Work with Baxter when you're off babysitting duty. Feeney, you and McNab can work here in the computer lab?'

'No problem.'

'I'll join you,' Roarke told them. 'But first, Lieutenant, a minute of your time.'

'That's about all I've got to spare. Peabody?'

'I'll head down with Trueheart, say hi to Nixie.'

Then, to Roarke, she said, 'I have to contact the commander, give him a report, so this has to be quick.'

He merely went to the door, closed it behind Peabody.

'What?' Eve's hands went automatically to her pockets. 'You pissed about something?'

'No.' Keeping his eyes, deep and blue, on hers, he walked to her. 'No,' he repeated, and taking her face in his hand, kissed her. Long, deep, soft.

'Jesus.' It took longer than it should have for her to pull her hands out of her pockets and nudge him back. 'I can't play lock the lips with you now.'

'Quiet.' He took her arms, and the look on his face, so strong, so serious, had her going still. 'I value my skin – a very great deal. I'll do what it takes to protect it. I'll do more yet, I promise you, to protect it so that you're not distracted from this with worry for me. I love you, Eve. I'll keep safe because I love you.'

'I shouldn't have hung that on you. I—'

'Quiet,' he repeated. 'I'm not finished. You'll keep yourself as safe as you can. You're courageous, but not reckless. I know. Just as I know there are risks you'll take, risks you'll feel duty-bound to take. Don't keep them from me. When you find a way to use yourself as bait on this, I want to know about it.'

He knew her, she thought. Knew her, understood her, accepted and loved anyway. You couldn't ask for more. 'I wouldn't do anything like that without telling you.' When his gaze stayed steady, she shrugged. 'I'd think about doing it without telling you, but then I'd cave. I'm not doing anything on that angle until I'm dead sure they won't get me. Because if they get me, they've got a better chance of getting her. And because I love you, too: I get sure, decide to try something, I'll tell you first.'

'Good enough, then. I didn't ask before, and I know you're pressed now, but were you able to speak to the Dysons about Nixie?'

'To her. He was out of it. She's not in much better shape. I'm going to give them another couple days. I know it's inconvenient, but—'

'It's not. I just assume that she'd feel steadier if she had those familiar faces, if she were able to have her friend's parents with her.' He considered telling her what he'd dug up regarding Nixie's remaining family, then let it go. She had enough on her plate. And for reasons he couldn't explain, even to himself, he wanted to handle that part of it. 'Summerset told me basically what Trueheart told you. She holds up, she breaks down, and holds up again. She's grieving, and there's no one here who can grieve with her, who knew her family.'

'I'll talk to Mira about it. Maybe she can speak to the Dysons. Might be better coming from her than me.'

'Maybe. I'll go join the EDD boys and leave you to your commander. Grab a nutribar at least with the next gallon of coffee you drink.'

'Nag, nag, nag,' she said as he walked out the door. But she got the nutribar out of her desk drawer.

10

After Mira and her security escort were cleared through the gates, Eve met her at the door. Since she had the extra men, she ordered security to do a patrol around the grounds, with electronic sweep.

'You're being very cautious,' Mira commented. 'Do you really expect them to try an invasion on this house?'

'Newman doesn't know where I took the kid, so trying a hit here isn't the next logical step.' She swept a glance down the hall. Trueheart had Nixie in the game room, but that didn't mean the kid couldn't come wandering out. 'Why don't we step outside for a minute?'

Eve led the way through the parlor and the doors to the side terrace. She had a momentary pause when she saw a little silver droid, a low, shiny box, busily sucking up fallen leaves. 'Huh, how about that.' At her voice, it glided off the terrace and slid down one of the paths into the garden. 'Wonder what it does with them once it sucks them up.'

'I think it chops them into a kind of mulch, or compost. Dennis talks about getting something like it, then doesn't. I think he secretly enjoys raking the leaves by hand.'

Eve thought of Mira's kind-eyed, absentminded husband. 'Why?'

'Mindless work that gets him outdoors. Of course, if we had grounds this extensive to deal with, it'd be a different story. It's lovely out here, isn't it, even so late in the year with so much of the gardens fading away toward winter.'

Eve looked over the gardens, through the ornamental and shade trees, past arbors and fountains to the thick stone walls. 'Lot of ways in, lot of ways out, but as secure as it gets.'

'And still your home. That makes it difficult.'

'I made the call. Look, it's cooler out here than I thought. You okay for a minute?'

'I'm fine.' Mira wore a jacket, and Eve was currently in shirtsleeves. 'It must be inconvenient, having so many people in your home.'

'Place is starting to smell like Central. Anyway, if they click on the idea Nixie's here, they might see it as a challenge, get revved at the idea. The bigger the mission, the bigger the payoff.'

'But you don't think they know Nixie's here.'

'I think your average CPS rep would spill data out like a gushing pipe under torture. And I wouldn't hold it against her. Best I can speculate, she doesn't know the witness is here, but knows I took her and bypassed regs. They could put it together. I would.'

'Taking a civilian witness into your personal residence isn't usual, or even standard procedure. But yes, they might put it together. And you also assume that under extreme duress, I would also gush like a broken pipe.'

'It's not a reflection on your standards or your integrity.'

'No.' Mira brushed back a wave of hair the breeze blew across her cheek. 'And I don't take it as such. I imagine you're right. While I'd like to think I'd suffer torture and painful death to protect another, it's much more likely I'd succumb. So you have me and my home under surveillance and security. Sensible of you, and I apologize for objecting.'

'I had you under security before, and Palmer got to you.'

Mira as psychologist and profiler and Eve as primary had helped put Palmer away. His revenge spree after his prison escape the previous winter had nearly cost Mira her life. Could have cost both of them, Eve remembered, when he'd abducted Mira and caged her in a basement to lure Eve to his sick New Year's Eve celebration.

'He didn't serve you a tea party, either, and you stood up.'

'He just wanted me to suffer and die. In this case . . . where is Nixie?'

'I've got Trueheart riding her. I didn't know where you wanted to set up with her.'

'Where do you think she's most comfortable?'

Eve stared, blank. 'Ah, I don't know. She did okay in the parlor last time.'

'A stunning room, and certainly comfortable. But maybe a little intimidating for a child used to less opulence. Where does she spend most of her time?'

'I don't know that either, exactly. She hangs with Summerset a lot, but he's all over the damn house. Like termites. She and Trueheart were hanging out in the game room before.'

'Game room?'

'Roarke's got a damn room for everything. Fancy toys, you know, arcade stuff.' She gave a shrug, though she had to admit, privately, she got a charge out of the deal. 'A lot of classic game stuff.'

'Child friendly, then. That sounds very good.'

'Okay.'

When Eve didn't turn back to the door, Mira asked, 'How do you feel she's coping?'

'Had a nightmare last night. A real screamer. Thought they were coming for her, hiding in the closet, under the bed.'

'Natural enough. I'd be more concerned if she wasn't afraid. If she was repressing.'

'Like I did.'

'You coped in your own way.' And because they'd come quite a distance in the last two years, Mira touched a hand to Eve's arm. 'And still do. This child has a firm foundation, which has been broken out from under her. But that foundation will mean she'll most likely have an easier time regaining her footing. With counseling, with care, and a return to normalcy.'

Eve gathered herself. 'There's a thing. The situation she's in, the one I was in, they're nothing alike. Not even close. But—'

'A young traumatized child.'

'She had murder done around her. I did murder.'

'Why do you call it murder?' Mira's voice sharpened. 'You know very well it was nothing of the kind. You were a child fighting for her life. If one of those men had found Nixie, and through some miracle she'd been able to kill him, save herself, would you call it murder? Lieutenant.'

'No.' Eve closed her eyes, bore down before the image could form. 'No. I know I did what I had to, like she did what she had to. I killed, she hid.'

'Eve.' Her tone gentle now, Mira laid a hand on Eve's cheek. 'Eve. You had nowhere to hide.'

'No, I had nowhere.' She had to step away from that touch, from that quiet understanding, or dissolve. 'It's good she did. Good she was smart enough to do what she did, strong enough to crawl through blood to survive.'

'And so did you, so were you smart enough and strong enough. And terrified enough. You can't help seeing yourself, as you were, when you deal with her.'

'I did see myself. When I found her, huddled in that bathroom, blood all over her. For a minute, I saw myself in that fucking freezing room in Dallas. And I nearly walked away from her. Hell, I nearly *ran* away from her.'

'But you didn't. And what you felt is normal. What similarities you see—'

'I'm projecting. I know the term.' She felt temper rise up in her, shoved it back. 'I'm handling it. I'm telling you because I figure you should know there's a thing. Off and on.'

'And I expect you to tell me if it becomes too much to handle. For your sake as well as hers. At this point, I believe your empathy with her is helpful – for her. She senses it, and it adds to her sense of safety. You're not just an authority figure. You're her savior.'

Eve turned to the door, opened it. 'She saved herself.'

After going back inside, Eve had to stand for a moment, orient herself and bring the location of the game room into her head.

'If you need to talk about this further—'

'I'll let you know.' She closed the door on it. 'This way. We keep her on monitor. Got a homer on her.'

'No precaution is overdone, in my opinion.'

'On authority figures, I talked with her legal guardians. Linnie Dyson's parents. They're still pretty torn up. I thought if you talked to them it might come easier than having a cop on their doorstep again.'

'I'll do what I can. It would be good for Nixie, certainly, to see them, to talk to them. And it would help them as well.'

Eve paused. She could hear the beeps and bells of machines. They'd left the door to the game room open. 'Listen, before you go in. Grabbing up Newman like that. It was ass covering, and a logical step. But it was strutting, too. Daylight, in front of witnesses. Pulling off something that risky, it's going to juice you up. Coolheaded, cold-blooded, organized planners, sure, but you're going to feel the juice.'

'Those who, even routinely, perform in risky professions or situations get the adrenaline kick. It's part of the reason they do what they do.'

'And the more they get out of Newman, the bigger the rush.'

'Yes.'

Eve let out a deep sigh. 'She's dead, isn't she? As soon as they determine they've gotten all the information out of her, there's no reason to keep her alive.'

'Unfortunately, I agree. You couldn't have saved her.'

'I could've thought ahead. I could've ordered this protection lockdown sooner on all connected parties. But I didn't.' Restless, she moved her shoulders. 'Hindsight doesn't change anything, so I'll think ahead now.'

She gestured toward the room. 'They're in there. You can tell by the insanity of noise.'

'You should come in with me. She needs to see you routinely,' Mira continued when Eve instinctively stepped back. 'To remember me in connection to you, so that she's comfortable with me. Once she's seen you, you can go.'

'All right. Jeez.'

Nixie was standing on a stool and pushing the buttons for the flippers on a pinball machine. The one, Eve noted, with cops and robbers – Roarke's particular favorite.

Trueheart was cheering her on, and looked about two years older than his charge.

'You got it now, you got it! Blast 'em good, Nix. In pursuit, armed suspects! You rock.'

The tiniest smile tugged at her cheeks, but her eyes were focused, her brow knitted in fierce concentration.

Eve smelled popcorn, and saw a bowl of it on one of

the tables. The wall screen was on, volume up to scream, with one of Mavis's videos blaring. Mavis Freestone herself, in little more than a sparkle of paint, cavorted on that screen with what looked to be a number of mostly naked pirates. Black patches weren't just worn over the eye in Mavis's world, Eve observed.

She recognized the song – so to speak. Something about having your heart sunk and your love shipwrecked.

'I'm not sure that video, however entertaining, is appropriate for a girl Nixie's age.'

'Huh?' Eve looked back at Mira. 'Oh, well, shit. Am I supposed to turn it off?'

'Never mind.' Mira patted Eve's hand, and waited until Nixie lost the ball.

'I *still* didn't get high score.'

'Beat the pants off of me,' Trueheart reminded her. 'But I can't beat Roarke. Maybe he cheats.'

'Wouldn't put it past him,' Eve said. 'But I've watched him on that thing. You just can't beat him.'

She'd hoped the casual, somewhat cheerful tone would keep Nixie in the game mood. But as soon as the kid stepped down from the stool, she stared at Eve, the question in her gaze clear.

'No.' Eve spoke tersely now. 'Not yet. When I get them, you'll be the first to know.'

'Hello, Nixie.' Mira stepped up to the machine. 'You may not have gotten high score, but that looks very impressive to me.'

'It's not good enough.'

'When it's the best you can do, it's good enough. But maybe Roarke will play it with you sometime. Maybe he'll show you some of his tricks.'

A spark of interest lit her face. 'Do you think?'

'You can ask him and see. Hello, Officer Trueheart.'

'Dr. Mira. Nice to see you.'

'Do you know all the police?' Nixie wanted to know.

'No, not all. But quite a few. I'd like to talk to you again, Nixie, but first I wonder if you could show me how to play that machine. It looks like fun.'

'I guess. If you want.'

'I do. I'll need to turn off the screen first.'

'But it's Mavis. She's the ult.'

'Oh, I think so, too.' Mira smiled at the cool suspicion in Nixie's eyes. 'I have quite a few of her discs myself. Did you know Lieutenant Dallas and Mavis are friends? Very good friends.'

'Get back!' Then she bit her lip. 'Excuse me, I'm not supposed to sass adults.'

'That's all right. You were just surprised. Eve?'

'Huh?' She'd been wondering why seeing a mostly naked Mavis, and company, on-screen was inappropriate for a kid who'd seen murder up close and personal. 'Oh, yeah. Yeah, Mavis and I are pals.'

'You talk to her, in person?'

'Well, sure.'

'Does she ever come here, right to the house?'

'All the time.' Eve was treated to that long, unblinking stare again. Shifted her stance. Thought about security and procedure. Felt her bones start to burn under that stare. 'Listen, if I can swing it, and she's not busy, I'll see if she can come by sometime. You can meet her and . . . whatever.'

'For real?'

'No, for false. Jesus, kid.'

'You're not supposed to swear in front of me.' Nixie informed her of this, quite primly.

'Then turn around so I can swear behind you. You straight here now?' Eve asked, just a little desperately, of Mira. 'I've got work.'

'We're fine.'

'Trueheart, with me.'

'Yes, sir. See you later, Nixie.'

But before she got to the door, Nixie trotted up behind her. 'Dallas. They all call you Dallas,' she said when Eve looked back. 'Except for her. For the doctor.'

'Yeah, so?'

'Are you going away to work?'

'No, I'm going to work here for a while.'

'Okay.' She walked back to Mira. 'I'll show you how to play now.'

'A while' was hours. McNab might've exaggerated about their ears bleeding, but Eve thought her eyes might. She ran search after search, waiting for names to cross. When the sun went down and the light in her office dimmed, she programmed more coffee, and kept going. 'Food.' Roarke walked in. 'You've sent your team home for food, to recharge, to rest. Do the same for yourself.'

'There's going to be a match. Has to be.'

'And the computer can continue the runs while you eat. We're going downstairs.'

'Why down – oh.' She scrubbed her hands over her face. 'Right. What are we supposed to talk to her about now?'

'I'm sure we'll think of something.'

'You know what? She's a little scary. I think all of that breed is. Kids I mean. It's like they know stuff you've forgotten, but they still hammer you with questions. She rocked up, though, when Mira told her I was friends with Mavis.'

'Ah.' He sat on the corner of the desk. 'A Mavis fan. Considerable conversation to be mined there.'

'And she wants you to play pinball with her. She's got a competitive streak, seems like. She's a little bent she can't meet your scores.'

'Really?' His smile bloomed. 'I'd enjoy that. I'll take her down for a bit after dinner. Good practice for when we have a brood of our own.' She didn't pale, but her eyes did go glassy. 'Are you trying to wig me?'

'It's fairly irresistible. Come on.' He held out a hand. 'Be a good girl and come to dinner.'

Before she could rise, her 'link beeped. 'Minute,' she said, and noted the commander's home data on the ID. 'It's Whitney.' Without thinking about it she straightened up in the chair, squared her shoulders. 'Dallas.'

'Lieutenant. The safe house on Ninety-second has been hit.'

'Ninety-second.' Not trusting her mental file, she flipped her fingers over the keyboard to bring up the data. 'Preston and Knight.'

'They're both down.'

Now she did pale. 'Down, sir?'

'DOS.' His face was grim, his voice was flat. 'Security was compromised. Both officers were terminated. Report to the scene immediately.'

'Yes, sir. Commander, the other locations—'

'Additional units have been dispatched. Reports are coming in. I'll meet you on-scene.'

When the screen went blank, she sat just as she was. Sat just as she was when Roarke came around the desk to lay his hand on her shoulder.

'I hand-picked them. Preston and Knight. Because they were good, solid cops. Good instincts. If there was going to be a hit on one of the locations, I wanted solid cops with good instincts covering them.'

'I'm sorry, Eve.'

'Didn't have to move a wit from that location. Didn't have anybody there, but it was one of the addresses Newman should have known, so it had to be covered. She's dead, too, by now. Stone dead. Tally's up to eight.'

She rose then, checked her weapon harness. 'Two good cops. I'm going to hunt them down like dogs.'

★　★　★

She didn't argue when he said he was going with her. She wanted him behind the wheel until she was more sure of her control.

As she jogged down the stairs, pulled her jacket on, Nixie came out into the foyer. 'You're supposed to come to dinner now.'

'We have to go out.' There was a firestorm raging in Eve's head she'd yet to be able to shut down to cold.

'Out to dinner?'

'No.' Roarke stepped to Nixie, brushed a hand lightly over her hair. 'The lieutenant has work. I'm going to help, but we'll be back as soon as we can.'

She looked at him, then focused on Eve. 'Is somebody else dead?' She started to fob it off, even to lie, but decided on truth. 'Yes.'

'What if they come while you're gone? What if the bad guys come when you're not here? What—'

'They can't get in.' Roarke said it so simply it could be taken as nothing less than fact. 'And look here.' He took a small 'link out of his pocket as he crouched down to her level. 'You keep this. If you're afraid, you should tell Summerset or one of the police we have in the house. But if you can't tell them, you push this. Do you see?'

She moved closer, her blonde hair brushing his black. 'What does it do?'

'It will signal me. You can push this, and my 'link will beep twice, and I'll know it's you, and you're afraid. But don't use it unless you really have to. All right?'

'Can I push it now, to see if it works?'

He turned his head to smile at her. 'A very good idea. Go ahead.' She pressed her finger on the button he'd shown her, and the 'link still in his pocket beeped twice. 'It works.'

'It does, yes. It'll fit right in your pocket. There.' He slipped it in for her, then straightened. 'We'll be back as soon as we can.'

Summerset was there, of course, hovering a few feet back in the hall. Roarke sent him their own signal as he put on his coat. 'Lieutenant,' he said, turning. 'I'm with you.'

When Summerset stepped forward to take Nixie's hand, she waited until the door shut. 'Why does he call her "Lieutenant"? Why doesn't he call her "Dallas" like most everybody else?'

'It's a kind of endearment between them.' He gave Nixie's hand a little squeeze. 'Why don't we eat in the kitchen tonight?'

It wasn't rage. Eve wasn't sure there was a word for what gripped the throat, the belly, the head, the bowels when you looked down at the slaughter of men you'd sent into battle. Men you'd sent to their death. Going down in the line was a risk they all took. But knowing that didn't loosen the grip, not when she'd been the one to give them their last orders.

The other cops were quiet, a silent wall. The scene had been secured. Now it was up to her.

The safe house was a post–Urban Wars construction. Cheap, never meant to last. But it had stood, a narrow box of two stories, bumped up against a few more narrow boxes that were all dwarfed and outclassed by the sturdiness of the buildings that had survived the wars, and the sleekness of those built since the hurried, harried aftermath.

She knew the city had bought this, and others, on the cheap. Maintained them on a shoestring. But the security was better than decent, with full-panning cams, alarms backed up by alarms.

Still, they'd gotten in. Not only gotten in, but had taken out two seasoned cops.

Knight's weapon was still holstered, but Preston's was drawn, lying useless at the base of the stairs while he was sprawled and bloody on them.

Knight's body was facedown, a full stride out of the kitchen. A broken plate, spilled coffee, a veggie ham on rye were scattered in front of him.

The miserly entertainment screen was showing an Arena Ball game. The security screen was black as death.

'Took Knight first.' Her voice was slightly hoarse, but she continued to record the scene and her impressions. 'Took him coming out of the kitchen. Surprised him. If they'd taken Preston, Knight would've come out with his weapon drawn. Preston heads down, ready, but they take him.'

She crouched, picked up the weapon. 'Got a blast off, at least one, before he went down. Officer, start a canvass. I want to know if anyone heard weapons' fire. If they heard shouts. If they saw a fucking cockroach pass this way.'

'Lieutenant—'

She merely turned her head, and the expression on her face had the uniform nodding. 'Yes, sir.'

'Cut their throats – their favorite game. But they didn't cut two cops' throats without a fight. Had to disable first. Long-range stunners,' she said, studying the faint singe on Preston's shirt. 'That's what they had. No chances this time. Not just killing little kids. So they come in the front. God *damn* how did they get through? How did they compromise this system so fast two cops are caught with their pants down?'

'It's a standard police system,' Roarke said quietly because he heard more than rage in her voice. He heard pain. 'A good system, but standard issue for cop houses. If they had the kind of knowledge we believe, they could have set for this, taken it out, got through the door in under two minutes. Very likely considerably under two minutes with the equipment they must have at their disposal.'

'These were good cops,' she reminded him. 'Too good to sit still for a breach like this. Knight's in the damn kitchen making a sandwich. There's a security monitor in there. There are security monitors upstairs. Screen goes out, you go straight to Code Red. So it didn't go out. Not at first. Why is Knight upstairs?'

She stepped over the body, over the blood, and went up to the second floor.

There were two bedrooms, one bath. All windows were privacy screened, barred, and wired. She looked at the 'link in the first bedroom, crossed to it and replayed the last incoming.

It was audio only, and it was her voice.

'Dallas, Lieutenant Eve. The suspects are contained. Repeat, the suspects are contained and being transported. Stand down and report to Central.'

'Fucking A.' Eve muttered.

'Lieutenant?' There was puzzlement, but no alarm in Preston's voice. 'You're on the house 'link.'

'I'm aware of that. Did you copy your orders?'

'Yes, sir, but—'

'Dallas out.'

'Well, shit.' Preston's voice was perturbed now, and he didn't immediately end the transmission on his end. 'Yo, Knight! Dallas collared the bastards. . . . How the hell do I know, she was her usual chatty self. Make me a damn sand—'

There was a blasting sound, a shout, then the sound of running feet. 'Voice simulator,' Roarke said from behind her. 'There was a tinny quality to it, and the lack of inflection in your tone. I suspect, if he had another moment or two, he'd have considered that, and checked in with you.'

'One working the simulator, two coming in. Pull one of them up here with the 'link call, keep him occupied just long enough. Good surveillance equipment, maybe body heat sensors. Knew where they were. One up, one down. Took Knight before he could blink, but Preston got a stream off. They've homed in on him, though, so he's down before he can signal there's trouble.'

'If they had sensors, they'd have known there were only two people here. Both adults.'

She tagged the 'link for EDD. 'Some of the safe houses have cold rooms, just to screw with that kind of surveillance. Subject under protection can be in the cold room. No point in not checking that out, once you've got the locations.'

She headed out, and down. Whitney came in the front as she reached the bottom of the stairs.

'Commander.'

'Lieutenant.' He nodded at Roarke, then crossed to the first body. He said nothing. Then, continuing to look at his fallen men, spoke in a voice dangerously soft. 'They don't yet know the wrath. But they will. Report.'

She went through the steps, reporting, recording, collecting, and repressed the storm inside.

She stood over Morris as he conducted his on-scene exam. 'Stunned first. Midbody hit on both.'

'Preston would have been four or five steps down. He got off a stream,' Eve added. 'Might've caught one of them. There's no sign of a hit on the walls, anywhere in the room. Crime Scene ran over it. No residue. No wasted shots here,' she noted. 'Everyone who fired hit something they were aiming at.'

'My guess would be he crumbled more than fell. I'll know more when I get him in, but the bruising, the position of the body indicates he was thrust back by the stream, then folded, slid. His throat slit where he lay.'

'They had to lift Knight's head to cut him. Blasted back, plate and cup flying. Hits the floor and rolls facedown.'

She walked back to the front door. 'Came in together, one high, one low. It's low guy who takes Knight, from the angle of the hit. High hits Preston. Moving fast, moving smooth.'

She simulated, weapon drawn, heading forward. 'One takes Knight.' Blood cold, she moved straight to the body, lifted the head by the hair, mimed drawing a knife over the throat. 'Left-handed this time. Versatile bastards. Had the stunners in the right, knives in the left.'

Morris said nothing, only watched.

'Second moves straight to Preston, bends down, slices. Combat grip, one quick stroke. Then he heads up, his partner takes the first floor. Place this size, they can confirm it's empty in under ninety seconds.'

'Have you walked it off already?'

'Yeah, I went through. They're in, they're out. Three minutes. The blood on the floor down here, going into the kitchen and into the toilet's going to be from Knight. Upstairs it's going to be Preston's. Coming off the knives, coming off the gear. The trail of it, the pattern, shows they were moving fast. See, look.'

She strode to the kitchen doorway, swung her weapon right, left. 'See the blood there? Pause, sweep the room, move in.'

She looked back up the stairs. 'Preston shouldn't have come down like that, exposed. Two seconds where he acts before he thinks – he's thinking about his partner instead of with cop instinct – and he's dead.'

She lowered her weapon, holstered it. 'Fuck.'

'Truer words. I'll take care of them now, Dallas.' He didn't touch her – his hands were smeared with blood – but the look in his eyes was as steady as the clasp of a hand.

'We're going to bury them for this, Morris.'

'Yes. Yes, we are.'

She went outside. Most of the reporters who'd gathered had scattered after Whitney had given them a brief statement. Stories to file, she thought.

But she saw Nadine over with Roarke by her vehicle. Some of the anger, the cold hard tips of it, clawed through. She strode toward them, ready to rake the reporter bloody – and have a few swipes left over for her husband – when Nadine turned.

Her face was streaked with tears.

'I knew them,' she said before Eve could speak. 'I knew them.'

'Okay.' The anger retracted, scraping those keen tips over her own gut on the way. 'Okay.'

'Knight . . . We used to flirt. Nothing serious, nothing that either of us meant to go anywhere, but we did the dance.' Her voice broke. 'Preston used to show off pictures of his kid. He's got a little boy.'

'I know. You ought to take some time off, Nadine. A couple of days.'

'After you get them.' She swiped her fingers over her cheeks. 'I don't know why it's hit me this way. It's not the first time somebody I know . . .'

'Preston may have hit one of them. I'm telling you that

friend to friend, not cop to reporter. Because you knew them. Because I knew them, and thinking he might've hit one of them helps me.'

'Thanks.'

'I've got to go finish up here, seal the scene, then go in,' Eve said to Roarke. 'I don't know when I'll be home.'

'Call, will you, when you do?'

'Sure.' She thought of what he'd said earlier about the risks she had to take. And what it might be like for him to see other cops, bloody and dead.

So despite Nadine, despite the other cops, the techs, the few gawkers who'd yet to be nudged on their way, she stepped to him, stepped into him. Laid her hands on his face, laid her lips on his.

'I can get you a ride in one of the black-and-whites.'

He smiled at her. 'There is nothing I'd like less. I'll take care of my own transpo. Nadine, I'll give you a lift.'

'If I could have a kiss like that, I'd be lifted into orbit. But I'll settle for a ride to the station. Dallas, if you need some research on the side, another pair of hands or eyes, mine are yours. No strings on this one.'

'I'll keep it in mind. Later.' She strode back up the sidewalk, and back into the narrow box that smelled of death.

11

Word spread quickly when cops went down. By the time Eve reached Central, that word had streamed through the maze, slid into cubes and offices, and had the air thick with fury.

She stepped into the bull pen, paused. She wasn't much for speeches. She preferred briefings or orders. But she was rank here, and the men deserved to hear from her.

They were at desks, in cubes, answering 'links, writing reports. A couple were taking statements from civilians who'd either been victimized or had victimized someone else.

There was the smell of bad fake coffee, sickly sugar substitute, sweat, and someone's greasy dinner. And under it was that fury, a ripe, rich, dangerous odor.

Most of the noise stopped when she came in, but one of the civilians continued to weep in soft, liquid sobs. 'Links beeped, and for the moment were ignored.

She knew she had blood on her, and she knew every cop in the room saw it and thought of where it had come from.

'Detectives Owen Knight and James Preston went down in the line at approximately twenty-fifteen this evening.

They were murdered while doing the job. Detective Knight leaves a mother, father, and sister. Detective Preston leaves a wife, a three-year-old son, his parents, grandparents. Donations to the Survivors' Fund can be made in their names. Detective Jannson,' Eve said, 'will you coordinate?'

The woman nodded. 'Yes, sir. Can you give us the status, Lieutenant?'

'We believe tonight's events are connected to the Swisher homicides. Five civilians, two of them minors, were murdered. Preston and Knight, and every one of us, is charged with protecting and serving the people of New York, of seeing to their safety. Those of us here, in Homicide, are equally charged to serve those whose lives have been taken, of searching out and apprehending those who take lives. We close cases here, and we'll close this one. For those five civilians, two of them minors, and the people they left behind. Now they've taken two of our own, and we will search them out and apprehend.'

She waited a beat, and there was only silence. 'Until such time any and all requests for personal time, vacation time, sick leave must be cleared by me or the ranking officer on shift. You'll be working this case in addition to your currents, reports to be filed daily. No exceptions. At change of shift, report to the ready room for a full briefing and assignments. We're going to hunt them down, and we're going to take them out. That's it.'

She heard no complaints at the additional load as she walked into her office, shut the door.

She got coffee, then just sat.

A police representative and department counselor would have delivered the news by now to the families of the dead. So she was spared that. She would have to speak to them at the memorials, offer some words.

She wanted the words to include: We got the sons of bitches who did this. Who left you a widow, who killed your son, your brother. Who left you without a father.

She pinched the bridge of her nose, then rose to pin the stills from the scene onto her board.

Then she sat to write her report.

None of the other safe houses had been hit. Didn't hit them, she thought, because you knew the target wasn't there. Knew that when you found two armed cops guarding an empty house.

Killing them was a flourish, she decided. A message. No need to finish them off when they were down. Already decided to do that, though. Part of the mission. Take out everybody inside, another clean sweep.

And what's the message? Why add cop killing to the mix when it brings down the full force of the NYPSD? Because you think you're better − smarter, slicker, better equipped. And you know we've made the connection. You know we've got the kid and you want her.

Newman would have told you the kid can't ID you. But she's a detail, she's a miss, and you can't risk it.

I wouldn't, Eve thought. *No, I wouldn't chance leaving that thread dangling when I'd been so careful. It's not squared away,*

217

and it's a little bit insulting. Some snot-nosed kid slips out from under you?

Pride in the work. She tipped back just a bit, rolled her shoulders. Got to have pride in the work to be that damn good at it. And the mission wasn't accomplished, is not complete until Nixie Swisher is dead. 'So what will you do next?' Eve asked aloud. 'What will you do?' There was a sharp knock on her door, then Peabody shoved it open.

'You didn't call me in. I heard it on the goddamn screen.'

'I need you tomorrow. I need you fresh.'

'Bullshit.'

Eve sat where she was, though a low vibration had begun to hum in her blood. 'Crossing a line, Detective.'

'I'm your partner. This case is mine, too. I knew those guys.'

'I'm also your lieutenant, and you're going to want to be careful before you end up with an insubordinate in your file.'

'Fuck my file. And fuck you, too, if you think I give a rat's ass about it.'

Slowly, Eve rose out of her chair. Peabody's chin jutted out, her jaw clenched – and so did her fists. 'Going to take a shot at me, Detective? You'll be on your ass and bloody before you finish the swing.'

'Maybe.'

In all the time they'd worked together, Eve had seen Peabody pissed, hurt, sad, and ready to rumble. But she'd never seen her boiling with all of it. A choice had to be made, and quickly. Plow in, step back.

And just as quickly, Eve decided to do neither. Her eyes stayed steady, her stance at the ready. 'You're beautiful when you're angry.'

There was a blink, then two. 'Dallas—'

'All hot and steamy. If I went for girls, I'd jump you right now.' There was a tremble along the jaw that rippled into a reluctant smile. And just like that, the crisis passed.

'I didn't call you in for the reasons I just told you. Plus this one.' Her hand snapped out, fast as a flicked whip and connected with Peabody's ribs.

Peabody's breath sucked in, and her face lost all color – until it came back with a faint tinge of green. 'That was just mean. Even for you.'

'Yeah, and telling. You're not a hundred percent yet. You don't get your downtime, you're no good to me.' Eve crossed to the AutoChef, ordered up a bottle of water as Peabody leaned against the desk and got her breath back. 'I can't afford to worry about you, and I am. I don't like seeing you hurting.'

'That nearly makes up for the punch in the ribs.'

'The fact that you called that tap a punch ought to tell you something.' She handed Peabody the water. 'You nearly died.'

'Well, Jesus, Dallas.'

'You nearly died,' Eve repeated, and it was partner to partner now, a unity tighter than most marriages. 'I was afraid you would. Sick and afraid.'

'I know,' Peabody replied. 'I get that.'

'I cleared you to come back because medical said you could handle light duty. This isn't turning out to be light. I'm not taking you off this case because I know if I were in your shoes – which would never happen, as I'd have to be beaten unconscious before you'd get those pink airboots on my feet—'

Peabody's lips twitched. 'Salmon.'

'What, you're hungry?'

'No.' Peabody took another sip of water and laughed, then winced and rubbed her ribs. 'The shoes. The color's salmon.'

'More the reason. I'm really going to wear fish shoes. So – God, what was I saying?'

'You're not taking me off because . . .'

'Because if it were me, the job's going to take my mind off the fact I nearly got taken out.'

'It does. I've woken up sweaty a few times the last weeks, which has nothing to do with mattress dancing with McNab. But it's getting better. I'm getting better. I need to work.'

'Agreed. In addition to the above reasons, I didn't call you in tonight because . . .'

She reached past Peabody to close the door. '. . . I sent them in. Knight and Preston. I knew them, too, and I sent them in, and now they're dead. I had to deal with that first, on my own. Now I have, so let's get to work.'

Peabody sat. 'I wasn't mad at you. Well, yeah, I was, but it was easier to be mad at you, to let it center there, than . . .'

'I know that, too. Get some coffee.'

'Hey, you actually offered me coffee.'

'I meant get some coffee for me, but you can have some, too.' Peabody pushed up, went to the AutoChef. While she programmed, she studied the board. 'What have we got?' It didn't take long to brief her.

'Have you got a copy of the 'link transmission? I'd like to hear it.' Eve took out a disc, plugged it in, called up the recording.

While it played, Peabody sipped coffee. 'It's off – just a little, but it's close. The way it says, "I'm aware of that," when he questions you contacting him on the house 'link. I'd have known it wasn't you, but he doesn't talk with you every day, so yeah, he'd have bought it. Initially. Then, give him another ten seconds, and he's going to think: blocked video, you never addressed him by name or rank, and you don't do drone work. You wouldn't be the one to contact all the plants and inform. You'd be too busy with the suspects.'

'He didn't have the additional ten seconds. He goes up to answer the 'link. Only house 'link in the place, and in that room because that room's secured, for police only when there's a witness on the premises. Good spy equipment, they can locate that, and it's good for them. Separate the two of them. Up and down, keeping one on the 'link just long enough to finish bypassing. He hasn't even ended the transmission when they're in.'

'Who called it in? Who called in the officer down?'

'They didn't make their required hourly check-in. Backup team sent in, found them. Canvass turned up zilch, so far.'

'Those locations are soundproofed. Nobody would have heard the weapons' fire.'

'It's street level, they had to close the door behind them. Don't miss a trick. In, one of them gives it a boot. Knight comes out, shouts the warning, and he's down before he can draw his weapon. Preston responds, gets off one stream, and he's down. Finish them off, do a quick search – not going to miss anything this time. Then they're out.'

'Had to have a vehicle somewhere, running the surveillance, the electronics.'

'The third man, at least one more. Possibly two now. One to drive, one to handle the equipment. Inside guys report the target's not there, the vehicle heads for a pickup spot, or just back to HQ. These guys walk away. Walk away from the scene because somebody might notice and remember seeing two guys get into a van outside a place where two cops got their throats cut. Too many people around there, walking, running shops, hailing cabs. It's not a pit like where they snatched Newman.'

'Somebody might've noticed two guys entering and leaving the scene.'

'Yeah, and we'll hope so, but it's less of a risk. A couple of pedestrians, as opposed to two men jumping into the back of a van – especially since the reports of how Newman was abducted are all over the screen. Better to mix things up than form too recognizable a pattern.'

'And we still don't know why.'

'We work with what we know. Extreme knowledge of

electronics and surveillance, commando-style hits. Multiple participants. This is a team, and well-lubed. This team, or a member of it, ordered or requested the hit on the Swishers. And there's a good chance they – What?' she called out, irritated at the knock on her door.

'Sorry, Lieutenant.' Jannson stood in the doorway. 'What is it, Detective?'

'I started making the rounds, for the Survivors' Fund.'

'We'll have to discuss that later.'

'No, sir. I was down in Booking, and when one of the uniforms was digging out a donation, he said they had an LC in the tank who was mouthing off about knowing something about what went down. He was pissed about it, the uniform, because she's a regular visitor – street level. Always looking for an angle, mostly full of it. He figured she heard some of the men talking about Knight and Preston and wants some attention, a little glory. It's a long shot otherwise, but I didn't want it overlooked. Lieutenant, she was picked up on West Eighty-Nine. Just blocks from the scene.'

'Bring her up, into Interview. We'll take her for a spin. Check which room's available.'

'I already did. Interview A's clear.'

'Bring her up. You want in?'

Jannson hesitated, and Eve could see the struggle on her face. 'Three of us in there, gives her too much thumb. I'll take the Observation Room.'

'Have Booking shoot up her sheet. Nice catch, Jannson.'

* * *

223

Ophelia Washburn was more than worn around the edges. She was heading for tattered. She was a wide-hipped black woman with breasts of such enormity and stature no angel of God had bestowed them. Her top was spangled and feathered and strained mightily to hold those mountains in place.

Her hair was a towering shock of white. Eve always wondered why street-levels felt huge hair was as big a drawing card as huge breasts. And why either were needed, when most customers either wanted a fast bang or a quick blow job.

Her lips were full, large, and dyed to match the top. A gold eye-tooth glinted between them, while the rest of her face was painted and slathered in a manner that shouted out, 'Whore here! Inquire regarding rates.'

But all the paint and polish didn't disguise the fact that Ophelia was past prime. Limping toward fifty, a decade beyond the age most street-levels burned out and took jobs as irritable waitresses or riders at sex clubs. Maybe bit actors in porn vids.

'Ophelia.' Eve kept her voice light, even friendly. 'I see you're operating on a suspended license and have three other violations within the last eighteen months.'

'No, see, that's the thing. That cop, he said I was carrying illegals and I *told* him the john musta put them on me. You can't trust a john, take it from me. But they don't pay any mind, and I get my license suspended. Now how'm I supposed to make a living I can't trick? Who'm I hurting out there? I get my health checks regular. You can see that in my file. I'm clean.'

'It also says you've tested positive for Exotica and Go.'

'Well, musta been a mistake, or some john, he slipped me some. Some rub Go on their dicks. Give a bj, and there you are.'

Eve cocked her head as if she found this information fascinating. 'You know with this last bust, they're going to lift your license permanently.'

'You can fix that. You can fix that for me, 'cause I got something for you.'

'What have you got for me, Ophelia?'

'First you fix it.'

'Peabody, do I look as if most of my brain has recently been surgically removed?'

'No. You certainly don't look nearly dim enough to fix a sheet of this length without first being given salient information.'

Ophelia sent Peabody a scowl. 'What she mean *salient*?'

'Ophelia, two cops are dead.' The light, friendly tone turned cold as Pluto. 'You heard about that. If you're using that, if you're playing me with that so you can get your license clear, I will personally see that it's not only lifted, but that you're hounded by the cops to the extent you won't be able to give away blow jobs for old times' sake.'

'No need to get pissy.' Ophelia's large lips seemed to gain weight with a pout. 'Just trying to help us both outtava jam.'

'Then you tell me what you know, and if it helps, you walk out.'

'With a license?'

'With a license.'

'Phat. So, here's what. I'm doing the stroll on Ninety-Two. My usual area of business is downtown, but with my current situation, I changed. And you get better tricks Upper West. That time of day, lots of nine-to-fives heading home after a quick drink. I give them a bj to go with it, maybe a fast bang.'

'On the street.'

'Well . . . See, I got an arrangement with a guy has a deli with a back room. He takes a cut, and I got some privacy for my business.'

'Okay. Keep going.'

Obviously cheered by the fact she wasn't going to get slapped for another violation, Ophelia beamed. 'So I'm starting the stroll. Got one quickie in, so I'm feeling pretty good. Nice night out, people walking around. Lots of potentials, you know? And I see these two. Mmmmmmm. Big, handsome guys. Look rough, look tough. Think maybe I can get me a twofer. I sway on up to them, leading with the champs here.' She laid her hands on her breasts, gave them a squeeze. 'And I say, how about you gentlemen and me have ourselves a party. Offer them a special rate. I'm standing in front of them. You gotta slow a john down, show off the merchandise, you gonna have a shot. And this one looks at me, hard. But not like he's thinking about doing me, but like he's thinking about kicking my sweet ass down and giving it a stomp. You been in the life long as I have, you know that look. They don't say nothing, just part ways and walk by on either side of me. That's when I smelled it.'

'Smelled what.'

'Blood. Fresh. So you best believe while they're walking that way, I'm walking quick, fast, and in a hurry in the other. It's 'cause I'm shaken up some that I end up offering to party with a cop in soft clothes, and he asks to see my license. And I end up in the tank where I hear talk about two cops getting dead on Ninety-second. And I'm saying how I have information, but—'

'Let's go back a minute. Did you see blood on these men?'

'No, smelled it.'

'How did you know it was blood?'

'Well, shit, you ever smelled it? Especially when it's fresh. You can almost taste it, like you sucked on an old credit. My granddaddy's got a little farm down in Kentucky. Raises pigs. I did some time there as a kid – hog slaughtering time. I know what blood smells like. And those guys had been bloody, you can take that to the bank.'

Eve felt that fizz in her own blood, but kept her tone even. 'What did they look like?'

'Big, built. White boys. Had to look up at them, but I don't have much height, even in my work shoes. But they looked big 'cause they were solid, you know?'

'Handsome, you said.'

'Yeah, good lookers, what I could see. Wearing sun shades and caps. I didn't see the eyes, but when they send that look at you, you don't have to. Sorta looked alike, I guess, but they were white boys and sometimes they just do.'

'What were they wearing?'

'Dark.' She lifted a shoulder. 'Didn't pay much attention, but they looked like good stuff – quality – so I figured they had fee and tip on them. Had bags, too, on long straps.' She held her hands about a foot apart. ''Bout that big. Now I'm thinking, one of the bags bumped me when they walked by. Felt solid, and that's when I smelled the blood.'

'Which way were they walking, west or east?'

'West, heading on over toward Broadway. One of 'em had a hitch in his stride.'

'Meaning?'

'Gimpy. Limping some. Like his leg was paining him or his shoes didn't fit right.'

Got one of them, Preston, Eve thought. Gave them a little pain. 'Hair color, distinguishing marks, anything else?'

'I don't know.'

Eve drew herself back. If she pushed too hard, the woman could start making things up, just to fill in the blanks. 'Do you think you'd recognize them if you saw them again?'

'Might.'

'I'd like you to work with a police artist.'

'No shit. Never did that before. I must've given you good stuff.'

228

'Maybe. Good enough I'll fix your license.'

'You're stand-up. I don't do girls as a rule, but you want a bang sometime, I'll give you a freebie.'

'I'll keep that in mind. Meanwhile, I need you to stay here while I arrange for an artist.'

'I don't gotta go back to the tank?'

'No.' As she rose, Eve decided she could do one better. 'There hasn't yet been a reward posted, but there will be by morning. There's a standard reward in cases of cop killing. If this information you've given us leads to an arrest, I'll see that you get it.'

This time Ophelia's jaw dropped. 'You are shitting me.'

'We appreciate your cooperation.'

The minute they stepped out, Peabody clutched a hand on Eve's arms. 'That's the real deal, Dallas. She saw them.'

'Yeah, she did. Goddamn street hooker. You just never know.' Eve nodded as Jannson came out of Observation. 'Nice work, Detective.'

'Back at you, sir. You drew that out of her like it was candy tied to a string. I can arrange for the artist.'

'Tag Yancy, he's the best. Call him in. I don't want this leaking to the media as yet. And the LC's name is now Jane Doe on any and all records.'

'On that.'

Eve turned to Peabody. 'I want her to stay in Central. I don't want her back on the street. They get wind, they'll find her. She gets out, she'll tell anyone who'll listen. No safe houses. We put her up in one of the cribs here. Get

229

her whatever she wants, within reason. Let's keep her happy.'

'On that,' Peabody said and returned to the interview room.

As she headed to her office, Eve yanked out her pocket 'link. Roarke's face filled the screen so quickly, she knew he'd been waiting.

'I may not make it home for a while. I got something.'

'What can you tell me?'

'Street LC, tried to solicit them a couple of blocks from the scene. I'll fill you in later, but I've got her here, bringing Yancy in to work with her. I'm going to stick, see if we can get a good picture.'

'What can I do?'

'Funny you should ask.' This time she walked straight through the bull pen, ignoring the questioning looks, into her office, and shut the door.

'You up for some drone work?'

'I prefer to call it expert computer tasking. You've got a look in your eye, Lieutenant, that I'm very pleased to see.'

'I'm on them.' Ophelia had smelled the blood, she thought. And now, so did she. 'I've been thinking, and was about to pursue the theory that the Swishers might not have been first. That's a kind of crescendo — isn't that the thing you call it when you drag me to symphonies and crap?'

'It is, my darling, uncultured Eve.'

'Crescendos, the big noise. But mostly, you lead up to

that, build up to it. So maybe they weren't the only. And maybe not the first.'

'Both you and Feeney have run IRCCA for like crimes.'

'Not like – not home invasion, necessarily, with a slaughter. But connected. So, here's a theory. If somebody was pissed enough or worried enough about one or more members of the Swisher household to wipe them out, could be there are one or more individuals this dick is pissed off at or worried about. So we need to go back, we need to do a search of logical connections – at least we'll stick with logical to start. School staff – anyone connected with the school who died or disappeared within, let's say, the last three years. These guys are patient, but they're cocky, too, proud. They wouldn't spread it out much longer than that.'

'Then there's health care workers and physicians Keelie or Grant Swisher worked with.'

'You do connect the dots. Lawyers who went up against Swisher in court, presiding judges, social workers. Clients on both – dead or missing.'

'Same time period?'

'Yeah – shit, let's make it six years. Better have a buffer. If I'm right and the Swishers were to be the big finish, we'll find something. What's happened since is cleanup, because of one small mistake. We connect something, that's going to connect to something else. Then I'll wrap them up and choke them with it.'

'Sexy talk.'

'Find me something, it'll get sexier. You're slicker than me on this stuff.'

'Darling, you're an amazon in bed.'

'Drone work, ace.' She could feel the juices bubbling inside now. 'I'll take the school angle, because it's the least likely. Anything pops, anything, tag me.'

She walked over to the AutoChef, then backed off. She was too damn revved for more coffee. Better to flush some of it out. She grabbed water instead before organizing what she needed for the ready room.

She opened her door, and stopped short before she walked into Whitney.

'Sir. I didn't realize you were in the house.'

'I've just come from paying condolence calls on Knight's and Preston's families.' He glanced down at the bottle in her hand. 'Does coffee now come clear and in bottles?'

'It's water, sir.'

'And has hell frozen over without me getting a report?'

'I'm sorry, I don't . . . Oh.' She gave the bottle a little frown. 'I thought I should offset the caffeine.'

'I, on the other hand, could use the jolt.'

'Yes, sir.' She set her things down, went to the AutoChef.

'I'm aware you have a briefing in a moment. It'll keep. I'm also aware you have an artist coming in to work a potential witness.'

'I think she's solid, Commander. I've requested Detective Yancy. I haven't yet written my report on the interview.'

He accepted the coffee. 'I saw Detective Peabody, so I

have the main points. I'll attend your briefing and expect to be filled in more completely at that time. But we need to discuss something else first.'

When he closed the door, her shoulders squared. When she realized it, she reminded herself of Trueheart.

'Sit down, Lieutenant.'

She took the visitor's chair, leaving him the marginally sturdier one at the desk. But he didn't sit, simply stood with the coffee in his hand.

'It's difficult to lose men. It's difficult to accept that your orders put them in harm's way.' He looked toward her board, toward the pictures of two cops. 'These aren't the first men either of us has lost.'

'No, sir.'

'But each is like the first. Each is difficult. Taking orders is less of a burden than giving them. You need to carry that weight, and stop yourself from asking if you should have done something different. You did what you had to do, just as your men did what they had to do. We may lose more in our pursuit of the scum who did this, and you are not allowed to hesitate to give the orders, you are not allowed to second guess what you know has to be done.'

'I've dealt with it, Commander.'

'You've started to. It'll come back on you when you stop, when you're away from here and the work. It'll come back on you, and you'll have to finish dealing with it. And put it away. If you have trouble doing that, speak with Mira or one of the department counselors.'

'I'll put it away. There isn't an officer in my division or in this department who should trust me if I can't. Or don't. I understood that I'd face this when I accepted the promotion to lieutenant. I understand that I'll be here again, with the faces of men I know on my board.'

'You should be captain,' he said, and she said nothing. 'You know there are reasons, mostly political, why you haven't yet been offered the opportunity to test for a captaincy.'

'I know the reasons, sir, and accept them.'

'You don't know them all. I could push it, push the chief, call in some markers.'

'I don't want markers called in on my account.'

He smiled a little. 'Markers are made to be called in. But I don't — not yet — because, frankly, Dallas, I'm not ready to have one of my best street cops riding a desk. And you're not ready to comfortably ride one.'

'No, sir. I'm not.'

'We'll both know when you are. Good coffee,' he said and took another swallow. 'I'll see you in the ready room.'

12

In his office, Roarke set up for his assignment. It continued to surprise him how much he enjoyed doing cop work. Most of his life had been spent avoiding, evading, or out-thinking cops.

Now he was not only married to one, ridiculously in love with one, but he spent a great deal of his time in a consultant capacity for the NYPSD.

Life was a bloody strange game.

Then again, perhaps it was the game of it that accounted for part of the entertainment. The puzzle that needed to be solved, with facts, with evidence, and with instinct.

They made a good team, he and his cop, he thought, as he poured himself a brandy before getting down to it. She with her ingrained cop senses, he with his ingrained crim-inal ones.

Just because he was retired from the shadier aspects of the law didn't mean the instincts weren't still humming.

He'd killed. Brutally, coldly, bloodily. He knew what it was to take a life, and what could drive one human to end the existence of another.

She accepted that in him, his justice-seeking Eve. Maybe

not forgave, but accepted. Even understood, and that was one of his miracles.

But even at his worst, he'd never killed an innocent. Never ended the life of a child. Still, he could comprehend it, even as Eve could. They both knew evil not only existed, it flourished and grew fat, and it reveled in its pursuit of the weak and the innocent.

He had an abrupt and crystal-clear image of himself – filthy shirt, bloody nose, hard and defiant eyes – standing at the top of the steps in the stinking dump where he'd once lived in Dublin.

And there was his father – big, strapping Patrick Roarke – weaving a bit from too much drink.

You think you can pass off a couple of thin wallets as a day's take? I'll have the rest of it, you buggering little bastard.

He remembered the boot coming up – he remembered that still – and his quick dodge. Not quick enough, though, not that time. He felt now as he'd felt then, the stomach-dropping sensation of falling, of knowing it would be bad. Had he cried out? Odd that he couldn't remember. Had he yelled in shock, cursed in fury, or just gone down those steps in a bone-banging roll?

What he could remember, and wasn't that a bitch, was the sound of his father laughing as the boy he'd been tumbled down the stairs. What was his age then? Five? Six? No matter.

And, well, hell, he had been holding back, hadn't he? And considered the cuts and bruises worth the ten pounds he'd stashed away.

Nixie had never been booted down the stairs by a drunken bastard who'd happened to share her blood.

And yet the child would understand about evil and cruelty, too. Poor little bit.

He glanced at his monitor, where he could see her curled under the covers of the bed they'd given her, in a room provided by strangers, with the light left dim.

She would come to understand it. Now there was only pain and confusion and grief. But she would come to, and make her choices to rebuild her life on that broken ground.

He'd made his, and didn't regret them. He could regret nothing that brought him where he was, that brought him to Eve. But he didn't wish the same for this small, fragile survivor.

The best that could be done was to win her some sort of justice.

He began a series of simultaneous searches. One on each of the Swisher adults, another cross-checking for duplicate names. Then one more on the Dysons. He doubted Eve would approve, but these were the people who would step in to raise the child. And the child was sleeping in his home, trusting him to keep her safe. He wanted to be sure they were clean.

At the same time, he continued the search for names of known terrorists, members of paramilitary or fringe military groups.

He intended to do one more, but would need the unregistered for that. Even with it, it would be tricky – which appealed to him. He wanted names of covert and special forces operators – military and government agencies who specialized in wet work and electronics. When he had those, he'd run another cross-reference on the Swishers.

He intended to leave his more standard work running while he took himself and his plan into his private office. But he glanced at the monitor again, and saw Nixie stirring in her bed.

He watched, hoping her subconscious wasn't tuning her up for another nightmare. And wondered if he hadn't made a mistake, insisting he take the night shift from Summerset. Nightmares may have become his province, but when it came to children, he was a pathetic novice.

But in another moment, she sat up in bed. She took the 'link he'd given her out from under her pillow, studied it, skimmed her fingers over it. Then she stared around the room, looking so small, so lost and sad it broke his heart.

He thought he should go in to her, try at least to soothe her back to sleep, but she climbed out of the bed. Just needs the loo or a drink of water, he decided. The sort of things a girl her age could handle on her own. He hoped.

But instead of walking to the bathroom, she went to the house scanner. 'Is Dallas here?'

There was a plaintive quality in her voice that touched him, even as he thought, 'Clever girl.'

Dallas, Lieutenant Eve, is not on premises at this time.

Nixie knuckled her eyes, sniffled, and again he thought he should go to her.

'Is Roarke here?'

Roarke is in his primary office.

'I don't know where that is. You have to tell me.'

Roarke rose, then sat back down as the computer relayed location and directions. Let her come to him, he decided. It seemed more normal somehow than having him intercept her, letting her know – though she was smart enough to know it anyway – that she was being monitored even while she slept.

He looked at the work yet to be done, rubbed the back of his neck. 'Computer, continue searches, text mode only, internal save. No display at this time.'

Acknowledged.

He opened other work, his own, and began to refine construction plans on another sector of the Olympus Resort while Nixie made her way to him.

He glanced up, cocked a brow, offered a smile when Nixie stepped into his doorway. 'Hello, Nixie. Late for you, isn't it?'

'I woke up. Where's Dallas?'

'She's still working. Would you like to come in?'

'I'm not supposed to be up in the night.' Her voice trembled, and he imagined she was thinking of what had happened the last time she'd wandered in the night.

'I wouldn't mind the company, since you're up. Or I can walk you back to your room if you'd rather.'

She walked over to his desk in her pale pink pajamas. 'Is she with the dead people?'

'No. She's working for them.'

'But my mom and dad, and Coyle and Linnie, and Inga, they were dead first. She said she would find out who. She *said* she—'

'She is.' Out of my sphere, he thought. Out of my bloody solar system. 'Finding out *who* is her priority. It's the most important thing she's doing. And she'll keep doing it until she knows.'

'What if it takes years and years?'

'She'll never stop.'

'I had a dream that they weren't dead.' The tears spilled over, slid down her cheeks. 'They weren't dead, and we were all there like we're supposed to be, and Mom and Inga were in the kitchen talking, and Dad was trying to sneak a snack and making her laugh. Me and Linnie were playing dress-up, and Coyle was teasing us. And they weren't dead until I woke up. I don't want them to be dead. They left me alone, and it's not fair.'

'It's not, no. It's not at all fair.' He came around, picked

240

her up so she could lay her head on his shoulder while she cried. This, he thought, was something a man could do. He could hold a child while she wept, while she grieved. And later he could do what he could to help piece her broken life back together.

'They left me alone.'

'They didn't want to. Still, I imagine all of them are so glad you weren't hurt.'

'How can they be glad when they're dead?'

Terrifying logic, he thought, and carried her around the desk, sat with her in his lap. 'Don't you think that when you die you might go to another place?'

'Like heaven.'

'Aye, like that.'

'I don't know. Maybe.' She turned her head, sighed. 'But I don't want them to be there. I want them to come back, like in my dream.'

'I know. I never had a brother. What's it like?'

'They can be mean sometimes, especially if they're bigger than you. But you can be mean back. But sometimes they're fun and they play with you and tell jokes. Coyle played baseball, and I like to go to the games and watch. Is there baseball in heaven?'

'I think there must be. It could hardly be heaven if it wasn't fun.'

'If I'd been in bed, I'd be in heaven with them. I wish—'

'You mustn't.' He drew her back so she could see his face. 'You mustn't wish for that, and they wouldn't want

241

you to wish it. There was a reason you didn't go with them. Hard as that is, you have to live your life and find out what it is. It hurts to be alone, I know.'

Her face bunched up like a fist. 'You don't. You're not.'

'There was a time I was. Someone took my mother from me before I was old enough to know her.'

'Is she in heaven?'

'I'm sure she is.'

'That's not fair either.' She laid her head on his chest again, patted him with her hand in a gesture of comfort that moved him, amazingly. She could offer him comfort, Roarke thought. Even now she had the heart in her to give solace. How did she come by that? Was it born in her or had it been instilled by her parents?

'I won't tell you I know how you're feeling, but I will tell you I know what it is to be alone and angry and afraid. And I'll tell you it'll get better, however much you don't think so, it will get better.'

'When?'

'Bit by little bit.' He touched his lips to her head.

She sighed again, then turned her head to study the painting on the wall. He shifted her, studied it himself. He and Eve, under the blossoming arbor on their wedding day.

'She doesn't look like police there.'

'Not on the outside anyway. She gave that to me on our anniversary. It's out in the garden here, on our wedding day. I hung it there, though it's a bit selfish of me, so I could

242

look at it whenever I'm working here. I can see her when I'm missing her.'

'We've got pictures at my house.'

'Would you like someone to bring some pictures to you?'

'I could look at them.'

'I'll see to it, then.'

'Can I stay in here for a while, with you?'

'You can. Do you want to see what I'm doing here?' He swiveled so they could both look at the wall screen. 'Those are plans for some developments on an off-planet resort and housing colony I've an interest in.'

'It says Olympus Resort. I've heard of that. It's got big hotels and amusement parks, and a beach and arcades. We were maybe going to go there one day. Maybe.'

'These are for a different sector than what's been done so far. See the first screen? Those are plans for villas, vacation villas. We're going to put a river in.'

'Do you build rivers?'

He smiled. 'I'm going to build this one.'

'How do you?'

'Well, why don't I show you what I have in mind?'

While Roarke showed Nixie how a river was built on an off-planet colony, Eve met with Yancy.

'Give me good news.'

'How about cautiously good?'

He was young, and what Peabody would have called a

cutie. And he was the best Ident artist in the city. Eve tracked him down in his domain, a generous cube filled with comp screens, portables, paper sketchpads, and pencils.

'How cautiously?'

'Your wit's enthusiastic, and she's got a good eye. Our favor. She's also prone to what I call dramination. She's rocking on the drama, and using her imagination to juice it all up. I can work with that, and we're making progress.'

'Where is she?'

'In the crib. Hey, Peabody.'

'Just settled her in,' Peabody said as she joined them. 'Got her an entertainment screen, extra pillows, a meal, a brew.'

'A brew?' Eve demanded.

'You said within reason,' Peabody reminded her. 'Not within regs. She's happy, though she squawked some about having to give up her pocket 'link, and not having access to another. Anyway, she's down, and I've got Invansky babysitting.'

'I wonder – just a thought that passes through my mind – why our wit is watching screen and drinking brew instead of giving us a picture of a couple of stone murderers.'

'My call, Lieutenant.' Yancy held up a hand. 'She was tapped for the night. She's given us a good start, but she was starting toward hyperbole. She comes back to what we've got fresh, it's a better chance other details will spring for her.'

'Okay, okay.' Eve raked both hands through her hair, at war with her own impatience. 'Show me what you've got.'

'Split screen,' he ordered, scooting over. 'Current images.'

Eve looked at rough sketches – rougher, she noted, than usual when working with Yancy. Both were of square-faced, square-jawed men she'd judge to be in their early forties to early fifties. The eyebrows were straight and pale, the mouths grim but sensuously full. Dark watch caps were pulled low over both foreheads, and most of their upper faces were concealed by them and the dark, wraparound shades.

'You've got to ditch the shades. I need best probability on the eyes.'

'I will. I'm going to work some from these, but I've got a better chance of hitting it closer after I have another session with Ophelia.'

'I can't go out with this, Yancy.'

'Give me until tomorrow. She's got a good eye, like I said, but it's more impressionistic, more big-picture. It'll take a little more work for me to finesse the details out of her.'

'Just how much is she going to forget while she's slurping down a brew and watching vids? I've got two cops in the fucking morgue.'

'I know what I'm doing.' For the first time in her memory, Yancy shoved up and into her face. 'Just because I never worked with Knight or Preston doesn't mean I'm stringing this out. You want results, get off my ass.'

She could have slapped him down for it. Nearly did. God knew she wanted to take a swing at someone. Close ranks, she thought, and sometimes you end up taking a bite out of one of your own.

'Step back, Detective.'

He vibrated, the muscles in his jaw worked, but he stepped back. 'You're right,' Eve said. 'You know what you're doing and I'm on your ass. We're all on edge about this. I requested you because I consider you the best we have. I also know you were off duty, and came in on your own time.'

'None of us are on our own time now.' His shoulders relaxed. 'Sorry for the spew, Dallas. It's frustrating for me not to be able to put this together faster. I pushed her a little longer than I should have first session. Now I've got to pull back.'

'How sure are you about the facial structure on these?'

'Sure as I get. She's got that big-picture style. I'd say the shape of the faces is on target – at least for one. If she's right on both, these guys might be brothers or cousins. Father and son.'

'Shoot me copies, will you? I'll start with what you've got – and try to stay off your ass until you have more.'

He smiled a little. 'Appreciate it.'

The house was quiet when she walked in. She'd nearly bunked at Central, would have if there wasn't a nine-year-old witness in her house. She had three cops patrolling the grounds, another three inside – a situation she imagined Roarke detested more than he would a stock market crash.

He might've built himself a fortress, but he wouldn't care to be under siege.

She checked in with all the night duties and got the all-clear before she went upstairs.

She'd thought he'd be in bed – it was closing in on three in the morning – but her house scan showed him in his office yet. She went into her own, dumped some files, then opened the connecting door to his.

She wasn't quite sure what to think when she saw the kid curled up in the spare bed Roarke must have brought out of its panel – and the man himself sitting beside her, eyes closed.

It was rare for her to see him sleep – he was so often up before her – but she didn't see how that position, with his back up against the wall, could be comfortable.

Even as she debated, he spoke. Eyes still closed. 'She was restless. I took the night shift, and let her come seek me out when she woke.'

'Nightmare?'

'Worse, really. She said she dreamed they were all still alive. Woke up, and they weren't.' He opened his eyes now, heavy and blue. 'She sat with me awhile, but was so worried about going back to her room, I put her here. She asked if I'd sit with her. Apparently we both nodded off. I've had the searches going on silent, haven't been able to check them.'

'Morning's good enough, since it's only a couple hours away. What do we do with her? Can't leave her here.'

'Well . . .' He looked over, studied Nixie. 'I could try carrying her back. If she wakes up, it's your turn.'

'Shit. Make sure she doesn't wake up.'

He slid off the bed. 'This usually works with you.' He

247

tucked his hands under her, lifted. Nixie gave a moan, stirred, and had them looking at each other in mild panic. Then her head dropped on his shoulder. 'Don't breathe,' Eve said in a whisper. 'Don't talk. And maybe you could sort of glide instead of walk.'

He merely cocked his head, then inclined it toward the elevator.

She used manual instead of voice, held her own breath until they'd completed the trip and he was easing Nixie into bed. They backed out of the room together as if the bed contained a homemade boomer.

'When does Summerset take over?'

'Six.'

'Three hours. We should be okay then.'

'I sincerely hope so. I need to sleep and so do you.' He rubbed a thumb on the smudges under her eyes. 'Anything new?'

'Yancy's working on a sketch, but he wants to get back to it in the morning.' In their bedroom, she shed her jacket, then her harness. 'I need a few hours down myself. Brain's mushy. I want to be back at Central around oh-seven hundred. You get any names that look good, you can shoot them to me there.'

She peeled out of her boots, her clothes. 'You tired enough not to argue if I ask you to work from here tomorrow?'

'At the moment. But I may revive by sunup.'

'We'll argue then.'

They crawled into bed, his arm came around her, snuggled her back against him. 'That's a date.'

He didn't wake before her – another surprise. The low beep from the monitor across the room woke her, and a check of her wrist unit confirmed it was six hundred hours.

The room was still dark, but she could see him, the shape of him. The line of cheek and jaw, the sweep of hair. She'd turned to face him sometime during that short rest. Seeking . . . what, she wondered. Connection, solace, warmth.

For a moment she wished she could simply close her eyes again, curl closer, escape everything but him in the silence of sleep. Her body, her brain, felt so heavy with fatigue. She'd have to dig in, dig deep to find the energy and purpose she'd need to face the day.

As her eyes adjusted to the dark, she could see more of him. The plane of his nose, his cheek, the curve of his mouth. Beautiful. And every plane, every line, every inch was hers.

It made her feel lighter, body and mind, just to look at him.

'I can feel you staring.' His voice was a sleepy murmur, but the thumb and finger of the hand resting on her butt gave her a sharp pinch. 'How come you're not up making another million and generally laying waste to the business world?'

'Because I'm sleeping. I'll make another million later, and let someone else start the day laying waste.'

249

Yes, she thought, lighter and lighter. 'Why are you tired?'

'Because someone won't shut up and let me sleep.'

'Batteries run down, huh? Maybe you need a recharge.' She wrapped her fingers around him, squeezed, and grinned when he hardened. 'Apparently, not running too low.'

'Reserves. You know what happens to sexual predators?'

'You bet. I'm a cop.' She rolled on top of him. 'My bats are on low, too. Need a jolt. You know how sex can rev you up?'

'I've heard rumors.' His hand stroked over her hair as she worked her way down – and his body flashed fully awake when her mouth replaced her fingers. 'I don't think that's playing quite fair, but keep it up.' She laughed, bit his thigh. 'Keeping it up's never been your problem.'

'You've got a smart mouth.' His breath caught when she used it again. 'Make that brilliant.'

She worked her way up, shifted to straddle him. And from across the room a child's voice demanded, 'Where is Dallas?'

'Shit! Shit a brick!' Eve sprang around, instinctively reaching for her weapon and slapping her own naked side. On the monitor she saw Nixie standing in the guest room by the house scanner. 'Jesus, does she ever sleep?'

'Summerset will go settle her down.' But he sat in the warm bed with his naked wife and watched the child.

'We can't have juicy sex with a kid right there. It's . . . perverted.'

'I don't mind perverted. What it is, is intimidating. It's

not like she can see or hear or . . . it's just that there she is. And now there's Summerset.' He sighed, pushed back his hair as he watched his major-domo go into Nixie's room. 'Bugger it. Let's try the shower. It could work in the shower, you know, with the door closed, the water running.'

'It's weirded me out now, him as much as her. I've got to slap it together and get to work. Go back to sleep.'

He dropped back on the pillows when she jumped out of bed and dashed toward the bath. 'Right. That'll happen.'

She was smart enough to get in and out of the shower in a blink, knowing he might try to talk them both into a quick water game. She was shutting the door on the drying tube when he came in.

'She wants pictures,' he said. 'Pictures of her family. Can you get some for her?'

'I'll take care of it. Gotta check some things in my office,' she added. 'See if anything came in while we slept. Then I've got to get back downtown.'

'I'll check the search results for you before you go – on the condition you have some breakfast.'

She watched him – the man had the best ass on the planet – step into the shower. 'Get something in the office.' She stepped out of the tube, combed her fingers through her hair as she reached for a robe. 'Update you in there if you want.'

'I'll come up as soon as I'm dressed. We'll have some breakfast while you do.'

251

'Deal.' She went into the bedroom, pulled out some underwear, grabbed some trousers, reached for a shirt. She was pulling it on when the in-house 'link beeped.

'Video off. What?'

'As you're up, Nixie would like a word with you,' Summerset said. 'I'm heading to my office in a minute.'

'As none of you has had breakfast, perhaps she could join you.'

Put me right in that corner, Eve thought with a snarl for the 'link. 'I'm still—'

'I can program coffee.' Nixie's voice piped through. 'I know how.'

'Okay, fine, sure. Do that. I'll be there in a minute.'

She buttoned the shirt, pulled on her boots, and muttered to herself about having to have conversations with witnesses before she'd had her coffee. Sex might've given her a charge, cleared the cobwebs, but no. Kid's got to start nagging at her before she's out of the damn bed.

She strapped on her weapon harness, strode to the closet for a jacket. She had work to do, damn it. Serious, concentrated work, and what was going to happen? The kid was going to start out the day with one of those long, soulful looks. And she'd have to tell her for the umpteenth time that no, she hadn't caught the murdering bastards who'd slaughtered her family.

'Oh fucking shit!'

The murder board, Eve thought, standing in plain sight in her office. She streaked out of the room, swung into the one Nixie was using. When she found it empty, she charged toward her office.

Still in her pink pajamas, the child stood, staring at the stark images of murder and death. Cursing herself, cursing Summerset, Eve strode across the room, put herself directly between Nixie and the board.

'This isn't for you.'

'I saw them before. I saw them for real. My mom and dad. I saw them before. You said I could see them again.'

'Not like this.' Her eyes were huge, Eve thought. So big in her face it seemed they'd swallow it whole.

'It's my mom and dad. They're not yours.' She tried to push pass Eve.

Going with instinct, Eve hauled Nixie up, turned around. 'It doesn't help to see them like that. It doesn't help them or you.'

'Why do you then?' Nixie pushed, shoved. Kicked. 'Why do you have pictures of them? Why do you get to look at them?'

'Because it's my job. That's it. You have to deal with that. Stop it. I said stop! Look at me.' When Nixie went limp, Eve tightened her grip. She wished desperately for Roarke, for Peabody, even – God – for Summerset. Then she fell back on training. She knew how to handle the survivor of violent death.

'Look at me, Nixie.' She waited until the child lifted her head, until those drenched eyes met hers. 'You want to be mad, *be* mad. They stole your family from you. Be pissed off. Be sad and sorry and outraged. They had no right. The bastards had no right to do this.'

Nixie trembled a little. 'But they did.'

'But they did. And last night, they killed two men I knew, men who worked for me. So I'm pissed off, too.'

'Will you kill them now? When you find them, will you kill the bastards because they killed your friends?'

'I'll want to. Part of me will want to, but that's not the job. Unless my life or someone else's life is in danger, if I kill them because I'm just pissed off and sad and sorry, it puts me in the same place as them. You have to leave this to me.'

'If they try to kill me, will you kill them first?'

'Yes.'

Nixie looked into Eve's eyes, nodded gravely. 'I can do the coffee. I know how.'

'That'd be good. I take mine black.'

When Nixie went into the kitchen, Eve grabbed the blanket off her sleep chair, tossed it over the board. Then she pressed her hands to her face.

The day, she thought, was already sucking large.

13

'That was just weird.' Eve went straight to her desk to check any incomings the minute Roarke poured the last of the coffee from the pot into his cup before he rose. 'Spending twenty minutes over breakfast is considered fairly normal in some primitive societies.'

'And now I'm behind.' She scanned the ME reports on Knight and Preston, the preliminaries on the security and electronics on the safe house. 'I've got to get out of here.'

'Let me see what I've got for you first.'

'Roarke? She saw the board.'

'Bloody hell. When—'

'I told Summerset to send her up, so I can't even blame him. I wasn't thinking – was just a little annoyed that I was going to have to deal with her before I got to work. And then—' She shook her head. 'By the time I thought of it, hauled ass up here, it was too late.'

He set the coffee down, forgot it. 'How did she handle it?'

'She's got more spine than you'd expect from a kid. But she's not going to forget it – ever. I'll need to tell Mira.' With no other target handy, she kicked her desk. 'Shit, shit,

shit! How could I be that stupid?' No need to ask how Eve was handling it, he thought. 'It's not your fault, or not exclusively. It's on all of us. We're not used to having a child in the house. I didn't think of it either. She might have wandered in here last night when she was coming up to see me. I never gave it a thought.'

'We're supposed to be smarter than this, aren't we? You know, responsible?'

'I suppose we are.' And he wondered just how hard he'd be kicking himself if Nixie had come through Eve's office to come to him the night before. 'Still it is a bit like diving straight into the pool without learning first how to swim a bloody stroke.'

'We need to get her with the Dysons, with people who know what they're doing with a nine-year-old girl. She's already got a cargo ship of issues she'll have to work through. I don't want to add to them.'

'You'll want them here and that's fine,' he said before she could speak. 'The sooner the better, I'd say, for her sake.'

'I'll put a call through to them, ask them to meet me at Central.'

'Let me get you the search results from last night.'

He moved into his office, called for the results on screen and on disc. 'Nineteen names,' he mused. 'More than you might expect, I'd think. Natural causes would cut that back considerably, but . . .'

'A lot of names.' She turned to study the wall screen. 'Five that cross with both of them. The Swishers weren't the first,' she said again. 'No way I buy that. I'll take these in, give them a run.'

'I can help you out in . . . later,' he decided when he checked the time. 'I'm behind myself. I've work I have to get to here, then I have some meetings in midtown starting at nine.'

'You said you'd work from here.'

'No, I said we'd argue about it this morning.' He reached out, skimmed a finger down her chin. 'My work can't stop any more than yours, Lieutenant – and if someone's paying attention, they might wonder why I'm hunkered down here when I should be out and about. I'll promise you to be careful, very. No unnecessary chances.'

'We might have different definitions of unnecessary chances.'

'Not so very much. Come here.'

'I am here.'

'A bit closer than that.' With a laugh he yanked her forward, into his arms. 'I'll worry about you, you worry about me.' He rubbed his cheek to hers. 'And we're even.'

'You let something happen to yourself, I'll kick your ass.'

'Ditto.'

Since she had to be satisfied with that, Eve fought the traffic downtown. Even the sky seemed more crowded this morning, jammed with sky trams and airbuses and the traffic copters that struggled to keep things moving.

However quicker they claimed it was to use the sky routes, she'd stick with the creep and stink of the streets.

257

She fought her way down Columbus and straight into a fresh log-jam caused by a glide-cart that had overturned into the street. A number of pedestrians were helping themselves to the tubes and food supplies that were rolling on the asphalt while the operator jumped up and down like a man on springs.

For a moment she regretted she didn't have the time to wade in to the potential riot. It would've been an entertaining way to start the day. Instead, she called the incident in, and solved her own commute dilemma by blasting her sirens – *wow!* look at those assholes scramble – and hit vertical mode.

Okay, she admitted, she loved her new ride.

She breezed over the jam – caught a glimpse of the glide-cart operator shaking a fist into the air – then settled back down three blocks south in relatively reasonable traffic.

She decided to trust auto long enough to make the calls on her list. She left messages for the Dysons, for Mira, reserved a conference room for ten, and left more voice mails for each member of the team she wanted in attendance.

And thought how much of this drone work she'd been able to avoid when Peabody had been her aide rather than her partner.

When she got to Central, there was Peabody right outside the bull pen, fit up against McNab like they were two pieces in some strange and perverted jigsaw puzzle.

'I actually had breakfast this morning.' Eve stopped beside them. 'This is the sort of thing that could make me boot.'

'Just kissing my sweetie good-bye,' Peabody said, and made exaggerated kissy noises against McNab's lips.

'Definitely booting material. This is a cop shop, not a sex club. Save it for after shift.'

'Still two minutes before shift.' McNab gave Peabody's butt a squeeze. 'See you later, She-Body.'

'Bye, Detective Stud.'

'Oh, please.' Eve pressed a hand to her uneasy belly. 'I want to keep the waffles down.'

'Waffles?' Peabody spun on the heels of her checked airskids. 'You had waffles. What's the occasion?'

'Just another day in Paradise. My office.'

'Tell me about the waffles,' Peabody begged as she scurried after Eve. 'Were they the kind with strawberries and whipped cream all over them, or the kind you just drown in syrup? I'm dieting, sort of. I had a low-cal nutridrink for breakfast. It's disgusting, but it won't expand my ass.'

'Peabody, I've observed – unwillingly and with considerable regret – that the person you have chosen to cohabitate with appears to have a nearly unnatural fondness for your ass.'

'Yeah.' She smiled, dreamily. 'He does, doesn't he?'

'So why – I ask unwillingly and with some regret – are you so obsessed with the size and shape of that particular part of your anatomy?'

'I've got the body type and metabolism that means I have to watch it or you'll be able to serve a five-course meal off the shelf of that particular part of my anatomy. It's a matter of pride. Not all of us are preordained to go through life skinny as a snake.'

'Now that we've cleared that up, I want coffee.'

She'd planned to wait a couple of beats, then give Peabody the Look of Destruction. But her partner moved directly to the AutoChef and programmed. 'I guess what happened last night with Knight and Preston got me and McNab both thinking, and just appreciating what we've got. Knowing what can happen sort of makes the moment more intense. He doesn't usually walk me to Division.'

She handed coffee to Eve, took one for herself. 'We just wanted a few minutes more.'

'Understood.' And because it was, Eve gestured to the chair before she leaned back against her desk. 'I left you a message, as well as leaving one for the rest of the team. Conference Room C, ten hundred. We'll brief, and hope Yancy's got a better picture of our suspects. Meanwhile, I have some names to be run. Potentials. Morris worked on Knight and Preston last night. Nothing new or unexpected there. Stun took them down, knife took them out. Tox was clear. I'm waiting for the lab to confirm that Preston's weapon was fired before he went down.'

'Hope he got off a good stream.'

'Ophelia said one of them was limping. I'd say Preston got some of his own in before the end. EDD doesn't give us anything new, but it establishes pattern. Let's see if we can find it again with any of the names on the list of people the Swishers knew who are now missing or dead.'

'I'll get started.'

'Your portion of the list is attached to the voice mail I sent you. You get any sort of a ring, I need to know.'

'I'm there.' She started out, paused. 'The waffles. Come on, Dallas, smothered in whipped cream or swimming in syrup?'

'Syrup, drowning.'

'Mmmmm.'

Peabody gave a little sigh and walked out. To satisfy her curiosity, Eve peered through the door and watched her go. She didn't think overmuch about female asses, but Peabody's looked fine to her.

She sat, called up her own list.

Brenegan, Jaynene, age 35 at TOD, February 10, 2055. Emergency care physician. Killed by multiple stab wounds in robbery attempt in parking lot of West Side Memorial Hospital. Suspect identified, apprehended, tested positive for Zeus. Currently serving twenty-five to life, Rikers.

Brenegan treated Coyle Swisher for a fractured arm — sports injury — and testified in Swisher's custody case Vemere v. Trent, May 2055, and Kirkendall v. Kirkendall, September 2053.

The addition was Roarke's, she noted. The guy was nothing if not thorough.

She'd take a look at Vemere and Trent and Kirkendall, and keep Brenegan on the active list for now. She was thorough, too.

Cruz, Pedro, age 72. Court reporter. Died of heart condition, October 22, 2058. Medical files confirm.

Cruz served as reporter in several of Swisher's trials in family court, and consulted Swisher regarding nutrition.

Unlikely, Eve decided, and bumped him down the list.

Hill, Lindi and Hester, ages 32 and 29 respectively. Same sex spouses. Died in a vehicular accident, August 2, 2057. Driver at fault, Fein, Kirk, charged with DWI, speeding, two counts of vehicular manslaughter. Serving term in Weitz Rehabilitation Complex.

Yeah, she thought, kill a couple of women because you're drunk and stupid and serve it out in a country club for ten years.

The Hills retained Swisher and Rangle to assist them in their plans to adopt a child. This was in process when they were killed. Both women also were clients of Keelie Swisher.

No motive, Eve thought, and crossed them off.

Mooreland, Amity, age 28 at TOD, May 17, 2059. Dancer. Killed by ex-cohabitation partner in rape/homicide. Lawrence, Jez, convicted. Serving life sentence, Attica.

Mooreland retained Swisher to terminate her cohabitation and to sue Lawrence for lost wages due to injuries. She consulted with Keelie Swisher on nutrition and health during her rehabilitation from injuries, and continued to consult until her death.

Lawrence, Jez, would bear another look. Mooreland stayed on the list. Moss, Thomas. Age 52 at TOD, September 6, 2057. Family Court judge. Killed, along with son, Moss, Evan, age 14, in car bomb explosion.

'Ring,' Eve mumbled.

Moss served as judge in several of Swisher's trials. His wife,

Suzanna, consulted Keelie Swisher. The homicide cases remain open.

'Computer, search and list all court cases wherein Swisher, Grant, served as attorney with Judge Thomas Moss presiding.'

```
Time frame for search?
```

'All cases.'

```
Acknowledged. Working . . .
```

She pushed up, paced. Car bomb. Not the same pattern, not up close and personal like a knife to the throat. But a military assassination technique. A terrorist tactic. So within the profile parameters.

Took a child out that time, too. By plan or circumstance?

She swung back to the computer, considering other health and medical types that might be on the list. Then pulled back. Her unit was going wonky, even though McNab had jury-rigged it. She didn't trust it to run complex multi-tasks.

'Dallas.' Peabody came to the door. 'I got a pop. I think. Social worker, attached to some of Swisher's cases. Strangled in her bed last year. Investigators looked hard at the boyfriend, they were having some trouble, but couldn't pin him. Case is still open. Her apartment showed no signs of forced entry. No sexual assault, no evidence of burglary. Manual strangulation. No trace evidence of anyone but the vic, the boyfriend, and a coworker, who were both alibied up.'

'Who worked it?'

'Ah . . .' She lifted her memo book. 'Detectives Howard and Little out of the six-two.'

'Tag them, get everything they've got. And check the vic's data. See if she was on one of Swisher's cases with a Judge Moss, Thomas, on the bench.'

'You got a pop, too.'

'It's looking that way.'

Search is complete.

Eve swung toward her screen. 'Display. Okay, Moss and Swisher had a lot of business together. We'll cross these with your vic. What's the name?'

'Karin Duberry, age 35 at TOD, single, no children.'

'Lieutenant? Sorry.' One of her detectives moved into the doorway. 'You've got a couple of visitors. A Mrs Dyson and a lawyer.'

Eve scooped up her hair. She was running hot, she thought, but couldn't put this off. 'Put them in the lounge. I'll be there. Peabody, do the cross. Work that list for names that have the kind of training or connections we're looking for. I'll be back as soon as I've dealt with this.' She called Mira's office, left a message with her admin when told the doctor was in session. Grinding her teeth, Eve decided she'd have to handle this one alone.

She found Dyson in what the Central cops lovingly – or sarcastically – called the lounge. It was a step up from the Eatery as far as the noise factor, and a step down on the food choices. Which, given the Eatery, wasn't saying much.

Dyson sat at one of the round tables, her head bent close to Dave Rangle's. Both of them looked as if they'd seen much better days.

'Mrs Dyson, Mr Rangle. I appreciate you making the time to come in.'

Jenny Dyson sat up, sat straight. 'I had planned to come today, before I got your message. I'd like to ask you first if there's any progress in the investigation.'

'We have what we believe may be a couple of good leads. We're pursuing them. In fact, Mr Rangle—'

'Dave,' he told her.

'Dave, if I could speak to you for a few moments when we're done here, I'd appreciate it.'

'Of course.'

Eve took a seat. 'Are you here as Mrs Dyson's legal representative or as Mr Swisher's partner?'

'Both. I'm aware, as you are, that Jenny and Matt were named as Coyle and Nixie's legal guardians should something happen to Grant and Keelie. I . . .' He shook his head. 'How's she doing? How's Nixie doing? Do you know?'

'She's dealing. She's being counseled. She's safe.'

'If you could somehow communicate to her that she's in my thoughts. Mine and everyone at the office. We—'

He broke off when Jenny laid a hand over his. 'I'll get to that later. We're here at this time to discuss the guardianship.'

'We can't take her,' Jenny blurted out.

'For her own safety and security, as well as the security of this investigation, I'd be unable to turn her over to you at this time. However—'

'Ever.'

'I'm sorry. What?'

'Jenny.' Dave spoke to her gently, and when his gaze came back to Eve's, it was full of sorrow and regret. 'Jenny has asked me to represent her in dissolving the guardianship. She and Matt feel unable to fulfill the terms. I've agreed to begin the process, and will file in Family Court today.'

'She has no one.'

'My child is dead.' Jenny's breath rushed out, rushed in. 'My baby is dead. My husband is devastated beyond any words I can use to tell you. We're burying her today, our Linnie, and I'm not sure he'll last through the service.'

'Mrs Dyson.'

'No. No! You listen.'

Her voice peaked up in a way that had other cops in the room glancing over, weighing the situation.

'We can't take her. It wasn't supposed to happen. If there'd been an accident, we would step in, we'd have taken Nixie and Coyle.'

'But it was murder, so you won't?'

'Lieutenant,' Dave began, and was silenced again.

'Can't. We're not capable of this. My baby is dead.' She

266

pressed both hands to her mouth. 'We loved Keelie and Grant, those children. We were almost like family.'

'The bits and pieces of family Nixie Swisher have left show no interest in providing for her welfare,' Eve put in. 'There was a reason you were named guardians.'

'Do you think I don't know that?' The words whipped out. 'That I feel nothing for that child, even through my own grief? Part of me wants to go to her, take her in my arms, and hold onto her. In that part of me, my arms ache to hold her. But the other part can barely say her name. Can't bear the thought of seeing her, of touching her.'

Tears slid down her cheeks. 'Part of me can't stop thinking it should have been her, and not my child. It should have been her we're burying today and not my Linnie. I may hate that part of myself, Lieutenant, but it's there.' She let out a shuddering breath. 'It's always going to be there. I'll never be able to look at her without wondering why, without wishing. And my husband . . . I think it would drive him mad.'

'Nothing that happened that night is her fault.'

'Oh, I know it. I know it. But I wonder how long, if I did what Keelie and Grant asked, it would take for me to have her blaming herself. I have to go.' She pushed to her feet. 'My husband needs me.'

'Jenny, if you could give me a few minutes with the lieutenant.'

'Take all the time you need. I'll get myself home. I want to be alone right now. I just want to be by myself.'

'I don't know if she should be.' Dave made to rise as she hurried out. 'Hold on.' She took out her communicator, gave Dyson's name, the description, her current location, and requested a plainclothes team follow her to make sure she arrived home safely.

'She's a good person, Lieutenant. I know how this must seem to you, but it's costing her to walk away from this.'

'It should. Don't you Family Court suits stand for the rights of the child?'

'For the family — and for what's in the best interests. After talking with Jenny, after seeing Matt, I can't state that trying to hold them to their agreement is in Nixie's best interests.'

'You could hold off a few days, see if they change their mind.'

'I have to file the papers, at her request. But I can slow things down a little. And I will. But I can tell you, they won't change their minds. They're leaving the city after the funeral. They've already made arrangements to move upstate, with her family. Matt's been given a leave of absence, and she's closed her practice. It's . . .'

He lifted his hands, let them fall again as he sat back. 'The lives they had are destroyed. They may build another — I hope they do. But it won't ever be the same. Nixie's part of what they lost. They can't — won't — have that reminder. I'll do whatever I can for Nixie. I can probably swing temporary custody. I'll speak with the blood relative she has left, see if that's the right direction.'

'I'll need you to keep me apprised of any movement or progress in the resolution of her guardianship.'

'I will. My God, I'm sorry. Sick and sorry for everyone. Look, can I get you something? I need some water. Gotta pop a blocker. I've got a headache coming on.'

Don't we all, she thought. 'No, I'm good. Go ahead.'

He rose, went to Vending for a bottle of water. When he returned, he popped a small pill, washed it down.

'Lieutenant, the Dysons are good people. It's costing Jenny to walk away from Nixie, from the promise she gave to people she loved. She's never going to forgive herself for it, but she just doesn't have anything left. And Matt, he's broken to pieces. I'm not having an easy time holding it together myself.'

'I need you to do just that. I need to ask you about some of Grant Swisher's cases.'

'Anything I can tell you.' He drank more water, capped the bottle off. 'If I can't, Sade can. She's got a brain like a motherboard.'

'Cases where Judge T. Moss presided.'

'Judge Moss? He was killed some years ago. Horrible tragedy. His boy, too. Car bomb. They never caught who did it.'

'I'm aware of that. Can you remember any cases, anything that stands out where Swisher was attorney of record, Moss on the bench, and a caseworker named Karin Duberry was involved?'

'Duberry.' He rubbed the back of his neck as he concentrated. 'Something vaguely familiar, but I don't know anybody by that name. Hold on.'

He reached for his pocket 'link. Within seconds, Sade was on-screen. 'Did Grant work with a CPS rep, Karin Duberry?'

'The one who was strangled last year?'

'I don't—' He looked toward Eve, got a nod. 'Yeah.'

'Sure. They were on cases – same side and opposing. Why?'

'How about both of them going before Judge Moss?'

'Had to, I'd think. Odds in favor. What's the deal, Dave?'

'I don't know.'

'Mind?' Eve asked, and before he could answer took the 'link herself. 'Lieutenant Dallas. Do you remember any threats by any participant in a case where Moss, Duberry, and Swisher were all involved?'

'Nothing springs. You've got copies of the case files. There'd be notes. Jesus, these are connected? You think the people who killed Grant blew up Judge Moss, killed the caseworker?'

'I'm looking into it. I'll need you available if I need to talk to you again.'

'You can count on it.'

Eve handed the 'link back.

'Thanks, Sade. I'll pick you up at two-thirty.' He shut off the 'link. 'We're going to the funeral together. Look, Lieutenant, I can go over the case files myself. See if any of them bring back any coffee-break chatter. Grant and I bitched to each other plenty. You know, partners.'

'Yes, I know partners. If you think of anything, get in touch.'

'I will. I wondered, before I go . . . I wondered if you could give me an idea when I could hold the memorial? I thought as Grant's partner, as their friend, I'd make the arrangements. I'd want to talk to Nixie, make sure we do this in a way that makes it as easy for her as possible.'

'You need to hold off awhile. I can't allow her to attend a memorial until we're satisfied she's no longer in any jeopardy.'

'All right, but could you just . . .' He lifted his briefcase, opened it. 'This is the picture Grant kept on his desk. I think she'd want it.'

Eve looked down at the four smiling faces, the family grouped together in what seemed to be a casual photograph at the beach. The father's arm slung around the son's shoulder – the hand reaching to lay on the wife's, his other drawing his daughter back to him. The mother with her arm around the son's waist – fingers hooked in the belt loops of her husband's jeans. Her other hand holding her daughter's.

Happy, she thought, carefree summer day.

'I took it, actually. It was one of those weekends at their beach place. I remember I said, "Hey, let me try out my new camera. You guys get together." They moved together just like that. Big smiles.' He cleared his throat. 'It was a good weekend, and Grant really loved that picture. Christ, I miss him.'

He broke off, shook his head. 'Nixie, I think Nixie would like to have it.'

'I'll make sure she gets it.'

When he left she sat there, looking at the summer moment, that frozen slice of careless family fun. They hadn't known there wouldn't be another summer.

What was it like to have that sort of bond? That sort of sunshine ease, as a family? To grow up knowing there were people there to lay an arm over your shoulder, reach for your hand. Keep you safe?

She'd never known that. Instead she'd grown up knowing there were people who would hurt you, just for the sport of it. Beat you, rape you, break you because you were weaker.

Until you got stronger, until there was that one mad moment when the knife was in your hand. And you used it until your skin, your face, your hands were slick with blood.

'Eve.'

She jolted, dropped the photograph, and stared up at Mira. Mira sat, turned the photograph around on the table to study it. 'A lovely family. Look at the body language. A loving and lovely family.'

'Not any more.'

'No, you're wrong. They'll always be a family, and moments like this one are what make that last. This will comfort Nixie.'

'Father's partner brought it in, along with Jenny Dyson. She and her husband are dissolving the guardianship. They won't take her.'

'Ah.' The sound came out as a sigh as Mira sat back. 'I was afraid of that.'

'You figured something like this?'

'Was afraid,' she repeated, 'that they might feel unable, unwilling to take Nixie into their home. She's too strong a reminder of their loss.'

'What the hell is she supposed to do now? End up in the system because some son of a bitch decided to massacre her family?'

Mira closed a hand over the fist Eve bunched on the table. 'It may very well be in Nixie's best interest to go into foster care, or with a relative, if possible. While she's a reminder of loss for the Dysons, they'd also be a reminder to her. She's still dealing with survivor's guilt, along with her shock, her grief, her fears.'

'Plunk her down with strangers, then spin the wheel,' Eve said bitterly. 'See if she gets lucky and gets somebody who actually gives a flying fuck, or isn't so lucky and gets one who's just in it for the fee.'

'She isn't you, Eve.'

'No, she by God isn't. Isn't even close. Maybe she's got it worse than I did.'

'How?'

'Because she had this.' Eve laid her hand on the photograph. 'And now she doesn't. You come from the bottom of the pit, there's no place but up. She's got a long way she can go down.'

'I'll help. As far as the process of placing her, finding the right family situation for her, I'll put my weight in. Yours wouldn't hurt either.'

'Yeah.' She leaned her head back, and for a moment, just

a moment, closed her eyes. 'I can't think about this now. We've got some leads that may pan out.'

'Was there something else you needed to speak with me about?'

'Need to walk and talk.' She rose, and told Mira about the incident with Nixie and the murder board.

'We'll talk about it in our next session.'

'Fine, good. I need to go harass Yancy about the composite.'

'Good luck.'

She could use some, Eve thought as she caught a glide. It was about time a little luck headed her way.

14

She found Yancy in a little glass box conference room in his sector, drinking station-house coffee with Ophelia. The LC wore the same feathers and paint as the night before. In the harsh lights she looked the way Eve had always thought carnies looked in daylight – a little worn, a little tawdry, and not particularly inviting.

But Yancy was chatting her up, flirting.

'So, asshole tells me he wants me to sing. Says it's the only way he can get the wood on. Wants me to sing "God Bless America." Can you dig it?'

'What did you do?'

'What you think? I sing. I got the tune okay, but I gotta make up the words mostly. Giving him a hand job, and he's singing with me, fixing the words. There we are, squeezed in a doorway, having ourselves a duet.'

'What happened?'

'He got up, got in, and round about the third time around the tune, got off. Got to be a regular after that. Every Tuesday night, we had ourselves a performance. I got me a red, white, and blue outfit, too. Give him a little more bang for his buck.'

'You see a lot of characters in your line of work.'

'Honey, you been on the stroll long as me, there's nothing you haven't seen. Why just last week—'

'Excuse me.' Eve's voice was hard as baked earth. 'Sorry to interrupt your chat, but I need to see Detective Yancy for a moment. Detective?'

'Be right back, Ophelia.'

'Oooh, she looks mean enough to chew rock and spit pebbles in your eye.' Voice low, Ophelia winked at Yancy. 'You watch that fine ass of yours.'

The minute they were outside, the door closed behind them, Eve tore in. 'What the hell are you doing? Drinking coffee, chatting about her exploits on the stroll.'

'I'm warming her up.'

'She had a bed, her meals, her entertainment, courtesy of the NYPSD. If you ask me, she's warm enough now to sweat. I need results, Detective, not amusing anecdotes for your case file.'

'I know what I'm doing, you don't. And if you're going to rip me a new one, wait until I'm finished.'

'I'll schedule that – as soon as you tell me when the hell you're going to be finished.'

'If I don't have something you can use in an hour, I'm not going to have it at all.'

'Do it. Get it. Bring it to Conference Room C.'

They turned their backs on each other. Eve walked away, ignoring the interested parties at desks and cubes.

When she arrived at the conference room herself, Peabody

was already there, setting up. At least she hadn't forgotten the duties of an aide. 'Got three names for you, Dallas, that fit the parameters of our profile.'

'At least somebody's doing what they're supposed to do today.'

Peabody preened a little as she arranged labeled discs. 'One still lives in the city, one is still on active and based at Fort Drum in Brooklyn. The last, is co-owner of a martial arts studio in Queens and has it listed as business and personal.'

'All still in New York. Handy. What was their deal with Swisher?'

'First one, retired sergeant, was a client – divorced with kids. Swisher got him a decent enough deal, at least when you're looking in from the outside. Reasonable split of marital property and assets, liberal visitation with minor children.'

'And where's the missus?'

'Westchester. Remarried. Spouse was the client with the second. Custody deal. She claimed emotional and physical abuse, and Swisher nailed him with it. Spouse got full custody and a stinging percentage of the guy's monthly as child support. She moved to Philadelphia, single-parent status.'

'Lost the wife and kiddies, and had to pay for it. That'll piss you off. The last?'

'Similar deal as the second, with the wife – Swisher's client – testifying under wraps. Regular and consistent abuse

277

claimed over a period of twelve years. Two minor children. Her documentation was shaky, but Swisher pulled it through. And she went into the wind.'

'She's missing?'

'No record of her or the kids the day after the court decided in her favor. I haven't got all the details yet, but it looks like she ran. Or—'

'He got to her. Any papers on her?'

'Sister filed a missing persons. Actively pursued. Sister and family moved to Nebraska.'

'Nebraska? Who lives in Nebraska?'

'Apparently they do.'

'Yeah, with the cows and sheep.'

'Parents live there, too. The missing woman and her sister's parents. Not the cows' and sheep's – though I'm sure there are lots of parental farm animals in Nebraska.'

The thought actually brought on a shudder. 'I don't like to think about those things. Cows banging each other in the field. Bizarre.'

'Well, if they don't, all we've got are manmade—'

'Don't go there. It's almost worse. Some science guy creating them in the lab.' Her voice darkened. 'One day they're going to make a mistake – a big one – and mutant clone cows are going to revolt and start eating people. You wait and see.'

'I saw this vid once where these clone pigs developed intelligence and started attacking people.'

'See?' She jabbed a finger in the air. 'From vid to reality

is one small, slippery step. I hope to Christ I don't have to go to Nebraska.'

'I've been there. It's actually very nice. Some good cities, and the countryside's interesting. All those cornfields.'

'Cornfields? Cornfields? Do you know what can hide in cornfields – what might be lurking in the corn? Have you thought about that?'

'No, but I will now.'

'Give me a nice dark alley. Okay.' She shook it off, looked at the murder board Peabody had set up for the briefing. 'We talk to all three of the guys you popped. We visit the investigators on the Duberry and the Judge Moss cases, and we review the missing-persons report and that case file. I want to talk to the primary on a robbery homicide. ER doc, taken out in the parking lot of her hospital. They got a guy for it, but she popped on this Kirkendall custody deal, too. We reinterview any witnesses to those cases, recanvass. And if we ever get a goddamn composite from Yancy, we find a match.'

'Yancy's sketches are gold,' Peabody reminded her. 'If he pulls a decent description out of the LC, we should be able to run it through the system, pop a name.'

'Step at a time.' She glanced over as Feeney walked in with McNab. She caught the suggestive look McNab sent Peabody, and tried to ignore it. They were in a cuddle stage of their relationship – new cohabs. She wasn't sure what it said about her to know she'd be relieved when they got back to sniping at each other.

'Put your hands, or your big, goofy mouth on my partner in this room, McNab, I'll rip those stupid hoops out of your ears so bloody strips of lobe fly around the room.'

In reflex, he lifted a hand to his ear and the quartet of bright blue hoops.

Feeney shook his head, spoke under his breath to Eve. 'Hornier now, you ask me, than before they moved in together. Wish they'd start swiping at each other like before. This shit's getting creepy.'

It was good, Eve thought, to have someone on the team who showed good sense. To show solidarity, she gave him a slap on one of his slouched shoulders.

When Baxter and Trueheart arrived, they got coffee, the updated files.

'Detective Yancy should be joining us shortly,' Eve began. 'If the wit comes through, we'll have faces. Meanwhile, we've found connections.' Using both the board and the screen, Eve briefed the team on the potential links between the Swishers and the two other victims.

'If this same person or persons killed or arranged to have killed Moss, Duberry, and the Swisher family, we can see by the time frame that these murders are not only carefully planned, but that the person or persons behind them are controlled, patient, careful. This is no psychopath on a spree, but a purposeful man on a mission. One with connections of his own, with skill and/or the money or resources to hire those with skill. He does not work alone, but as part of a well-honed team.'

'Cop killers,' Baxter said without any of his usual humor.

'Cop killers,' Eve confirmed. 'But the fact that they were cops was irrelevant. They were obstacles, nothing more.'

'But not collateral damage.' Trueheart looked surprised, even slightly embarrassed to realize he'd spoken aloud. 'What I mean, Lieutenant, is that Detectives Knight and Preston weren't bystanders or innocent victims from the killers' points of view. They were what I guess we could call enemy guards?'

'Agreed. This is a small, very personal war. With very specific objectives. One of those objectives has not been met. Nixie Swisher.' She brought the child's ID image on-screen.

'Given what we know, we can speculate that the survivor is no threat to them. She is a child, one who saw nothing that can lead to the identification of the individuals who killed the family. In any case, what she saw, what she knew, had already been reported. Her death gains nothing. It is probable they abducted Meredith Newman, likely they interrogated her, under duress, and gained the knowledge that the survivor knew nothing that would lead us to their identity.'

'But they don't give it a wash.' Baxter studied the child. 'They don't move on, consider it done. They put together another operation to try to find and eliminate her, and instead take down two cops.'

'The mission isn't complete, therefore the mission has not been successful. What did they want from the Swishers?'

'Their lives,' Baxter answered.

'Their family. The destruction of their family. You take mine, I'll take yours. So they continue to hunt the last remaining member, illustrating a need for completion, for perfection, for a fulfillment of the work. With the murder of Knight and Preston, a message was sent. They will engage the enemy, they will eliminate obstacles. They will complete their mission.'

'Hell they will,' Feeney voiced. 'Hell they will. Detective Peabody?' Peabody jolted, blinked at Eve. 'Sir?'

'Brief the rest of the team on the results of your recent search.'

'Ahhh.' She cleared her throat and rose. 'At Lieutenant Dallas's orders, I conducted a search for any individuals who fit our current profile who were involved in a trial or case that included Swisher, Moss, and Duberry. The search resulted in three individuals. The first, Donaldson, John Jay, Sergeant USMC, retired.'

She ordered image and data on-screen and relayed the details of the divorce case.

'Looks like a jarhead.' Baxter shrugged when Eve frowned at him. 'That's what my grandfather called marines. He was regular army during the Urbans.'

'You and Trueheart will take the jarhead. It's possible he wasn't satisfied with the court's decision. Peabody, next up.'

'Next is Glick, Viktor, Lieutenant Colonel, US Army, active and based at Fort Hamilton, Brooklyn.'

When Peabody finished the data, Eve gestured to Feeney. 'You and McNab up for some field work in Brooklyn?'

'Can do. I'm going to enjoy seeing what the army makes of our E-Division fashion plate.'

'Peabody and I will take the last. Peabody?'

'Kirkendall, Roger, Sergeant, US Army, retired.'

When the data was complete, she sat down with obvious relief.

'Kirkendall,' Eve continued, 'also has a connect to a Brenegan, Jaynene, who was stabbed to death in a parking lot outside the health center where she served as an ER doc. They got a guy for that, but it bears looking at. Baxter, reach out to the investigators on that. Let's see if anything rings.'

'You thinking they hired somebody to hit the doctor?'

'No. They're too smart to hire some junkie and leave him alive after. Just covering all the ground. We'll need clearance in order to acquire the full military records of these three individuals,' Eve added. 'Which, let's face it, isn't going to be a snap. I'll start fighting through the red tape there. Unless I get clear to handle it myself, I want you to talk to the primary on the Duberry case.'

She stopped when Yancy entered.

'Lieutenant.' He walked over, handed her a disc. 'As ordered.'

'Have a seat, Detective. Give us the rundown.'

She plugged in the disc herself, called up the images on two screens.

On each screen a nearly identical face appeared. Squared, tough, pale brows, close-cut hair. The lips were firm, noses sharply planed.

Ears close to the head, she noted. Eyes cold and pale. She judged them both to be early fifties.

'The witness was cooperative, and got a good, close-up look at both men. However, she, at least initially,' Yancy added with a flick of a glance at Eve, 'had trouble with details. Both men wore watch caps and sun shades which can be seen in the next sketch. But working with the witness, and adding probability of certain details, i.e, natural eye color, given the lightness of the brows, eye shape given the facial structure, we can assume.'

'How close an assumption?'

'Close as I can get. I ran probabilities on these, with the data received from the wit. It comes to ninety-six and change. I was also able to get full-length composites. The witness recalled the body types in detail. Next sketch.'

Now Eve studied two muscular, well-built men, wide at the shoulders, narrow at the hip. Both wore black – turtleneck-style shirt; loose, straight pants; jump boots – and carried bags cross-body. Yancy had added projected heights and weights.

Six foot one, and one-ninety to two hundred on suspect one, five foot eleven, same weight range on suspect two.

'You confident in these, Detective?'

'I am, yes, sir.'

'None of them match the men Peabody dug up,' McNab said. 'Body type's close enough on her first guy and her last, but the faces aren't.'

'No, they're not.' And that was a severe disappointment. 'But that doesn't preclude the possibility that these were soldiers – hirelings or under orders – and that one of the men we've found is in a command position. We'll put these images and the data through the system, see what we find.'

She hesitated briefly. 'You can take that, Yancy. You'd have the best eye for it.'

The rigor eased out of his shoulders. 'Sure.'

'Then let's get started. You do good work, Yancy, even when you're dealing with a pain in your ass.'

'Would that be my witness, sir, or you?'

'Take your choice.'

She walked it by Whitney first, compiling copies of all data along with her oral. 'I've done the first pass at both military branches for full disclosure of records, and as expected on first pass, request was denied. I'm working my way up with the second.'

'Leave that to me,' Whitney told her. He studied the sketches. 'You'd have to say brothers. The resemblance is too strong otherwise. Or your witness projected the resemblance.'

'Yancy was thorough. He's standing by the composites. Brothers isn't far out of reach, sir, considering the smoothness of the teamwork. Twins, as they appear to be, often have a close, almost preternatural bond.'

'We'll give them adjoining cages when you bring them in.'

Brothers they were, a unit of beliefs, desires, and training. Machines. Though they were human, though they ran on blood, humanity was lost in them.

The obsession of one was the obsession of the other.

They rose at the same hour every day, retired at the same hour in their identical rooms. They ate the same food, worshipped the same gods, in a sychronicity of discipline and objective.

They shared the same cold, harsh love for each other that each would have termed loyalty.

Now, as one worked, sweat streaming down his face while he executed punishing squats and lunges on his injured leg, the other sat at a command console, pale eyes tracking screens.

The room where they worked had no windows and a single door. It contained an emergency underground exit, and the capability for self-destruct should their security be compromised.

It was outfitted with enough supplies to last two men a full year. Once, they had planned to use it as both shelter and command post when the primary vision of the organization they both had served had been met, and the city above was in their hands.

Now, it was shelter and command post for a more personal vision. They had worked together for the larger cause for nearly a decade, and this more personal one for six years. They had seen the larger fractured, scattered. But the smaller, the personal, they would complete. Whatever the cost.

One stopped, sweat still dripping as he reached for a jug containing filtered water and electrolytes.

'How's the leg?' his brother asked.

'Eighty percent. A hundred by tomorrow. Bastard cop was fast.'

'Now he's dead. We'll terminate more, strike the other locations, but that can wait until we've hit the primary target.'

On one of the screens, Nixie's young face smiled out at the spartan room and the two men who wanted her life.

'They might have moved her out of the city.'

His brother shook his head. 'Dallas would want her close. All the probabilities indicate she's still in the city. Cops coming and going out of Dallas's home location, but the probabilities are low that she'd take the target there. But she'll be close.'

'We bring Dallas in, ascertain the target's location.'

'She'll be ready for it, waiting for it. We can't rush it. Roarke's security and intelligence may be as good as ours. It may be better. His pockets are deeper, even with our contingency funds.'

'They have nothing that leads to us. That gives us time. It would be a coup, the kind that would boost morale and bring the primary mission back in place, if Roarke's home location was breached, if he was terminated in his own bed, and the cop taken. We'd have the message needed to regroup our members, and the information needed to complete our mission here.'

The man at the console turned. 'We'll start on tactics.'

The martial arts studio in Queens was more of a palace, in Eve's opinion. Or a temple.

The entrance was decorated in a spare yet somehow

lustrous style – an Asian flavor with the Japanese sand gardens she'd never understood, gongs, the whiff of incense, a glossy red ceiling against cool, white walls and floor.

Tables were low, and the seats were red cushions decorated in gold thread that formed symbols.

Doorways were the papery screens she'd seen in Asian restaurants. The woman who sat cross-legged on a cushion by a neat and tiny workstation nodded, placed the palms of her hands together, and bowed.

'How can I serve you?'

She wore a red robe with a black dragon flying across the bottom. Her head was shaved clean, the shape of her skull somehow as tidy and lustrous as the room.

'Roger Kirkendall.' Eve showed her badge.

She smiled, showing white, even teeth. 'I'm sorry, Mr Kirkendall isn't with us. May I inquire as to the nature of your business?'

'No. Where is he?'

'I believe Mr Kirkendall is traveling.' Despite the clipped response, the woman's tone never altered. 'Perhaps you'd like to speak with Mr Lu, his partner. Should I inform Mr Lu that you'd like to speak with him?'

'Do that.' She turned, rescanned the room. 'Pretty kicked for a dojo. Must do a hell of a business. Not bad for former Army.'

'Mr Lu will come out and escort you. May I serve you some refreshments? Green tea, spring water?'

'No, we're good. How long have you worked here?'

'I've been employed in this capacity for three years.'

'So you know Kirkendall.'

'I have not had the pleasure of meeting him.'

One of the screens slid open. The man who came out wore a black gi, with the black belt around it scored in a way that told Eve he was a master.

He was no more than five-eight in his bare feet. Like the woman, his head was hairless. And like her, he put his palms together and bowed. 'You are welcome here. You inquire about Mr Kirkendall. Do you require privacy?'

'Never hurts.'

'Please, then.' He gestured to the opening. 'We will speak in my office. I am Lu,' he told them as he escorted them down a narrow white hallway.

'Dallas, Lieutenant. Peabody, Detective. NYPSD. What are these rooms?'

'We offer privacy rooms for meditation.' He bowed to a white-robed man who carried a white pot of tea and two handleless cups on a tray.

Eve watched the man slip through one of the sliding screens and close it behind him.

She caught the sounds of hand-to-hand ahead. The slap of flesh, the thud of bodies, the hiss of breath. Saying nothing, she moved passed Lu and walked to another opening.

The studio spread out, in sections. In one she saw a class of six executing the sharp, silent movements of an elaborate and graceful kata. In another, several students of various ranks fought under the supervision of another black belt.

'We instruct in tai chi, karate, tai kwon do, aikido,' Lu began. 'Other forms and methods as well. We offer instruction to novices and continuing instruction and practice to the experienced.'

'You offer anything but tea and meditation in those privacy room?'

'Yes. We offer spring water.' He neither smiled nor seemed insulted by the question. 'If you would like to examine one of our meditation rooms, not currently in use, I would only request you remove your boots before entering.'

'We'll leave that for now.'

He led her through another doorway, into a small, efficient, and attractive office. More low tables and cushions. Painted screens on the walls, a single white orchid bowing out of a red pot.

His desk space was stringently ordered with its compact d and c unit and a miniature 'link.

'Would you care to sit?'

'Standing's fine. I need to speak with Kirkendall.'

'He's traveling.'

'Where?'

'I can't tell you. He is, to my knowledge, traveling extensively.'

'You don't know how to reach your partner?'

'I'm afraid I don't. Is there a problem that involves my business?'

'He lists this as his address on his official data.'

'He does not live at this address.' Lu's voice remained smooth and untroubled. 'There is no residence here. I fear there is some mistake.'

'When's the last time you spoke with him?'

'Six years ago.'

'Six years? You haven't spoken with your partner in six years.'

'That is correct. Mr Kirkendall approached me with a business opportunity that I found interesting. At that time I owned a small dojo in Okinawa. I was afforded this by some success in tournaments and instructional discs.'

'Lu. The Dragon. I recognized you.'

There was the faintest of smiles, the slightest of bows. 'I am honored.'

'You kicked some serious ass. Three-time Olympic gold medalist, world record holder. They use some of your vids at the Academy.'

'You are interested in the art?'

'Yeah, especially when it's executed by a master. You were undefeated, Master Lu.'

'The gods favored me.'

'Your signature flying kick didn't hurt either.'

A gleam of humor brightened his eyes. 'It occasionally hurt my opponent.'

'Bet. What business opportunity did Kirkendall bring to you?'

'Partnership, with considerable funds, this location, and

291

the freedom to operate this school personally. His money, my expertise and reputation. I accepted.'

'You don't consider it odd that he hasn't come to check up on you in six years?'

'He wished to travel and not to be encumbered by business. He is, I believe, eccentric.'

'How does he get his cut?'

'The business reports and figures are sent to him electronically, as is his share of the profits, which goes to an account in Zurich. I am sent confirmation of the receipt of these. Has there been some difficulty with the funds and their transfer?'

'Not that I'm aware of. That's it?' Eve asked. 'You don't speak with him at all, don't deal through an intermediary, a representative?'

'He was specific in his requirements for this arrangement. As it benefits me, and harms no one, I agreed to it.'

'I'm going to need the paperwork, the information on all e-transfers and communications.'

'I must ask the reason before I agree or refuse.'

'His name has come up during an investigation of several homicides.'

'But he is traveling.'

'Maybe, or maybe he's a lot closer to home. Peabody, show Lu the composites.'

Peabody took them out of her file bag, offered them. 'Mr Lu, do you recognize either of these men?'

'They appear to be twins. And no, they are not familiar to me.' The first sign of distress eked through his considerable calm. 'Who are they? What have they done?'

'They're wanted for questioning on seven murders, including two children.'

Lu drew in a breath. 'The tragedy, the family, a few days ago. I heard of it. Children. I have a child, Lieutenant. My wife, who greeted you, we have a child. He's four.' His eyes weren't calm now, nor did they show distress. They were simply cold. 'The media reports that this family was in their home, in their beds, sleeping. They were unarmed, they were defenseless. And the throats of these defenseless children were slashed. Is this truth?'

'Yes, it's truth.'

'There is no punishment that will balance this scale. Not even death.'

'Justice doesn't always balance the scale, Master Lu, but it's the best we have.'

'Yes.' He stood very still for a moment. 'You believe the man I call partner may be in some way involved with these deaths?'

'It's a possibility.'

'I will give you whatever you require. Do whatever can be done. A moment.' He moved to his desk, gave his unit several commands in what Eve took to be Japanese.

'When would Kirkendall expect to hear from you again, to receive a report or a payment?'

'Not until December, and the last quarter of this year.'

'Do you ever contact him otherwise? With a question, a problem?'

'It's not usual, but there has been the occasion.'

'Maybe we can work with that. I'd like to send someone from our E-Division in to do a scan on your unit, on any unit you might have used to send communication to Kirkendall.'

'Only this one, and you may send an officer. Or you may take it with you. I apologize that this will take a few moments. I have ordered all communications and transmissions since the beginning of the partnership.'

'No problem.' He was upset, Eve thought. Holding it in, but struggling with the emotion of realizing he may have done business, years of business, with a murderer. His cooperation could very well lead them to close the case.

'Master Lu.' She spoke with respect and his eyes lifted toward her. 'It takes more than skill – even the level of yours – it takes more than training and discipline to go undefeated, to accomplish what you have without once falling to an opponent. How did you do it?'

'Training, yes, skill developed through that training and through discipline – both physical and mental. Spiritual, if you will. And with that, instinct. Anticipation of the opponent and a belief that you can, indeed must, prevail.'

Now he smiled, quickly, charmingly. 'And I like to win.'

'Yeah.' Eve grinned back at him. 'Me, too.'

15

The shuttle trip to Philadelphia played hell with Roarke's schedule. He'd just have to put in some long hours, perhaps make a few out-of-town trips, to make up for it. It couldn't be helped.

He couldn't – wouldn't – discuss Nixie's situation, her custody, her life, via 'link or holo. In any case, he wanted a face-to-face with Leesa Corday, a personal meeting that would give him a sense of her rather than just straight background data.

His name had cleared the way, gotten him an immediate appointment with her. He imagined she thought he was considering putting her and her firm on retainer. That could be arranged.

It would be simple enough for him to throw some of his business her way as support for Nixie. Money had its uses, after all.

The firm had a strong reputation – he'd checked on that, as well. And while the nature of his business was unknown, he was given what he recognized as the VIP treatment as he was met in the black and silver lobby by Corday's assistant, whisked across the marble floor, and into a private elevator.

The assistant – young, male, in a conservative gray suit – offered him coffee, tea, beverages of any nature. Roarke imagined he'd been primed to arrange to have a trio of LCs deliver it – and anything else – should it be requested.

It was the sort of brown-nosing that irritated him.

Corday's office level was done in strong reds and frothy creams. Lots of translucent automatic doors and a single massive workstation manned by five more assistants.

He was shown through a set of doors into what he recognized as one of the power centers. Corday hadn't yet climbed to the corner office, but she was next in line.

And waiting for him, standing – strategic position – behind her L-shaped black desk, the city's skyline behind her.

Her ID photo had been a good one, reflective of the woman. He knew her to be thirty-eight. He knew where she had her hair styled and where she'd bought the black pinstriped suit she was wearing.

He knew she'd be financially able to hire good child care providers, to afford good schools. And if she needed a bit of incentive, he would offer to set up a trust fund for Nixie's care and education.

He was willing to negotiate.

She had an attractive, soft-featured face, which she sharpened with enhancements – discreet ones. Her hair was a quiet brown worn short, with a kind of triangle at the nape.

The suit showed off a good body as she came around

the desk to offer her hand and a welcoming smile. 'Mr Roarke. I hope your trip in was uneventful.'

'It was.'

'What can we offer you? Coffee?'

'Thanks, if you're having some.'

'David?' She turned away from the assistant, obviously expecting him to jump into action.

A point in her favor, in Roarke's opinion.

She gestured to a seating area, waited until he chose one of the wide, black chairs.

'I appreciate you seeing me on such short notice,' he began. 'It's my pleasure. Do you have other business in Philadelphia?'

'Not today.'

The assistant hurried over with a tray, the coffeepot, cups and saucers, a little bowl of sugar cubes, and a small pitcher of what might have been actual cream.

'Thank you, David. Hold my calls. Now, how would you like your coffee?'

'Just black, thanks. Ms. Corday, I'm aware your time is valuable.' Her smile was easy as she crossed her legs. 'I'm happy to invest as much of it as you need.'

'Appreciated.' He accepted the coffee, and cut through the amenities. 'I'm actually here on a personal matter. I'm here on behalf of your niece.'

Her eyes, as quiet a brown as her hair, met his. The brows above them lifted in puzzlement. 'My niece? I don't have a niece.'

'Nixie, your stepbrother's daughter.'

'My stepbrother? I assume you're speaking of . . .' He could almost see her flip through her files for a name. 'Grant. My father was married to his mother for a short time. I'm afraid I don't consider him my stepbrother.'

'Are you aware that he and his wife, and his son, were recently murdered?'

'No.' She set her coffee down. 'No. God, that's horrible. How?'

'In a home invasion. They were killed, along with a young girl who was spending the night with their daughter, with Nixie. Nixie wasn't in her bedroom, but in another part of the house, and survived.'

'I'm very, very sorry to hear this. Tremendously sorry. I did hear something in the media about these murders. I'm afraid I didn't put it together. I haven't seen or had contact with Grant in years. This is shocking.'

'I'm sorry to tell you this way, but my concern now is for Nixie.'

'I'm a little confused.' She shook her head, touched her fingers to the seed pearls at her throat. 'Did you know Grant?'

'I didn't, no. My involvement in all this happened after the murders.'

'I see.' Those quiet eyes sharpened. 'Your wife is with the NYPSD, isn't she?'

'She is, yes. This is her case.' He waited a beat, but she failed to ask what the status of that case might be. 'At the moment, Nixie is in an undisclosed location, in protective custody. She can't stay there indefinitely.'

'Surely Child Protection—'

'Your stepbrother and his wife named legal guardians, but circumstances prevent those guardians from fulfilling the agreement. As a result, this child has no one who knew her family, no one who had a connection with them, with her, to care for her. I'm here to ask you to consider doing so.'

'Me?' Her head snapped back as if he'd slapped her. 'That's impossible. Out of the question.'

'Ms. Corday, you're the closest thing she has to family on planet.'

'Hardly family.'

'All right, then. A connection to family. And her family was murdered, all but in front of her eyes. She's a child, grieving and frightened, and innocent.'

'And I'm sorry, truly sorry for what happened. But it's not my responsibility. She's not my responsibility.'

'Then whose?'

'There's a system in place for circumstances like this for a reason. Frankly, I don't understand your involvement, or why you'd come here expecting me to take on a child I've never even met.'

He knew when a deal had gone south, and when it was best to let it go. But he couldn't quite make himself. 'Your stepbrother—'

'Why do you insist on calling him that?' Irritation snapped in her voice. 'My father was hooked up with his mother for less than two years. I barely knew the man. I wasn't interested in knowing him, or his family.'

'She has no one.'

'That's not my fault.'

'No. It's the fault of the men who walked into her home, slit the throats of her parents, her brother, her young friend. So now she has no home.'

'Which is a tragedy,' Corday agreed, with no emotion. 'However, I'm not interested in stepping in to save the day – even for the possibility of Roarke Industries as a client, and I resent you coming here, pushing this on me.'

'So I see. You didn't even ask if she'd been hurt.'

'I don't care.' Anger, or perhaps just a hint of embarrassment colored her cheeks. 'I have my life, I have my career. If I wanted children, I'd have my own. I have no intention of fostering someone else's.'

'Then I've made a mistake.' He got to his feet. 'I've taken up too much of your time, and wasted my own.'

'Grant's mother booted my father out when I was ten, and she was just one of many. What possible reason would I have to take responsibility for his daughter?'

'Apparently none at all.'

He walked out, more angry with himself than with her.

Eve stepped out of the dojo, surveyed the street, eyes tracking over parked vehicles, pedestrians, street traffic.

'Odds are low they'd have been able to trail us here,' Peabody said from behind her. 'Even if they had the equipment, and the man power, to keep round-the-clock surveillance on Central, they'd have to be really good or really lucky to make our unit.'

'So far they've been really good and really lucky. We don't play the odds on this one.' She drew the scanner out of her pocket.

'That's not standard issue.'

'No, it's Roarke issue. Cop issue would be what they'd expect, and they could have planted any number of devices with that in mind.'

'Dallas, you make me feel all safe and snuggled. And hungry. There's a deli right next door.'

'I'm off delis for a while. I'll always wonder if somebody's getting a blow job in the back room, with the extra veggie hash.'

'Oh, well, thanks. Now I'm off delis, and I didn't have waffles this morning. Chinese place across the street. How about an egg roll?'

'Fine, just make it fast.'

She ran the scan for explosives, homing devices, while Peabody hot-footed it. She gave a shoulder roll – the light body armor irritated her – then slid into the car as Peabody dashed back across.

'Didn't have Pepsi.'

'What?' Eve stared at the take-out bag. 'Is this America? Have I crossed over into some dark continent, some alternate universe?'

'Sorry. Got you a lemon fizz.'

'It's just not right.' Eve pulled away from the curb. 'It should be illegal to run a food-service operation and not offer Pepsi.'

'Speaking of food-service operations, you know what Ophelia told me she's going to do with the reward?'

'If she gets it.'

'If. Anyway, she and the deli guy talked about going in together if she ever got enough scratch. So, with the reward, she'd be solid. They want to open a sex club.'

'Oh, like New York doesn't have enough of those.'

'Yeah, but a sex club deli. It's pretty innovative. Get your salami hard, get your hard salami, all in one venue.'

'Christ, I'm never eating in a deli again.'

'I think it might be interesting. Anyway.' Peabody popped a mini eggroll. 'You want me to tag Feeney, have him start trying to trace the transmissions?'

'No. I'll take that. Tag Baxter, tell him to prioritize the Brenegan case. And contact the commander, see if he's had any luck cutting through the red tape. Let him know Kirkendall is now prime, and we've got Baxter looking into a closed case that may connect. No, not the 'link,' she added. 'Let's mix up the communication devices. Use your personal for this. Then do a check with the rest of the team, using your communicator.'

'You think they might try to triangulate our location through communication?'

'I think we'll be careful.' Eve used the dash unit for Sade Tully's home address. Her next stop.

It was a modest building, easy walking distance to the law firm. No doorman, Eve noted. Average security. A scan of her badge got them through – and she imagined a couple of buzzes on various apartment intercoms would have done the same. In the narrow lobby, she pushed the button for Sade's floor and studied the setup.

Dual security cams – that may or may not have been working. Fire-door leading to stair access. There was another cam in the single elevator, and the standard set of them on opposite sides of Sade's floor.

The apartment door was fitted with an electronic peep and a sturdy police lock. Eve buzzed, saw the peep engage a few moments later. Locks snicked, and Sade opened the door.

'Has something happened? Oh, Jesus, did something happen to Dave?'

'No. Sorry to alarm you. Can we come in?'

'Yeah, yeah.' She pushed a hand through her hair. 'I guess I'm on edge. Getting myself together for Linnie's funeral. I've never been to one for a kid. You should never have to go to one for a kid. We closed the office for the day. Dave's going to pick me up soon.'

The apartment was pretty and bright, the trendy gel sofa done in shimmering shades of blue and green with a small eating area set up in front of a pair of windows framed with fabric. Inexpensive posters of some of the city's high-lights decorated the walls.

'Dave says you've got a good memory for names, for details.'

'That's why they pay me the big bucks. You want to sit?

Do you want . . . God, I don't know what I have. I haven't been to the market since . . .'

'It's all right, we're fine.' Peabody went into comfort mode. 'This is a nice place. Great sofa.'

'I like it. I mean the whole shot. It's a quiet building, close to work. And when I want to play, I can scoot half a block to the subway and head toward the action.'

'Full apartment in this neighborhood doesn't come cheap,' Eve commented.

'No. I have a roommate. Had,' she corrected. 'Jilly's a flight attendant – handles the New York to Vegas II route, mostly. She's gone so much we don't get in each other's way, or on each other's nerves.'

'Had?' Eve prompted.

'She got in touch a couple of days ago. She's going to base on Vegas II now, so . . .' Sade shrugged. 'No big for me. I can handle the rent now on my salary. Grant and Dave – hell. Dave's not stingy. I've gotten raises along the way.'

She looked down at herself. 'Do you think this is the right thing to wear? Maybe it's too morbid. Black suit. I mean, a funeral's morbid, but maybe—'

'I think it's very appropriate,' Peabody told her. 'Respectful.'

'Okay. Okay. I know it's a stupid thing to worry about. Why the hell should they care what I'm wearing when . . . I'm going to get some water. Do you want any water?'

'No, go ahead.' But Eve rose, wandered toward the trim galley kitchen. 'Sade, do you remember a case Grant worked on? Kirkendall. His client was Dian.'

'Give me a sec.' She got a bottle of water from a mini-friggie, leaned back on the lipstick-red counter. 'Divorce and custody deal. Guy used to knock her around. Army guy – well, he was retired army by then. But one mean son of a bitch. They had a couple of kids – boy and girl. Dian finally got her butt in gear when he started on the kids. Well, not straight off.'

She opened the bottle, sipped thoughtfully. 'Seems he ran the show like he was the general. More the tyrant. Schedules, orders, discipline. Had the three of them pretty well cowed. She went into a shelter, finally, and one of the people who ran it recommended our firm. Woman was terrified, seriously terrified. We see that sometimes. Too many times.'

'The court ruled in her favor.'

'All the way. Grant worked hard on that case.' Her eyes went shiny, and she paused to take a long drink, fight back the tears. 'She'd screwed herself pretty good along the way, a lot of them do. Not calling the cops, or telling them that there was no trouble if somebody else called them. Going to various health clinics so she wouldn't send up a red flag. But Grant, he put a lot of hours in – pro bono, too – finding doctors, health techs, getting psych evals. The guy had some slick lawyers. Tried to make it like Dian was unstable, that her injuries were both self-induced and a result of affairs with abusive men. It didn't wash, especially when Grant put Jaynene on the stand.'

'Jaynene Brenegan?'

'Yeah.' Sade frowned. 'You knew her?'

'Why was her testimony important?'

'Trauma expert – and she just blew the bastard's lawyers out of the water. Made it clear that her exam of Dian showed consistent and long-term physical abuse, impossible to self-inflict. They couldn't shake her, and it was one of the things that really turned the tide. She was killed two, no, must be three years ago now. Some goddamn junkie knifed her after her shift. Bastard claimed he found her dead, just helped himself to her money, but they slapped his ass away.'

'Dian Kirkendall got full custody.'

'Right, with him getting monthly supervised visits. He never got the chance to make one. She whiffed a day or two later. Grant was sick about it, we all were. Worried he might have gotten to her somehow.'

'You believed he might've done her violence.'

'Grant did. Cops never found a trace of her, or the kids.'

'Did Kirkendall make any threats to her, or to Grant?'

'He was too cool for that. Like arctic. Never broke a sweat, never said a word that you could construe as threatening. But believe me, you could see he had it in him.'

Eve nodded to Peabody who drew the sketches out of her bag. 'Do you recognize these men?'

Sade set the bottle down, took a good long look. 'No. And I'd remember if I'd seen them. Scary. Are these the men who—' She broke off. 'Kirkendall? You think he had something to do with what happened to Grant and his family? That bastard son of a bitch!'

'We have questions we'd like to ask him.'

'He could have done it,' she said softly. 'He's capable. You know how you see someone, or brush up against them on the street, and everything in you freezes? That's the thing with him. Makes your blood run cold. But, Jesus, it was so long ago. It was years ago. I'd just started with the firm, was living in this one-room box up on One Hundred and Seventh.'

'We're checking several leads,' Eve said. 'Thanks for the details on this. Oh, just curious. How'd you find this place, the roommate?'

'They found me, basically. I met Jilly at this club I used to hang at. Friend of a friend of a friend sort of thing. We hit it off. Then she told me she had this place, was looking for a roommate since she was away so much. Just wanted somebody there, you know, so it wasn't empty half the time. I snapped it.'

'And this was after the trial?'

'Right after, now that you mention it. Just a couple of weeks.' Sade's hand trembled a little as she reached for her water. 'Why?'

'Did you ever talk with Jilly about work? About cases? Details.'

'Nothing confidential, but yeah. Oh shit, yeah. Just the broad strokes of something hot or funny. I talked about the Kirkendall case – no names. Just about how hard Grant worked on it, how much he'd wanted to get what was right for this poor woman and her kids. Oh God, oh God. But we lived here together, for six years. Almost six years.'

'I'd like her full name.'

'Jilly Isenberry,' Sade said dully. 'She went with me to Grant's place. I don't know how many times. She went to parties there, to barbecues. She had dinner at their table. I got in touch with her when this happened, and she cried. She cried, but she's not coming back. I took her into their home.'

'You're not responsible. This may be nothing, but if it's not, you're still not responsible. What you've just told us may help us find the people who are.'

Eve stepped back, drew Sade out of the kitchen. 'Sit down. Tell us more about her.'

'Sharp-looking woman,' Peabody commented. She brought Jilly Isenberry's data and image up on the dash screen so Eve could see. 'Thirty-eight, mixed race, single. No marriage or cohab on record. Employed as flight attendant, Orbital Transportation, since 2053. Previous employment listed as – hoohaw—'

Eve, fighting traffic, only furrowed her brow. 'Hoohaw?'

'I think it's a military exclamation. Maybe. Which fits, as prior to her employment at Orbital, she was Corporal Isenberry, US Army. Put in twelve years. You'd think she'd make more than corporal in a dozen.'

'And you'd think a dozen years as a soldier would point her toward something other than serving drinks and passing out vids to yeehaws heading to the gambling world.'

'Yeehaws?'

'Another military term. We get the military records, you can bet she served with Kirkendall somewhere, sometime.'

'And that kind of coincidence—'

'Isn't. She didn't change her data, change her name, nothing. They thought they'd be gone by the time we got this far, *if* we ever got this far. We've got our who, we've got our why. Now we find the son of a bitch. Dallas,' she said into her communicator when it signalled.

'A legal adjutant for military services requests a meeting,' Whitney informed her. 'My office. ASAP.'

'Heading toward Central now, sir.'

Eve judged the traffic, the distance, then hit the sirens and went in hot. Peabody was still catching her breath when they caught the glide to Whitney's floor. 'Are my eyes back down where they belong? I don't like to go into a meeting when they're rolled up white. Looks bad.' For the hell of it, Eve gave her a thump on the back firm enough to have Peabody nearly wheeling off the glide. 'There. They're back.'

'I don't think that was funny. I don't think that was funny especially after you nearly killed us three times flying back here.'

'It was twice, and really, it was only maimed. People don't respect sirens in this city, that's the problem. They just keep *la, la, la,* when an emergency vehicle needs to get the hell where it's going.'

'The Rapid Cab you nearly creamed wasn't going *la, la, la.* It was more a scream of abject terror.'

'Yeah.' It made Eve smile to remember it. 'So he should've gotten the hell out of my way.' She bounced her shoulders a couple of times. 'You know, that little ride buzzed me up. Almost as good as coffee.'

They were passed straight into Whitney's office, where her commander and the rest of the team were already in place. Along with a holo-projection of a woman in dress whites.

Spruced up for it, Eve thought, but couldn't bother to be here in person. 'Lieutenant Dallas, Detective Peabody, Major Foyer, United States Armed Forces, legal branch. Major Foyer requires further incentive to release the full military records of the individuals we have requested.'

'Those records are the property of the US government,' Foyer said in clipped tones. 'We have a duty to protect the men and women who serve.'

'And we have a duty to protect the citizens of this city,' Eve put in. 'Information has come into my hands during the course of a multiple homicide investigation that leads me to believe Kirkendall, Roger, former sergeant, US Army, is involved.'

'Disclosure of this nature requires more than the belief of an officer in the civilian sector, Lieutenant. The Revised Patriot Act, section 3 implemented 2040, specifically—'

'Gives the government carte blanche to demand and receive personal data on any citizen, while secreting data on their own. I know how it works. However, when a member of the armed forces is under suspicion for acts against the government or its citizenry, those records can be turned over to both military and civilian authorities.'

'Your suspicions, Lieutenant, are not enough. Evidence—'

'Commander, with your permission?'

He raised his brow when Eve stepped toward his computer, then nodded.

Eve ordered the file on the Swishers. 'Images of victims, crime scene, on-screen.'

They flashed on, stark and bloody. 'He did that.'

'You believe—'

'I know,' Eve corrected. She ordered the images of Knight and Preston on screen. 'He did that. You trained him, but that's not on you. He twisted his training. But it's on you if you don't cooperate, if you don't assist this department, this investigation. If you hamper in any way our pursuit of Roger Kirkendall, then the next one he kills is on you.'

'Your evidence is far from conclusive at this stage of your investigation.'

'Let me give you some more. And since you look like a woman who does her job, not a lot of what I'm going to give you is news. He owns part of a successful business in Queens, but hasn't been seen by his partner in six years. Grant Swisher represented his wife in a custody suit – and won. Judge Moss, presiding, was assassinated, along with his fourteen-year-old son, in a car bomb two years ago. Karin Duberry, the case worker from Child Protection Services, was strangled in her apartment last year. I believe when I complete the investigation into the stabbing of the medical authority who testified for Mrs Kirkendall, we will find that Kirkendall was also responsible for this death.'

'Circumstantial.'

'Bullshit, Major. Jilly Isenberry, former corporal in the US Army, was until recently the roommate of Sade Tully, the paralegal in Swisher's office. Isenberry spent time in the Swisher home, was considered a friend. Isenberry arranged to meet Tully shortly after the Kirkendall trial, with the happy coincidence of a nice apartment within walking distance of Swisher's office. She, like Kirkendall, seems to travel a good deal. And I'll bet my next month's salary against yours that Kirkendall and Isenberry not only knew each other, but served together.'

'One moment, Lieutenant.' The holo vanished.

'Checking it now, aren't you? Tight-assed bitch.' Eve caught herself, turned to Whitney. 'I beg your pardon, Commander.'

'No need.'

'You've been busy,' Feeney said. 'Good going, kid.'

'We're rolling. We don't really need the military details at this point, but I'm not going to let her stonewall us. I want them.'

'Holes in the ER doc's case,' Baxter put in. 'If you're looking at them. Guy who went down for it claimed he found her that way, just decided to rob the body – and got himself busted with her wallet and personal effects before he got off the lot. Her blood all over him. But they never found the murder weapon.'

'Anything in his statement? He claim to see anything?'

'He was juiced. Had a homemade stunner in his pocket. No evidence vic was stunned. Already had a sheet. He'd gone down for illegals, and for assault, and for robbery. Cops find him a hundred feet from a dead body, dead body's possessions and blood on him, they didn't look elsewhere.'

'I want copies of the case file, the ME's report, the whole shot.'

'Already done.'

The holo shimmered back on. 'The records requested will be made available to you.'

'Add Isenberry's.'

'Along with former Corporal Isenberry's. These officers are no longer under military jurisdiction. If either or both are responsible for these deaths, I hope you get them.'

'Thank you, Major.' Whitney gave the holo a nod of acknowledgment. 'My department and the city of New York appreciate your help in this matter.'

'Commander. Lieutenant.' The holo faded away.

Whitney settled at his desk again. 'I'd like an update while we wait for the data.'

Eve ran through it for him, for the team.

'Patient isn't the word.' Baxter huffed out a breath. 'Patient's a cat at a mouse hole. This guy's like a spider who'll work for years to spin a web from the Bronx to the Bowery. Our retired USMC seemed clean. He was out of town the night of the Swisher murders. Golf tourney in Palm Springs. Transpo checked out, hotel, and he's got plenty of witnesses.'

'Ours was running night maneuver drills the night of.' McNab spread his hands. 'He's got a whole platoon to back

313

him up. Maybe they had solids because they needed to cover, but they seemed straight.'

'This is our man.' Again, Eve called on Whitney's computer, and brought Kirkendall's image on-screen. 'Swisher helped cost him his wife and kids. And that wife, those kids, went missing directly after the trial.'

'He got them.'

'Maybe. Maybe. But then why spend years planning and executing the assassinations of those he blamed for the loss? Payback maybe, for the time and trouble, but if you got them back, or punished them, why plant a cohort with Swisher's paralegal? For six years.'

'Because they got away from him,' Peabody put in. 'Whiffed. Vanished.'

'I'm thinking they did just that. She probably planned to go, no matter how the trial came out. So that's a pisser. She not only gets custody, she gets away, with his kids. He loses his control over them. So, plant somebody with Tully, and maybe she talks about where they went. Except she didn't know, she figures they're dead. Only thing left to do is take out the enemy. The people who went up against him, and won.'

'Data incoming.' Whitney checked his unit. He removed the images currently on-screen, replaced them with the new data.

'Eighteen years in,' Eve read. 'Went in a fresh young kid. Why didn't he do his twenty? Yeah, yeah, there it is. Special Forces, covert ops. Grade-five rating.'

'That would be termination grade.' Baxter lifted a shoulder. 'My grandfather does a lot of yapping about this stuff. Non-wartime termination level. Means you can off somebody outside of a declared situation. You can be ordered to assassinate targets.'

'Continue, Lieutenant. Split screen, Isenberry data.'

'They served together. Based in the same unit in Baghdad. He's listed as her sergeant during her covert training. Bet they were good pals. War buddies. Jilly and the good old Sarge. They both stepped out of uniform about the same time, too.'

'They both have a couple of conducts not becoming,' Feeney pointed out.

'Dallas,' Peabody interrupted. 'There are no siblings listed under Kirkendall's data. No male cousins.'

'We'll need to study this further. I have to see what Yancy's got for us, and I've got a meet.' Eve checked her wrist unit. 'Feeney, I've got the go-ahead from Tully for EDD to check all her communication equipment at home. Off chance Isenberry might have used it to contact someone involved in this. Also, I've requested an expert consultant, civilian, to work on other electronic traces.'

'If it's your usual ECC, no objections.'

'Baxter, Trueheart, Linnie Dyson's funeral is starting shortly. Attend as reps from the department and keep your eyes peeled.'

'Kid's burial.' Baxter shook his head. 'We get the choice assignments.'

★　　★　　★

'Nothing,' Yancy told her. 'Nothing above a seventy-two percent match, so far. I've got another hour or two to run, but I've gone through IRCCA – so no criminal matchups.'

'We've got cooperation from the military. Request Whitney contact them re doing a search for a match with members of any of Kirkendall's units during his stint. Guys with the same training as his. Ah, start with the inactive and retired. These two don't have time to answer reveille.'

'Okay. But I've been thinking. Doing this sort of search gives you plenty of time to think, to speculate. Look at these guys again.'

He brought them up on a secondary screen. 'These faces are close. Twin close.'

'We've agreed on that. Most likely brothers, but Kirkendall's got no bro. Hirelings maybe.' But she didn't like it. Where was the rush if you paid someone to do the job?

'Well, thinking twins, identical faces – but not identical heights. That's not a stretch, but what don't you see when you look at them?'

'Humanity.'

'Besides. I spend most of my time with faces. What you don't see, Dallas, are lines or scars, bumps, flaws. You said they'd had strong physical training, most probably military. Seen action. But you don't see action on their faces. You don't see wear. She'd have given it to me,' he said almost to himself. 'Ophelia would, because you nudge them along there instinctively. You want identifying marks when you can get them. But other than the one favoring his leg, they were perfect.'

'I considered droids, but the probability's low. Two of that caliber would cost, and it's difficult to program one for wet work, for covert and assassinations. That's why the military doesn't use them for intricate work.'

'I'm not thinking droids. I'm thinking sculpting, surgery. They could look so much alike, so unmarked and identical, if they paid for it.'

'Shit. Shit. The height, the weight of the first one runs with Kirkendall's data. The coloring's close.'

'The face isn't,' Yancy continued. 'But if he had it built up here . . .' He pulled out a copy of Kirkendall's ID photo and began to change it. 'Widen, square off the jaw, plane down the nose. Build up the lower lip. It would take a top guy, *mucho dinero,* but you could do it. I know the eyes don't match, but—'

'They were wearing shades, you were going with probables.'

'You can have the shape changed, too, and the color.'

'I got a friend changes her eye color as often as she does her underwear.' She paced away, paced back. 'It makes more sense to me. Why go through all the years of planning, the perfecting, the anticipation, then not be in on the kill?'

'If we're right, who's the other one?'

Eve studied the twin images. 'Good question.'

317

16

Leaves, going crisp, skittered across the sweep of the drive as Eve drove through the gates. New sets of possibilities, probabilities, and the action required for both circled in her mind.

'Wind's coming up,' Peabody observed. 'Rain's coming in.'

'Thank you for the forecast.'

'It's going to strip the trees. I always hate to see that happen. Then they're all naked out there, at least until we get the first snow.'

'You're that worried, maybe you and some of your Free-Ager relations can knit them some sweaters.'

'I'm better at weaving.' Peabody's voice remained placid while Eve parked in front of the house. 'Haven't hit the loom in a good long while, but I bet I could pick it up again. I should think about that, with Christmas right around the corner.'

'Oh, stop. It's fricking October.'

'Nearly November. I'm not going to let it get away from me this year. I've already started picking up gifts. Easier to afford it now because – hey, I made detective.'

'The fact of which you never forget to remind me, and anyone else within hearing.'

'I added time in due to being injured in the line. Still, I've cut it back to once or twice a week.' She climbed out, drew in a deep breath. 'Don't you love the way it smells?'

'What smells?'

'The air, Dallas. The it's-almost-November-and-the-rain's-rolling-in-on-the-city air. All brisk and damp. And you got those mums and asters going over there – just a little spicy. Makes me want to rake up a big pile of leaves and jump in them.'

That put a hitch in Eve's stride, enough for her to stop and stare. 'Christ' was all she could think of, and she strode to the door and in.

Summerset was there, the specter of the foyer, with his stark black suit and thin, disapproving face.

'I see you've decided to make an appearance.'

'Yeah. And for my next act I'll boot your ugly ass out of my way.'

'You brought a child into this home, who needs and expects some of your time and attention.'

'I brought a witness, minor, into this home, who needs and expects me to find out who killed her family. If you can't deal with her while I'm doing that, I'll bring in a child care droid to handle it.'

'Is that all she is to you?' His voice was a blade, edgy and slicing. 'Witness, minor. A droid has more feeling. She's a child, one who isn't through her first decade and who has endured unspeakable horror and suffered unspeakable loss. And you have to be manipulated into spending a few spare moments with her over the morning meal.'

'I know just what she's endured and suffered.' She matched him tone for tone, even as her fingers dug hard into the newel post. 'I'm the one who walked through the blood they left behind. So don't you get in my face on this. You son of a bitch.' She started up the stairs, stopped, looked down at him. 'She's not yours. You better remember that.'

Peabody stayed where she was a moment, breathing in air that was no longer brisk and damp but thick and seething. 'You were off.' She said it quietly, drawing Summerset's gaze to her. 'I make it a policy to stay out between the two of you. But you were off. Her mind's on that kid, one way or the other, every minute, every day.'

She crossed to the steps, followed Eve up.

Long, angry strides had carried Eve to her office and taken her on one turn around it when Peabody came in.

'Dallas—'

'Don't talk to me.'

'He was wrong. I'm going to say it.'

'Just don't talk to me for a minute.'

She had to burn it off – the rage, the insult, and the damning suspicion creeping under it that he was right.

She'd taken that step back, the step away necessary to maintain professional objectivity. She wouldn't apologize for it. But she'd taken another step back, a personal one. The one she needed to keep herself from projecting, from seeing too much of herself in the girl she needed to protect. Lost, alone, terrified, damaged.

It was different, different, different, Eve repeated to herself as she paced. As she yanked off her jacket, heaved it toward a chair. But the results, weren't they horribly the same?

They'd toss her into the system, as she'd been tossed. Maybe she'd get lucky. Maybe she wouldn't. And maybe she'd spend the rest of her life reliving what Summerset had called *the unspeakable* in nightmares.

She stepped to the window and, looking out, didn't see the leaves dancing in that rising wind, or the burnished fall color that was already fading toward November dull. She saw the face of the cop who'd stood over her hospital bed when she'd been eight.

Who hurt you? What's your name? Where's your mom and dad?

Give me the facts, she thought now. Give me some data so I can help you. I'm not going to feel too much, standing here over this broken kid, because I've got to do the job.

She closed her eyes a moment and pulled it back in. So did she have to do the job.

'Start running Kirkendall for known associates, for other family members,' she said without turning. 'Do the same on Isenberry. You get any who cross, we push it.'

'Yes, sir. Want coffee?'

'Yeah I want coffee, as I'm still among the living. Thanks.'

She turned just as Roarke came into the room. Something must have shown on her face still, as he stopped, frowned. 'What's wrong?'

'A pile of dead bodies at the morgue. Same old same old.'

'Eve.'

'Leave it, would you?'

He started to speak again, she could see the struggle. Then he gave a quick nod. 'All right. Where do I sign up for my assignment?'

'Gotcha covered right here. Suspect, Kirkendall, Roger, former army, rank of sergeant. Swisher repped the spouse in a custody suit, won. Presiding judge was hit a couple years back. Vehicular explosion device. CPS rep was strangled in her bed. Expert medical wit stabbed, and it looks like the asshole they pinched for it might have just been wrong place, wrong time.'

'Looks like you've got your man.'

'He's not in a cage yet. He co-owns a dojo in Queens. Flash place with Master Lu, his partner.'

'Lu the Dragon?'

'Yeah.' She was able to smile now, though it didn't quite move up into her eyes. 'Who says we've got nothing in common? You catch him wiping the floor with the Korean to take his third Olympic gold?'

'I did, yes. Front row.'

'Okay, not so much in common, as I caught it on a screen in a bar in Hell's Kitchen. Anyway, Lu comes up clean. He deals with Kirkendall through the magic of E. Sends required paperwork and profits electronically. Says he hasn't seen his partner in six years. I believe him.'

'And you'd like me to trace the transmissions and deposits.'

'Check. Lu's equipment's in your comp lab. Pickup officer confirmed its delivery.'

'I'll get started.' But he crossed to her first, stroked his fingers down her cheek. 'I don't like to see you sad.'

'I'll have a big, toothy smile on my face when I close this case.' He kissed her lightly. 'I'll hold you to that, Lieutenant.'

Discreetly, Peabody waited until he'd left before coming out with the coffee. 'You want me to set up on your secondary unit?'

'Yeah.' Eve took the coffee. 'I'm going to take a poke at Yancy's theory. If Kirkendall's had major face sculpting, wouldn't he trust – first – a military surgeon? Guy spends nearly twenty in, it doesn't seem like he'd go to a civilian.'

'That kind of change has to be recorded,' Peabody pointed out. 'You can't radically change your appearance without filing fresh ID. If Yancy's right, and he did, we wouldn't be looking for a surgeon on the up.'

'Covert ops, guys have work done. Temp and permanent. We'll see if he had any before, and who he trusted to do the job.'

She sat at her desk, called up Kirkendall's military data. And Mira walked in.

'I'm sorry to interrupt you.'

'Yeah, yeah, yeah.' Teeth set in frustration, Eve sat back, lifted her hands. 'What?'

'I need to speak with you regarding Nixie.'

'Look, you're in charge of her counseling. You want to do a session, pick your spot. As long as it's not in here.'

'We've had a session. She's having a difficult day.'

'She should get in line.'

'Eve.'

'I'm doing what I need to do.' Her earlier rage began to bubble back. 'And I can't do it if somebody's forever in my face telling me I've got to go pat the kid on the head and give her a there, there. I can't—'

'Lieutenant.'

Safely across the room, Peabody hunched her shoulders. It was the same tone her own mother used to stop any one of her children in their tracks.

'Fine. What? I'm listening. I'm all fricking ears.'

And *that,* Peabody thought as she slid down another inch in her chair, was the tone that would have resulted in immediate annihilation should she, or a sibling, have dared to use it.

'I hope you find it cathartic to take your frustration out on me.'

If she'd been sure no one would notice, Peabody would have chosen that point to slink out of the room.

'However,' Mira continued in a voice cool enough to scatter frost on the windows, 'we're discussing a child in our charge, not your poor manners.'

'Well, Jesus, I'm just—'

'Regarding that child,' Mira interrupted. 'She needs to see her family.'

'Her family's in the damn morgue.'

'I'm aware of that, and so is she. She needs to see them, to begin to say good-bye. You and I are both aware of the importance of this step with survivors. The stages of her grief require this.'

'I told her I'd fix it so she'd see them. But for Christ's sake, not like this. You want to take a kid to the morgue so that she can see her family pulled out of containment drawers?'

'Yes.'

'With their throats cut.'

Impatience rippled over Mira's face. 'I've spoken with ME Morris. There are ways, which you very well know, to treat wounds and injuries on the dead, to spare their loved ones. He's agreed to do so. It's not possible for her to attend any sort of service or memorial for her family until this case is closed and her safety is insured. She needs to see them.'

'I've got her here in lockdown for a reason.' Eve dragged her hands through her hair when Mira only stood, gaze cool and level. 'Okay, fine. I can get you secure transpo there and back. I'll need to coordinate it with Morris. We get her in the delivery door – no record, no ID scans. He clears the area so you can take her straight into a view room. Out the same way. It'll have to be quick. Ten minutes.'

'That's acceptable. She'll need you there.'

'Wait a minute, wait a minute.'

'Like it or not, you're her touchstone. You were there when she last saw them. You're the one she believes will find the people responsible. She needs you to be there in order to feel safe. We'll be ready to leave as soon as you arrange secure transportation.'

Eve sat, too stunned to work up a glare as Mira walked out.

She decided on Roarke's jet-copter. It would be fast, and it wasn't unusual for him to buzz off in it to a meeting. It meant she had to pull him away from the trace as she didn't trust anyone else to get them there and back without incident. Not only the crashing sort of incidents she tried not to obsess over when zipping along a couple hundred feet above street level, but the assault incident she was risking by following Mira's edict.

'Risks are minimal,' he told her as the copter landed gracefully on the lawn. 'We'll engage the privacy shields and the antiscan equipment. Even if they're watching, they wouldn't be able to jam – in the amount of time we'll need – to detect her on board.'

Eve frowned pessimistically at the sky that was beginning to bruise with Peabody's predicted rain. 'Maybe they'll just blow us out of the air.' He smiled at her dour tone. 'If you thought that a possibility, you wouldn't be sending her up.'

'Okay, no. I just want this the hell over with.'

'I'll be doing my own scans. I'll know if anyone's trying to track us or jam the equipment. We should be able to do this in thirty minutes. Not an appreciable delay in your schedule.'

'Then let's do it.' She signalled for Mira to bring Nixie out while Roarke exchanged a quick word with the pilot, then took the controls himself.

'I've never been in a copter,' Nixie said. 'It's mag.' But her hand crept over the seat, found Mira's.

Roarke looked over his shoulder, smiled at her. 'Ready?' When she nodded, he lifted off.

Smoother, Eve noted, than he did when she was the only passenger. He liked to cowboy it, bursts of speed, quick dips – just to make her crazy. But this time, he piloted the copter with the care and grace, despite the speed, of a man hauling precious cargo.

He'd think of that, she realized. The little things. Is that what she lacked, the ability to consider the compassionate, because she was so focused on brutality?

Trueheart played with her, Baxter joked with her. Peabody had no trouble finding the right words, the right tone. Summerset – frog-faced demon from hell – he was handling her overall care and feeding without a single bump.

And there was Roarke being Roarke – no matter what he said about the kid being scary and intimidating. He interacted with her as smoothly as he drove the damn copter.

And, Eve admitted, every time she got within five feet of the kid she wanted to walk the other way. She didn't know how to deal with the *entity* of a child. Just didn't have the instincts.

And just wasn't able to – bottom line – close out the horror of her own memories the kid pushed into her head.

She glanced down, saw Nixie watching her.

'Mira says they have to be in places that are cold.'

'Yeah.'

'But they don't feel cold any more, so it's okay.'

Eve started to nod, dismiss it. Jesus, she thought, give her *something*. 'Morris – Dr. Morris,' Eve corrected, 'has been taking care of them. There's nobody better than Dr. Morris. So yeah, it's okay.'

'Tracking us,' Roarke said softly and she swung around to him. 'What?'

'Tracking.' He tapped a gauge bisected with green and red lines. 'Or – more accurately – trying. Can't get a lock. Ah, that must be frustrating.'

She studied the dash gauges, tried to decipher the symbols. 'Can you track it back to source?'

'Possibly. I engaged the tracking equipment before we took off, so it's working on it. It's mobile, I can tell you that.'

'Ground or air?'

'Ground. Clever. They're attempting to clone my signal. And yes, detected me doing precisely the same to theirs. They've shut it down. We'll call that one a draw, then.'

Still he detoured, spent a few minutes cruising to see if they'd attempt another trace. His equipment continued to sound the all-clear when he landed on the roof of the morgue.

As arranged, it was Morris himself who opened the by-air delivery doors. Closing and latching them when everyone was inside.

'Nixie.' He offered his hand. 'I'm Dr. Morris. I'm very sorry about your family.'

'You didn't hurt them.'

'No, I didn't. I'll take you to them now. Level B,' he ordered, and the wide elevator began its descent. 'I know Dr. Mira and Lieutenant Dallas have explained some of this to you, but if you have any questions you can ask me.'

'I watch a show about a man who does work on dead bodies. I'm not really supposed to, but Coyle can, and sometimes I sneak.'

'Dr. Death? I watch that sometimes myself.' The doors opened into the long, cool white corridor. 'It's a little more entertaining than it is accurate. I don't chase the bad guys, for instance – I leave that in the capable hands of the police, like Lieutenant Dallas.'

'You have to cut them open sometimes.'

'Yes. I try to find something that will help the police.'

'Did you find something with my mom and dad, with my brother?'

'Everything Morris has done has helped,' Eve said.

They stopped by double doors, their small, round observation windows screened now. Nixie reached for Eve's hand, but they were jammed in pockets. She settled for Mira's. 'Are they in there?'

'Yes.' Morris paused again. 'Are you ready to go in?' She only nodded.

She would smell it, of course, Eve thought. No matter

what sterilizer they used, it never quite masked the smell of death, the fluids and liquids and flesh.

She would smell it, and never forget it. 'Can I see my daddy first? Please.'

Her voice trembled a little, and when Eve looked down she saw Nixie was pale, but her face was set with a concentrated determination.

So nor would she forget it, Eve thought. She wouldn't forget this kind of courage, the kind it had to take for a child to stand, to wait while her father – not a monster, but a father – was drawn out of a steel drawer.

Morris had masked the throat wound with the magic of his enhancers. He had draped the body with a clean white sheet. But dead was dead.

'Can I touch him?'

'Yes.' Morris set a stool by the drawer, helped her climb onto it, and stood by her, his hand lightly on her shoulder. She brushed her fingers – light as a wish – over her father's cheek.

'He has a scratchy face. Sometimes he rubs it on mine to make me laugh. It's dark in the drawer.'

'I know, but I think where he is now, it's not.'

She nodded, silent tears trickling down her face. 'He had to go to heaven, even though he didn't want to.' And when she leaned over, touched her lips to her father's cheek, Eve felt the hot ball of tears in her own belly.

'You can put him back now.' She climbed off the stool, took the tissue Mira offered her. 'Maybe I can see Coyle now.'

She touched her brother's hair, studied his face in a way that made Eve think she was trying to see him alive again. 'Maybe he can play baseball all the time now. He likes baseball best.'

She asked for Inga, touched her hair as well. 'Sometimes she baked cookies – the ones with sugar. She'd pretend it was a secret, but I knew Mom told her it was okay.'

She stepped off the stool again. Her face wasn't pale now, but flushed from the tears. Eve could see her chest tremble with the effort to hold them back.

'Linnie's not here. They took her already. They didn't let me see her or say good-bye. I know they're mad at me.'

'They're not.' Eve looked down when Nixie turned to her. 'I saw Linnie's mother today, and she's not mad at you. She's upset, like you are. She's sad and upset, but she's not mad at you. She asked about you. She wanted to make sure you were okay.'

'She's not mad? You swear?'

Her belly churned but she kept her eyes steady. If the kid could maintain, by God, so could she. 'She's not mad. I swear. I couldn't let you go say good-bye to Linnie, so that's on me. It wasn't safe, and it was my call.'

'Because of the bad guys?'

'Yeah.'

'Then it's on them,' Nixie said simply. 'I want to see my mother now. Will you come with me?'

Oh Christ, Eve thought, but she took Nixie's hand and stepped toward the drawer Morris pulled out.

Eve knew the face well now. Pretty woman who'd passed the shape of her mouth on to her daughter. White as wax now, with that faint tinge of unearthly blue, and soft as wax as well, in the way the dead go soft.

Nixie's fingers trembled in hers as the girl reached down to touch that soft, white face. And the sound she made as she lay her head on the sheet over her mother's breast was a low, painful keening.

When it quieted to whimpers, Mira stepped forward, stroked her hand over Nixie's hair. 'She'd be glad you came to see her, proud that you could. Can you say good-bye to her, Nixie?'

'I don't want to.'

'Oh, baby, I know, and so does she. It's so hard to say good-bye.'

'Her heart doesn't thump. If I sat in her lap and leaned my head here, I could hear her heart thump. But now it doesn't.' She lifted her head, whispered good-bye, and stepped off the stool for the last time.

'Thank you for taking care of them,' she said to Morris.

He merely nodded, then walked to the door to hold it open. When Eve passed behind Mira and Nixie, he murmured to her, 'You think you can handle anything in this job.' His voice was thick and raw. 'Stand anything, stand up to anything. But my sweet Christ, that child almost had me on the floor.'

' "Grace was in all her steps, heaven in her eye, In every gesture dignity and love." '

332

Looking at Roarke now, Morris managed a small smile. 'Well said. I'll get you out.'

'What was that from?' Eve asked. 'What you just said.'

'*Paradise Lost.* Written by a poet named Milton. It seemed apt as what we just witnessed was a wrenching form of poetry.'

She drew in a breath. 'Let's get her back.'

When they returned, Mira sent Nixie upstairs with Summerset and the promise to be up in a moment.

Gauging the ground, Roarke excused himself and went back to work.

'I know that was difficult for you,' Mira began.

'It's not about me.'

'Every case is about you, to some extent, or you wouldn't be able to do what you do so well. You have the gift of being able to mate your objectivity with compassion.'

'That's not the way I hear it.'

'She needed what you gave her. She'll heal. She's too strong not to. But she needed this to begin.'

'She'll need a hell of a lot more since the Dysons won't take her.'

'I'd hoped . . . well, it may be for the best on all sides. She would remind them of their loss, and they of hers.'

'It's not best for her to end up a ward of the court. I may have another possibility. I know some people who'd qualify to take her on. I was thinking maybe we could contact Richard DeBlass and Elizabeth Barrister.'

'It's a good thought.'

'They took that kid, the boy, we found on a murder scene last year.' Eve shifted, not entirely comfortable with the role of family planner. 'I figure they decided to foster him because their daughter was murdered. Though she was an adult, and—'

'Your child is always your child. Age doesn't factor.'

'If you say so. Anyway, I guess they wanted another chance to . . . whatever. I know Roarke waded in with that kid, ah, Kevin. Gave them a little nudge to take him in. From what I know, it worked out okay, and like I said, they're qualified. Maybe they'd consider taking in another.'

'I think it's a very good idea. You'll talk to them.'

Boggy area, Eve thought. 'Ah...I need to talk to Roarke because he knows them better. I'm the cop who closed their daughter's murder case – and uncovered some ugly family secrets. He's their friend. But if this pans out, I'm going to need you to add your weight with CPS.'

'You've given this considerable thought.'

'No, but it's the best thought I've had on it since Mrs Dyson dropped the boomer on me this morning. She's been kicked around enough. I don't want her kicked around by the system that's supposed to protect her.'

'Once you've talked to Roarke, let me know. We'll work to get what's best for Nixie. I should go up to her now.'

'Ah, just one more thing.' Eve got out the photograph Dave Rangle had given her. 'Her father's partner sent this for her. Swisher kept it on his desk. His partner figured Nixie would want it.'

'What a lovely family,' Mira said as she took the photograph. 'Yes, she'll want this. And it couldn't come at a better time. She'll see this, remember this, and imagine them this way rather than as they were at the morgue.'

She looked back at Eve. 'Wouldn't you like to give this to her yourself?' When Eve only shook her head, Mira nodded. 'All right, then. I'll take it to her.'

Mira turned toward the steps, stopped at the base. 'She doesn't know how hard that was for you, to stand with her while she said good-bye to her family. But I do.'

Upstairs, Summerset sat with Nixie in his lap.

'They didn't look like they were sleeping,' she said, with her head on his chest, his heart beating in her ear. 'I thought maybe they would, but you could tell they weren't.'

His long, thin fingers stroked through her hair. 'Some people believe, as I do, that when we die the essence of ourselves – the spirit or the soul – has choices.'

'What kind?'

'Some of those choices might depend on how we've lived our lives. If we've tried to do our best, we might then decide to go to a place of peace.'

'Like angels on a cloud.'

'Perhaps.' He continued to stroke her hair as the cat padded into the room, then leaped up to join them on the arm of the chair. 'Or like a garden where we can walk or play, where we see others who made this same choice before us.'

Nixie reached out, petted Galahad's wide flank. 'Where Coyle can play baseball?'

'Yes. Or we might decide to come back, live again, begin a new life at the very start of it, inside the womb. We may decide to do this because we want to do better than we did before, or right some wrong we may have done. Or simply because we're not quite ready to go to that place of peace.'

'So maybe they'll decide to come back, like babies?' The idea made her smile a little. 'Would I know them if I got to meet them some time?'

'I think you would, in some part of your heart. Even if you don't realize it, you *recognize* in your heart. Do you understand?'

'I guess. I think so. Did you ever recognize somebody who had to die before?'

'I think I have. But there's one I keep hoping I might recognize one day.' He thought of his daughter, his beautiful, lost Marlena. 'I haven't found her yet.'

'Maybe she made the choice to go to the garden.'

He bent to touch his lips to Nixie's hair. 'Maybe she did.'

Summerset waited nearly an hour, monitoring Eve's office until he saw Peabody leave the room. He hoped whatever task she'd been sent to perform took long enough for him to finish what he had to do. When he stepped into Eve's office, she was just coming out of the kitchen with another mug of coffee. Her hand jerked slightly, lapping hot liquid over the rim.

'Oh, fuck me. Consider this area police property and restricted to tight-assed fuckwits I don't want around. Which is you.'

'I only need a moment of your time. I would apologize.'

'You would what?'

His voice was as stiff as hers and only went more rigid. 'I would apologize for my remarks earlier. They were incorrect.'

'As far as I'm concerned, your remarks are always incorrect. So fine. Now make tracks. I'm working.'

He would *damn* well finish swallowing this hideous crow. 'You brought the child here for safe-keeping, and you've seen that she's been safely kept. I'm aware that you're working diligently to identify and capture the people who killed her family. It's visibly apparent that you're giving this considerable time and effort as you have circles under your eyes and your disposition is even more disagreeable than usual due to lack of proper rest and nutrition.'

'Bite me.'

'And your clever repartee suffers as a result.'

'How's this for clever repartee?' She jabbed her middle finger into the air.

'Typical.' He nearly turned and left. Very nearly. But he couldn't forget that Nixie had told him Eve stood with her when she'd said good-bye to her mother.

'She had a very hard day, Lieutenant. Grieving. And when I coaxed her to take a nap, she had another nightmare. She asked for you, and you wouldn't . . . couldn't,' he corrected,

337

'be here. I was overwrought when you arrived, and I was incorrect.'

'Okay. Forget it.'

When he turned to leave, she took a deep breath. She didn't mind giving as good as she got, when it came to cheap shots. It was harder to give as good when it was conciliatory. But if she didn't, it would itch at her and distract her from the work.

'Hey.' He stopped, turned. 'I brought her here because I figured it was the safest place for her. And because I figured I had someone on site who'd know how to take care of a nine-year-old girl. Knowing she's comfortable with you gives me the space I need to do what I have to do.'

'Understood. I'll leave you to do it.'

It's about time somebody did, Eve thought as he left. Then she sat down, propped her feet on her desk, sipped her coffee. And studied her murder board while the computer ran the next search.

17

Eve made notes from search results, ran probabilities, continued her notes. She was tired of riding a desk on this one. She wanted action. Needed to *move.*

Instead, she rolled her shoulders, went back to her notes. Kirkendall v. Kirkendall to Moss.

To Duberry. To, most likely, Brenegan.

To Swisher, Swisher, Swisher, Dyson, and Snood. To Newman.

To Knight and Preston. Kirkendall to Isenberry.

Isenberry to Tully and Tully to Rangle.

No harm to Tully or Rangle, with countless opportunities. Target specific.

And all circling back to Kirkendall v. Kirdendall. 'What time is it in Nebraska?'

'Ah.' Peabody blinked her tired eyes, rubbed them. 'Let's see, it's five-twenty here, so I think it's an hour earlier there? Do they do daylight savings? I think. An hour. Probably.'

'Why does it have to be an hour earlier there, or an hour later here? Why can't everybody just run on the same time and end the madness?'

'It has to do with the earth turning on its axis as it

orbits the sun and . . .' She trailed off, catching Eve's narrowed glare. 'You're right. Everybody should run on the same time. Dallas time. I'd vote for it. Are we going to Nebraska?'

'I'm going to do everything in my power to avoid it.' Going out in the field didn't mean she wanted to go out in actual fields. With hay or grass or spooky corn. 'Let's try the wonder of the 'link first.'

She opened Dian Kirkendall's file, found her sister's data. 'Turnbill, Roxanne. Age forty-three. Married to Joshua, mother of Benjamin and Samuel. Professional Mother status. Okay, Roxanne, let's see what you know about your brother-in-law.'

The face that popped on her screen was a child's – a boy, Eve thought, despite the sunny halo of hair. He had a big, wide open face with the dazzle of green eyes. 'Hello, hi, this is Ben. Who are you?'

'Is either your mother or your father' – or any rational adult – 'at home?'

'My mom's here, but you're supposed to say who it is, then say if you can – if you *may*,' he corrected, 'speak with somebody.'

Now kids were lecturing her on manners. What had happened to her world? 'This is Dallas. May I speak with your mother?'

'Okay.' There was a blur and a jumble on-screen, then a piercing shout. '*Mom!* Dallas is calling you. Can I have a cookie now?'

'One cookie, Ben. And don't shout near the 'link. It's rude.' The mother had the son's curls, but in a deep brunette. Her smile wasn't as open, but polite, and just a little annoyed around the edges. 'Can I help you?'

'Mrs Turnbill?'

'Yes. Look, we've blocked solicitations, so I'm sorry, but if you've—'

'I'm Lieutenant Dallas with the New York City Police and Security Department.'

'Oh.' Even that polite smile faded. 'What is it?'

'I'm calling regarding your former brother-in-law, Roger Kirkendall.'

'Is he dead?'

'No, not to my knowledge. I'm trying to locate him for questioning in connection with a case. Do you have any information as to his whereabouts?'

'No. I can't help you. I've very busy so—'

'Mrs Turnbill, it's very important that I locate Mr Kirkendall. If you could tell me if you've had any contact—'

'I haven't, and I don't want any contact with him.' Her voice was strained, like a wire snapped tight. 'How do I know you're who you say you are?'

Eve held her badge to the screen. 'Can you read my ID and my badge number?'

'Of course I can, but—'

'You can verify by contacting Cop Central in Manhattan. I can give you a contact number that won't cost—'

'I'll get the number. You'll have to hold.'

'Careful,' Peabody noted when the screen went to holding blue. 'And a little pissy.'

'Not just careful, not just pissy. A little scared on top of it.' As she waited, Eve considered. She began to calculate how long a round trip to Nebraska, including interview time, might take.

Roxanne came back on screen. 'All right, Lieutenant, I've verified your information.' Her face was pale now. 'You're with Homicide.'

'That's correct.'

'He's killed someone. Dian—' She broke off, bit down on her lip as if to block words. 'Who has he killed?'

'He's wanted for questioning in the murders of at least seven people, including two police officers.'

'In New York,' she said carefully. 'He killed people in New York City?'

'He's wanted for questioning for murders that occurred in New York.'

'I see. I'm sorry. I'm very sorry. I don't know where he is, I don't know what he's doing. Frankly, I don't want to know. If I did, if I knew anything, I'd tell you. I can't help you, and this isn't something I want to discuss. I have to get back to my children.'

The screen went black.

'She's still scared of him,' Peabody commented.

'Yeah. And her sister's still alive. That's what she thought, just for an instant there. Oh God, he finally got to Dian.

She may know more than she realizes. She needs a face-to-face.'

'We're going to Nebraska?'

'No, but you are.'

'Me? Just me? Out there in the wilderness?'

'Take McNab. Backup and ballast.' And, Eve thought, as someone who'd keep Peabody from overdoing. 'I want you there and back tonight. You'll do better with the mother type, the family type, than I would first shot. She'll trust you faster.'

Eve used the house 'link, interrupted Roarke in the computer lab.

'I need fast, secure transpo.'

'Where are we going?'

'Not we – Peabody. Nebraska. I'm sending McNab with her, so something that'll hold two. But quick and small. They shouldn't need to be there more than a couple of hours. I've got the exact location.'

'All right, I'll arrange it. Give me a minute.'

'Wow, just like that.' Peabody gave a little sigh. 'What's it like being with a guy who can snap his fingers and get you pretty much whatever you need?'

'Convenient. Use the sister on her if you have to. Show her the dead kids.'

'Jesus, Dallas.'

'She's got kids. It'll help crack her if she's hiding anything. We can't play nice. Have McNab take the edge if you need one. Can he handle bad cop?'

'He does it really well during personal role-playing games when I'm the reluctant witness.'

'Oh crap.' Eve pressed her fingers to her eyes and prayed the image wouldn't form. 'Just work her, Peabody. She must know where to find the sister. Kirkendall's ex would be a valuable tool in this investigation.'

Roarke walked in, handed Peabody a memo cube. 'There's your transpo. The pilot will be waiting for you.'

'Thanks.' She gathered her file bag. 'I'll contact McNab, have him meet me there.'

'I want to know when you arrive, when you leave, and when you get back,' Eve told her.

'Yes, sir.'

'Safe trip,' Roarke said, then turned to Eve when Peabody headed out. 'I've got some bits and pieces, but I'm going to need the unregistered to pull them together.'

'Show me what you've got.'

'Let's take it in there.' He ran a hand down her arm as they walked. 'You're tired, Lieutenant.'

'Some.'

'It's been a stressful, emotional day.'

She jerked a shoulder when he unlocked his private office with palm and voice ID.

'And Nixie?'

'Mira came by on her way out. She said the kid was doing a little better. That the trip to the morgue . . . Jesus.' She covered her face with her hands. 'God, I didn't think I was going to be able to hold it together in there.'

'I know.'

She shook her head, struggling even now to maintain. 'The way she looked at her father, touched him. What was in her eyes when she did. Sorrow, something beyond sorrow. And you knew, seeing that, how much she loved him. That she was never afraid of him, never had to worry if he'd hurt her. We don't know what that's like. We can't. I can find the man who did this, but I can't understand what she feels. And if I can't understand, how can I make it right?'

'Not true.' He brushed her face with his fingers, took away tears. 'Who are you weeping for, if not for her?'

'I don't know. I don't know. She doesn't know what I do, but she's living through it. I can't know what she knows. That kind of bond? It's different than what we've got. It's got to be. Child to parent, parent to child. That was taken from her.'

She reached up with her own hands, wiped the tears away. 'I stood over my father, with his blood all over me. I can't really remember what I felt. Relief, pleasure, terror – all of it, none of it. He comes back, in my head, in my dreams, and he tells me it's not over. He's right. It's not over. It's never going to be. She makes me see it.'

'I know.' He rubbed an errant tear away with his thumb. 'Yes, I know. It's wearing on you, I can see that, too. There doesn't seem to be anything either of us can do about it. You won't pass the case to someone else.' He lifted her chin with his hand before she could answer. 'You won't, and I wouldn't want you to. You'd never forgive yourself for stepping aside because of personal distress. And you'd never trust yourself again, not fully, not the way you need to.'

'I saw myself when I found her. Saw myself, instead of her, huddled in a ball, coated in blood. Not just thought of it, but saw it. Just a flash, just for an instant.'

'Yet you brought her here. You face it. Darling Eve.' His voice was like balm on the burn. 'The child isn't the only one who shows grace in her steps.'

'Grace isn't the issue. Roarke.' She could tell him, say this to him. 'On days like this, part of me wants to go back there, to that room in Dallas. Just so I can stand over him again, with his blood all over me and the knife in my hand.'

She closed her fist as if she held the hilt. 'Just to kill him again, but this time to know what I feel when I do, to feel it because maybe then it'll be done. Even if it doesn't, to feel that moment when I carved him up. I don't know what that makes me.'

'On days like this, all of me wants to be the one to go back to that room in Dallas. To have his blood on me, and the knife in my hands. I know exactly what I would feel. And what it makes us, Eve, is who we are.' She let out a long breath. 'I don't know why that helps when it should probably scare me. She won't feel this way, because she had that base. Because she could lay her head on her mother's dead heart and cry. She'll have sorrow, and nights when she's afraid, but she'll remember why she was able to touch her father's face, her brother's hair, and cry on her mother's breast.'

346

'She'll remember a cop who stood with her, and held her hand when she did.'

'They're going to throw her into the system, Roarke. Sometimes it's salvation, sometimes it's good, but not for her. I don't want her to be another case file. To cycle through that like I did. I have an idea what could be done, but I wanted to run it by you.'

His face went absolutely still, absolutely blank. 'What?'

'I was thinking we could approach Richard DeBlass and Elizabeth Barrister.'

'Oh.' This time it was Roarke who let out a long breath. 'Of course. Richard and Beth, good thought.' He turned away, walked away from her to stare out the window.

'If it's a good idea, why are you upset?'

'I'm not.' What was he? He didn't have the name for it. 'I should've thought of them myself. I should have thought more clearly.'

'You can't think of everything.'

'Apparently not.'

'Something's wrong.'

He started to deny it, push it aside. And had to accept that it would just be one more mistake. 'I can't get my mind off the child. No, that's not it, not altogether. I can't get it out of my head, all of it, not since I went to that house with you. Stood looking at those rooms where those children had been sleeping.'

'It's rougher when it's kids. I should've thought of that before I asked you to do the walk-through.'

'I'm not green.' He whirled around, his face lit with fury. 'I'm not so soft in the belly I can't . . . Ah, fuck me.' He broke off, ran his hands through his hair.

'Hey, hey, hey.' Obviously alarmed, she crossed over quickly, rubbed his back. 'What gives?'

'They were sleeping.' Christ Jesus, would that single thing always sicken him the most? 'They were innocent. They had what children are supposed to have. Love and comfort and security. And I looked in those rooms, saw their blood, and it tears at me. Tears at my gut. Tears at the years between. I never think of it. Why should I, goddamn it.'

She didn't ask of what, not when she could see it on his face. Had it only been a short time ago he'd told her he hated to see her look sad? How could she tell him what it did to her guts to see him look devastated?

'Maybe we should sit down a minute.'

'Bloody hell. Bloody buggering hell.' He stalked to the door, booted it closed. 'You can't forget it, but you can live with it. And I have. I do. It doesn't beat at me as it does you.'

'So maybe when it does, it's worse.'

He leaned back against the door, stared at her. 'I see myself lying in a puddle of my own blood and puke and piss after he beat me unconscious. And yet here I am, aren't I? Damn good suit, big house, a wife I love more than life. He left me there, probably for dead. Didn't even bother to throw me away as he had my mother. I wasn't worth the trouble. Why should I give a damn about that now? But I wonder, what in God's name is the purpose, Eve? What is the purpose when I come to this, and those children are dead? When the one who's left has nothing and no one?'

'You don't deal the cards,' she said carefully. 'You just play them. Don't do this to yourself.'

'I cheated and stole and connived my way to what I have, or to the base of it in any case. It wasn't an innocent lying in that alley.'

'Bullshit. That's just bullshit.'

'I'd have killed him.' His eyes weren't devastated now, but winter cold. 'If someone hadn't done it before me, when I was older and stronger I'd have gone for him. I'd have finished him. Can't change that either. Well.' He sighed, heavily. 'This is useless.'

'It's not. You don't think it's useless when I flood it on you. I like your dick, Roarke, like it fine. But it's irritating when you think with it.' He opened his mouth, hissed out a breath just before a choked laugh. 'It's irritating when you point it out. All right then, let's finish this out with me telling you I went to Philadelphia today.'

'What the hell for?' She snapped it out. 'I told you I needed to know where you were.'

'I wasn't going to mention it, and not to spare myself your wrath, Lieutenant. I wasn't going to mention it because it was a waste of time. I'd thought I could fix it – I'm good at fixing, or buying off if fixing won't work. I went to see Grant Swisher's stepsister. To talk to her about stepping in for Nixie, now that the legal guardianship's been voided. She couldn't be less interested.'

He sat now, on the arm of a chair. 'I decided to make all this my concern. Magnanimous of me.'

'Shut up. Nobody rips on you but me.' She stepped to him, caught his face in her hands, kissed him. 'And I'm not because – even being pissed off about you taking an unscheduled trip – I'm proud that you'd try to help. I wouldn't have thought of doing it.'

'I'd have bought her off, if that had been an option. Money fixes all sorts of problems, and why have so bloody much if you can't buy what you like? Such as a nice family for a little girl. I'd already eliminated the grandparents – found the grandfather, by the way – on my high moral grounds. But the one left, the one I hand-selected, wouldn't fall in.'

'If she doesn't want the kid, the kid's better off somewhere else.'

'I know it. I might've been disgusted with this woman's callousness, but I was furious with myself for assuming I could just snap fingers and make it all tidy. And furious that I couldn't. If it was tidy, I wouldn't feel guilty, would I?'

'About what?'

'About not considering, not being able to consider keeping her with us.'

'Us? Here? Us?'

He laughed again, but the sound was weary. 'Well, we're on the same page there anyway. We can't do it. We're not the right people for it – for her. The big house, all the money, it doesn't mean a damn when we're not the right people.'

'Still on the same page.'

He smiled at her. 'I've wondered if I'd be a good father. I think I would be. I think we'd be good at it, either despite or because of where we came from. Maybe both. But it's not now. It's not this child. It'll be when we know we'll be good at it.'

'That's nothing to feel guilty about.'

'How does it make me any different from Leesa Corday? Swisher's stepsister?'

'Because you tried to make it right. You'll help to make it right.'

'You steady me,' he murmured. 'I didn't even know how far off-balance I'd been, and here you steady me.' He took her hands, kissed them. 'I want children with you, Eve.'

The sound she made brought on a quick and easy grin. 'No need for the panic face, darling. I don't mean today, or tomorrow, or nine months down the road. Having Nixie around's been considerable education. Children are a lot of bloody work, aren't they?'

'Big duh.'

'Emotional, physical, time-consuming work. With undoubtedly amazing rewards. That bond you spoke of, we deserve to have it. To make it, when we're ready. But we're not, either of us, ready. And we're not equipped to parent a girl nearly ten. It would be like – for us, anyway – starting a twisty, laborious, fascinating task somewhere in the middle, without any time for that learning curve.'

He stepped to her again, laid his lips on her brow. 'But I want children with you, my lovely Eve. One day.'

'One day being far, far in the future. Like, I don't know, say a decade when . . . Hold on. Children is plural.'

He eased back, grinned. 'Why so it is – nothing slips by my canny cop.'

'You really think if I ever actually let you plant something in me – they're like aliens in there, growing little hands and feet.' She shuddered. 'Creepy. If I ever did that, popped a kid out – which I think is probably as pleasant a process as having your eyeballs pierced by burning, poisonous sticks, I'd say, "Whoopee, let's do this again?" Have you recently suffered head trauma?'

'Not to my knowledge.'

'Could be coming. Any second.'

He laughed, kissed her. 'I do love you, and the rest is all in the vague and misty future. In any case, we're talking about this child. I think Richard and Beth are a fine thought.'

She locked the rest away – where hopefully it would stay in some deep, dark mind vault. 'They took that kid last year.'

'Kevin. Yes, they recently finalized the adoption.'

'Yeah, you mentioned it. Kid had it rough – bouncy for all of that, but he had it rough. Junkie LC of a mother who knocked him around, left him alone. They have to know how to handle kids with baggage, so . . .'

'They may be a good choice for Nixie. I'll talk to them, tonight if I can manage it. They'll need to meet her, and she them.'

'You could give that a push. With the Dysons bowing

out, CPS is going to start squawking about fostering pretty soon. Okay. Let's get down to it. What've you got for me?'

'Some names I've ferreted out that intersect in one way or another with both Kirkendall and Isenberry.' He moved over to his console as he spoke. 'Some connect to CIA, some to Homeland Security.' He glanced over at her, and thought this would be one more punch to her psyche. 'Are you going to be all right with that?'

'Are you?'

'I've made my peace there, best I can. They watched an innocent, desperate child suffer for what they deemed a bigger cause. I don't forget it, but I've made my peace with it.'

'I don't forget it,' she said quietly. Eve knew it was for love of her that he'd walked away from taking vengeance on the HSO operatives who'd witnessed her abuse those many years ago in Dallas – they'd witnessed a man beating and brutalizing his own daughter, and done nothing to stop it. 'I don't forget what you did for me.'

'Didn't do, more accurately. In any case, to nudge this any further, to access the data on these people through these organizations, I'll need this. Roarke,' he said, laying his hand on a palm plate. 'Open operations.'

Roarke, ID verified, command acknowledged.

The console came to life, lights flashing on, equipment going to a low, holding hum. She came around the console to stand with him. And saw the framed photo he kept here.

The baby, all vivid blue eyes and dark thick hair, held close to the young mother with her bruised face and bandaged hand.

That was private, too, she thought, and why he kept it here in this room. Something else he was making his peace over.

'Another thing I found interesting,' he told her. 'Take a look.' He ordered an image on a wall screen.

'Clinton, Isaac P., US Army, retired. Sergeant. Looks like Kirkendall,' she commented. 'Around the eyes, the mouth. Same coloring.'

'Yes, that caught me, too. Particularly when I noticed the birth date.' He brought up Kirkendall's image and data.

'The same date. Same health center. Son of a bitch. Different parents listed. But if the records were altered. If—'

'I think someone was naughty, and decided it would be worth a bit of hacking into those health center records.'

'Illegal adoption? Twins separated at birth. Could it be that strange?'

'Strange,' Roarke agreed, 'but logical for all that.'

'They have to know. They end up in the same regiment, the same training. Guy's got your face – or close enough to make people notice – you're going to ask questions.'

'I take it you'd like that as first order of business.'

'Go.'

'This won't take long.'

He sat, began to work by voice command and manual while she paced. Brothers, she thought. Teamwork. Twins, pulled apart, then brought back together. By fate? Luck? A higher power's vicious sense of humor? Would the bond be stronger then, somehow? The anger deeper. And the murders even more personal. Denied their rightful family at birth. Denied one's rightful family by the courts.

Life's a bitch, so you kill.

'Was this Clinton ever married?'

'Shush,' was Roarke's response, so she looked for herself.

'Lot of mirrors here,' she noted. 'He was married – the same year as Kirkendall. One kid for him, male. Both son and wife are listed as missing, the year before Kirkendall's punching bag and kids whiffed. They take off?' she wondered. 'Or not get the chance?'

'Birth mothers on hospital records are the same as on later data,' Roarke said as he worked.

'Poke around, find others listed for that same day. Twin boys, deceased.'

'Already there, Lieutenant. Another moment. And here. On-screen. Smith, Jane – original – delivered twin boys, stillbirths. I imagine the health center, and the doctor of record, gained a healthy fee on this.'

'Sold them. Yeah, betcha that's what she did. It happened. Happens,' she corrected, 'even with the laws coming down on women getting themselves inseminated and incubating fetuses for big, fat fees, it happens.'

'Target couples – with the finances for it – can outline the physical characteristics they'd like, the ethnicity and so on, bypass mainstream routes with their screenings and regulations.' Roarke nodded. 'Yes, healthy newborns are always a hot commodity on the black market.'

'And this Jane Smith hits the jackpot with twins. The Kirkendalls, the Clintons, walk away with bouncing boys – and their baby broker collects the fees, divvies up the rest of the shares. I'll pass this data to somebody in Child Protection Services. They'll want to dig into it, see if they can find the birth mother, the brokers. Long shot since we're talking fifty years, and I can't take time out for it unless it leads to Kirkendall. Selling kids. Pretty low.'

'It could be better to be wanted, even bought and paid for, than to be unwanted, discarded.'

'There are legitimate agencies to handle this stuff. Even ways to conceive – if that's what you want – if you have physical limitations. People like this want to cut corners, want to ignore the law and the system in place to protect the child.'

'I agree with you. And I'd say, in these cases, the ones who were wanted, bought and paid for, when learning of it, reacted badly.'

She paced. 'I had a brother, and you stole him from me. I lived a lie that was beyond my control. I *will* take charge. So, we've got a couple of pissed-off guys who've been trained with our tax dollars to kill. Brothers, brotherly loyalty along with *semper fi.*'

'I think that's the marine corps, not the army.'

'Whatever. They meet up at some point, figure it out. Or one of them figures it out and seeks out the other.

You're going to end up with two halves of one coin kind of deal, and the worse for it. They've changed their faces. Not only to avoid detection, but to look more alike, to what, honor their bond? Not just fraternal twins, identical. Or as close as can be to identical. Two bodies, one mind. That's how it looks to me.'

'Both their files, as well as a few others I found, indicate assignments from both CIA and Homeland, as well as Special Ops.'

I see you now, Eve thought. I *know* you now. I'll find you now.

'How long will it take you to get in, pull it out?'

'A bit. You're restless, Lieutenant.'

'I need . . .' She rolled her shoulders. 'Something physical. A good workout. Haven't managed one in a few days. More, I just want to pound on something awhile. Something that hits back.'

'I can help you with that.'

She lifted her fisted hands. 'Want to go a round, ace?'

'Actually, no, but give me a minute to set this up.' He gave the machines orders, in the e-speak Eve could never fully translate. 'It can start without me, then I'll come back to finish it off. Come with me.'

'It'd go quicker with you working it.'

'An hour or so won't make much difference.' He drew her into the elevator. 'Holo-room.'

'Holo-room? What for?'

'A little program I've been playing with. I think you'll

like it. Especially considering our recent discussion of Master Lu and our mutual admiration for his skill.'

He stepped with her into the blank square of the holo-room. 'Initiate martial arts program 5A,' he said with a smile whispering around his lips. 'Eve Dallas as opponent.'

'I thought you said you didn't want to—'

The room shimmered, swam, and became a dojo, with a wall of weapons and glossy wood floor. She looked down at herself, studied the traditional black gi.

'Icy' was all she could think of saying.

'How much of a workout do you want?'

She rolled to the balls of her feet, back on the heels. 'Hard and sweaty.'

'I've got just the thing. Triple threat,' he ordered. 'Full cycle. Have fun,' he added to Eve when three figures appeared.

Two male, Eve noted, one female. The woman was small, with her siren red hair pulled back in a sleek tail to leave her stunning face unframed. One male was black, well over six feet, solid muscle, good long reach. The second was Asian, black eyes like marbles, and the lithe sort of build that told her he'd be quick and agile as a lizard.

They waited for her to step forward, then with a snap of their gis, bowed. She mirrored the gesture, then shifted smoothly to fighting stance as they began to circle.

The woman came first, a graceful handspring followed by a scissoring kick that whizzed by Eve's face. To counter, Eve dived, swept out her legs, and landed the first blow on the Asian. Gained her feet on a roll, blocked with a forearm.

And felt the smack of flesh to flesh vibrate.

Testing moves at first, backhand, jump kick, pivot, punch.

She parried, caught the movement out of the corner of her eye, and spun to meet the woman with a stomp on her instep, a hard elbow jab to the jaw.

'Nicely done,' Roarke called out, and leaned against the wall to watch.

She took a blow that knocked her down, used her hands and her quads to flip herself back before the next landed. And the Asian spun in, caught her with a flying kick to the kidneys that sent her skidding over the floor on her belly.

'Ouch.' Roarke winced. 'That one stung a bit.'

'Woke me up is all.' Breathing through her teeth, she pushed up on her arms, kicked back, and took the black guy down with two hard heels to the groin.

'That stung more,' Roarke decided, and ordered himself a glass of cabernet from the AutoChef.

He sipped contemplatively while watching his woman battle. Outnumbered, and in two cases well outweighed. But holding her own.

And she needed this, this hard, physical challenge. To help vent some of those hard, emotional fists pummeling inside her.

Still, he hissed in sympathy as she took a punishing blow to the face. Well, he thought, she was more or less holding her own.

359

They came at her at once, and she blocked one by flipping him over her back, evaded another with an agile shoulder roll, but the third caught her with a sharp backward kick that sent her down again.

'Why don't I tone it down a bit,' Roarke suggested.

She gained her feet, blood in her eye now. 'You do, and I'll kick your ass when I'm done with these.'

He shrugged, sipped. 'Your call, darling.'

'Okay.' She shook her arms, circling as they did, noting the female was favoring her left leg now, and the black male was winded. 'Let's finish this up.'

She went for the black guy. He might've been the biggest, but the groin shot had hurt. Using the woman as a decoy, Eve flew into a double spin, a snapping side kick, easily blocked, and used the momentum to carry her around, push her forward so that her upper body, head, and fists all connected with the black man's crotch.

This time he went down, and stayed down.

She blocked blows with her forearms, her shoulders, gauging her ground, taking the defensive and drawing both her opponents in close.

A short-armed punch to the jaw snapped the female's head back, and the elbow Eve jabbed into her throat took her out.

Eve grabbed her falling body and shoved it at her last opponent.

He had to spin away, but came back at her. They were both puffing now, and the sweat stung her eyes. She doubled over when his foot landed in her gut. And he was fast – but not quite fast enough to snap his leg back before she gripped his ankle and heaved.

He used the move to carry himself over into a flip, punched the landing with a grace she admired. Even as she was hurling at him, springing up to a flying kick. Her heel landed on the bridge of his nose, and she heard the satisfying crunch.

'That's game,' Roarke said. 'End program.'

The figures faded away, as did the dojo. She stood, in her work clothes now, catching her breath. 'Good fight,' she managed.

'Not bad. You finished them up in . . . twenty-one minutes, forty seconds.'

'Time flies when you're . . . ow.' She rubbed her right inner thigh. 'What I get for not warming up.'

'You pull something?'

'No.' She bent to stretch it out. 'Just a little tender.' She blew her hair out of narrowed eyes as she glanced toward Roarke. 'Twenty minutes?'

'Twenty-one forty. Not quite the high score. I did it in nineteen twenty-three.'

She lifted her head, squinted at him as she pulled the heel of her right foot to her butt in a stretch. 'Under twenty first time out?'

'All right, no, not the first time. That took me twenty and change.'

'How much change?'

He laughed. 'Fifty-eight.'

'I'd say the difference is negated as you programmed the game. Gimme a sip of that.'

He offered her the glass. 'Feel better?'

'Yeah. Nothing like punching your fist into a face to brighten up the day. I don't know what that says about me either, but I don't care.'

'Then we'll have another game. Recreational hour's not up,' he said before she could protest. 'Initiate Program Island-3.'

They were on a white sand beach that flowed into water of blue crystal. There were flowers – pink, white, rosy red – strewn along the shoreline. Jewel-colored birds winged into a sky as clear and blue as a glass bowl.

Floating gently on the sea was a wide white bed. 'There's a bed on the water.'

'I've never made love to you on the water. In it, somewhat under it, but never on it. You like the beach.' He lifted her hand to his lips. 'I like the idea of floating away with you.'

She looked at him. He wore a thin white shirt now, unbuttoned so it rippled in the breeze, and loose black pants. His feet were bare, as hers were.

He'd programmed her for white as well, she noted. Floating white dress with wire-thin straps. There were flowers in her hair. A long way from a black gi and flying fists. 'From combat to romance?'

'Can you think of anything that suits us more?'

She laughed. 'Guess not. I wouldn't have been able to

step away like this for an hour, not a couple of years ago. I hope I'm better for it, all around.'

She took his hand, walked with him into the warm, clear water. And laughed as they rolled onto the bed. 'It's like a really sexy raft.'

'And infinitely more comfortable.' He brushed his lips over hers. 'I stepped away whenever I chose. But I was never able to take myself away, as I can with you. I know I'm better for it.'

In another world there was death and pain, grief and rage. And here was love. The white sand and blue water might have been fantasy, but this world was as real as the other. Because he was real, they were real.

'Let's take ourselves away, then. Float away.'

She drew him to her, mouth to mouth, heart to heart. The bed dipped gently on the blue water, and the restlessness inside her eased.

She tasted the wine on him, rich, and felt the warm, moist air bathe her skin as he touched her.

A dreaming time now, she thought. Without the hard brightness of that other world. Without the pain and the blood and the incessant violence of the everyday. Calming and soothing, a kind of easy arousal that steadied the heart and fed the soul.

When she held him like this, when her mouth was on his in a long, long kiss, she could forget what it was to be hungry and hurting. Being held like this, she knew she could go back to the hurt stronger.

She slid the shirt from his shoulders, let her hands explore warm skin, tough muscle, let herself float as the bed floated, when he nudged those thin straps down her arms.

The warrior was his. The woman who had only moments before waged combat, defeated foes with a concentrated and fearsome violence, was soft beneath him, pliant and eager and impossibly sweet.

She would battle again and again, shed blood and spill it. Yet, miraculously, she would come back to him, again and again. Soft and pliant and eager.

He murmured in Irish. *My love.* And trailed kisses over those strong shoulders, those long arms where muscles were carved in alabaster. He slipped a flower from her hair. Tracing it over her even as his lips traced. Making her shiver.

'This is something special.'

'The flower?'

'The flower, yes. Extra.' He twirled it on its stem while he watched her. 'Will you trust me?'

'I always trust you.'

'I want to give you this. To give it to both of us.'

He flicked the petals over her breast. And with his tongue he tasted them, and her.

She arched up, floating still, still floating, but higher now as if the wave of heat lifted her. Desire shimmered through her like the wine. She could hear birdsong, some exotic, erotic music with the quiet underscore of water lapping against the shore. She could hear his voice, the music of it, as he drew the white gown away.

The sun, his hands, his lips, all on her skin – as hers were on his. The bed rocked on the water, soothing as a lullaby.

Then he swept the flower between her legs.

The sensation had her fingers digging into him. 'God.'

He watched her, watched that baffled pleasure run over her face. His cop, his warrior, and still oddly innocent about her own pleasures.

'It's called the Venus Bloom, and is grown on a colony on Green One. Hybridized,' he said, brushing it over her, watching her eyes blur, 'with certain properties that enhance and heighten sensation.'

Her breasts were tingling from it as if the nerves were raw-edged and exposed. And when his mouth closed over her, his teeth a light nip on her nipple, the shock of it had her crying out. He pressed the flower against her as he suckled.

Her body erupted.

She lost her mind. It was impossible to think through the barrage of sensations, the unspeakable pleasure. The shock of it had her body pulsing, plunging as the orgasm gushed through her.

'When I'm inside you . . .' His voice was thick with Ireland now, his eyes wild and blue. 'When I'm in you, Eve, it will do the same to me. Taste it.' His mouth crushed to hers, his tongue sweeping in. 'Feel it.' He crushed the flower against her. 'Come again, I want you to come again, while I'm watching you.'

She bucked, riding out the storm, brilliantly aware of

every cell in her body and the pleasure that flooded them. 'I want you inside me.' She gripped his hair, dragged his mouth back to hers. 'Feel what I feel.' He eased into her, slowly, so slowly she knew from the tremors in his body how rigidly he controlled himself. Then his breath caught, and his eyes, his beautiful eyes, went blind. 'Christ.'

'I don't know if we'll live through it,' she managed, and wrapped her legs around him. 'Let's find out. Don't hold back.'

He wasn't sure he could have, not now, not with the sensations that pounded him, not with her reckless words ringing in his ears. He let the chain snap and rode it with her, wave by hot, towering wave.

When the last swamped him, it swamped them both.

She wasn't sure she would ever get her breath back, or the full use of her limbs. Her arms had slid away from him, limply, until her fingers trailed in the water.

'Is that thing legal?'

He was flat out on top of her, breathing like a man who'd climbed up, or fallen off, a mountain. And his laugh rumbled against her skin. 'God, only you.'

'Seriously.'

'We really ought to have Trina tattoo that damn badge on your breast permanently. Yes. It's been tested, and approved, and licensed. A bit tricky to acquire yet. And as you can see, its effects are transitory.'

'Good thing. Wicked effective.'

'Erotic, arousing, enhancing, without taking away the will

or choice.' He lifted the flower, twirled it, then tossed it into the water where it floated. 'And pretty.'

'Are all of these like that?'

'No, just the one.' He kissed her again, savored the fading heat on her lips. 'But I can get more.'

'I bet.' She started to stretch, and frowned at the sound of a beep. 'Ah. Looks like we're through the first levels, and my attention's required.'

She sat up, shoved at her hair. She took one last look at blue water, white sand, and flowers strewn like jewels on the shoreline. 'Playtime's over.'

He nodded. 'End program.'

18

Eve sat at one of Roarke's substations and began to pick her way through the lives of Kirkendall and Clinton. They needed a base of operations, a place to set up, to store equipment, to plan strategies and do sims.

A place to take someone like Meredith Newman.

She started with childhood – Kirkendall in New Jersey, Clinton in Missouri. Kirkendall relocating to New York with custodial parent at the age of twelve. Clinton doing the same, to Ohio, at the age of ten. And both had enlisted in the army at eighteen. Both had been recruited into Special Forces at twenty.

Corporals Kirkendall and Clinton had both trained at Camp Powell, Miami.

'It's like a mirror,' Eve said. 'No, like magnets. They just kept duplicating each other's moves until they slapped together.'

'No talking.'

Eve frowned over at him. Sleeves rolled, hair tied back, he hammered at a keyboard with one hand and tapped icons on a viewboard with the other. And for the last ten minutes, he'd been muttering in a stylish combination of

Gaelic – she supposed – and the weird Irish slang he fell into when revved up.

Bugger this, bollocks to that, shagging, bloody, and a heavy sprinkling of fucks that sounded more and more like *fook* as he geared up.

'You're talking.'

'Feisigh do thoin fein!' He rattled that off, sat back for a moment, and studied his board. 'What? I'm not talking, I'm communing. Ah yes, there you are, you bitch.'

Communing, she thought as he hunkered over the keys. Get him. But she turned back to her own work. If she wasn't careful, she'd get caught up watching him. He made a hell of a picture when he was in the zone.

The army had – as the army did – shuffled them around over the next few years. They'd lived in military housing, even after they married their respective spouses – within three months of each other. And when they had opted to leave the military, to buy homes, they'd plunked down in the same development.

She toggled back and forth between locations, financials, added Isenberry into the mix. And slid into her own zone.

When the in-house 'link beeped beside her, she wished *she* could curse in Gaelic.

'Detective Baxter and Officer Trueheart have arrived and would like to speak with you.'

'Have them wait in my office.' She clicked off, then shot the data and the notes she'd been working on to her office unit. 'I've got some stuff,' she said to Roarke.

'So do I. I'm in Kirkendall's CIA file right now. Busy, busy boy.'

'Tell me one thing. Do agencies like that pay fees – outside fees – for wet work? For special assignments?'

'Apparently. I'm finding a number of what's listed as "op fees" in his file. His top seems to be a half mil – USD – for the termination of a scientist in Belingrad. He worked fairly cheap.'

'How do we manage to live in the same world when you actually exist on a plane where half a million is cheap?'

'True love hobbles us to the same post. Freelancers can get double that for an assassination. Easily.' He looked up from his work. 'I was once offered that, at the tender age of twenty – to do away with the business rival of a weapons' runner. A bit difficult to turn it down – quick money – but murder for pay has always struck me as tacky.'

'Tacky.'

He just smiled at her. 'I'm in now, so I'll keep with it, and run through Clinton's and Isenberry's. It won't take long now, as I've already punched through.'

'I'll be in my office. Just for curiosity, what does . . .' She paused, brought the Gaelic phrase back in her mind, and mangled it in the repeating.

Surprise flickered over his face as he angled his head. 'Where did you hear that?'

'Out of your mouth a little while ago.'

'I said that?' He looked mildly shocked – and if she

wasn't mistaken, a little embarrassed. 'Well, what does come back to you. Just a flash from my youth. A very crude one.'

'Oh, then, as a cop who's worked the tidy and genteel streets of New York for eleven years and counting, I'd be shocked by crude language.'

'Very crude,' he repeated. Then shrugged. 'Basically, it's fuck yourself in your own ass.'

'Yeah?' She brightened. 'How do you say it again – the right way? I could use it on Summerset.'

He laughed, shook his head. 'Go to work.' She walked out, mumbling the phrase.

And walked into her office in time to see Baxter take a big bite of a loaded burger. Since there were no takeout bags in evidence, and the smell was real meat, she deduced it came from her own kitchen.

'Help yourself.'

'Thanks.' He grinned and chewed, and gestured toward Trueheart, who was chewing on an identical meal – with the grace, at least, to look slightly shamefaced. 'We didn't stop for fuel. Eats are better here.'

'I'll give your compliments to the chef. Are you going to report, or just push dead cow in your mouth?'

'Both. Reached out to the primary on Moss, and on Duberry. Team working Moss, they crossed all the hatches. Nothing to go on. No specific threats filed. Moss hadn't mentioned anything to his wife, his associates, friends, neighbors, about any threats. He and his kid drove upstate to this cabin he owned one weekend a month. Man-to-man time.

Fishing and shit. Vehicle was parked, private garage – full vid surveillance, droid security. Droid on showed no tampering, but had a thirty-minute break on his disc. Same with the security cams.'

'What kind of cabin?'

Baxter nodded, picked up one of the fries he had ordered along with the burger. 'We thought the same. Why go through all that when it'd be easier to take him out in a cabin upstate. Troy?'

Trueheart swallowed hastily. 'The cabin's in a gated, recreational community, and the security is good. The investigators believed, due to the nature of the explosive device and the ability to jam the lot security, that the possibility was strong on urban terrorism. Several other vehicles were destroyed, and the lot suffered some structural damage.'

'Yeah,' she murmured. 'Smarter. Add the urban terrorism element to murk the waters.'

'There was no evidence to conclude Moss was target specific, but if so, they concluded it was because he was a judge, not because of any particular case. Moss had also been approached as a possible mayoral candidate, so the team factored in politics.'

He cleared his throat, and continued when no one commented. 'There was no evidence, no reason for them to look at Kirkendall at that time. He'd made no threat, and his case had been resolved about three years prior to the incident. With, ah, what we have now, we can look at Kirkendall, his pattern and pathology, and conclude that he hit Moss in the city rather than at the cabin because it, um, murked the waters. And it was more of a challenge. More of a statement.'

'Agreed,' Eve said and watched Trueheart take an easing breath. 'What about the device?'

'Well, that's pretty interesting.' Baxter gestured with his burger. 'And another reason the primary and team concluded urban terrorism. What they were able to sweep up from scene, then sim, indicated a military-style device. This wasn't any homemade boomer some yahoo stuck together in his basement because he was pissed off some judge made him pay child support. Lab guys creamed over it − primary's words − plaston base, and it don't come cheap, electronic trigger designed to blow when the engine engaged, and . . .' He made a wide gesture, pulling his arms apart. '. . . explode outwards for additional damage.'

Something flickered in her mind. 'Okay, how could they be sure Moss would be the one to engage the engine? What about the wife?'

'Didn't drive.'

'Not good enough. Even private lots can make a few extra fees by renting out a vehicle. You got to factor that in. And Kirkendall would want a hundred percent success rate. I want the lab to take another look. I'm betting there was a fail-safe on it. That he had control, and could detonate or abort by remote if necessary. Clinton's their E and B man,' she stated. 'That's the specialty that pops out of his data, but Kirkendall would want the control.'

'I'll give the lab a push,' Baxter agreed. 'We also spoke

with the primary on the Duberry murder. Now there's a guy who's dug in.'

'Meaning?'

'He figured the ex-boyfriend. He still figures the ex-boyfriend. I'm not going to say he missed anything on the investigation, but I'll be going over it again myself. He homed on this guy and that's that.'

'Boyfriend alibied?'

'Right and tight. Get this.' He wiggled a fry at her, bit it in two. 'He's home alone, and the building's scan cams are crap. So yeah, you might think, hey, he could slip out, do the deal, slip back, no big. But in the apartment above him, there's this guy with this big-ass water bed. Snuck that in past building regs. Weighs a fricking ton. Top it off, he likes to party. Got himself two economy-sized ladies up there for a three-way. And while they're surfing, they get pretty enthusiastic. Bed pops, and you got yourself a frigging ocean. Water comes gushing through the ceiling, and nearly drowns the guy below. Big altercation between upstairs and down, all witnessed by neighbors – and taking place at the time Duberry was strangled.'

'Huh.' Eve stepped over, stole one of Baxter's fries.

'Primary's sure the guy was behind it. You got a woman with no known enemies, ordinary life. You got no sexual assault, no burglary, so you gotta figure personal.'

'Ex-boyfriend's going to rape her – high probability,' Eve put in. 'Do some damage to her face, too. *That's* personal.'

'Yeah, but the primary figures he hired somebody to do

her. But the guy doesn't have the financials for a hit. He's barely making rent. And this was a prime hit. He's got no priors, no known association with the dark side. The guy's not in it, Dallas. We started the interviews again. Nobody comes up with any motive, nobody remembers the vic talking about any worries. Her communication and data equipment is long gone, but EDD did the scans, and came up zip.'

'Okay, clock out for the night. Peabody and McNab are out talking to Kirkendall's former sister-in-law. We'll brief here, oh eight hundred.'

'Good enough. Listen, Trueheart and I thought we could take the night shift on the kid. We can bunk here.' He shrugged a shoulder when Eve frowned at him. 'She's a cutie. Gets to you. Rough day for her. We could hang out with her awhile, take her mind off it.'

'Talk to Summerset about where you should bunk. I appreciate the extra duty.'

'No problem.' He lifted the burger to his mouth again, then paused. 'Where did Peabody head to interview the sister-in-law?'

'Nebraska.'

'Nebraska.' He bit in, chewed thoughtfully. 'Do people really live there? I thought it was one of those myths. You know, like Idaho.'

'People live in Idaho, too, sir,' Trueheart told him.

'Step out.' Baxter laughed, and swept a fry through ketchup. 'The stuff you learn.'

* * *

The two-passenger shuttle landed in a small cargo station in North Platte. As per Roarke's memo, there was a vehicle waiting for the last leg of the trip.

Peabody and McNab stood in the chilly evening air, staring at the sleek black jewel.

'Oh my God. I thought the shuttle was mag.' Heart skipping, Peabody circled. 'You know, the sleep chairs, the comp stations, the menu on the AutoChef.'

'The speed,' McNab added with a dopey grin.

Peabody sent him one back. 'Yeah. Way uptown. But this—'

'It's a beast.' McNab trailed his fingers over the hood. 'Man, this baby's gotta wing.'

'Bet your ass.'

But when she started to open the driver's-side door, he took her arm. 'Wait. Who says you get to pilot?'

'My partner's primary.'

'Not good enough.'

'Her husband provided the transpo.'

'Not even,' he said with a shake of his head. 'I've got a grade on you, Detective Baby.'

'I wanna.'

He laughed, and dug into one of the many red pockets on his baggy pants. 'I say we flip for it.'

'Let me see that credit first.'

'This level of trust is sad,' he said, but handed it over.

She studied it, turning it over, and back. 'Okay, you call, I flip.'

'Tails, due to how much I like yours.'

'Fine, I'll take heads due to the fact yours is so empty.' She tossed the credit, snatched it out of the air, and slapped it on the back of her hand. 'Damn it!'

'Woo-wee! Strap it in, She-Body, 'cause we're going to orbit.'

She sulked as she walked around to settle in the passenger's side. Not that it wasn't bodacious, even in that position. The seat molded to the tail McNab admired, like a lover's hands, and the dash was a gleaming curve armed with enough gauges to make his claim of going into orbit not out of the realm.

Still pouting, she engaged the map, programmed the desired location. And was told in the computer's melodious male voice the most direct route, given an ETA of twenty minutes at posted speed limits.

Beside her, McNab put on black-framed sun shades with hot red lenses. 'We gonna beat that down cold.'

He was right, she thought. The beast did wing. The thrill of it infected her enough to order the sky roof open.

'You pick the tunes,' McNab shouted over the roar of engine and wind. 'And pump it up!'

She went for trash rock – it seemed to fit – and screamed along with the song as they tore south.

The insanity that was McNab cut the travel time nearly in half. She took a portion of the time saved to rake at what was now a bird's nest on her head, and tame it down to her usual ruler-straight bowl cut. McNab pulled a folding brush out of another pocket and whacked at his knotted ponytail. 'Nice place,' he commented, looking around the yard, the field of corn that ran alongside it. 'If you go for rural.'

'I do. To visit anyway.' She studied the neatly painted red barn, the smaller, trimmer outbuilding, and the pasture where a few spotted cows grazed. 'Somebody takes good care of this.'

She got out, looked at the narrow patch of lawn, the ordered beds of fading fall flowers that led to a two-story white house with a covered porch.

There were festive pumpkins, two with grinning faces carved out, on the steps, reminding her Halloween was only days away.

'Do some dairy,' she observed. 'Some row crops. Probably got some chickens out back.'

'How do you know?'

'This stuff I know. My sister's farm's bigger than this, and she does okay. Hard work, you have to love it to do it, I think. Place like this is small, but well-run. Mostly they self-provide, sell some of the harvest and the by-products at a local market for transport. Maybe they got a hydro out back, too, so they can grow through the winter. But that costs.'

He was out of his element. 'Okay.'

'She was an exec at one of the top communication companies in New York. Fast track. Husband was a producer – daytime drama. Individually they were pulling down double our combined salaries.'

'Now they're working a farm in Nebraska.' He nodded. 'I get you.'

'Somebody already knows we're out here.'

'Yeah.' Behind the shades, his gaze tracked to the dot of yellow blinking above the front door. 'They got motion and cams, bet it's a three-sixty scan. More on the fence lines, east and west. A lot of security for a little farm in West Bumfuck, Nebraska.'

They went to the door, knocked. Steel-reinforced, McNab thought, and noted the shimmer on the windows. Lockdown alarms.

'Yes?' The voice through the intercom was female, and firm.

'Mrs Turnbill? We're the police. Detectives Peabody and McNab with the New York City Police and Security Department.'

'That's not a police vehicle.'

'No, ma'am, it's private.' Peabody held up her badge. 'We'd like to speak with you, and will wait until you verify our IDs.'

'I don't—'

'You spoke with my partner, Lieutenant Dallas, earlier today. I understand your caution under the circumstances, Mrs Turnbill, but it's important we speak with you. If you refuse, we'll contact the local authorities and arrange for a warrant. I don't want to do that. We've gone to some trouble to keep this visit quiet, to insure your safety.'

'Wait.'

Like Peabody, McNab kept his badge up, and watched the thin red light shimmer out, scan both. Somebody, he thought, isn't just cautious, but scared. Right into the bowels.

The door opened. 'I'll speak with you, but I can't tell you any more than I told Lieutenant Dallas.' As she spoke a man came down from the second floor. His face was grim, his eyes cold.

'Why can't you people leave us alone?'

'The kids?' his wife asked him.

'Fine. I told them to stay upstairs.'

He was stocky in the way that told Peabody he did manual labor routinely. His face was tanned, squint lines scoring out from his eyes, his hair bleached by the sun.

Six years, she thought, had made him more farmer than urbanite. And the way he kept one hand in the pocket of his work pants warned her he was carrying.

'Mr Turnbill, we've come a long way, and not to harass you. Roger Kirkendall is wanted in connection with seven homicides.'

'Only seven.' His lips twisted. 'You're way off.'

'That may be, but it's the seven that concern us at the moment.' Taking his cue, McNab kept his voice as brittle as Turnbill's, and drew crime scene photos from his field bag. 'Here's a couple to start.' He'd gone straight to the kids, and saw by the way Roxanne paled, it had been the right move. 'They were sleeping when he cut their throats. I guess that's a mercy.'

380

'Oh God.' Roxanne wrapped her arms around her belly. 'Oh my God.'

'You've got no right to come in here and do this.'

'Oh yeah.' McNab's eyes were merciless as they met Turnbill's. 'We do.'

'McNab.' Peabody murmured it, deliberately reached out and pulled back the photos. 'I'm sorry. Sorry to disturb you, sorry to upset you. We need your help.'

'We don't know anything.' Turnbill put his arm around his wife's shoulders. 'We just want to be left alone.'

'You left high-powered, high-paying jobs six years ago,' McNab began. 'Why?'

'That's none of your—'

'Joshua.' Roxanne shook her head. 'I need to sit down. Let's just sit down.'

She turned into a living room showing the chaotic debris of young children, the comfortable wear of family. Roxanne sat, gripped her husband's hand. 'How do you know he did it? He's gotten away with so much for so long, how do you know?'

'We have evidence linking him to the crimes. Those children, their parents, and a domestic were all murdered in their beds. Grant Swisher was your sister's attorney in her divorce and custody case.'

'Six years ago,' she replied. 'Yes, he could wait six years. He could wait sixty.'

'Do you have any idea where he is?'

381

'None. He leaves us alone now. He leaves us alone. We're not important any more. We don't want to be.'

'Where's your sister?' McNab demanded, and Roxanne jerked. 'She's dead. He killed her.'

'We believe he's capable of doing so.' Peabody kept her eyes level on Roxanne's. 'But he hasn't. Not yet. What if he finds her before we find him? What if you have some information and refuse to cooperate with us, impede our investigation long enough for him to hunt her down?'

'I don't know where she is.' Weary tears filled Roxanne's eyes. 'Her, my nephew, my niece. I haven't seen them in six years.'

'But you know she's alive. You know she got away from him.'

'I thought she was dead. For two years. I went to the police, but they couldn't help. I thought he'd killed them. And then—'

'You don't have to do this, Roxie.' Her husband drew her closer. 'You don't have to go through this again.'

'I don't know what to do. What if he comes here? What if he does, after all this time? Our babies, Joshua.'

'We're safe here.'

'You've got a good security system.' McNab drew Turnbill's attention back to him. 'So did the Swishers. The nice family on the Upper West Side he slaughtered. Their good security system didn't help them.'

'We'll help you,' Peabody assured them. 'We'll arrange for police protection for you, for your family. We took

382

private transpo out of New York, under the radar. He doesn't know we're here. He doesn't, at this time, know we're looking for him. The longer it takes to find him, the better the chance he'll know.'

'When will this be over?'

'When we find him.' McNab shut down on compassion as the tears slid down Roxanne's cheeks. 'We'll find him sooner with your help.'

'Joshua. Please, would you get me some water?'

He studied her face, then nodded. 'Are you sure?' he asked as he rose. 'Roxie, are you sure?'

'No, but I know I don't want to live like this.' She took slow breaths as he left the room. 'It's worse for him, I think. Worse. He works so hard for so little. We were happy in New York. Such an exciting city, full of so much energy. We both had careers we loved, we were good at. We'd just bought a townhouse. Because I was pregnant. My sister . . .'

She trailed off, managed a smile when her husband came in with a glass of water. 'Thanks, honey. My sister was damaged, I guess you could say. He damaged her. Years of abuse, physical, emotional, mental. I tried to get her to leave, to get help. I'd talk to her, but she was too afraid, or too entrenched, and I was the little sister who didn't understand. It was her fault, you see. I did a lot of studying on battered syndrome in those days. I'm sure you've seen your share of it.'

'Too much,' Peabody agreed.

'He was worse than anything, than anybody. Not just

because she was my sister. It's not that he likes to cause pain, to harm. It's that it means nothing to him. He might snap the bone in her finger for having dinner on the table two minutes late – according to his schedule – then sit down and eat a hot meal without a single flicker of emotion. Can you imagine living like that?'

'No, ma'am. No,' Peabody repeated, 'I can't.'

'She was property to him, Dian and the children. It was when he began to hurt the children that she was able to pull out of the mire. He'd already damaged them, too, but she thought she was protecting them, keeping the *family* together. He brutalized them, punishments, his brand of discipline. Solitary confinement, he'd call it, or he'd make them stand in cold showers for an hour, deny them food for two days. Once he cut off all of my niece's hair because he said she'd taken too long brushing it. But then he began to beat Jack, my nephew. Toughen him up, he claimed. One day, when Roger was out, she found her son with Roger's army-issue stunner. He'd put it on full, he was holding it here . . .'

She pressed her fingers to the pulse in her throat. 'He was going to kill himself. This eight-year-old boy was going to end his own life rather than face another day with that monster. It woke her up. She left. She took the kids, nothing else. She didn't even pack a bag. There were shelters I'd told her about, and she ran to one.'

Roxanne closed her eyes, drank deeply. 'I don't know if she'd have gone through with it, expect for the children. But once she did, it was like a miracle. She got herself back.

And a few weeks later, she hired a lawyer. It was horrible, going through the trial, but she did it. She stood up to him, and she won.'

'She never intended to adhere to the conditions, to stay in New York, to allow him to see the kids again,' Peabody said.

'I don't know. She never told me, never even hinted, but no, I think not. I think she must have planned to run all along. I don't know how else she could have managed to get away from him.'

'There are undergrounds, for people in her situation.'

'Yes. I didn't know then. When she vanished, I was sure he'd killed her and the kids. He's not only capable, but he has the means, the training. Even when he took me, I thought—'

'He abducted you?'

'I was on the subway coming home, and I felt a little sting.' She cupped a hand around her biceps. 'I felt sick and dizzy – and I don't remember. I remember waking up, still sick. It was a room, a big room. No windows and just this ugly greenish light. He'd taken my clothes, all of my clothes.'

She pressed her lips together until they went white, reached blindly for her husband's hand. 'I was on the floor, my hands in restraints. And as I woke I was lifted up, by some sort of pulley, so that I was standing, had to stand on my toes. I was six months pregnant with Ben.'

Turnbill pressed his face into his wife's shoulder, and Peabody could see now that he wept.

'He stepped in front of me. He had some sort of rod. He said, "Where is my wife?" Even before I could answer, he pressed the tip of the rod here.' She laid a hand between her breasts. 'Horrible pain, electrical shock. He told me, very calmly, that he had the rod on low, and would up the power every time I lied.

'I told him I knew he'd killed her, and he shocked me again. And again and again. I begged, I screamed, I pleaded, for myself, for my baby. He left me there, I don't know how long, then he came back and did it all again.'

'He had her over twelve hours.' Turnbill sucked in breath, ignored the tears on his face. 'The police – you can't file a report, a missing person's, that soon. I tried, but they said it wasn't enough time, when I called. But it was a lifetime, for both of us. It was a miracle she didn't miscarry. When he was done with her, he dumped her on the sidewalk in Times Square.'

'He believed me, finally. He must have known that I would've told him anything just to stop the pain. So he believed me, and before he knocked me out again, he told me if I went to the police – if I implicated him in any way – he would find me again. He would cut the brat out of my belly and slit its throat.'

'Roxanne.' Peabody spoke quietly. 'I know this is very hard for you to speak about. But I need to know: Was Kirkendall alone when he held you?'

'No. He had that bastard with him. They were joined at the hip, claimed to be brothers. Isaac, Isaac Clinton. They were in the army together. He . . . he sat at some sort of console, controls. I don't know. I think he was studying some kind of readout. They had some sort of hookup on me, like in a hospital. He sat, the whole time Roger tortured me, and he never spoke. Not one word. At least not when I was conscious.'

'Was there anyone else?'

'I'm not sure. Sometimes I thought I heard voices, maybe a woman's. But I was out of my mind. I didn't see anyone else, and I was unconscious when they took me out, when they tossed me onto the street.'

'You didn't tell the police that you knew your abductors?'

'When I . . . when I came out of it, I was in the hospital. I was afraid for my life, for my baby's life. So I said nothing. I told them I couldn't remember anything.'

'What do you expect—'Turnbill began, but Peabody sent him a look of such sympathy his voice broke.

'I expect I would have done exactly the same,' she told him. 'I expect my only clear thought would be to protect my child, my husband, myself.'

'We said nothing,' Roxanne continued, her voice a little stronger.

'We left New York, we left our lives there, and came here. My parents live nearby. I realized she'd run – Dian— but I thought he'd find her. Kill her. Two years, I was sure she was gone. Then I answered the 'link. She'd blocked the video, but she said my name. She said my name and we're safe. That's all. She broke the connection. I get those calls every few months, sometimes more than a year between. That's all she ever says.'

'When was the last time she contacted you?'

'Three weeks ago. I don't know where she is, and if I did I wouldn't tell you, for the same reasons I said nothing after the abduction. We've made a life here. We have two sons now, and they're happy. This is their home. And still, we live in a prison because of this one man. I'm afraid every day, every single day.'

'We're going to find him, Roxanne, and when we do, you won't have to be afraid again. Tell me about the room where they held you,' Peabody said. 'Every detail you remember.'

19

Eve was back at her desk when Roarke came into her office. He immediately sniffed the air.

'What? No. Baxter, Trueheart. Let cops loose near food, it's a free-for-all. They'd want a place in the city, wouldn't they?'

'Baxter and Trueheart? Is there something about their relationship I've missed?'

'What?'

'You keep saying that. You need to eat.'

Her mind cleared slightly as he moved into the kitchen. 'I'm not talking about Baxter and Trueheart.'

'I'm perfectly aware of that. And yes, I agree. Kirkendall and associates would want a place in the city. Why risk running into pesky commuter traffic, or pesky commuter traffic cops?'

'I bet it's Upper West.'

'We agree again.' He came back in with two plates, and this time Eve sniffed the air. 'What is that?'

'Lasagna.' Veggie lasagna, he thought. One of the easiest ways to get something green in her system that wasn't a gumdrop was to disguise it in pasta.

'Why do you agree? About the Upper West?'

He set one of the plates in front of her, the other across the desk. Then went to get a chair, and two glasses of wine. When a man wanted to eat a meal with his wife, and his wife was Eve, Roarke thought, the man learned to make adjustments.

'Considerable time and effort went into casing out the Swisher property. Not only the electronics, but lifestyle. They knew where to go and when to go. So—'

He set her wine down, tapped his glass against it, then sat. 'More efficient to have a location near the target point. You can do drive-bys, walk-bys, test your jammers and so on against their system. And you'd want to watch them.'

She watched him as she cut into the lasagna. 'Because you'd want to see them alive before you saw them dead.'

'Oh yes. It's personal. So though the kill is clean and quick, you'd want the rush beforehand. Look at them, they don't know I have the power to end them. When and how I like.'

'It's a little strange being hooked up with someone who can think that much like a killer.'

He lifted his glass to her. 'I'll say precisely the same. And make a considerable wager that your thoughts ran parallel to mine.'

'Yeah, you win.' She sampled the lasagna. Something in there tasted like spinach. But it wasn't half bad. 'You come up with anything for me?'

'I'm a little hurt you'd have to ask. Eat first. You've heard from Peabody?'

'They're on their way back. Want to hear the roundup?'

'Of course.'

She told him while they ate.

'Torturing a pregnant woman,' Roarke commented. 'Lower and lower. But he should've killed her, in hindsight. It seems his long-suffering wife learned enough from him to keep her location – more likely locations, as she'd be smarter to move every few months at least – from everyone. He kept the sister alive assuming that his wife would, at some point, run to her family.'

'Then they'd all be dispensable. I really want this guy.'

This time Roarke reached over, laid a hand on hers. 'I know.'

'Do you? He's not like my father. There's a world of difference, but somehow they're exactly the same.'

'Brutalizing his children, day after day. Training them in his own sick fashion. Breaking their spirit, destroying their innocence, driving a young boy to contemplate suicide. The difference between him and your father, Eve, is Kirkendall has more skill, more training, and a sharper brain. But inside, they couldn't be more alike.'

It helped that he saw that, and understood why her mind kept circling around it. 'I have to get past it, or I'll mess up. Location.' She nodded toward the map on her screen. 'Lots of prime property Upper West. Have to be solo occupants. He can afford it. All those hefty fees, combined with his brother's hefty fees – and possibly Isenberry's. Investments like the dojo show me he likes business, making money from money. Yeah, he's plush. You have any luck with the money?'

'Again, my sensitive feelings are bruised.'

'You can take a punch, ace. Let me have it.'

He merely sent a meaningful glance at the food still on her plate. 'Jeez.' She forked up a huge bite, stuffed it in. 'Spill.'

'He has what we'll call his dumping account, which coordinates with the profits from the dojo. Hefty, but not enough to finance this sort of operation.'

'So he's got other accounts.'

'Has to. He doesn't dip into this one, just dumps the funds, and his personal data on it leads to a law firm out of Eden.'

'Eden? Like the garden thereof?'

'Based on. A manmade island in the South Pacific created ostensibly for recreation and in reality for tax evasion, money laundering. It takes considerable doing to get past the legal blocks there to gain information. And it takes considerable funds to open accounts there, or utilize any of their legal protection.'

'You've used it.'

'Actually, I helped create it. Before I saw the light of truth and justice.' He grinned when she just stared at him. 'I sold out my interests there before we were married. However, since I did have some part in the design, I have ways of getting to information. Kirkendall's covered himself very well. His law firm there leads to an off-planet financial firm, which leads – Do you want to hear all this?'

'Bottom-line it for now.'

'It all circles back to other numbered accounts. Five. All very plush indeed, and all under various aliases. The most interesting is one with a single deposit of just under twenty million.'

'That's million? Two-oh.'

'A tad under. But doing the math, that's well over and above any of the recorded fees I've found so far – that is, including the other accounts, which jibe with those fees, and expenses.'

'He hired out to more than sanctioned US agencies.'

'There will be other accounts, I haven't swept them all up yet. It's going to take some time. But this account is interesting for a couple of reasons. The lump-sum deposit, for one. Have a look at this.'

He drew a disc out of his pocket, plugged it in her unit himself. 'Data on-screen.'

Eve skimmed the data – another CIA file on Kirkendall. 'Subject is considered nonsecure. Get them,' she muttered. 'Train yourself a killer, then oops, he's no longer secure. Last psych eval, eighteen months ago. Sociopathic tendencies – another huge surprise. Suspected ties to Doomsday – and the big surprises keep rolling. Suspected ties to . . . Cassandra.'

Doomsday Group, she thought. Techno-terrorist organization she'd brushed up against, by default, on a recent case.

But Cassandra, they'd been more flexible in the terrorist game, and her involvement with them the year before much more personal.

They'd nearly killed her, and Roarke, in their quest to destroy New York's landmarks. Took out a couple, too, she remembered with some bitterness, before she'd put the hurt on the ring leaders.

'And the bell rings. They were keeping him active as much to watch him as to utilize his skills. Look at the dates.' Roarke gestured with his fork. 'When they lost him. When he went rogue according to both this file and the one I dug out of Homeland – which also coordinates with the same entries on his brother's file and Isenberry's.'

'September of last year. Just a few months before we got the first Cassandra letter. Before things started blowing up in the city.'

'And the date of the hefty deposit.'

'After we broke their back. We got most of them – figured we got most of them, but you never get all the rats crawling off the sinking ship. We got to most of the money, too, but they were a well-financed terrorist organization.'

'And it appears Kirkendall scooped up a chunk of the funds, or was given them for safekeeping.'

'One more reason to take him down. I don't like leaving rats outside the cage.'

'He went rogue,' Roarke pointed out. 'All three of them are on various agencies' lists. Though, again, you can see by the file that the status was lowered after Cassandra scattered. And there's no indication he's had any facial surgery.'

'We had doctors on Cassandra. I'll pop up that file, start looking at them. He's left a trail. Everyone does.' When Roarke gently cleared his throat, she slid her gaze in his direction. 'Even you, ace. If I wanted to find yours, I'd just put you on as consultant.'

It made him laugh. 'I imagine I could find myself, if I tried hard enough. I'll get back to it. I have to say the ins and outs are fairly fascinating.'

'You find any connection to a building in the city – especially Upper West – to any of those aliases or blinds, you get a big bonus.'

Those blue eyes went wicked. 'Of my choosing.'

'Pervert.' She swung back to her computer.

'I got the meal, you deal with the dishes.' He rose, then waited when her communicator beeped.

'Dallas.'

Dispatch, Dallas, Lieutenant Eve. The body of a woman identified as Newman, Meredith, has been discovered. Report Broadway and Fordham as primary. Scene is being secured.

'Acknowledged. Dallas out. Up to eleven – twelve if we add Jaynene Brenegan,' she said as she rose. 'That's nearly to the Bronx.'

'I'll go with you.'

'No. She's found because he wanted her found. Takes manpower away from the Swisher case. No big if we make that connect, because it doesn't connect him with Moss

395

and Duberry or Brenegan. So he thinks. I need you here doing that thing you do. I'll take Trueheart. It's good training for him. I'd rather have Baxter here on the kid.'

'He knows they'll pull you in on this. Primary on Swisher, she's the caseworker on Nixie. He could be waiting for you.'

She walked to the closet, pulled out a vest. She stripped off her shirt, put it on. 'I hope so. I won't be going in blind,' she added as she tugged the shirt back in place.

She moved to her desk, took out her clutch piece and strapped on her ankle holster. 'I know he's hoping to get a shot at me.'

'Then make sure he doesn't get one.' He walked over, buttoned her shirt himself. 'And make sure you come home.'

'I'll be back.' She hitched on her weapon harness, motioned toward her desk. 'Your bad luck. You're stuck with the dishes.'

'You've got good eyes,' Eve said to Trueheart. 'Use them. Suspects may be observing the scene. They may be mixed with the lookie-loos, or based farther away using long-range. You spot anything that gives you a tingle, I hear about it.'

She stepped out of her vehicle, looked at him over the roof. 'At this point, Baxter would add, "Especially if the tingle comes from seeing a hot skirt loitering in the vicinity who looks like she'd put out for a couple of overworked cops." '

She waited a beat while Trueheart's face reddened.

'I, however, am not interested in that kind of tingle.'

'Yes, sir. I mean, no, sir.'

She saw the scene was secured with police barricades. And that, as expected, the usual gang of gawkers had gathered. It was the sort of area, she thought as she scanned street, sidewalk, windows, roofs, where a good percentage of the gawkers would be pickpockets, and another good percentage would go home with those pockets handily emptied.

Their problem.

She hooked her badge to her waistband, headed in.

'Suit's here,' one of the uniforms called out, and she stopped in her tracks.

She turned, very slowly, caught him in the crosshairs of her cold gaze. 'Don't ever call me a suit.'

She left him, withered, and moved toward the crumpled body of Meredith Newman. 'First on scene?' she asked the uniform standing by. 'Yes, sir. My partner and I responded to a call from this location, reporting a body in the alley between the buildings. One of the owners of the restaurant stepped out in the alley on her break, and observed what appeared to be a body. Upon responding, we—'

'I got it. Have you secured the witness?'

'Yes, sir, along with other kitchen staff who also entered the scene in response to the first witness's screams.'

Eve puffed out her cheeks as she looked around the alley. 'How many people have tromped around on my scene?'

'At least six, Lieutenant. I'm sorry, they'd already come

out, looked around – and moved the body – by the time we arrived. We moved the civilians back into the restaurant and secured the scene.'

'All right.' She did another study of the alley. Short and narrow, dead-ending into the graffiti-laced wall of another. Confidence, arrogance again, she decided. They could have dumped her anywhere, or simply destroyed the body.

Still, there was no security here. No cams on any of the exit doors. Pull in, dump, pull out. And wait for somebody to trip over what's left of her.

'Seal up, Trueheart,' she ordered, and continued to examine the body as she drew out her own can of Seal-It. 'Record on. What do you see?'

'Female, early thirties, clothes removed.'

'You can say naked, Trueheart. You're of age.'

'Yes, sir. Ligature marks, wrists, ankles. What appear to be burn marks on shoulders, torso, arms, legs, indicate torture. The throat's been deeply cut. There's no blood. She wasn't cut here, but killed elsewhere and put here.'

Eve crouched, turned one of the dead hands at the wrist. 'She's cold. Like meat you put in a friggie to keep it fresh. They had her stowed. She's been dead since the day they grabbed her.'

But she got out her gauge to estimate the time of death and confirmed. 'Burn marks on her back and buttocks as well. Bruising might be from the grab. Abrasions are consistent with the body hitting the pavement, rolling. Way postmortem.'

She fit on her goggles, examined the area around the mouth and eyes. 'It looks like they taped her up. Skin's reddened here, shows a pattern that would match tape, but there's no residue.'

She sat back on her heels.

'What else do you see, Trueheart?'

'The location—'

'No, the body. Focus on her. She's been dead for days now. There's evidence of considerable torture. She had her throat cut, and going with previous pattern, she was alive when the knife went in. What do you see?'

Concentration settled over his face. Then he shook his head. 'I'm sorry, sir.'

'She's clean, Trueheart. What do you do when somebody inflicts burns on your body strong enough to singe flesh? You don't just scream your lungs out and beg for mercy. You piss yourself, you soil yourself, you puke. Your body erupts, and it voids. But she's clean. Somebody washed her down, even to removing the residue from whatever they used to blindfold and gag her. We won't find any trace on her.'

She bent close, sniffed the skin. 'Smells like hospital. Antiseptic. Maybe the lab boys can give us more there. For what it's worth. She bit right through her own lip,' Eve observed, then pushed to her feet.

She put her hands on her hips, studied the alley. The usual overworked recyclers, but it was clean, too, as alleys went. Some graffiti – sort of artsy – but none of the nasty debris left behind by sidewalk sleepers or junkies, even the street LCs and their clients.

She turned to the first on-scene. 'What do you know about this place – this restaurant here, this business next door.'

'Actually, it's a Free-Ager center – classes, crafts, like that. And the restaurant's run by the group. Grow a lot of the stuff in Greenpeace Park, bring it in from some of their communes. Run a clean place, even if it is mostly health food.'

'Run a clean alleyway, too.'

'Yeah. I mean, yes, sir. We don't get many calls here.'

'The woman who found her, what's her name?'

He had to consult his book. 'Leah Rames.'

'Trueheart, stay here, sweepers should be on-scene momentarily.' Eve walked into the storeroom, took a quick glance at the tidy shelves of supplies, and moved into the kitchen beyond.

Tidy was the watchword here, as well. Something was steaming on the stove, but that stove was huge and scrubbed to a gleam. Counters were simple white, covered with signs of meal prep in progress. Who knew it took so much stuff to make food? There were friggies and cold boxes, some kind of gargantuan oven, and not a civilized AutoChef in sight.

Several people, all wearing long white aprons, were seated on stools around an island counter. Some of them were chopping at things with wicked-looking knives. Others just sat. And all looked at her when she entered.

'Leah Rames?'

A woman, mid-forties, lean, long sandy hair thickly braided, lifted a hand like a schoolgirl. Her face was milk-white.

'I'm Leah. Do you know what happened to that poor woman?' The gash in the throat should've been a clue, but something about the earnest question and the earnest setup of the kitchen sucked up Eve's sarcasm.

'I'm Lieutenant Dallas, with Homicide. I'm the primary on this matter.'

'You're Dee's boss – partner,' Leah corrected with an attempt to smile. 'Is she with you?'

'No, she's on another assignment. You know Detective Peabody?'

'Yes, and her family. My life partner and I lived near the Peabodys until we moved here.' She reached out to lay her hand over the hand of the man who sat beside her.

'We opened our center and restaurant about eight months ago. Peabody and her young man came for dinner once or twice. Can you tell us what happened? We know everyone in this area. We've made a point of it. I know there are some rough characters, but I can't believe anyone who comes here could have done this.'

'You don't have security on your alley exits.'

'No.' It was the man who spoke now. 'We believe in trust. And in giving back.'

'And in community relations,' Leah added. 'We give food out in the alley after closing every night. We spread the word that we would provide this service as long as the alley was kept clean, that no one used it to do illegals, to harm anyone else, or littered. The first few weeks it was touch and go, mostly go, but eventually the food, given freely, turned the tide. And now . . .'

'Why did you go out in the alley?'

'I thought I heard something. Like a thud. I was in the storeroom getting some supplies. Sometimes people come, knock on the door early. I opened the door, thinking if they didn't seem in dire need, I'd tell them to come back at closing. She was right there, right by the door. She was naked, and facedown. I thought, By the goddess, someone's raped this poor woman. I bent down, I spoke to her. . . . I touched her, her shoulder, I think, I'm not sure. I touched her, and she was so cold. I didn't think dead, not immediately. I just thought, oh, poor, poor thing, she's so cold, and I turned her over, calling for Genoa.'

'She called.' The life partner took up the story. 'I could tell something was wrong, by the tone, and I stopped what I was doing in here. She started screaming before I got to the storeroom. Several of us rushed out then. I thought she was injured – the woman – and tried to pick her up. Then I saw she was dead. We called for the police. I stayed with her, with the woman, until they came. I thought someone should.'

'Did you see anyone else in the alley? See any vehicle or person leaving the alley?' she asked Leah.

'I saw, just for a second, taillights. They were gone so fast, I just saw the blocks of them.'

'Blocks?'

'Like building blocks. Three red squares, one on top of the other on either side. It was only a glimpse, I'm sorry. I wouldn't have seen even that if I'd looked down instead of over first.'

'Did you hear them drive in, drive out?'

'I might have. I'm not sure. We have music playing back here while we work. I'd only been in the storeroom a minute or so, and I was humming. You can hear the street traffic from there, but you tune it out. You understand? You hear it, but you don't. I think — I wish I could be sure — but I think I might've heard an engine in the alley before I heard the thump, and then the sound of driving away. I'm almost sure, now that I put myself back there, almost sure.'

'Have you ever seen this man?' Eve offered the composite of Kirkendall.

'No, I'm sorry. Did he—'

'Pass this around,' Eve interrupted. 'See if anyone else recognizes him. Or her.' She handed Leah a copy of Isenberry's ID photo.

When she exited, Eve gestured to Trueheart. 'Any tingles?'

'No, sir. So far the canvass hasn't turned up anybody who saw a vehicle entering or leaving the alley.'

'Witness heard the body hit — and caught a glimpse of the taillights at the mouth of the alley. Three vertical squares on each side. Little bits and pieces. If the witness hadn't been all but on top of the exit door when she hit, nobody would have seen even that much.'

403

'Bad luck for them,' Trueheart said.

'Yeah, bad luck for them. We'll let the CSU and sweepers do their thing, for what it's worth, and write this up from my home office. We've got another face to pin to our board, Trueheart.'

She looked at the black bag being loaded into the morgue wagon. 'Bad luck for her.'

'I didn't mean any disrespect before, Lieutenant, regarding the bad luck comment.'

'I didn't hear any disrespect.' As she walked back toward her vehicle, she scanned as she had before. Street, sidewalks, windows, roofs, faces. 'Meredith Newman was dead the minute they laid hands on her. There was nothing we could do for her. So we do for her now.'

'I shouldn't have missed the points on-scene. The fact that the body had been sanitized.'

'No, you shouldn't have. You won't next time.' She drove south, taking her time. 'You learning anything working under Baxter?'

'He pushes the details, and he's patient. I'm grateful you gave me the chance to work in Homicide, Lieutenant, and to train under Baxter.'

'He hasn't corrupted you yet.' She turned east, cruised.

'He says he's working on that,' Trueheart said with a quick smile. 'He speaks highly of you, Lieutenant. I know he kids around, that's his way. But he has nothing but the greatest respect for you as a police officer.'

'He didn't, he wouldn't be on this investigative team.'

She checked the rearview, the sideview, back to the front. She turned south again. 'And if I didn't have the same for him, he wouldn't be on this team.'

She pulled up at a bodega, dug out credits. 'Run in, will you, get me a tube of Pepsi. Whatever you're drinking.'

The fact that he didn't appear to find the request odd told her Baxter sent the kid off on similar errands routinely. While he dashed out and into the shop, Eve sat, watched, tapped her fingers lightly on the butt of her weapon.

Trueheart came out with her Pepsi, and a cherry fizzy for himself. She waited until he'd strapped in, then began to cruise as before.

'Do we have another stop to make, sir?' he asked a few moments later.

'Why do you ask?'

'You're well east now of your home.'

'That's right. Keep drinking that fizzy, Trueheart, keep facing front. But check the side mirror. You see that black panel van about five vehicles back?'

He did as ordered. 'Yes, sir.'

'Same one's been on us since we left the scene. Not all the time, didn't pick us up until we were about four blocks south, but it keeps sliding in, four, five, six back. Gave them a chance to come at me when I sent you in for refreshing beverages.'

'Sir!'

'They didn't take it. They're just watching awhile. Just watching, maybe trying to catch a transmission, maybe thinking I might lead them to wherever we've got the kid stashed. Careful, careful, careful. Me, I'm getting a little tired of watching.'

'I'll call it in.'

'No! They're close enough, maybe they can monitor transmissions. You don't call anything in until I say different. You strapped in all right and tight, Trueheart?'

'Yes, sir.'

'Good. Hold on to your fizzy.'

She'd gone as far east as Second, and now at an intersection, whipped the wheel, slapped into a steep vertical lift, and executed a rapid and airborne three-sixty.

'Hit the sirens,' she snapped at Trueheart. 'Call it in now! Street and air support. Black panel van, New York plates. Abel-Abel-Delta-4-6-1-3. And up they go.'

The van shot into vertical, then blasted like cannon shot down Second. A white light exploded in front of Eve's windshield and shook the air like thunder.

'Shit on a stick. They've got laser rifles. Fricking armed and fricking dangerous, heading south on Second at Seventy-eight. Make that west on Seventy-seven, approaching Park. Look at that bastard *move*.'

'Juiced up.' Trueheart's voice was even as he spoke, as he gave dispatch a rapid-fire report of their direction. But it had gone up a full octave.

The van shot out another blast, then dropped to street level, punching up speed in a shower of sparks as they streamed onto Fifth and aimed south.

She saw two black-and-whites cut over from the west at Sixty-fifth, move to intercept. Pedestrians scattered, and some of them went airborne as the next blast boomed out. One of the black-and-whites was flung into the air to spiral like a top.

Eve was forced to slap vertical again to avoid collision and panicked civilians. She lost nearly half a block before she could set down and increase speed. Then she screamed downtown after the building-block red squares of the van's taillights.

Another blast knocked her back, had her fighting to keep control. Icy red liquid splattered over the dash.

She was gaining. The shops of midtown were a colorful blur as she careened south. Lights and animated billboards were nothing but sparkle.

Overhead, one of the ad blimps boomed out about a buy-one-get-one-half fall sale on winter coats.

She stayed on him, weaving, dodging, matching maneuver to maneuver as he swung west again. She heard the scream of sirens, her own and others.

She would tell herself later she should have anticipated, should have seen it coming.

The maxibus was lumbering in the right-hand lane. The blast from the van rolled it like a turtle, had it skidding over the street. Even as she switched to a straight lift, the maxi's spin caught a Rapid Cab, flipped it into the air like a big yellow ball.

On an oath, Eve whipped right, dived down, managed

to thread between the bus, the cab, and a pocket of people on the sidewalk who were standing with eyes and mouths wide open at the free show.

'Abort standard safety factors!' she shouted and prayed the computer would act quickly enough. 'Abort cushioning gel, goddamn it!' An instant later, she landed with a bone-crunching slap of tires to pavement.

Safety factors aborted. Please reset.

She was too busy swearing, shooting into reverse. But when she pulled out on Seventh, she saw nothing but chaos. And no sign of the van.

She yanked the harness clear, shoved out of the door, and slammed a fist on the roof. 'Son of a bitch! Tell me air support's still got him. Tell me one of the black-and-whites still has him.'

'That's a negative, sir.'

She studied the overturned bus, the wrecked cars, the still screaming pedestrians. There was going to be hell to pay.

She looked over at Trueheart, and for one moment her heart stopped. His face, his uniform jacket, his hair were covered with red.

Then she let out a breath. 'Told you to hold on to that damn fizzy.'

20

Summerset glanced up from his book when Roarke tapped on the jamb of his open parlor door. It was rare for Roarke to come into his private quarters, so he put the book aside, rose.

'No, don't get up. I . . . have you got a minute?'

'Of course.' He looked over at the monitor, saw that Nixie was in bed, sleeping. 'I was about to get a brandy. Would you like one?'

'Yes. I would, yes.'

As he picked up the decanter, Summerset pondered over the fact that Roarke continued to stand, trouble written on his face. 'Is something wrong?'

'No. Yes. No.' Roarke let out a frustrated laugh. 'Well now, I've been stepping on my own feet quite a bit the last days. I've something I want to say to you, and I'm not sure quite how to start it.'

Stiffly now, Summerset handed Roarke a snifter of brandy. 'I realize the lieutenant and I have had a number of difficulties. However—'

'Christ, no, it's nothing to do with that. If I came around every time the two of you locked horns I'd put in a bleeding revolving door.' He stared down at the brandy a moment, decided maybe it would be better done sitting.

He took a chair, swirled the brandy while Summerset did the same. And the silence dragged on.

'Ah, well.' It annoyed him that he had to clear his throat. 'These murders. This child – the children – they've made me think about things I'd rather not. Things I make a point of not thinking of. My father, my own early years.'

'I've gone back a few times myself.'

'You think of Marlena.' Of the daughter, the young, pretty girl who'd been murdered. Raped, tortured, murdered. 'I told Nixie the pain lessens. I think it must. But it never goes completely, does it?'

'Should it?'

'I don't know. I'm still grieving for my mother. I didn't even know her, and I'm still grieving when I thought I'd be done. I wonder how long that little girl will grieve for hers.'

'In some part of her, always, but she'll go on.'

'She's lost more than I ever had. It's humbling to think of. I don't know how . . . You saved my life,' Roarke blurted out. 'No, don't say anything, not until I manage this. I might have lived through that beating, the one he gave me before you found me. I might have survived it, physically. But you saved me that day, and days after. You took me in, and tended to me. You gave me a home when you had no obligation. No one wanted me, and then . . . You did. I'm grateful.'

'If there was a debt, it was paid long ago.'

410

'It can never be paid. I might have lived through that beating, and the next, and whatever came after. But I wouldn't be the man I am, sitting here now. That's a debt I'm not looking to pay, or one you're looking to collect.'

Summerset sipped brandy, two slow sips. 'I would have been lost without you, after Marlena. That's another debt that's not looking for payment.'

'There's been a weight inside me,' Roarke said quietly. 'Since this began, since I found myself faced with the blood of children I didn't know. I could shift it aside, do whatever I needed to do, but it kept rolling back on me. I think, like grief, it might stay there awhile. But it's less now.'

He drank down the brandy, got to his feet. 'Good night.'

'Good night.' When he was alone, Summerset went into his bedroom, opened a drawer, and took out a photograph taken a lifetime ago.

Marlena, fresh and sweet, smiling out at him. Roarke, young and tough, with his arms slung around her shoulder, a cocky grin on his face.

Some children you could save, you could keep, he thought. And some you couldn't.

She got home late enough to consider just going up and dropping fully dressed onto the bed. A headache clamped the back of her neck, digging its hot fingers into the base of her skull. To avoid increasing it with sheer irritation, she pushed Trueheart at Summerset the minute they came in the door.

'Do something with his uniform,' she said, already heading up the stairs. 'And put him to bed. I want him daisy fresh by seven hundred.'

'Your jacket, Lieutenant.'

She peeled it off, still walking, and tossed it over her shoulder. He probably had some household magic that got cherry fizzy off leather.

She aimed straight for the bedroom, then only stood, rubbing the back of her neck, trying to dissolve the rocks that were forming a small mountain range from that point and out to her shoulders. The bed was empty. If he was still working, and likely on her behalf, she could hardly crawl into bed and pull the covers over her head until morning.

She turned, her hand automatically slapping to her weapon, when she saw the movement behind her.

'Christ on airskates, kid. What *is* it with you and skulking around in the dark?'

'I heard you come in.' Nixie stood, this time in a yellow nightgown, with those sleep-starved eyes locked on Eve's face.

'No, not yet.' Eve watched the gaze drop to the floor and didn't know whether to curse or sigh. 'But I know who they are.'

Nixie's eyes flew up again. 'Who?'

'You don't know them. I know who they are. And I know why.'

'Why?'

'Because your father was a good man who did good work. Because he was good, and these people aren't, they wanted to hurt him and everyone he loved.'

'I don't understand that.'

She looked, Eve thought, like a wounded angel with all that tangled blonde hair surrounding a face haunted by fatigue, and worse. 'You're not supposed to understand it. Nobody's supposed to understand why some people decide to take lives instead of living decent ones of their own. But that's the way it is. You're supposed to understand that your father was a good man, your family was a good family. And the people who did this to them, to you, are wrong people. You're supposed to understand that I'll find them and put them in a goddamn cage where they'll spend what's left of their miserable, selfish lives. That has to be good enough, because that's all we've got.'

'Will it be soon?'

'Sooner if I'm working instead of standing here in the damn hallway talking to you.'

The slightest flicker of a smile curved Nixie's lips. 'You're not really mean.'

Eve hooked her thumbs in her front pockets. 'Am, too. Mean as spit, and don't you forget it.'

'Are not. Baxter says you're tough, and sometimes you're scary, but it's because you care about helping people, even when they're dead.'

'Yeah? Well, what does he know? Go back to bed.'

Nixie started toward her room, then paused. 'I think,

413

when you catch them, when you put them in a goddamn cage, my dad and my mom, and Coyle and Inga and Linnie, I think they'll be okay then. That's what I think.'

'Then I better get working on it.'

She waited until Nixie was back in her room, then walked away.

She found Roarke still working with the unregistered, and with barely a grunt of greeting crossed over to take the coffee he had on the console and gulp some down.

A second later she was coughing and shoving it back in his hand. 'Oh, blech. Brandy.'

'If you'd asked, I'd have warned you there was brandy in it. You look a bit worse for wear, Lieutenant. Brandy might be a good idea.'

She shook her head and got herself a cup, strong and black and without additives. 'How's it going here?'

'He's very good – or one of them is very good. Every thread I tug on leads to another knot, which leads to another set of threads. I'll unravel it – I'm bloody determined now – but it won't be quick. But a thought occurred while I've been picking these threads apart. I wonder how he'd feel if his funds were frozen.'

'I've got no forensics, nothing solid tying him to the murders. The best I've got is a composite from a street LC's perspective, which looks nothing like him. I know it's him, but I'll never get the flag to freeze his assets based on nothing much more than my gut.'

'It would be a fairly simple matter for me, at this point, to make a sizable withdrawal from these accounts.'

'Steal the money.'

'Let's say transfer the money. Steal is such a . . . Well, it's a fine word, isn't it? But transfer would be more to your taste.'

She thought it over. Tempting, tempting, tempting. Still, it wasn't only not by the book, it exploded the book entirely. 'Nixie intercepted me, for a change. She said she thought her family would be okay once I caught these guys, once I put them in a goddamn cage.'

'I see.'

'She probably shouldn't swear, I'm a bad influence. Spank me. But—' She broke off at the wide grin that spread over his face, and found herself laughing. She covered her face, rubbed it. 'Just stop. Anyway, that kind of thing gives me a nudge to go out of bounds – more out of bounds,' she added, looking around the room. 'But say you did. Say it pisses him off enough to make the kind of mistake that opens him up to me. Hooray for our side. But it could, given his profile, piss him off enough to have him taking out a couple of Swiss bankers first, or a lawyer in – what was it? Eden. So let's just hold that in reserve.'

'You make a point.'

'You know, this day has just been crap.' She sprawled in the chair, stretched out her legs. 'Making progress, I can feel it, but overall it's been weighed down with big piles of crap. And I finished it up with a cargo ship of shit.'

'Would it have something to do with the blood on your trousers?' She looked down, saw the streaks and sprinkles of red. 'It's not blood. It's cherry fizzy.'

She drank her coffee and began to take him through. 'So when I made them, I pulled up at a twenty-four/seven, sent Trueheart inside for drinks, and—'

'Hold.' He held up a hand. 'You realized one or more of these people, people responsible for several murders and who are, very likely, hoping to get to you, were trailing you, and you sent your backup off for sodas?'

She didn't squirm under his gaze, one she imagined he aimed at underlings who'd cocked up some deal and were about to be demolished by his iciest wrath.

But it was close.

'I wanted to see what they'd do.'

'You were hoping they'd move on you, and got Trueheart out of the way.'

'Not exactly. Close, but—'

'I asked one thing, Eve. That when you decided to use yourself as bait you'd tell me.'

'I wasn't – it was an immediate sort of . . .' She trailed off as the headache moved along from the base of her skull to squeeze into the top of her head. 'Now you're pissed, at me.'

'What gave you your first clue?'

'You'll have to be pissed, then.' She shoved to her feet to prowl. 'You'll just have to be pissed because I can't stop and check every move with you when I'm out there. I can't

416

stop and say, "Hmm, would Roarke approve of this action, or gee, should I tag Roarke and run this by him?" '

'Don't you swat away my concerns like they're gnats around your ears.' He got to his feet as well. 'Don't you dare make light of them, Eve, or what it is to me to sit and wait.'

'I'm not.' But of course she was, a knee-jerk defense mechanism. Before she could say anything else, he was plowing on.

'I bury my own instincts every bloody day to stay out of your way as much as I do. Not to let myself think, every minute of every bloody day you're out there if tonight's the night you don't come back.'

'You can't think that way. You married a cop, you took the package.'

'I did, and I do.'

It wasn't ice in his eyes, she noted. It was fire, strong and blue. And that was somehow worse. 'Then—'

'Have I asked you to change what you are, what you do? Have I complained when you're called away in the middle of the night, or when you come home smelling of death?'

'No. You're better at this than I am. Media flash.'

'Bollocks. We've both managed to fumble our way through nearly two years of each other, and quite well. But when you give your word to me, I expect you to keep it.'

The headache had reached behind her eyes now, stabbing fingers gleefully poking. 'I guess that cargo ship hasn't quite

417

finished dumping shit on me today. And you're right. I broke my word. It wasn't intentional. It was of the moment. And it was wrong. I let it get to me. The kid, the body in the alley, dead cops, children killed in their beds. I let it ball up in my throat, and I know better.'

She shoved the heels of her hands into her temples in a desperate attempt to relieve the pressure. 'It was worth the chance, I believe it was worth the chance, but it turned out to be the wrong call. You're not the first one to scrape me over about it tonight. Whitney's already taken off a few layers of skin.'

Saying nothing, he moved back behind his console, pressed a button. He took a small bottle out of a drawer, tapped two little blue pills into his hand. Then he fetched a small bottle of water out of the friggie behind a panel.

'Take the blockers. Don't argue,' he snapped when she opened her mouth. 'I can see the fucking headache pounding as I'm standing here.'

'It's past headache. It feels like my brains are being squeezed out my ears.' She took the blockers, dropped back into the chair, and dropped her head in her hands. 'I fucked up. Goddamn clusterfuck. Cops and civilians in the hospital, private and city property damage up the wazoo.

Three murder suspects still at large. Because I made the wrong call.'

'I guess that's why they call you lieutenant instead of God. Sit back now, relax a minute.'

'Don't baby me. I don't deserve it. I don't want it. They

were too close. Had to figure they'd stick that close
they were trying to monitor any communication
vehicle has screens, but they've got choice toys, so I h
figure they were within visual for a reason. If they c
track me or monitor me, they needed to be close. I did
want to risk calling it in.'

'That seems reasonable. Logical.'

'Yeah, seems. I call it in, they catch the signal, they poof.
So I pulled over, sent Trueheart into the twenty-four/seven
so it looked like I had a reason, so it looked casual. To see
what they did. They drove by, circled around, and picked me
up again. So then I figure I'll switch it on them. Get behind
them, call in support, keep on them until we can box them
in, take them down. But Jesus Christ, that van *moved*. I don't
know how they've juiced it up, but I clocked it at one-
twenty-six, airborne. Then there were the laser rifles, and
God knows. They took out a couple of black-and-whites, a
number of civilian vehicles, and a maxibus. And I lost them.'

'All by yourself?'

'It was my call. The wrong call. Best I got was make and
model of the van. And the plate. Turns out the plate belongs
to a black panel van of that make and model, but not *that*
panel van. Dupe plates, and they were smart enough to
dupe them from the same type of vehicle. Guy who owns
the legal van – which was legally parked at his place of
business – is a licensed home handy. He's clean, and he was
home watching screen with his wife.'

She took a swig of water. 'So we got injuries, property

because
s. The
ad to
ould
n't

hell, probable — civil suits against the

pects know I've made their ride.'

sed you down right and proper.'

have done differently than you, under the

tances.'

not. Probably not. Still a wrong call. And the mayor
ew out the chief, the chief will chew out the
mander, and down to me. Nobody below me on this
rticular feeding chain. The media will have a feeding frenzy.'

'So, you got your ass kicked a bit. A little ass kicking
from time to time builds character.'

'Hell it does. It results in a sore ass.' She let out a sigh.
'I've got data on all purchases of that make and model.
Popular. I left the color open. Figured it'd be easy to paint.
I don't expect to have bells ring on that angle. If it were
me, I'd've bought it out of town. Or jacked it off some lot
outside New York. There won't be a record, there won't be
a bill of sale.'

'You're discouraged.' And he hated to see it. 'You shouldn't
be.'

'No, just feeling a little beat up tonight. Sorry for my
sorry self.'

'So get some sleep. Start fresh in the morning.'

'You're not.'

'Actually, I will.' He gave commands to save, lock, and
shut down.

'You've got your own work tomorrow.'

'I've rescheduled some things.' He walked her out, secured the doors. 'I spoke with Richard and Beth. They're coming to meet Nixie tomorrow.'

'Tomorrow? I'd asked for quick but I didn't expect immediate.'

'Actually, they've been talking about taking another child. Have just put in applications. And Richard tells me Beth hoped for a girl this time. They both see this as a kind of sign.'

He laid his hand on the base of her neck as they walked to the bedroom and rubbed what she thought of as his magic fingers on the dulling ache. 'Fate's a fickle and often insensitive bitch, isn't she?' he commented. 'And yet, there are moments you see the work. If their daughter hadn't been murdered, they would never have looked to take a child into their home. If a friend of mine hadn't met the same fate, I wouldn't have met that little boy, or paid mind to him, thought of suggesting they might give him a home.'

'If Grant Swisher hadn't helped Dian Kirkendall, he and his family would still be alive.'

'Insensitive, yes. Still, now Nixie will have a chance for a life with Richard and Beth. She'll grow up knowing there are people in the world who try to balance the scales.'

'You don't say if Sharon DeBlass hadn't been murdered, you and I wouldn't have met in the first place.'

'Because we would have. Another time, another place. Every step of my life was bringing me to you.' He turned her, kissed her forehead. 'Even the ones on the darkest road.'

'Death brought us here.'

'No. That's discouragement talking. It's love that brought us here.' He unhooked her weapon harness himself. 'Come now, you're asleep on your feet. Into bed.'

She stripped, climbed the platform, slid in. And when his arm came around her, she closed her eyes. 'I would've found you,' she murmured, 'even on the darkest road.'

The nightmare crept in, stealthy feet tiptoeing over her mind. She saw herself, the small, bloody child, packed into a blinding white room with other small, bloody children. Fear and despair, pain and weariness were thick in the room, crowding it like yet more small, bloody children.

No one spoke, no one cried. They only stood, bruised shoulder to bruised shoulder. Waiting for their fate.

One by one they were led away by stone-faced adults with dead eyes. Led away without protest, without a whimper, the way sick dogs are led away by those charged with ending their misery.

She saw this, and waited her turn.

But no one came for her. She stood alone in the white room, with the blood that coated her face, her hands, her arms, dripping almost musically onto the floor.

It didn't surprise her when he walked into the room. He always came, this man she'd killed. The man who'd broken her and ripped her and beaten her down into a quivering animal.

He smiled, and she smelled it on him. The whiskey and candy.

They want the pretty ones, he told her. *The good ones, the sweet ones. They leave the ones like you for me. No one will ever want you. Do you wonder where they go when they leave?*

She didn't want to know. Tears slid down, mixed with the blood. But she didn't make a sound. If she was quiet, very quiet, maybe he would go and someone else would come. Anyone else.

They take them to the pit, didn't I tell you? Didn't I warn you if you screwed with me, they'd throw you into the pit with the spiders and snakes? They say: Oh, let me help you, little girl. But what they do is eat you alive, bite by chomp by bite. But they don't want you. You're too scrawny for them, too bony. Do you think they don't know what you did?

He came closer, and now she could smell something else. Rot. And her breath began to hitch even as she fought to hold it in.

Killer. Murderer. And they leave you to me.

When he fell on her, she screamed. 'No. Eve, no. Shhh.' Fighting for breath, she locked her arms around him. 'Hold on. Just hold on to me. I've got you.' He pressed his cheek to hers. 'Easy now. I won't let go.'

'They left me alone, and he came for me.'

'You're not alone. I won't leave you alone.'

'They didn't want me. No one ever did. He did.'

'I want you.' He stroked her hair, her back, calming the tremors. 'From the first moment I saw you, I wanted you.'

'There were so many other children.' She loosened her

423

grip, let him lay her back, hold her close. 'Then only me, and I knew he'd come. Why won't he leave me alone?'

'He won't come back tonight.' Roarke took her hand, pressed it to his chest so she could feel his heart beating. 'He won't come back because there's the both of us here, and he's too much the coward.'

'Both of us,' she repeated, and left her hand on his heart while she slept.

He was up and dressed when she woke, and monitoring the stock reports on-screen in the sitting area over a cup of coffee. He turned as she rolled out of bed. 'How are you?'

'About half,' she said. 'I think I can make three-quarters after a shower.'

She started to walk toward the bath, then paused, changed directions, and walked to him. She bent, touched her lips to his forehead in a simple gesture of affection that left him moved and puzzled.

'You're there with me even when you're not. So thanks.'

'You're welcome.'

She crossed to the bath, glanced over her shoulder. 'Sometimes you being there is annoying. But mostly it's not.'

The worry in his own mind cleared. With a laugh he turned back to the financial news and drank his coffee.

Just before seven, Eve opened her own office door to find Baxter at her desk, enjoying what appeared to be a hearty breakfast.

'Detective Baxter, your ass seems to have somehow ended up in my chair. I'd like it removed immediately so I can kick every inch of it.'

'Soon as I'm done. This is actual ham in these actual eggs.' He jerked a chin toward the wall screen where updated reports were displayed. 'You don't sleep much, do you, Dallas? Damn busy night. I see you took my boy for a hell of a ride.'

'Your boy complain?'

'Hey, Trueheart's no whiner.'

His instinctive defense of his aide cooled Eve's temper. 'Oh right. I must've mixed him up with you.'

'Must've been some flight.'

'Yeah, fun while it lasted.' Since he'd been courteous – or greedy – enough to program an entire pot of coffee, she poured herself a cup. 'Whitney ripped me a new one over it.'

'He's been off the street a long time. You had a call to make and made it.'

She jerked a shoulder. 'Maybe he'd have done the same, and maybe he knows I'd do the same again, given the same circumstances. But it was a hell of a screwup, and a right-eous ripping. It won't come down on Trueheart.'

'He'd handle it if he had do. Appreciate you seeing it doesn't. How much of a punch are you going to take?'

'Written and oral reports to the review board. Fuck. Might get myself a departmental censure in my file. I can back up my actions, justify the call, but they won't like it, and will like it less when the civil suits start piling up.'

425

'You collar three mercenary terrorists responsible for the deaths of twelve people – including cops – the heat gets turned way down.'

'Yeah. The same way if I don't get them soon, the heat keeps heading up. I'll handle it; I'm not a whiner either. But I want these fucking guys, Baxter.'

She turned to the door as the rest of the team began to arrive. 'If you're going to eat, get it and chow it down fast,' she ordered. 'We've got a lot to go over in a short amount of time.'

Briefings and reports, cop chatter and coffee. And the chatter cut off, as if a knife had sliced down, when Don Webster, Internal Affairs Bureau, strolled in.

'Morning, boys and girls. Dallas, you should've sold tickets to that show last night.'

'I thought this briefing was reserved for real cops.'

At Baxter's comment, Eve shook her head in warning. She'd been expecting IAB to poke its sharp nose in. If it had to be IAB, Webster was a mixed bag. She trusted him, as she trusted no one else in that sector. But they had a dicey personal history, and she didn't need a former lover and Roarke butting heads again.

'There's data on this case that's on a need-to-know basis,' she began. 'The Tower,' he said, referring to Chief of Police Tibble's office, 'has decided I need to know. You've got considerable OT banked on this, multiple injuries civilian and department, property damage. You've got multiple dead civilians and two dead cops.'

He waited a moment, scanned the faces in the room. 'You've been questioning the investigating officers on other cases, one of which is closed. IAB needs to know. And I'm going to say this here and now, to all of you before the record goes on, that I'm not here to bust anybody's balls for doing what needs to be done to get the bastards responsible for Knight and Preston. I pulled some levers to get this duty. I've worked Homicide. I've worked with you,' he said to Eve. 'It's me or somebody who hasn't.'

'The devil we know,' Eve said. 'That's right.'

'Find a seat. You'll have to catch up.'

She continued the briefing, picking her way carefully now through data Roarke had gained. 'We believe Kirkendall, Clinton, and Isenberry executed individuals on a freelance basis for various covert agencies. We have reason to believe they were connected to the terrorist group Cassandra.'

'How do you come by that?' Webster asked.

She'd barely hesitated when Feeney spoke up. 'It's data we were able to extrapolate from the military files provided,' he said smoothly. 'EDD knows how to do its job, and this team knows how to put a case together.'

'With the Cassandra connection,' Eve continued, 'these individuals had access to weaponry, electronics, and funds. The philosophy of this group – a world order in their image – correlates to the personal philosophy displayed by Kirkendall. His family was made to perform according to his specifications, his orders, or was disciplined accordingly.

We know, through the statement given to Detectives Peabody and McNab by Roxanne Turnbill, that she was abducted and tortured by Kirkendall after his wife's disappearance. The time elapsed makes it likely she was taken to a location in or near the city. Cassandra operated and had a base in New York last year.'

'The current murders don't seem to be part of a terrorist threat,' Webster put in.

'No, they're personal. Screw with me, I don't just screw with you – I kill you and your whole family. It's not revenge. It's pride. Who insulted his pride?'

'Everyone he's killed had a part in it,' Peabody commented. 'No, not everyone.'

'Well, the kid.' McNab glanced toward the door as if she might be listening on the other side.

'No. He wants her dead because his mission isn't complete until that time. His wife. It's his wife who dared to oppose him, dared to not only walk out with his kids, but who took him through the embarrassment of a custody trial. Who won. And who got away clean.'

'He can't find her.' Peabody spread her hands. 'Neither can we.' Eve thought of Roarke. He could, given the time, he could. But she wasn't going to endanger another family. 'We can make him think we have her. It'll take a while to set up. Find a female cop who can handle it, one close to her build. We can use some enhancements, but she doesn't have to look identical. If he can have facial sculpting, he'd buy she could, too. We'd have to leak it so he didn't suspect it's a leak. And we've been pretty damn careful so far, so we'd need to trickle it.'

'Need a location.' Feeney pulled on his lip as he took up the thought. 'Secure, so he'd buy we were holding her. Lure him in, box him in, shut him down. With the equipment and know-how he's got, you've got a hell of a trick on your hands, Dallas.'

'We put it together. I want it together within thirty-six hours, another twelve for sims. When we lay this trap out, I want it to spring shut right on their necks. Feeney, you and McNab take the computer lab.'

'We'll get on it.'

'The rest of you, give me five minutes with Lieutenant Webster.' She waited until the room emptied and the door clicked closed.

'This investigation, and last night's events, are my responsibility. The chief, IAB, or God Himself wants to file a complaint, it's on me.'

'So noted. I said I wasn't here to bust balls, and I meant it. The Duberry case, I've had a look at the files. While I wouldn't call the investigation sloppy, I'd call it narrow. Brenegan? It looked like a righteous bust that resulted in a righteous conviction. But this data calls that into question.'

'The cops on those cases complained to IAB?'

'Cops don't complain to IAB,' he returned with the slightest of sneers. 'You avoid us like a case of the clap. But we get wind. Fact is, Dallas, if the primary on Duberry had done a more thorough job, scratched out that connection to Moss, then back to Brenegan, this hunt might've started a year ago.'

'Figuring a connect between a strangulation and a car bomb's a stretch.'

'You made the stretch.'

'I had more. If you're looking for fuel against another cop on this from me, you're not going to get it.'

'That's up to his superiors, not IAB. Regarding the media that's going to . . . has already started to explode on the incident last night, you spin that right – and you've got excellent media connections – you can circle it into a positive. Heroic cop risks life to protect the city from baby killers.'

'Oh fuck that.'

'Don't think that's not just how Tibble will have it spun. Not just your ass in the sling if you don't get some shine on this. Turn it around, get that sexy, fierce-eyed face on camera. Shake this off so you can get back to work.'

'I am back to work.' But she considered. 'The spin lower the heat on the rest of the team, on the investigation?'

'Couldn't hurt. It couldn't hurt if you tell the rest of your team to cut me some serious slack. I was a good murder cop.'

'Yeah, too bad you didn't stick with that.'

'Your opinion. I can help, and that's why I'm here. Not to roust you, and not because I've still got a torch going. Maybe just a little smoulder now and then,' he added with an easy smile.

'Cut it out.'

430

The door between the offices opened. Though Roarke leaned against the jamb, he looked about as lazy as a wolf eyeballing quarry. 'Webster,' he said in the coolest of tones.

Eve had a flash of the two of them beating the crap out of each other right where she now stood. She felt the tickle that might have been panic in the back of her throat as she stepped between them.

'Lieutenant Webster is here – at the directive of Chief Tibble – as a representative of IAB and for the purposes of—'

'Christ, Dallas, I can talk for myself.' And he held his hands up, palms out. 'Never touched her, don't intend to.'

'Good. She's on a difficult investigation, as I'm sure you're aware. She hardly needs either of us complicating things.'

'I'm not here to complicate things for her, or you.'

'Standing right here,' Eve said sharply. 'You can stop talking around me.'

'Just clearing the air, Lieutenant.' Roarke nodded to her, to Webster. 'I'll let you get back to work.'

'A minute,' she muttered and stalked into the office behind Roarke, shut the door with a decisive click. 'Listen—'

He cut her off, pressing his lips to hers, then eased back. 'I like to wind him up – and you as well. It's small of me, but there you are. I know perfectly well that he won't move on you, and if he lost his mind and did, you'd bloody him. Well, unless I got there first, which I sincerely hope would be the case. Actually, as I've told you before, I like him.'

'You like him.'

'Yes. He has superb taste in women, and a rather fine left jab.'

'Great. Good.' She shook her head. You figured you knew what made men tick, she thought. But you never did. 'I'm going back to work.'

21

With a frown on her face, Eve surveyed Roarke's computer lab. Several of the units were up and running, several of the screens had words, codes, strange symbols that might as well have been hieroglyphics whizzing over them. Computerized voices intoned incomprehensible statements, questions, comments.

And the rumpled Feeney, the neon McNab, scooted around on wheeled chairs, somehow miraculously avoiding collision with work stations and each other, like a couple of kids in a strange, strange game.

Stepping into the room was, for her, like stepping into an alternate universe.

'Yo.' Feeney gave her a finger point, then tapped icons on a screen that slid up out of the counter. 'Got something going.'

'Okay. I assume it's not Maximum Force 2200.'

'Hey.' McNab looked over. 'You cruise MF?'

'No.' Well, maybe she'd played it a couple of times, but just to test her comp skills. 'What's going?'

'What we've got over here is a diagnostic on the Swisher security system. We ran all the standards on it, stripped her down. Nice system, by the way.'

'We already know it was jammed, remote. Bypassed the failsafes and backups.'

'Yeah, yeah, but not how, not what they used. We're getting that. You work back from the system, code by code, signal by signal, and maybe you put together, code by code, signal by signal, the device that pulled it off.'

'They had to get it somewhere.' Eve nodded. 'Even if they reconfigured, added flourishes, they had to get the basic device somewhere.'

'Yep. And what we got going over there is the security on the hospital lot where Jaynene Brenegan was taken out – and the system on the apartment where Karin Duberry was murdered. Hitting correlations. Gonna be the same device, or one configured the same way. When you get them, it'll help burn them.'

'Have you got room for one more deal?'

'Shoot.'

'I need you to alter my communicator. A fault, but nothing that I'd reasonably notice as a non-EDD cop. Just a blip, so that someone who's trying to monitor communications might get through, catch a transmission.'

'You want to leak data?'

'Once we get this set up, select our location, put the op together, I want them to be able to monitor my communicator. Maybe it's fuzzy, but they should get the details. Like the communicator's going bad on me. Like the shield's thinning out. It happens, right?'

'Yeah, but there's a default warning.'

'Wouldn't be the first time departmental equipment went bad. You should see my damn computer.'

'Still giving you grief?' McNab asked.

'It's holding. I haven't gotten any foreign porn when I ask for a file. Lately.'

'Hand it over.' Feeney held up his palm. 'We'll play with it. You got your backup?'

'Yeah.' She pulled both out of her pocket. 'Just dink with the one. Can you make it so the signal coming into it is still shielded? So they only get bits of what I transmit?'

'We'll get you covered.'

There were enough rooms in the house to billet a military battalion. It was risky tucking Webster away with Baxter, but she didn't want IAB strolling around her office. He wanted to observe, she thought, he could observe Baxter and Trueheart. Before rounding up Peabody, Eve slipped into her bedroom to make a private call.

'How about some more tit for tat?' she asked when Nadine came on-screen. 'I need a spin, apparently. An incident last night—'

'Your air show through midtown?' Nadine gave a wicked laugh. 'We got some extreme footage on that. Bought it off a tourist from Tokyo. It's aired twice this morning.'

'Great.'

'You're taking some heat on that? I've never known you to worry about a little sweat.'

'They've sicced IAB on me, and it could get in the way

435

of the investigation. Trueheart was with me, and shit trickles even if you plug the dam. I'm advised to spin this around so it's the courageous cop in pursuit of kid killers. Risking life and limb to apprehend cop killers and protect the known universe.'

'Boy, that's killing you.' But Nadine angled her head. 'That's what you were doing, wasn't it?'

'The point is this kind of thing doesn't reflect well on the department.'

'And the department will take a sacrifice, if deemed necessary.'

'It'll be Trueheart, Nadine. They'll give me a slap, maybe a smudge on my record, but if they have to roast somebody, it'll be him. He's more disposable. I put him on the line.'

'So you're asking me to spin the story so the crap doesn't clog up the momentum of your investigation, and so the cutie-pie doesn't get his tight little ass fried.'

'That's the idea. And in return—'

'No, don't tell me.' Nadine sat back, held up both hands. 'Because it'll kill me to turn it down.'

'Look, Nadine, it's not that big a spin.'

'Obviously you didn't catch my pithy and insightful morning report. Spin's already spun. The cool-headed, nerveless Lieutenant Dallas and the young, dedicated Officer Trueheart, risking their lives in pursuit of the vicious killers of children and their fellow officers. Killers who discharge weapons with no thought to the welfare of innocent strangers – men, women, and children who live in or visit our great city. And so on.'

'Okay. You've got another IOU.'

'Slate's clear. This played better – and the vid showed the blasts coming out of that van. Most of the competition worked the same angle, but there's still some heat, some stirring of the urban terrorism pot and why aren't we safe walking the streets, in our own homes.'

'It's a good question. Could it be because a portion of society sucks?'

'Can I quote you? Better, how about a quick talking head while you repeat that?'

Eve considered. 'How about you say, "When contacted, Lieutenant Dallas stated that every member of the NYPSD will work diligently to identify and apprehend those responsible for the deaths of their fellow officers, for Grant, Keelie, and Coyle Swisher, for Inga Snood, for Linnie Dyson. We serve them, we serve New York. We serve Nixie Swisher because surviving the brutality that was brought into her home isn't enough. She deserves justice, and we'll get it for her." '

'Good. Got it. As for the other IOU, toasting these bastards from my media vantage point? I'd be doing it now anyway. I'd be doing it for Knight and Preston. Both of their memorials are tomorrow.'

'I'll see you there.' Eve hesitated. 'An unnamed source at Cop Central has confirmed that the abduction and murder

437

of Meredith Newman has been connected to the recent home invasion and murder of five people, including two children, on the Upper West Side. Meredith Newman, a Child Protection Services caseworker, was abducted – fill in the rest.'

'Can I say Newman was assigned to the invasion survivor, nine-year-old Nixie Swisher?'

'Yes, get it out there. And that multiple premortem burns on Newman's body indicate she was tortured before her throat was cut in the same manner as the members of the Swisher household. Ms. Newman's body was discovered in an alley—'

'We've got all that.'

'Say it again. Say it again – her naked body, covered with electrical burns, with its throat slit, was discovered after being dumped in an alley. Witnesses saw a black FourStar van, forged New York license AAD-4613, exiting the alley moments before the body was discovered. Lieutenant Eve Dallas, primary, and Officer Troy Trueheart, acting as aide, encountered a van of this description when leaving the scene.'

'And pursued,' Nadine finished. 'Which leads right back to the flight show. Good. Solid. Thanks. How many witnesses?'

One, Eve thought, and only on the taillights. But why quibble. 'When contacted, Lieutenant Dallas would neither confirm nor deny the report.'

'A formal one-on-one would round this off sweet.'

'I'm cutting back on sweets. Later.'

Juggling plans in her head, Eve headed to her office, then swung toward Roarke's. She gave a quick knock, opened the door. And winced.

It was full of people. Or more accurately, it was full of Roarke and holos. His admin, Caro, sat in her tidy way, her hands folded in her lap.

Two men in square, collarless suit jackets, and three women in similar conservative corporate gear studied yet another holo of some sort of elaborate development, complete with winding river and a sheer tower ringed with people glides.

'Sorry.' She started to back out, but Roarke lifted a hand. 'Ladies, gentlemen, my wife.'

They all looked over at her. She saw, clearly enough, the measuring of the females – and the reactions of puzzlement, even amusement. And she could understand it. There was Roarke, rangy and stunning in his dark suit, power like an aura around him.

And here she was, banged-up boots, hair she couldn't quite remember if she'd even finger-combed that morning, and a weapon harness over her shirt.

'We're just wrapping up,' he told Eve, then turned back to the group. 'If you have any further questions, relay them through Caro. I want the changes discussed and implemented by this time tomorrow. Thank you. Caro, stay a moment.'

The holos, save Caro's, winked off. Caro rose. 'Lieutenant Dallas. It's good to see you.'

'Good to see you, too.' Now, Eve thought, she'd have to make chatty talk. 'Ah, how's Reva?'

'She's very well. She's moved back to the city.'

'Well, good. Tell her hi.'

Caro turned to Roarke. 'You're conferencing again at eleven with the engineers on the project. And have a one o'clock with Yule Hiser that we've switched to 'link. Your two o'clock is Ava McCoy and her team. Then you're clear for your five o'clock. The Fitch Communications meeting is tentatively scheduled for nine p.m., via holo.'

'Thank you, Caro. Anything urgent, you know where to reach me.' She nodded. 'Lieutenant,' she said, and winked out.

'Who were the suits?' Eve asked.

'Architects. I'm still making some refinements on a new development on Olympus.'

'Six architects for one development.'

'A rather large and complex one – and that includes buildings, landscape, water, interiors . . . And you don't care.'

She felt a little pinch of guilt, right between the shoulder blades. 'Not much, but that's not the same as not being interested. Which I am, in a supportive kind of way.'

He chuckled. 'What do you need?'

Now annoyance slapped over the guilt. 'Just because I said I was interested and supportive doesn't mean I need something from you.'

'It doesn't, no.' He leaned back on his desk. 'But you came in here because you did. There's no need to feel guilty about it, or to start worrying that I'm carving off my own

440

worktime to help with yours. I wouldn't if I didn't want to do it.'

'Well, how do you feel about giving me a building downtown?'

'Which would you like?'

This time she chuckled. 'Showoff. Have you got something untenanted? Something we can secure and wire up within twenty-four?'

'I imagine we can come up with something. That's your trap. Why downtown?'

'Because I know they're based uptown. Because when this goes down, I want it as far away from the kid as I can make it and stay in the city. I need a place where I can post up to a dozen men inside, where I can place snipers and tech response in select locations. I need to make it look like a safe house – cop security on doors and windows. And I need to be able to lock the place down tight as soon as I have them inside.'

'I'll give you some possibilities by this afternoon. That soon enough?'

'Good. There's this other thing. I'll make it quick. You said Richard and Elizabeth were coming today.'

'Yes, at four. I'll take care of that.'

'Much as I'd like to let you, it's not right.' She didn't have to be told the meetings Caro had rattled off weren't all he had on the big, shiny plate of Roarke Industries. 'I dumped her here, I've got to do my part in it. I figure you've dealt with their security.'

'It's done.'

'I'm bringing Mavis in.'

'Excuse me?'

'The kid's a big fan. She brightened up when she heard I knew Mavis, and before I knew it I'd said something about yeah, she could meet her. Anyway, it seems like if I had Mavis come in, Mira – we'd need Mira to give an opinion on the kid's reaction to the fostering – it would look more causal. Like we're having guests over.'

His communication system beeped and buzzed, lights signalling incoming data. She wondered how he stood all the interruptions. Of which, she knew, she was one.

'In the real world of good and evil, good doesn't have a party if they've got a reason to think evil might try to crash.'

He gave her an easy nod. 'Thereby giving the impression that there's certainly no young girl evil might want to get its hands on around here.'

'It's sort of braining a lot of birds with one stone. Leonardo's in Milan or Paris or someplace over there.' She gestured vaguely in what might've been the direction of Europe. 'So if I bring her in, it'd be best to keep her here. Just in case.'

'I'd say the more the merrier – and merrier it tends to be with Mavis around – but it's not quite the phrase that comes to mind with a houseful of cops.'

There came the guilt again, with a more enthusiastic pinch. 'I'll get them all out as soon as I can.'

'Holding you to that. Oh, I caught your performance on a media flash right before my meeting.'

'Yeah. Heard it got screen time.'

'Some impressive maneuvers, both air and ground. Still you're lucky you didn't splat that new police issue of yours into the face of a building.'

'I couldn't. I wreck another ride this soon, even with Peabody offering a variety of perverted, possibly illegal sexual favors, I'd be lucky to score an airboard out of Requisitions.'

'An offer of a variety of perverted, possibly illegal sexual favors would score you any vehicle you might like from me.'

'Peabody doesn't need the incentive. She already wants to jump you.'

'Flattering. But I was actually thinking of you in regard to those favors. But I'm sure Peabody and I can work something out.'

'I'd hate to put her back in the hospital this soon. Catch you at four.'

With Peabody, Eve made a point of going back to every crime scene she attributed to Kirkendall. She stood on the sidewalk, studied the building where Judge Moss and his family had once lived. Another family lived in the pretty brownstone now.

Did they think about it? Talk about it? Entertain their friends with the horror story?

'Baxter and Trueheart recanvassed here,' Peabody

commented. 'Showed off the composite and the military ID photos. Nobody remembers seeing them around. Two years since,' she added. 'It was a long shot.'

'He didn't go after the wife on this one. You could speculate that he was more focused in on the judge. Or that he opted to leave her alive, to suffer. But he knew the routine, so he'd watched them.' She turned a circle. 'A lot of places around here a guy could rent or buy, settle in, stake out. Isenberry probably handled this end. Smarter. Original canvass probably interviewed her. We'll re-evaluate the reports, see if we see anything on that.'

She got back in the car, drove toward the Swisher's. 'Property around here's a good investment. He likes good investments. Maybe he bought in somewhere near the Moss residence, held on to it, rents it out. He partners up with Master Lu for investment, for income. Why not do some real estate?'

'Vary your portfolio.'

'Let's tug that line. See if we can find a property bought after the trial, before the bomb. It may not lead us to him, but it builds evidence. When these bastards go to trial, I'm going to have them sewn in a titanium shroud. Goddamn it!' She punched the accelerator as the Swisher house came into view. 'Look at those idiot kids.'

The trio – teenagers, at her guess – were huddled together at the police seal on the front entrance. Their lookout, a curvy little number in a black skin-suit and wrap shades, let out a shout and took off on a silver airboard.

Kids scattered, leaping solo or in tandem on other boards, plowing through shrubbery, onto the sidewalk, into the street between vehicles that squealed and honked.

Eve heard looney, loopy laughter as they whipped around the corner. 'You're not going after them?' Peabody asked when Eve zipped to the curb. 'Squish them like bugs?'

'No. It's just as likely one of them will end up getting squished by a cab while I'm chasing them. Pricks.' She slammed out, jogged to the entrance to check the seal. 'Tinkered with it, didn't get through far enough to set off the alarm. Slap on a fresh one anyway, Peabody. Asshole kids. What did they plan to do, break in and have a party in the death house? Why aren't they in school, or better yet in juvie?'

'Saturday.'

'What day?'

'Today's Saturday, Dallas. No school on the weekends.'

'There ought to be,' she said darkly. 'There ought to be school twenty-four/seven for little disrespectful creeps like that. Give them a day out, all they do is cause trouble.'

'You'd have felt better if you'd gone after and squished them.'

'Yeah.' She let out a breath. 'Next time.' She forced herself to set it aside. 'Recanvass was zip here, too. But we know Isenberry used the paralegal to get inside, get close to the family. We know the killers walked away, headed down the block, not into a neighboring building. Still, we'll try the same investment angle here, too. They might have bought one, rented one, used it for stakeout previously.'

Her last stop was the hospital parking lot. 'Not just a quick slice here. Multiple stab wounds, defensive wounds. She put up a fight, or tried to. Played with her some. Jab here, jab there. I think this was girl on girl. They let Isenberry do this one. Her file says she likes to mix it up. Clinton, he likes a silent kill – manual strangulation a specialty. Kirkendall let his brother take point there. But the other kills were his. Cold and clean. But everybody got bloody. You trust your comrades more when they get bloody along with you.'

'Easiest one to take here.' Peabody frowned at the lot, the health center. 'You either hack in, get her schedule, or you hang around – who notices? – get a feel. Both, probably. You do it end of shift, late. And yeah, if it's another woman walking your way, you don't get the alarm bells. Little friendly nod, or Isenberry stops her, asks for directions. How do I get to the surgery wing? Vic turns, knife comes out. Sticks here, vic tries to block or run, gives her another jab. Works her back, away from the building. Some of the wounds were shallow, just nasty little sticks. Finishes her off. Rendezvous, and you're gone.'

Yeah, Eve thought, that was the way. 'They'd have watched. Kirkendall and Clinton. Close enough for visual, or Isenberry wore a recorder. You're not part of the kill unless you see the kill. We find their base, we're going to find vids of every murder. They'd study them like Arena Ball players study the vid of a game. Looking for flaws, for moves, ways to improve.'

'Sick. Dallas, it's going on fifteen hundred.'

'And?'

'We're due to get Mavis at fifteen hundred.'

'Right. I got this buzz.' She rocked on her heels, studying the spot where Brenegan's body had been found years before. 'I know we're close. We push the right buttons, we pull them in, and they're gone. They're smart, they're crafty, but they're vulnerable because they won't walk away until they're done. They'd rather fail than walk away without the mission complete.'

'It's hard to stop, change tracks, and deal with the other areas.'

'Yeah, it's a pisser all right. Let's go get Mavis.'

Eve had been to some of Mavis's concerts. She'd been backstage and watched the adoring fans lucky enough to gain entrance. But she'd never seen a nine-year-old girl rendered speechless by the mere sight of her friend.

Not that the sight couldn't render anyone incapable of speech. Mavis wore her hair in hundreds of ringlets, bright gold and shimmery green, that spilled around her face like some sort of electric mop. Her eyes were gold today as well, tipped with green lashes. She wore a deep purple calf-length coat, which she peeled off upon entering the house to reveal a crotch-length dress in swirls of purple and gold. Her green tights were accented with shiny knee and ankle bracelets and a pair of gold shoes with transparent heels filled with those same colorful swirls.

Her pregnancy had progressed far enough that her belly popped out of the swirls in a small, neat lump.

Her bracelets – knee, ankle, wrist – rang like bells as she danced across the floor toward a slack-jawed Nixie.

'Hi! I'm Mavis.'

Nixie only nodded, her head like a puppet's on a string. 'Dallas says you like my music.'

At the next nod, Mavis grinned. 'I thought maybe you'd like this.' Apparently there was a pocket somewhere in the dizzying swirls as Mavis drew out a disc. 'It's my new vid, for "Inside Out Over You." It's not hitting until next month.'

'I can have it?'

'Sure. You want to watch it? Okay if we go plug it in, Dallas?'

'Go ahead.'

'This is the ult,' Nixie exclaimed. 'The serious ult. Linnie and I . . .' She trailed off, stared hard at the disc. 'Linnie's my best friend, and we watch your vids all the time. But she's . . .'

'I know.' Mavis's voice softened. 'I'm really sorry. Dallas is my best friend. I'd feel so bad if anything happened to her. It would hurt for a long time. I guess I'd have to think about the fun we had together whenever I could, so it didn't hurt so much.'

She nodded. 'You're having a baby. Can I touch it?'

'You bet. Sometimes it bumps around in there, and it feels really frosty.' Mavis laid her hand over Nixie's. 'Gotta cook a while longer. In the new vid I've got this totally mag belly painting going on. Why don't you go plug the disc in. I'll come watch it with you.'

'Okay, thanks.' Nixie looked up at Eve. 'You said you'd bring her, and you did. Thanks.'

When Nixie raced off to the parlor, Eve stepped up, laid a hand on Mavis's shoulder. 'I appreciate this.'

'Poor kid. Man, makes you misty.' She laid a hand on her belly, blinked her emerald lashes. 'Look, if I can give her a couple hours of fun, that's what it's all about. Hey! Bump!' She grabbed Eve's hand, slapped it to the side of her belly.

'Jesus, don't! Whoa!' She jerked when something kicked against her palm.

'Is that uptown or what?'

'Or what.'

But curiosity had her eyeing the ball of Mavis's belly as the little kicks continued. It was kind of . . . she wasn't sure. A happy little beat, and not nearly as creepy as she'd expected. 'What the hell's it doing in there, dancing?'

'It's swimming and stretching and rolling. I'm so knocked up now its nostrils are opening, and he's got these little air sacs—'

Eve whipped her hand clear, tucked it safely behind her back as Mavis laughed. And her own hands gently caressed her belly as she looked toward the stairs. 'Hi, Dr. Mira.'

'Mavis. I'd say you're glowing, but I've never known you otherwise. I will say you look wonderfully healthy.'

'Feeling TIT these days. Totally In Tune.'

'I didn't know you were already here,' Eve said.

'A few minutes before you. I've been upstairs speaking

to Roarke. He'll be right down. Ms. Barrister, Mr DeBlass, and their son have just been cleared through the gate.'

'I'll go keep Nixie entertained.' Mavis gave Eve a bolstering pat on the arm and swirled her way into the parlor. 'Hit it, Nix!' she called out, and there was a blast of what could be called, in some cultures, music. 'I guess that's showtime,' Eve declared, and walked to the front door.

22

It was an odd group under any circumstances, Eve supposed.
Odder yet when she was trying to pay attention to the
chitchat, watch the kid for reactions, structure a major
operation, coordinate her team, and play hostess.

Richard and Elizabeth had weathered the storm of
murder, scandal, and horror, and looked the stronger for it.
She watched them both engage Nixie in conversation,
together and separately. The kid was polite, and distracted
enough, Eve thought, by both Mavis and a child near her
own age, to enjoy herself.

It was a strange group. But from the sound of conversation, Eve seemed to be the only one who thought so.

She slipped away long enough to check on Peabody's
progress with the real estate angle, and thought it showed
strength of character to leave the comfort of cop work to
head back down to social hour.

Elizabeth Barrister waylaid her in the foyer. 'She's a
beautiful child.'

'She's got spine.'

'She must, and she'll need it as time goes on. Grief

451

comes in waves. Just when you think you've weathered one, another swamps you again.'

Elizabeth Barrister, Eve thought, knew plenty about grief. 'It's a lot to take on, from your position.'

Elizabeth shook her head as she glanced toward the parlor. 'We made mistakes, Richard and I. So many. Too many. And we've accepted that our daughter paid for them.'

'Senator DeBlass was responsible.'

'From your position,' Elizabeth agreed. 'But she was our child, and we made mistakes. We've been given another chance with Kevin. He's lit up our lives.'

There was no question of that, Eve noted, when just saying his name lit Elizabeth's face.

'We'd give Nixie a home, if she wants it. Give her a chance to heal. We'd be good for her, I think. Kevin certainly would. They're already making friends. She's been telling him about the game room, which is, apparently, the ult. I wonder if I could take them in for a while.'

'Sure. I'll show you where it is.'

Eve remembered Kevin as a scrawny kid of about six with ragged clothes and a bony cat in tow. He'd filled out, cleaned up, grown a couple of inches, and showed a gap-toothed grin as he clutched a pudgy Galahad in his arms.

'He's fat,' Kevin said cheerfully. 'But he's soft.'

'Yeah, well . . .' Galahad aimed his dual-colored eyes at Eve in a way that promised payback for the indignity. 'You don't have to carry him.'

'I like to. I have a cat named Dopey, and now I have

a puppy, too, named Butch. I go to school and I eat like a horse.' Behind them, Elizabeth laughed. 'He certainly does.'

'If I *had* a horse.' The way Kevin slid his eyes slyly in his mother's direction told Eve he knew where the butter was best slathered. 'I would ride him like a cowboy.'

'One step at a time, little man. Let's see how you handle Butch. Do you like horses, Nixie?'

'I got to pet one that pulls a carriage around the park. It was nice.'

At his first sight of the nirvana of Roarke's game room, Kevin let out a shout, dumped Galahad on the floor, and raced to the closest arcade game.

'I'll take it from here,' Elizabeth told Eve. 'I've become an expert in this arena.'

With considerable relief, Eve left her to it. And took the opportunity to head back upstairs.

This time, Webster was leaning over Peabody's shoulder. 'Stop crowding my partner,' Eve snapped.

Webster straightened, but held his ground. 'I have to head downtown shortly, give my report.'

'Don't let the door hit you in the ass on the way out. What've you got?' she asked Peabody.

'Looks like you hit on something with the properties. I've got what you call a townstone on the Moss's block. Purchased three months after the custody resolution in the name of the Triangle Group. No financing, so they plunked down the whole – considerable – shot. No income until

453

six weeks after Moss's death. Got rentals coming in after that. Tenants are clean and unconnected as far as I can tell. Triangle Group also owns, since March 2054, a two-family building two blocks south of the hospital where Brenegan was murdered. Tenants in and out, every six months like clockwork. I think we might find some of the names from Cassandra or Doomsday in here.'

'Kirkendall, Clinton, Isenberry. Triangle Group. Cute. We tie them to it.'

'It's a tangle, Dallas.'

She paced away, paced back. Webster was a solid cop, she knew. But he was still IAB. Overtime was racking up, and nothing made the review board, the brass, the nut crunchers bitch like unauthorized OT.

But there were ways around it.

'You're past shift,' she said to Peabody. 'You and the rest of the team. Clock out.'

'But we've got—'

'You're off the clock.' She smiled thinly at Webster as she spoke. 'What you do with your own time, in your own home, isn't my business. Or the department's. You want to do something useful,' Eve told Webster. 'Go file your report. Get them off my back for the next forty-eight.'

'I can do that. Give the detective her orders. I've gone suddenly and strangely deaf.'

'Shoot this to your desk unit and get down to Central.'

'Do you want to move on these buildings?'

'Tomorrow. Try for at least six hours' downtime. We're

going to put this in place tomorrow. We move this team back to Central, avoid inquiries from IAB about what the hell we're doing here. Get a conference room booked for seven hundred tomorrow. Tell the rest of the team to do the same or work from home.'

She could see it, and in her head was already outlining strategy.

'Start looking for other properties under that name or similar ones. Under any of the tenants' names who lived in the building near the hospital. I want their base. We get their base, we change this op around, and that's where we move on them.'

'Will you work from here?'

'I'll be pursuing the same data. I want your unit talking to mine. Something breaks, I'll come downtown. Got all that?'

'Got it.'

'Then get all these cops out of my house.'

'Dallas.' Webster stopped her as she turned to the door. 'Nobody's business what I do on my own time, either. If I happened to get copies of this data Detective Peabody's finessed, I could entertain myself by seeing if I could beat her, or you, to the rest.'

'Peabody, have you got any problem having a race with an IAB suit?'

'I thrive on competition.'

'There you go. Beat his ass.'

Better yet, she thought as she walked out. She'd get Roarke to work unraveling. And she'd work with him, and they'd ring the goddamn bell. There had to be enough civilians in the damn house to ride the controls on a couple of kids while she worked.

She swung by the computer lab, and the lounge where Baxter and Trueheart were set up to relay the data. 'Check out the owners before the buy,' she ordered. 'See if there's a connect – military, paramilitary – siblings, spouses, offspring in same. Get current status. Let's see if we can squeeze out a weasel. But do it from home. You're officially off the clock.'

She veered off to start downstairs, and Summerset intercepted. 'Lieutenant, your guests require some of your attention.'

'Cram the etiquette lesson. Tell Roarke I'm working in his office and I require some of his attention. Now.'

Pleased to save time, and to have been able to tell Summerset to cram anything, she backtracked and sat at Roarke's desk.

'Engage computer.'

One moment, please, to verify authorization by voice scan. Verified, Darling Eve. Engaged.

'Christ, what if somebody hears that? Don't you know there are cops in the damn woodwork around here? Search all data, Triangle Group.'

Searching . . . Triangle Group, licensed real estate brokerage company, subsidiary of Five-By Corporation.

'Location or locations of Triangle Group's offices or company headquarters.'

Working . . . Triangle Group is listed as an electronic company with base office 1600 Pennsylvania Avenue, East Washington.

'Display map, East Washington. Highlight given address.'

Map displayed. Highlighted location is The White House.

'Yeah, even I knew that. Little power trip. Search data on Five-By Corporation.'

She leaned back as the computer fed her data, then glanced over as Roarke came in.

'You needed something?'

'Kirkendall acquired real estate near two of the targets. Prime stuff, good investment. Looks like he kept them. Using a couple of blinds, or a couple we've got so far. Triangle Group out of Five-By Corporation.'

'Triangle.' He moved toward her, brushed her out of his chair. 'Logical. Five-By? Is that an indication there are two more prime players in this?'

'Five-by-five.'

'Is twenty-five?'

'No, not math. Military term.'

'You've got one on me.'

'It's like loud and clear. Like I hear you fine. Everything's solid. Like that.'

'Ah.' He looked over what she'd already done. 'The White House. Don't we think a lot of ourselves? And the parent organization is ostensibly housed in the Pentagon and the UN, and I believe this is Buckingham Palace. However grand their delusions, they don't make much of a blip in the business world. I've never heard of either company. Let's just see what we see.'

'Can I leave you on this a minute? I need to update the commander. It might keep them off my ass a while longer.'

'Go on, but pop downstairs and see if all's well, will you? I left Mavis as acting host, and Christ knows what she might think up.'

She made the call, and put off her social obligations long enough to pop in on Feeney as he was wrapping up.

Once she made it down, she found all the adults, including Elizabeth, in the parlor.

'They're fine,' Elizabeth told her. 'Having such a good time I thought I'd let them hang together, as Kevin says, for a little while.'

'Good. Okay. Fine.'

'Don't worry about us,' Mira told her. 'It's obvious you've had something come up. We can easily entertain ourselves for a while.'

'Even better.'

★　　★　　★

458

In the game room Nixie and Kevin took a break from the machines. She liked having another kid around, even if he was a boy. And his mother and father seemed nice. His mother had even played Intergalactic War with them. And nearly won, too.

But she was glad she'd gone away for a while. There were things you couldn't say with adults around.

'How come you don't talk like your mom and dad?' Nixie wanted to know.

'I talk like everybody.'

'No, they have a sort of accent. It's different. How come you don't?'

'Maybe because they haven't been my mom and dad the whole time. But they are now.'

'They, like, adopted you?'

'We had a party when they did. Almost like a birthday. There was chocolate cake.'

'That's nice.' She thought it was, but there was a jittery feeling in her stomach. 'Did somebody kill your real mom and dad?'

'My other mom,' he corrected. 'Because I have a real mom. You get to be real when you're adopted.'

'I mean your other. Did somebody kill her?'

'Nuh-uh.' He began to pet Galahad, who'd deigned to stay and have his belly rubbed. 'Sometimes she'd go away, and I'd get hungry. Sometimes she'd be nice, and sometimes she'd hit me. "Smack the crap out of you, little bastard." ' He grinned when he said it, but it wasn't a pleasant expression. 'That's how her face looked when she hit. But my mom now, she never hits, and she never has that face. My dad either. Sometimes they get this one.'

He drew his eyebrows together and tried to look stern. 'But mostly they don't. And they don't go away, and I don't get hungry, not like before.'

'How did they find you?'

'They came and got me from the place where you have to go if you don't have a mom or something. You get to eat there, and they've got games, but I didn't want to stay there – and I didn't for very long. Then they came and we got to go live in Virginia. We have a big house. Not as big as this,' he said, stringently honest. 'But it's big and I have my own room, and Dopey came with us.'

Nixie moistened her lips. 'Are they going to take me to Virginia?' She knew where that was, sort of. She knew the capital was Richmond because she had to learn all the states and their capitals in school. But it wasn't New York. It wasn't here. It wasn't home.

'I don't know.' Obviously intrigued, Kevin cocked his head and studied her. 'Don't you live here?'

'No. I don't live anywhere. People came in our house and killed my mom and dad.'

'Killed them dead?' Kevin's eyes popped wide. 'How come?'

'Because my dad was good and they were wrong people. That's what Dallas said.'

'That's the doom.' He gave her a pat, as he had Galahad. 'Were you scared?'

'What do you think?' she snapped back, but the sympathy on Kevin's face didn't fade.

'I think I'da been so scared I wouldn't even be able to *breathe.*'

The little flash of anger died. 'I was. They killed them, and they didn't kill me, and I have to stay here for protection. Dallas is going to find them and put them in a goddamn cage.'

He slapped a hand over his mouth and slid his gaze to the door.

'You're not supposed to say goddamn,' he whispered. 'Mom gets that look on her face if you forget and say it.'

'She's not my mom.'

When tears glimmered, Kevin scooted over and put an arm around her. 'It's okay. She can be your mom, too, if you want.'

'I want my own mom.'

'She got dead.'

Nixie dropped her head to her drawn-up knees. 'They won't let me go back to my house. They won't let me go to school. And I don't know where Virginia is, exactly.'

'We have a big yard, and we have a puppy. Sometimes he pees on the floor. It's pretty funny.'

She sighed, rested her cheek on her knees. 'I want to ask Dallas if I have to go to Virginia.' She swiped at her cheeks, rose, and used the house scanner. 'Where is Dallas?'

Dallas is in Roarke's office.

461

'You have to keep this.' Carefully, she unpinned the homer from her shirt, pinned it on Kevin's. 'It's how Summerset knows where I am. I just want to talk to Dallas and nobody else, so you have to stay here and play games until I get back.'

'Okay. When you come back, we can look Virginia up on a map, then you can see.'

'Maybe.'

She knew the house, or at least the parts of it Summerset had shown her. To avoid the parlor, she took the elevator up a floor, then dashed down the corridor, and used the steps.

Part of her wanted to run away. But where would she go? She didn't want to be alone. She knew kids were sometimes. Coyle had told her there were places like Sidewalk City where kids nobody wanted lived in boxes and had to beg for food.

She didn't want to live in a box, but it wasn't right, it wasn't fair that they were going to send her away. No one even asked.

Creeping past a door, she paused to listen.

She heard nothing inside, so eased around to look. It was Dallas's office, and no one was there.

She crept to the next door.

'Gonna nail those sons of bitches. Look at the tenant list, two blocks from the Brenegan murder scene, and we've got a fucking revolving door.'

There was a sound in Dallas's voice, Nixie thought. Kind of mean, and kind of excited, too. Like she'd heard one of

462

the bigger kids sound at free-time in school when he talked about punching another kid.

'Two of those names are known aliases for Cassandra disciples. And one of them's a face sculptor – a dead one. Bet your excellent ass he's the one who did the work on Kirkendall and Clinton. The other's off planet doing life. I'm going to have to go squeeze him, and I *hate* going off planet.'

'We get lucky here, you won't have to. Every property or company I find is one away from pinning their base. Just give us some room here, Lieutenant.'

'Right, right.'

Nixie heard footsteps, crouched.

'And stop pacing about. It's annoying. Why don't you leave me to this for a half hour, go downstairs – or at the very least go hound someone.'

'I sent my team home. You're what's left for me to hound.'

'Just my lucky day.'

There was a beeping, an oath that would have gotten Nixie grounded for a month if she'd so much as thought it.

'Dallas.'

Dispatch, Dallas, Lieutenant Eve. Compromised police seal, main front entrance, Swisher murder scene.

'Goddamn kids.'

Patrol dispatched. Acknowledge you have been informed of compromise. 'Acknowledged. Have the patrol hold at scene. Have officers in light armor as precautionary measure. I want to check it out myself. ETA, ten minutes.'

Acknowledged. Seal requires replacement. Dispatch out.

'If there's a patrol heading there, it seems unnecessary for you to go as well.'

'I chased a bunch of kids away earlier. Should've kicked some butt, but I didn't want to chance another chase. If they're inside, I want to correct that error in judgment, personally. If they're nearby, I'm going to take a few minutes of my time to round them up, and kick said butt.'

'I'll go with you, then.'

'Jesus, Roarke, it's a kid butt-kicking detail. I can handle it.' There was a long pause, a hiss of breath. 'Okay, okay, no unnecessary risks. I'll catch Baxter, take him along. I need you to stay on this and coordinate with Peabody once she gets to Central.'

'Wear your vest.'

'Oh Christ!' There was a sharp thud, as if something had been kicked. 'Yes, mommy.'

'And later when I take it off of you, you'll be calling me something entirely different.'

'Ha-ha. Ten minutes there, ten back, ten to kick teenage butt. Back in thirty.'

In the hall, Nixie streaked away. With her heart drumming, she raced down the stairs, found an elevator, and ordered it to take her to the ground-floor library.

There was an outside door there, and she knew which car Dallas drove.

★   ★   ★

464

Eve caught Baxter on the stairs. 'I need you to ride with me. Seal's compromised at the Swisher house. I chased a bunch of teenagers away from it this afternoon. Looks like they came back. Trueheart, take the vehicle. I'll stick your partner in a cab when we're done slapping around a bunch of kids.' She tossed Baxter a vest. 'Suit up. I take no chances.'

He started to take off his jacket.

'Upstairs. Jesus, you think I want to see what you refer to as your manly chest?' She took a small remote out of her pocket, tapped in a code.

'What's that?'

She felt the heat rise up the back of her neck. 'It's a remote, brings my ride around on auto.'

'Sweet. Let me—'

She stuck it back in her pocket. 'Just suit up, Baxter. I'd like to get this annoying little detail accomplished so I can get back to work.'

She took enough time to signal Mavis out of the parlor. 'Listen, I've got to go out for a few, and I might be pretty jammed up when I get back. Can you keep everybody happy?'

'It's what I do best. Hey, maybe I'll get everybody down to the pool before we eat. That chilly with you?'

'It's great.' She tried to envision Mavis cavorting in the water with Elizabeth and Mira. 'Ah . . . But wear a suit, okay?'

Outside, Nixie dashed behind a tree when she heard the engine. She watched, breath quick and short as Dallas's car streamed out of the garage and toward the front of the house. She watched it stop, heard locks click.

It was wrong. She shouldn't do it. But she wanted to go *home*. Even for a little while. Before they sent her away, before they made her have another mom and dad.

She took one last glance toward the house, then ran for the car and crawled onto the floor of the backseat. She pulled the door shut only a moment before the door of the house opened. And she lay there, eyes squeezed shut.

'Some smooth ride you scored this time, Dallas.'

Baxter. He was nice, funny. He wouldn't be too mad if they found her.

'Don't play with my controls. When we're done with this, I need you to hook up with Peabody, keep pushing the property angle. We're going to find them Upper West. Shit, they could be a fucking block away.'

'There goes the neighborhood. We scattering for the night because of the IAB hound?'

'Webster's okay – but if I've got the team officially on the clock, and working out of my home, it's a gray area. Politicians grumbling, and they don't like gray unless they're painting it. We got dead cops, we got injured cops, we're poking into other cops' cases – one of them closed with a guy doing cage time for it. And I'm not shutting it down fast enough to suit them. I'm not going to give them a reason to pull me off.'

'Taking the kid into your place opened you up to it.'

'I know it.'

'It was the right thing, Dallas. The right thing for her. Kid didn't just need protection. She needed . . . comfort.'

'She needs me to close this thing, and I can't if I get jammed up with bullshit. So we straddle the line, and Webster will keep the brass off our ass until we do. There's the black-and-white. Let's get this done.'

Eve strode to the two uniforms. 'Either of you go inside?'

'No, sir. We were ordered to hold. Light was on up there, right front window, second floor.' One of them nodded toward the house. 'Switched off when we pulled up. No one's come out.'

'You check the back?'

'We were told to hold.'

'Jesus, don't either of you have possession of a brain today? Kids've probably scrambled. Baxter, go around the back. I'll take the front. The two of you stand here and give the appearance of being cops.'

She approached the front entrance, examined the seal and lock. Both had been hacked and mangled. It screamed kids, but she followed the suggestion of the tingle at the base of her spine and drew her weapon before she booted the door.

She swept, center, right, left, back to center. Called for lights and listened.

There was some debris scattered around. Home brew bottles, bags of soy chips. Snack food littered the floor, and had been crushed underfoot. It all said kids, disrespect, party.

When she heard a soft creak overhead, she crossed to the stairs. Because she couldn't hear anything, Nixie risked

467

easing her head up, peeking out the window. She saw the two policemen and bit her lip when her eyes welled with tears. They wouldn't let her go inside. If she tried to, they'd see her.

Even as she thought it, there were two bright flashes, and the policemen flew backwards and fell down the steps to her mother's office. So quickly it seemed like pretend, two figures in black ran across the sidewalk and into her house.

The shadows.

She wanted to scream, to scream so loud, but nothing came out of her throat as she squeezed her body down onto the floor again. The shadows would kill Dallas and Baxter, just like they'd killed everybody. While she hid. They would cut them up while she hid.

Then she remembered what was in her pocket, and fumbled out the 'link Roarke had given her. She pushed the button, hard, and began to weep as she crawled out of the car. 'You have to come, you have to help. They're here! They're going to kill Dallas. Hurry and come.'

Then she ran home.

At his desk Roarke felt the cool satisfaction of outwitting a foe. He was peeling away layers. He didn't have the core yet, not yet, but it was only a matter of time. Dig deeply enough, and there were always footprints under the muck. He could follow them now. Triangle to Five-By, Five-By to Unified Action – another military term. And all the crisscrossing threads between. He came across the name Clarissa Branson, listed as president of Unified. Jolt from the past, he thought. One of Cassandra's top-level operatives.

Eve had caught her, he remembered, before the crazy bitch could kill them both and blow up the Statue of Liberty for good measure. Clarissa and William Henson, the man who'd trained her. Both dead now. But . . .

He pulled up another program and ordered a search for New York properties under Clarissa Branson, William Henson, or any combination thereof.

He checked the time, judged Eve would have arrived at the Swisher house. No point in interrupting her fun, he decided. Which she would gain, whatever she said, from busting down on a bunch of foolish kids. 'Ah, well now, there you are you shagging bastards. Branson Williams, West Seventy-third. My cop's right again. Best interrupt her after all.'

'Roarke.' Summerset, normally the most restrained of men, rushed into the office without knocking. 'Nixie's missing.'

'Be specific.'

'She's not in the house. She took off the homer, put it on the boy. She told him she wanted to talk with the lieu-tenant, and left him in the game room. I've checked the scanners. She's not in the house.'

'Well, she could hardly get off the property. Likely she's just . . .' He thought of Eve leaving with Baxter. 'Oh bloody hell.'

As he swung to his desk 'link, the one in his pocket signalled. He yanked it out, heard the child's voice.

'Call for backup,' he snapped out and uncoded a drawer. 'Contact Peabody and the rest, give them the situation.'

'I'll do it on the way. I'm going with you. That child was my responsibility.'

Rather than argue, Roarke checked the weapon he'd taken out, tossed it to Summerset, and chose another. 'You'll have to keep up.'

23

As she reached the steps, Eve eased her communicator out of her pocket. She keyed in a code, ordering Baxter in as backup. Where there was no response, she let the curses roll in her head. She tapped into Dispatch, keyed in for officer-needs-assistance. If it was kids playing hide-and-seek upstairs, she'd live down the humiliation.

She backed down, made her way quietly toward the rear of the house. She'd call Baxter again, and she'd use the domestic's steps.

She'd reached the kitchen when the lights shut off.

She crouched in the dark, and though her heart gave three solid bumps, her mind stayed cool. They'd sprung a trap before she did, but it didn't mean she'd wouldn't take the cheese and walk away.

She keyed her communicator again, intending to order armed response, and found it dead in her hand.

Jammed all electronics. Smart. Goddamn smart. Still, they had to find her before she found them. She thought briefly of Baxter, and blocked emotion. He was down, no question. The cops out front, too.

Just me and you, then. Let's see who brings it first.

471

She stayed low, and with her eyes adjusting to the dark, slipped toward the domestic's quarters. A movement from behind had her swinging around with her finger trembling on the trigger.

She recognized Nixie by scent almost before she recognized the small shape of girl. Biting off curses, she slapped her hand over Nixie's mouth and dragged her into Inga's parlor.

'Are you fucking crazy?' Eve whispered.

'I saw them, I saw them. They came in the house. They went up the stairs.'

No time for questions. 'You listen to me. You hide in here, you hide good. You don't make a sound, not a fucking sound. You don't come out until I say so.'

'I called Roarke. I called him on the 'link.'

Oh Christ, what was he walking into? 'Fine. Don't come out until one of us says so. They don't know you're here. They won't find you. I've got to go up.'

'You can't. They'll kill you.'

'They won't. I've got to go up, because my friend's hurt.' Or dead. 'Because it's my job. You do what I tell you, and you do it now.'

She half-carried Nixie across the room, shoved her under the sofa. 'Stay there. Stay quiet, or I'm going to beat the crap out of you.'

Eve eased open the door to the stairs, breathing again when she found the housekeeper had kept the hinges well-oiled. Take it to the second floor, she thought. Away from the kid. Take it to them.

Roarke would get backup, she could trust him for that. Just as she could trust he was already on his way – fighting back worry for her. And he might not fight it off well enough.

She slipped up the steps like a shadow, and listened at the door.

Not a sound, not a breath. Night-vision, certainly. They'd spread out now, looking for her. Cover the exits, sweep room by room. She'd lied to Nixie. They'd find her. They'd find her because they were looking for a cop, and they'd look everywhere.

Unless she showed herself.

They thought she was looking for kids, so they wouldn't expect she'd have her weapon out – or even so, that she'd be primed.

Time she gave them a surprise.

She rolled her shoulders and, laying down a stream right and left, went through the door.

There was answering fire from her left, but it was high and she was already down and rolling. She was blasting in the direction of the returning stream.

She saw the shadow, heard the thud of it when the blast kicked it back against the wall.

She leaped forward. One of the males – she couldn't tell which. Good and stunned. She ripped off his night goggles, grabbed both his blaster and his combat knife. And was running for cover when footsteps pounded up the stairs.

She fixed on the goggles, and it was light, that faint green tinge that made everything look surreal. She slipped the knife into her belt, gripped both blasters, and came out firing.

She barely made the movement behind her, was able to pivot, but not quickly enough to avoid the knife. It sliced through the leather of her jacket, missed the vest, and ripped into her shoulder.

Using momentum and pain, she swung, back-fisted, and heard the satisfying crunch of cartilage.

She blasted toward the main steps again – keep him off me! – as her assailant leaped at her again.

The kick landed in Eve's sternum, stole her breath, and had the blasters squirting out of her fingers like soap.

She could see Isenberry, blood streaming out of her nose, grinning. Her blaster was holstered, her knife in combat grip.

Likes to party, she thought. Likes to play.

'Unfriendlies approaching!' Isenberry's cohort shouted from downstairs. 'Abort!'

'Like hell. I've got her.' The grin widened. 'I've been looking forward to this. Get up, bitch.'

Drawing the knife out of her belt, Eve pushed through the pain and rose. 'Lieutenant Bitch. I broke your fucking nose, Jilly.'

'Going to pay for that now.'

She came in with a swipe, spun, and missed Eve's face with a vicious back-kick by a breath. The knife slashed down toward Eve's chest, ripped cloth, and skidded over shield.

474

'Body armor?' Isenberry spun back, planted her feet. 'Knew you were a pussy.'

Eve feinted, jabbed, then rammed her fist into Isenberry's grin. 'Sticks and stones.'

In fury, Isenberry reached for her blaster. Eve rose on her toes to leap. And the lights flashed on, blinding them both.

Roarke came in the front like lightning, rolled to his left an instant before the blast hit – two instants before Summerset engaged the lights.

He saw the man ripping off goggles, pivoting behind a doorway.

He could hear the sound of combat up the stairs. She was alive, and she was fighting. The cold fear that had squeezed his heart loosened. He sent out another blast, rolled in the opposite direction.

'See to Eve!' he ordered Summerset and bolted through a doorway to intercept his quarry.

The lights were bright now, and he listened for any sound. There might have been sirens, far off yet. It was best to wish for them, he knew. But there was that cold, hard center of him that wanted the fight, and the blood.

Leading with his weapon, he started to ease around a corner when the scream, the sound of tumbling bodies, broke his concentration for an instant.

In that instant the blast seared across the top of his shoulder, singeing skin, tearing pain. He smelled blood, burned flesh, and – gripping the weapon in his left hand now – shot out streams, somersaulting under them.

Glass imploded. Shards flew. He saw a blast knock his opponent back, and was on him like a dog.

Eve lay at the base of the steps in Inga's parlor, body vibrating with pain, hands slick with blood. The knife was still in her hand, gripped as if her fingers had welded around it. Isenberry was beneath her, their faces so close Eve could see the life drain out of her eyes.

She heard the child under the sofa whimpering, but it was like a dream. Blood, death, the knife hot in her hand.

She heard footsteps rushing down the stairs and forced herself to roll off Isenberry.

Pain screamed through her arm, her shoulder, so her vision wavered. She saw a room washed with red light, heard herself pleading for mercy.

'Lieutenant.' Summerset crouched until she saw his face. 'Let me see where you're injured.'

'Don't touch me.' She lifted the knife, showed him the blade. 'Don't touch me.'

She saw the child huddled under the sofa, face white. White so that some of the blood that had spilled on the fall dotted it like red freckles.

She saw the eyes, glassy with shock. Somehow they were her own eyes.

She pushed herself up, stumbled into the kitchen.

He was alive. Blood on him, too. Well, there was always blood. But Roarke was alive, standing up now, turning toward her.

She shook her head, dropped to her knees as her head spun and her legs trembled. And crawled the last few feet to where Kirkendall was sprawled.

Blood on him, too. But he wasn't dead. Not yet. Not yet. She turned the knife in her hand, gripping it blade down.

Was her arm broken? Had she heard it snap? The pain was there, but it was like a memory. If she put the knife in him, if she drove it through him, again and again, knowing what she did, *feeling* what she did, would the pain go away?

She watched the blood drip from her fingers and knew she could do it. She could, and maybe it would end.

Killer of children, raper of the weak. Why was a cage good enough? She laid the point over his heart and her hand shook. It shook until her arm shook, until her heart shook. Then she drew it back.

Pushing up to her knees, she managed to shove the knife into her belt. 'I've got men down. We need the MTs.'

'Eve.'

'Not now.' There was a sob − or it might've been a scream − trying to claw out of her throat. 'Baxter went around back. He's down. I don't know if he's still alive.'

'Cops out front were stunned. I don't know how bad, but they were alive.'

'I need to check on Baxter.'

'In a minute. You're bleeding.'

'He—' No, no not he. 'She caught me a little. The fall was worse. I think I dislocated the shoulder.'

477

'Let's have a look.' He was gentle, helping her to her feet, and still she went pale.

'Get a good hold,' she told him.

'Baby, you'd do better with a blocker first.'

She shook her head. 'Get a good hold.' She got a strong grip on him as well, hissing out three readying breaths as she stared into his eyes.

Wild blue eyes, concentrate.

And with a jerk, one that brought her stomach to the base of her throat, turned her vision bright white, he snapped the shoulder back in place.

'Shit. Shit. Shit.' She caught her breath, nearly nodded, and was grateful he was holding her upright. 'Okay. That's okay. It's better.'

And she'd needed the jolt, she thought, not just to dull the pain in the shoulder, but to bring her back, fully, to where she was.

'The kid,' she began. 'Summerset.'

He came out with Nixie clinging to his neck. 'She hasn't been hurt.' There was the faintest of tremors in his voice. 'Only frightened. She needs to be taken out of here.'

'I want to see him.' Nixie's voice was thick when she lifted her face from Summerset's neck. Her cheeks were wet, her eyes still streaming. But they met Eve's. 'I want to see who killed my family. Dallas said I could.'

'Bring her over here.'

'I don't think—'

'I'm not asking you to think.' Eve crossed over herself,

and when she wiggled down, took one of Nixie's hands in her bloody one. 'The woman's dead,' she said flatly. 'Neck snapped when we took that header down the steps.'

Not my arm, Eve thought, though it ached like a rotten tooth. 'There's another upstairs.'

'He's unconscious, unarmed, and restrained,' Summerset said. 'This one's hurt bad,' Eve went on. 'But he'll live. He'll live a long time – the longer the better – because he'll never be free again. He'll eat and piss and sleep where and when he's told. Where he's going . . . you getting this, Kirkendall?' she demanded. 'Where he's going, it's like death. Only you live through it, day after day after day.'

Nixie looked down, and her fingers tightened on Eve's. 'She's going to put you in a goddamn cage,' she said, clearly now. 'Then, when you die, you're going to hell.'

'That's quite right.' Summerset went to Nixie again, picked her up. 'Now let's go outside and let the lieutenant do her job.'

Peabody rushed in, a few strides ahead of an army of cops. 'Jesus loving Christ.'

'Baxter's down. Out in the back most likely. See if he's alive.' She turned to a uniform as Peabody raced out. 'One suspect down on the second floor, unconscious and restrained. A second in that room over there, dead. This one makes three. I want MTs, CSU, the ME, sweepers, and Captain Feeney from EDD.'

'Sir, you don't look so good yourself.'

'Get that going, I'll worry about how I look.' She started to go out to check on Baxter herself, and saw him being helped toward the house by Peabody.

Her knees trembled in relief. 'Should've known the sick bastard wouldn't be dead. Where the hell was my backup, Baxter?'

'Got me dead in the shield. Must've.' He pressed a hand to the back of his head, showed the smear of blood. 'Gave me a whale of a kick. Cracked my head on the frigging patio. Got the mother of all headaches.'

'Concussion,' Peabody said. 'Needs a health center.'

'See he's transported.'

'What the hell happened here? Anybody dead?'

'One of them,' Eve told him.

'Okay then. Tell me later. Peabody, my beauty, get me drugs.' Roarke touched her lightly on the back. 'Let's have a look at that arm then, and the rest of you.'

'Got a couple of jabs in past my guard. I got a couple of sticks into her. Tit for fricking tat.'

'Your nose is bleeding.'

Eve swiped at it. 'I broke hers. See who's the pussy now. Kicked her ass right through the door, but she was just quick enough to take me on a ride down that flight of stairs with her. Fall – I think it was the fall – snapped her neck. She was dead when we landed.'

She wrapped a hand around her bloody shoulder, turned toward him. And really saw him for the first time. 'You're hit. How bad?'

'He got a couple of streams past my guard,' he said, and smiled. 'Hurts like a bitch, too.'

She touched his cheek with her bloody fingers. 'Got a black eye coming on.'

'He got worse. Why don't we – oh, well now, that's extreme,' he said when she ripped away the tattered sleeve of his shirt.

'It was trashed anyway.' She poked and prodded at his wound and made him curse in two languages. 'Shoulder's nasty.'

'As is yours.' He lifted his brows as two MTs came through. 'Ladies first.'

'Civilians first. And I ain't no lady.'

He laughed, and kissed her solidly on the mouth. 'You're mine. But we'll suffer through the first-aid together.'

It seemed fair enough, and she could bitch at the MTs, threaten them with violence if they so much as thought of tranqing her. She could coordinate the various teams, get her report on record, and watch three killers – two live, one dead – hauled away.

She'd take her shot at the live ones in the morning.

'I'll go in, take care of the paperwork,' Peabody told her. 'There are too many cops volunteering to handle it. One of them's bound to try to get in some kicks for Knight and Preston.'

'We'll take them in separate interviews tomorrow.'

'You might want to send a team over to secure this address tonight. One on West Seventy-third.' Roarke

481

handed her a memo. 'I believe you'll find their head-quarters.'

She took the memo, and standing in her bloody shirt-sleeves now, grinned. 'I *knew* it. Peabody, find uniforms you can trust and have them sit over Kirkendall and Clinton. Call in the team and screw the OT. We're moving on this tonight.'

'Hot damn!'

'E-men first,' she added. 'And I want, let me think, I want Jules and Brinkman from Bombs and Explosives. We don't know how they may have that place wired, or what booby traps they might've set inside. I want body armor on everyone, full riot gear. These three may not be it. I'll contact the commander and clear it.'

She turned to Roarke. 'You're in if you want it.'

'I can't think of a more entertaining way to spend the evening.'

'Give me five.' She walked away, yanking out her commu-nicator. 'That's my weapon, you putz,' she snapped at one of the Crime Scene techs as he bagged it. 'Give it back.'

'Sorry, sir, it has to go in.'

'Goddamn it, do you know how long it takes to get – Commander, we have two suspects in custody and one suspect DOS.'

'I'm on my way to the scene now. I'm told four officers, including yourself, are injured.'

'MTs treated on-scene, three are being transported to the hospital. The suspects are secured. We have what we believe is the location for their base of operations. I've called in my team, as well as two members of B and E. As it's more efficiently located to both this scene and the suspected base, I'll be coordinating the maneuver from my home office. With permission, sir.'

'I'll meet you there. How extensive are your injuries, Lieutenant?'

'I'll do, sir.'

'Yes, you will.'

'Okay then,' she muttered when he clicked off. 'I want the evidence from this scene so clean I could eat off it,' she told anyone from CSU within hearing. 'I want this scene secured so tight a fucking flea couldn't squeeze under a doorway. Any screwups, I'll be eating asses for breakfast.'

She nodded to Roarke, who fell into step beside her. 'I love when you snarl. Stirs me up.'

'You'll be plenty stirred before the night's over.' She stepped out, amused when he draped her ruined jacket over her shoulders.

And the smile fell away when she saw Summerset sitting in one of Roarke's vehicles with Nixie in his arms. The window rolled down as she approached.

'I had to promise we wouldn't leave until she'd spoken to you.'

'I don't have time to—' She broke off when Nixie lifted her head. 'What?'

'Can I talk to you, just you, for a minute? Please.'

'Sixty seconds and counting. Come on then.'

When Nixie climbed out, Eve started to walk down the sidewalk. Gave a snarl Roarke would've enjoyed as she stared down the gawkers already pressed against the barricades. She detoured to her vehicle, gestured Nixie in.

'You hid in the backseat?'

'Uh-huh.'

'I ought to pound every square inch of you. I won't because my arm still hurts, and because – maybe – by being a stupid ass you helped. I could've taken the three of them.' She pressed a hand to the throb of her shoulder. 'But it was handy having Roarke pull down the third.'

'I wanted to go home.'

Eve laid her head back on the seat. Taking down three armed and dangerous was easier than picking through the minefield of a child's emotions.

'You did. What did you find there? It sucks wide, the widest, but that's not home any more.'

'I wanted to see it again.'

'I get that. It's just a house, building materials. It's what you had there before the bad stuff happened that counts. That's how I see it.'

'You're going to send me away.'

'I'm going to give you a chance, the best I've got to offer.' She lifted her head, shifted in the seat. 'You got kicked hard. You can get up, or you can stay down. I'm saying you're going to get up. Elizabeth and Richard are good people. They know about getting kicked hard. They want to give you a place, give you a family. It's never going to be what it was, but it can be something else. You can make it something else and never forget what it was like in that house there, before the bad stuff happened.'

'I'm afraid.'

'Then you're not as stupid an ass as I thought. Another thing you're not is a coward. You've got to give this a chance, see how it goes.'

'Is Virginia really far away?'

'Not all that much.'

'Can I see you and Roarke and Summerset sometimes?'

'Yeah, I guess. If you actually want to see Summerset's ugly face again.'

'If you promise, I know you mean it. You said you'd find them, and you did. You keep promises.'

'I promise, then. I have to go, finish this.'

Nixie knelt on the seat, leaned over, and kissed Eve's cheek. Then she laid her head on Eve's good shoulder, sighed once. 'I'm sorry you got hurt helping me.'

'No big.' She found her hand lifting to stroke over the soft, pale hair. 'Just part of the job.'

She sat where she was when Nixie got out. Sat and watched the little girl walk to Roarke, and him bend down as they spoke. The way he gave the child a hug when she kissed him.

Summerset put her in the car, secured her himself, brushed those bony fingers gently over her cheek. As they drove away, Roarke got in beside Eve.

'All right?'

She shook her head. 'Need another minute.'

'Take all you need.'

'She'll be okay. She's got guts, and heart. Scared ten years off me when she came running in, but she's got guts.'

'She loves you.'

'Oh, Jesus.'

'You found her, you protected her, you saved her. She'll love you more for it as her life heals. You were right to let her see his face.'

'I hope, because I wasn't thinking clear yet. The fall down the stairs—' She broke off, hissed. 'Not just the fall. The blood, the knife, the pain. I heard her neck snap, and it was like an echo in my head. When I came out and saw you, there was this dull relief. Distant, in another part of me.'

She drew a long breath. 'You'd have let me do it. You'd have stood back and let me put that knife in him.'

'Yes. I'd have stood back and let you do what you needed to do.'

'Even cold-blooded murder.'

'Nothing cold-blooded about it, Eve.' He touched her face, turned it to his. His eyes weren't wild and blue now, she thought, but calm and deep and sure. 'You couldn't have done it.'

'I nearly did, I could feel the way it punched through his body.'

'Nearly did. And if something had snapped that clean inside of you, we'd have dealt with it. But what's inside of you, what you are down to the bone, wouldn't have allowed

486

it. You needed to kneel there with that knife in your hand, and to know that.'

'Guess I did.'

'Tomorrow, you'll face him, both of them, in Interview. What you do will be worse to him than a knife in the heart. You beat him, you stopped him, you caged him.'

'Cage him, and another crawls out from under the next rock.' She pressed her shoulder, gave her arm a testing turn. 'So I guess I'd better get back in shape, so I can go after the next one.'

'I love you, madly.'

'Yeah, you do.' She smiled and, praying nobody was watching, touched her lips to his burned shoulder. 'Let's go clean up, and get back to work.'

She flicked a glance in the rearview as they drove away. Just a house, she thought. They'd clean up the blood, sweep out the death. Another family would move in.

She hoped they had a nice life.

Read an extract from

DELUSION
IN DEATH

The new J.D. Robb thriller, out
September 2012

After a killer day at the office, nothing smoothed those raw edges like Happy Hour. On The Rocks, on Manhattan's Lower West Side, catered to white collar working stiffs who wanted half-price drinks and some cheesy rice balls while they bitched about their bosses or hit on a co-worker.

Or the execs who wanted a couple of quick belts close to the office before their commute to the 'burbs.

From four-thirty to six, the long bar, the hightops and lowtops bulged with lower-rung execs, admins, assistants and secretaries who flooded out of the cubes, pools and tiny offices. Some washed up like shipwreck survivors. Others waded ashore ready to bask in the buzz. A few wanted nothing more than to huddle alone on their small square of claimed territory and drink the day away.

By five, the bar hummed like a hive while bartenders and wait staff rushed and scurried to serve those whose work day was behind them. The second of those half-price drinks tended to improve moods so the laughter, amiable chatter and pre-mating rituals punctuated the hum.

Files, accounts, slights, unanswered messages were

forgotten in the warm gold light, the clink of glasses and complimentary beer nuts.

Now and again the door opened to welcome another survivor of New York's vicious business day. Cool fall air whisked in along with a blast of street noise. Then it was warm again, gold again, a humming hive again.

Midway through that happiest of hours (ninety minutes in bar time), some headed back out. Responsibilities, families, a hot date pulled them out the door to subways, airtrams, maxibuses, cabs. Those who remained settled back for one more, a little more time with friends and co-workers, a little more of that warm gold light before the bright or the dark.

Macie Snyder crowded at a plate-sized hightop with her boyfriend of three months and twelve days Travis, her best work pal CiCi, and Travis's friend Bren. Macie had wheedled and finagled for weeks to set CiCi up with Bren with the long view to double dates and shared boy talk. They made a happy, chattering group, with Macie perhaps the happiest of all.

CiCi and Bren had definitely *connected* – she could see it in the body language, the eye contact – and since CiCi texted her a couple times under the table, she had it verified.

By the time they ordered the second round, plans began to evolve to extend the evening with dinner.

After a quick signal to CiCi, Macie grabbed her purse. 'We'll be right back.'

She wound her way through tables, muttered when someone at the bar stood up and shoulder bumped her. 'Make a hole,' she called out cheerfully, and took CiCi's hand as they scurried down the narrow steps and queued up for the thankfully short line in the rest room.

'Told ya!'

'I know, I know. You said he was adorable, and you showed me his picture, but he's *so* much cuter in person. And so funny! Blind dates are usually so lame, but this is just mag.'

'Here's what we'll do. We'll talk them into going to Nino's. That way, after dinner, we'll go one way, and you'll have to go the other to get home. It'll give Bren a chance to walk you home – and you can ask him up.'

'I don't know.' Always second-guessing with dates – which was why she didn't have a boyfriend of three months and twelve days – CiCi chewed at her bottom lip. 'I don't want to rush it.'

'You don't have to sleep with him.' Macie rolled her round blue eyes. 'Just offer him coffee, or, you know, a nightcap. Maybe fool around a little.'

She dashed into the next open stall. She *really* had to pee. 'Then text me after he leaves and tell me *everything*. Full deets.'

Making a bee-line for the adjoining stall, CiCi peed in solidarity. 'Maybe. Let's see how dinner goes. Maybe he won't want to walk me home.'

'He will. He's a total sweetie. I wouldn't hook you up

with a jerkhead, CiCi.' She walked to the sink, sniffed at the peachy-scented foam soap, then beamed a grin at her friend when CiCi joined her. 'If it works out, it'll be so much fun. We can double-date.'

'I really like him. I get a little nervous when I really like a guy.'

'He really likes you.'

'Are you sure?'

'Abso-poso,' Macie assured her, brushing her short curve of sunny blond hair while CiCi added some shine to her lip dye. Jesus, she thought, suddenly annoyed. Did she have to stroke and soothe all damn night?

'You're pretty and smart and fun.' I don't hang with jerkheads, Macie thought. 'Why wouldn't he like you? God, CiCi, loosen up and stop whining. Stop playing the nervous freaking virgin.'

'I'm not—'

'You want to get laid or not?' Macie snapped and had CiCi gaping. 'I went to a lot of trouble to set this up, now you're going to blow it.'

'I just—'

'Shit.' Macie rubbed at her temple. 'Now I'm getting a headache.'

A bad one, CiCi assumed. Macie never said mean things. And, well, maybe she was playing the nervous virgin. A little. 'Bren's got the nicest smile.' CiCi's eyes, a luminous green against her caramel skin, met Macie's in the narrow mirror. 'If he walks me home, I'll ask him up.'

'Now you're talking.'

They walked back. It seemed louder than it had, Macie thought. All the voices, the clattering dishes, the scraping chairs ground against her headache.

She told herself, with some bitterness, to ease off the next drink.

Someone blocked her path, just for a moment, as they passed the bar. Annoyed, she rounded, shoved at him, but he was already murmuring an apology and moving toward the door.

'Asshole,' she muttered, and at least had the chance to snarl as he glanced back, smiled at her before he stepped outside.

'What's wrong?'

'Nothing – just a jerkhead.'

'Are you okay? I probably have a blocker if your head really hurts. I've got a little headache, too.'

'Always about you,' Macie muttered, then tried to take a calming breath. Good friends, she reminded herself. Good times.

As she sat again, Travis took her hand the way he did, gave her a wink.

'We want to go to Nino's,' she announced.

'We were just talking about going to Tortilla Flats. We'd need a reservation at Nino's,' Travis reminded her.

'We don't want Mexican crap. We want to go somewhere nice. Jesus, we'll split the bill if the tab's a BFD.'

Travis's eyebrows drew together, digging a thin line

between them, the way they did when she said something stupid. She *hated* when he did that.

'Nino's is twelve blocks away. The Mexican place is practically around the corner.'

So angry her hands began to shake, she shoved her face toward his. 'Are you in a fucking hurry? Why can't we do something *I* want for a change?'

'We're doing something you wanted right now.'

Their voices rose to shouts, clanging with the sharp voices all around them. As her head began to throb, CiCi glanced toward Bren.

He sat, teeth bared in a snarl, staring into his glass, muttering, muttering.

He wasn't adorable. He was horrible, just like Travis. Ugly, ugly. He only wanted to fuck her. He'd rape her if she said no. He'd beat her, rape her, first chance. Macie knew. She *knew* and she'd laugh about it.

'Screw both of you,' CiCi said under her breath. 'Screw all of you.'

'Stop looking at me like that,' Macie shouted. 'You freak.'

Travis slammed his fist on the table. 'Shut your fucking mouth.'

'I said stop!' Grabbing a fork from the table, Macie peeled off a scream. And stabbed the prongs through Travis's eye.

He howled, the sound tearing through CiCi's brain as he leaped up, fell on her friend.

And the bloodbath began.

★   ★   ★

Lieutenant Eve Dallas stood in the carnage. Always something new, she thought. Always something just a little more terrible than even a cop could imagine.

Even for a veteran murder cop swimming in the bubbling stew of New York in the last quarter of the year 2060, there was always something worse.

Bodies floated on a sea of blood, booze and vomit. Some draped like rag dolls over the long bar or curled like grisly cats under broken tables. Jagged hunks of glass littered the floor, sparkled like deadly diamonds on what was left of tables and chairs – or jabbed, thick with gore, out of bodies.

The stench of blood, piss, vomit, emptied bowels clogged the air and made her think of old photos she'd seen of battlefields where no side could claim clear victory.

Gouged eyes, torn faces, slit throats, heads bashed in so violently she saw pieces of skull and gray matter only added to the impression of war waged and lost. A few victims were naked, or nearly, the exposed flesh painted with blood like ancient warriors.

She stood, waiting for the first wave of shock to pass. She'd forgotten she could be shocked. She turned, tall and lean, brown eyes flat, to the beat cop, and first on scene.

'What do you know?'

She heard him breathing between his teeth, gave him time.

'My partner and I were on our break, in the diner across the street. As I came out, I observed a female, late twenties, backing away from the door of the location. She was screaming. She was still screaming when I reached her.'

'What time was that?'

'We logged out for the break at seventeen-forty-five. I don't think we were in there over five minutes, Lieutenant.'

'Okay. Continue.'

'The female was unable to speak coherently, but she pointed to the door. While my partner attempted to calm the female, I opened the door.'

He paused, cleared his throat. 'I've got twenty-two years in, Lieutenant, and I've never seen anything like this. Bodies, everywhere. Some were still alive. Crawling, crying, moaning. I called it in, called for medicals. There was no way to keep the scene undisturbed, sir. People were dying.'

'Understood.'

'We got eight or ten out – the medicals, Lieutenant. I'm sorry, I'm not clear on the number. They were in pretty bad shape. They worked on some of them here, transported all survivors to the Tribeca Health Center. At that time we secured the scene. The medicals were all over it, Lieutenant. We found more in the bathrooms, back in the kitchen.'

'Were you able to question any of the survivors?'

'We got some names. The ones able to speak all said basically the same thing. People were trying to kill them.'

'What people?'

'Sir? Everybody.'

'Okay. Let's keep everybody out of here for now.' She walked with him to the door.

She spotted her partner. She'd parted ways with Peabody less than an hour before. Eve stayed back at Central to catch up on paperwork. She'd been on her way to the garage, thinking of home when she'd gotten the call.

At least, for once, she remembered to text her husband, letting Roarke know she'd be later than expected.

Again.

She moved forward to block the door and intercept her partner.

She knew Peabody was sturdy, solid – despite the pink cowgirl boots, rainbow-tinted sunshades and short, flippy ponytail. But what was beyond the door had shaken her, and a beat cop with over twenty on his hard, black shoes.

'Almost made it,' Peabody said. 'I'd stopped by the market on the way home. Thought I'd surprise McNab with a home-cooked.' She shook a small market bag. 'Good thing I hadn't started. What did we catch?'

'It's bad.'

Peabody easy expression slid away, leaving her face cold. 'How bad?'

'Pray to God you never see worse. Multiple bodies. Hacked, sliced, bashed, you name it. Seal up.' Eve tossed her a can of Seal-it from the field kit she carried. 'Put down that bag and grab your guts. If you need to puke, get outside. There's already plenty of puke in there, and I don't want yours mixed in. The crime scene's fucked. No way around it. MTs and the responding officers had to get the survivors, treat some of them right on scene.'

Have you read them all?

Eve and Roarke are back in September 2012 with
DELUSION IN DEATH

Have you
read them all?

Eve and Roarke are back in September 2012, with
DELUSION IN DEATH